Alexandra Connor was born in Lancashire and educated in Yorkshire. She has had a variety of careers, including photographic model, cinema manager, and personal assistant to a world-famous heart surgeon. Yet it was only after being stalked and assaulted in London that she found her real forte — during her convalescence, she discovered an ability to paint, and a further relapse resulted in the writing of her first novel. Although traumatic, Alexandra believes that the assault changed her, and gave her a life she could never have imagined before. She still has strong connections to Lancashire today; and as well as being a highly popular novelist, she is a presenter on television and BBC radio.

You can discover more about the author at www.alexandra-connor.co.uk

MASK OF FORTUNE

As a child, Zoe Mellor craved her mother's
love, but her mother only had eyes for her
first child, Victor — and died without
revealing why she had directed such rancour
at her daughter. Motherless at sixteen, Zoe
spends her young days looking after her
father and adored brothers in Lancashire.
Here, she discovers she has a talent for
painting and art appreciation — which the
conniving Victor persuades her to put to
nefarious use. Zoe's meteoric rise in the
glamorous world of international art is
mirrored by her success as a forger, which
makes the family a fortune — but also
engenders jealousy and greed. Now Zoe risks
losing everything she has always worked for:
her reputation, and the love and security she
has found . . .

Books by Alexandra Connor
Published by Ulverscroft:

THE MOON IS MY WITNESS
MIDNIGHT'S SMILING
THE SIXPENNY WINNER
THE FACE IN THE LOCKET
THE TURN OF THE TIDE
THE TAILOR'S WIFE
THE LYDGATE WIDOW
THE WATCHMAN'S DAUGHTER
THE SOLDIER'S WOMAN
THE WITCH MARK

ALEXANDRA CONNOR

MASK OF FORTUNE

Complete and Unabridged

CHARNWOOD
Leicester

First published in Great Britain in 1990

First Charnwood Edition
published 2016

C463795069

A catalogue record for this book is available
from the British Library.

ISBN 978–1–4448–2923–5

Published by
F. A. Thorpe (Publishing)
Anstey, Leicestershire

Set by Words & Graphics Ltd.
Anstey, Leicestershire
Printed and bound in Great Britain by
T. J. International Ltd., Padstow, Cornwall

This book is printed on acid-free paper

This book is for JC

Prologue

She held her breath to the end of the street. Running. Past Mrs Reynolds, past Mrs Cluff's and the old man Riley, past the ginnel and towards the corner shop. Past Whittaker's and the lorry driver with the pigeons. Her feet stamped on the pavement as she ran, her chest burning with effort . . .

At the corner she stopped and took in her breath quickly, the air damp, November-cold, making her cough, making everyone cough when it came from the moors already scratched with snow. Rubbing her hands together, she banged her feet on the pavement and looked round. The street was deserted, bleak, cold, the night dead. Suddenly, she took in her breath and closed her eyes, the memory scalding her.

No one should let a child out, not at night, not even at six o'clock. No one should leave a child alone.

Zoe slowly opened her eyes but the street looked the same. Still empty, no figure coming towards her, not Victor, or Alan. No one calling for her, looking for her. Not even her father.

On Christmas Eve 1967, Zoe Mellor stood alone on the street and wondered why Christmas had been cancelled.

PART ONE

The Start

1

The front room was cold when Zoe returned, the fire nearly out, the settee and chairs pushed back against the wall, a vase of honesty overturned, and, staring her full in the face, the blank corner. Blank and huge. Zoe looked over her shoulder and then glanced back to the corner. Only hours earlier there had been a Christmas tree standing there, complete with lights and a few cheap, well-used ornaments. It had been bushy, dense, wickedly green, so high that it had almost lacerated the ceiling.

Zoe swallowed and listened, her heart banging. The house was quiet, as it always was after one of her mother's scenes. 'Scenes' she thought, repeating the word as though there was a clue in it — as if, by understanding the word, she would understand something of what happened. She knelt suddenly and touched a pine needle with her gloved hand, relieved that it was real. There *had* been a tree after all, she hadn't dreamt it.

The coal shuffled in the grate and startled her, making her jump to her feet and look to the door. But no one walked in and so she waited, in the centre of the room, her mind slipping back to that afternoon.

'Help me with this,' her mother had said,

5

passing the vase full of honesty to Zoe and smiling. Smiles and kindness. 'Put it on the table there, love. Careful.'

Eagerly she had helped, grateful for her mother's good mood and the gentleness which soothed her so much that she sidled over and clasped hold of her hand.

'Come here, sweetheart, and let Mummy cuddle you.' Jane Mellor had knelt down by her daughter and hugged her. She was wearing her best winter clothes, her dark hair freshly washed and loose on her shoulders, her face smooth with make-up. 'You're such a baby,' she continued, kissing Zoe's cheek, her voice crooning, gentle, without any trace of the tone which swung down from the bedroom and woke her daughter, frightened, in the early hours.

Zoe clung on to her mother fiercely then felt her stiffen and draw back. 'Come on now, I've things to do. I must get on,' her mother said, suddenly irritated.

And the tone in her voice was there. The warning, the harbinger. Zoe heard it, but chose to ignore it.

'Mum . . . ' she said simply, making the word a plea for affection and wrapping her small arms around her mother, thinking stupidly that she could stop what was bound to happen, believing that she could love her enough to prevent the inevitable.

Swiftly, Jane Mellor got to her feet and pushed her daughter away, unfastening the little hands which were clutching at her cardigan. Peeling her off.

6

'Zoe! Stop it! Let go of me!'

Her face had altered, the hair swinging around a livid expression, all gentleness gone. With a ferocity which frightened Zoe, she bent to face her daughter, her eyes burning. 'Get off me! You want too much! You're always hanging on to me!'

Zoe began to cry helplessly as her mother snatched angrily at the vase of honesty and pulled it on to the floor where it fell, soundlessly, on to the worn carpet. With terrifying intensity the change in mood escalated, following the pattern familiar throughout Zoe's childhood. Trembling with fear, she watched as her mother looked about her frantically and then began pushing around the furniture, hurling chairs against the walls, slamming them back so hard that the wooden mirror rattled above, and a picture swung evilly from its hook.

Zoe stepped back, pressing herself against the door as she watched. Round and round the room her mother went, then suddenly she stopped and glanced to the corner.

'No!' Zoe cried out hoarsely, running towards her mother and catching hold of her skirt. 'No! Please, no!'

But her mother didn't hear her; she saw only the tree — and that inflamed her. Defiantly it stood in the corner of the ruined room, a celebration of Christmas. Of family life. High, wide and handsome, almost indecently cheerful with its lights. Without a moment's hesitation she lunged for it, her hands gobbled up into the greenery, her whole body straining with effort.

And down it fell. Down went the lights, the

little illuminated coaches smashing on the floor, the faded ornaments falling around them, gold baubles rolling round Jane Mellor's shoes, the branches spitting rotten fruit from a rotten tree. Unbalanced, it tipped against the wall and then slid despairingly against the window, the bucket which had supported it bleeding a pool of Rochdale earth.

Incredibly there had been no sound. Zoe knew there must have been, that the fall of the tree must have vibrated throughout the house, but all she remembered was silence — and the look on her mother's face as she turned to her.

'Christmas,' she said, breathing heavily, 'is cancelled.'

2

Rochdale
June 1970

'He's too bloody fat!' Bernard Mellor said for the second time as Alan's hand moved towards the cake. 'Too bloody fat by half.'

'It's his glands.'

Bernard spun round on his wife. 'Glands! Glands, my eye, it's his bloody mouth that's the trouble.'

Silence swung down on all of them. On Zoe, her brothers — Alan, Victor and Ron — and her parents. The clock chimed, the sound coming muffled from the front room. With timid obstinacy, Alan's hand moved towards the cake again. Bernard's eyes were fixed on him.

'He's — '

' — too bloody fat,' Victor finished for his father, pushing his own plate away.

'And you can mind what you say!' the old man retorted, turning his anger on his elder son as Alan sneaked the cake into his mouth. 'It's a shame you don't get paid money for every one of your words. The amount you talk we'd all be bloody rich by now.'

'Bernard, stop it!' his wife interrupted, her hands clenched together on the table. 'Let's just finish our meal in peace.'

Instantly, Bernard Mellor stopped. Nearly

9

twenty years older than his wife, he was besotted and terrified of her at the same time. Before their marriage Jane Mellor had been the hugely attractive, but highly strung, only daughter of Rochdale's town hall clerk; a tall young woman, with fair skin and blue eyes, the lashes black and even, the eyebrows straight. Always excitable, her passionate response to the world around her seemed only intriguing then, and fascinated the older, steadier Bernard Mellor. Even after one violent argument when she had been unreasonably vicious, he was quick to forgive, and when she broke down later he wilingly transferred all blame to himself. Absenting her from guilt, he thereby set the pattern for their life afterwards.

The wedding day had begun well, Jane dressed in violent white, her blue eyes brilliant against the surrounding barren lace, her gaze fixed upon her husband to be. Afterwards, her mood shifted, almost imperceptibly, her hands frantic to clasp his while the guests looked on, amazed by the intense feeling between such an ill-assorted couple. To outsiders, her choice of husband was curious, but Jane realised that although she had not found a man either handsome or good-tempered, she *had* found safety. Maybe Bernard Mellor was not destined for greatness as the foreman in the local engineering factory, but he was protective, committed, and reliably in love with her . . . which was all she had hoped for.

So she bore the mean little wedding, and her widowed father's disappointment, and answered her vows firmly, so there should be no mistake. Her final acceptance of her lot in life came later, in the dark. Understanding Bernard Mellor, she realised his needs and bound him to her finally on their wedding night. With intense gratitude, she returned and matched his passion, supplying her husband with the beauty and excitement of a young wife whilst paying forty-one-year-old Bernard Mellor the finest compliment of his life by simply making love to him. To *him* — not a younger man, not a richer one. But him. It was a compliment he never forgot.

It would have been a match made in heaven if the devotion had been mutual, but as the marriage wore on, Jane's feelings for her husband were erratic. She veered between tolerant indifference and violent affection, whilst he remained unchangingly besotted. Nights spent in fretful tears slipped without logic into luminous mornings when she would rise and have his breakfast prepared before he woke, her long hair loose over her shoulders, a penitent look on her face until he caught hold of her.

'I'm so sorry,' she said, clinging to him. 'Sorry.'

'Don't fret, luv,' he replied, responding to her affection and coaxing her into laughter, fooling himself into believing that one day the black moods would lift and she would be like this always.

She knew, of course. Intelligent and reasonably well educated, Jane Mellor had no illusions about her behaviour. But although she might recognise the symptoms, she could not control them, and simply resigned herself to living each day as it came. In fact, she was almost ruthless with her illness and when she was most troubled she segregated herself, taking refuge in the spare bedroom and locking the door, her tall figure curled on the bed, her arms wrapped around herself as the small hours had their sport with her.

Then the mood lifted, sometimes for weeks on end, and a more familiar Jane Mellor looked back from the mirror and made her lightheaded with relief.

'I am myself,' she said. 'I am myself.'

With the euphoria which followed she was more affectionate and more giving, and when Bernard and she made love his desire was all the more intense and desperate because he was making love to her not the interloper who frightened them both. Later, when she slept, he would lie beside her and watch her face, searching to find any sign of the depression which dogged her, to discover a birthmark, or some other outward manifestation of her difference. There was none, all her agony was inside, and he loved her for it.

Her feelings of love continued to oscillate until her first child arrived, and with the advent of Victor, the moods lifted. Week after week passed without tears, violence, sharp words — nothing, only a sense of having come home. Bernard watched her and held his breath, but when the next son, Alan, was born, Jane's character remained even, the depression seemingly obliterated by the births. She bloomed, her looks maturing, the grinding unease of her illness gone from her, her troubles past. When Bernard

Mellor opened the door at night he knew what to expect, and when Jane opened her eyes on a new morning she recognised the world for what it was and thought she had her place in it. The house was still a mean house at the end of Buck's Lane, and Bernard Mellor was still only a foreman, but the darkness had lifted, and they revelled in it. Aware of their good fortune, both of them began to believe that the black moods were past and that the children had finally laid that uneasy ghost to rest. Then Zoe was born.

★ ★ ★

Bernard could see that something was wrong almost immediately, noticing how his wife's fingers plucked at the bedsheets, and the bright, high colour on her cheeks. Oh God, he thought, not now, not now. Please.

'I want something to read.'

The voice he knew had gone. *Her* voice had gone. The interloper was in its place, giving orders.

'Jane, why don't you rest?'

She looked up at him, her face unreadable, unrecognisable. I don't know you, he thought, clenching his hands.

'I want something to read,' she repeated, glancing quickly to the baby in the cot beside the bed. 'And a bottle.'

He frowned. She had breastfed the other children, insisting on the closeness, binding them to her from the start. 'Get the nurse!'

'Jane — '

13

She glanced up at him, her hair pulled away from her face, the blue eyes closed off, the mouth a deadening memory from the past. 'Don't argue with me! It's your bloody child, after all.'

★ ★ ★

Ron was born two years later, during which time Jane Mellor's illness had altered course, her moods becoming less frequent, but when depression did swamp her she was more vicious and struck out physically, first at Bernard and then at the children, hard slaps handed out for minor misdemeanours, and then, when the gloom had lifted, overwhelming tenderness was offered in compensation. There was no talk of doctors — it had been suggested once and a violent argument had taken place, Jane hurling a packed suitcase at her husband and ordering him to leave. From then on, there had been no mention of doctors. Besides, what would people think? A man should be able to control his wife, shouldn't he, Bernard reasoned. A man should be able to keep his wife happy.

The children reacted in their own ways. The eldest, Victor, adapted easily, his character independent from the first, whilst Alan and Ron adopted their own defence. When their mother was moody, they simply got out of the way. But for Zoe, it was never so simple. She knew from her earliest memories that she had been responsible for something profound, that her presence had somehow altered her parents' lives.

She knew it; and her mother did too.

Shrewd and sensitive, Zoe discovered early on that her mother was devoted to her brothers, and absorbed by Victor. She also recognised that Jane Mellor's black moods were turned on her far more often than on them. Yet, even knowing this, when her mother was affectionate she clung to her desperately, picking up each particle of loving, treasuring every word, or smile — cherishing each kindness for the moment, because the next was uncertain. Their relationship staggered from day to day. A hand, held out and grasped when they crossed the road, could strike out in irritation at another time; the same voice which might read a bedtime story could alter and become savage, her mother's cries echoing as Zoe hid, cowering, in the back yard.

In an attempt to secure some constant affection in her life, Zoe turned to her father, but his devotion began and ended with his wife. Detached, merely tolerated, she changed her tack and her target, and by the time she reached ten both Alan and Ron were mesmerised by her.

Victor was another matter. Ten years older than his sister he was sharply attractive, blisteringly confident, and irresistible to women. Used to his mother's adoration he expected, and received, similar devotion from most of the women with whom he came in contact. Hearts fluttered when he went into the bread shop, conversation ceased in the grocer's, and only the jealous intervention of the butcher prevented grand passion on a truly operatic scale.

15

Blissfully aware of the effect his presence caused, Victor also developed a useful skill with his fists and could defend himself physically when his tongue failed to get him out of trouble. To his mother he was a most handsome, most intelligent, and most charming man — to Zoe, he was a hundred per cent fake.

'You're not going out again, Victor?' his mother asked, putting down some shopping on the table. 'I've got unsmoked bacon, your favourite.'

Victor checked his reflection in the mirror over the fire, turning his head from side to side and smoothing back his dark hair.

'I'm busy. Give it to the others,' he replied, leaning towards the glass and rubbing the end of his narrow nose.

'They don't enjoy it like you, love. Have a little, just to please me.'

Taking a deep breath, Victor turned. 'Not just now, Mum.' He kissed her cheek, his lips resting momentarily on the responsive skin. 'I have to go. Could you . . . ?' The words trailed off. Smiling, his mother laid the plates she was carrying on the table and pulled some money out of her purse.

★ ★ ★

'I don't see why he always gets extra money,' Alan grumbled in the garage, his huge frame leaning against the wall, his hands dismantling a large orange. 'I asked for some the other day and got sod all for my trouble.' He frowned and

16

peered at the segments of fruit. 'It's gone off!'

Zoe swung herself on to the work bench. Bernard Mellor had never made enough money to buy a car so the garage had been used as a storeroom until Alan began working with his uncle, the local stonemason. Uncertain of what to do with a son who had enormous strength and little brain, Bernard had hit upon the idea of apprenticing Alan out to his brother. With typical equanimity, Alan had accepted the situation, hardly daring to hope that he might grow to like the job.

'What's it like working here?' Zoe asked. She was fascinated by everything Alan did. Her giant brother, quiet and safe and constant. 'D'you get to see dead bodies?'

'There's no bodies there, just headstones,' he said patiently, fingering a rough piece of marble. 'It's hard work, but I can do it. Anyway, I'll be as good as him one day.'

Zoe thought of her uncle. Tom Mellor, fifty-seven years old, living near Heywood, his hair white and his eyes always red-rimmed as though he'd been crying.

'What's he like?'

Alan rummaged in his pocket. 'Bad-tempered.' Half a biscuit materialised in his fleshy hand and a slow smile of contentment washed over his face as Zoe watched him.

'How can you eat that? It's got fluff on it!'

'I'm hungry,' Alan responded vehemently, leaning against the bench next to her. 'He carves all kinds of things — even angels.' His eyes flicked away from her towards the garage

17

window. 'And urns, like they had in the olden days.'

'What's an urn?'

The question caught Alan off guard. 'A pot.'

'A pot!' Zoe replied, mystified. 'What would someone want with a pot?'

'It's for the body.'

Zoe frowned. 'Babies?'

Baffled, Alan stood his ground. 'Babies? What d'you mean?'

'Well, how could you get a grown-up in a pot?'

Alan was still laughing when Zoe ran out.

★   ★   ★

The nights were short suddenly, winter moving in, the damp remaining constant, the aching cold which set in until March or sometimes April. The Mellor house was set well back from its neighbours at the end of a cutting called Buck's Lane — aptly named after Victor, some wag said. The street lamps stopped on the main street, the short run to the house dark unless the lights were on in the front room and the kitchen. Then you could see your way clearly, but otherwise there were a few yards of dense blackness punctuated only by the garage light burning well into the night as Alan worked.

Sometimes Zoe would creep up and, climbing on to the bucket outside, peer through the window to watch her brother. It fascinated her, the way he could lift huge blocks of stone, or, at other times, carve precise lettering into the marble, his massive hands working carefully in the cold, the same hands which swung her high up on to his shoulders, offering precious affection and protection. Having only been with his uncle for a few months, Alan was not allowed to do any work for customers, although he could practise at home on the pieces of crude marble Tom Mellor let him buy out of his wages. And every night Alan worked, the light burning out into the alleyway.

'He thinks I'm made of bloody money!' his father grumbled. 'Not content with eating me out of house and home, he wants to beggar me with the flaming electricity bill as well.'

'He's working,' Zoe said, rising to Alan's defence as ever.

'He's making headstones,' Victor said smoothly. 'You wouldn't catch me dead doing that job.'

'You *couldn't* do it!' Zoe snapped.

The oven door banged closed. 'That will be enough, my girl,' her mother replied. 'I'm sure Victor could do anything he set his mind to.'

Zoe knew she should have left it there, but instead she turned round, her face burning with indignation. 'Why?'

'Why *what*?'

'Why do you always think Victor's so perfect?'

The words left her lips too quickly, their meaning striking her mother full on the face. She drew herself up to her full height and looked down on her daughter. 'How dare you!'

'I only meant — '

'You're a wicked girl!' Jane Mellor hissed. 'You're jealous of your brother and it'll do you no good. You mark my words!' The punishment

19

was not slow in coming. 'Go upstairs and stay there until I tell you otherwise.'

Zoe rose to her feet, her eyes filling. For an instant she hesitated and turned to her father in mute appeal. Bernard Mellor looked at his daughter for a long moment. 'You've upset your mother again,' he said sharply. 'You ought to control that temper of yours.'

Without another word, Zoe ran up the narrow stairs to her room. The bedspread was cool and unwelcoming against her skin, the evening crowding round her. With a sense of intense loneliness she waited, alternately longing for, and then dreading, the sound of her mother's feet on the stairs. After an hour she realised that she would not come, and, excluded from the rest of the family, she lay listening to the muffled voices from below and the sound of the letter-box rattling as the evening paper was delivered.

'One day when I'm grown up,' she whispered, catching hold of the doll next to her, 'one day I'm going to have children and love them.' She rocked herself. 'Whatever they do, I'll love them,' she said, stroking the doll's face.

But it was bland, expressionless, and offered no comfort, and with a sense of cruel disappointment, Zoe dropped her hand on to the bed beside her, her fingers brushing against a feather jutting out from the eiderdown. Slowly, she pulled it out and looked at it, and then, with an impatient gesture, she pushed the doll away from her and rolled on to her stomach, plucking the feathers out one by one. It was her version of an old game, the one usually played with the petals of a flower, but in Zoe's mind the litany of 'he loves me, he loves me not' had changed for ever to something darker with no joy in it.

'Love me,' she said, pulling out a feather, 'hate me,' drawing out another. 'Love me, hate me, love me, hate me . . . ' she repeated, over and over as the minutes and hours passed.

3

It was the eve of Zoe's fifteenth birthday when Jane Mellor fell down the stairs and landed heavily on the tiled floor of the lobby. The noise brought Zoe rushing out of her bedroom, Ron materialising at the same instant across the landing.

'Mum!' Zoe shouted, taking the stairs two at a time and kneeling down. 'Mum, are you all right?'

Her mother's face altered, the pallor deepening to a dull crimson on her cheeks, her lips purple. Alarmed, Zoe rubbed her hands and asked Ron to fetch a blanket. Slowly, her mother's breathing began to settle, becoming more rhythmic from the livid mouth. In silence, Zoe held on to her hands.

'I'm . . . better now,' her mother said finally, glancing away from her. 'Get Victor.'

He was whistling, the lighted end of his cigarette glowing in the dark as he approached the house. The anger burning in her throat, Zoe ran towards him and stopped.

He faced her, his eyes straining to read her expression. 'Well, what's up?'

'Mum's fallen.'

She expected him to respond, for shock to galvanise him. Instead he flicked back his hair with his hand and nodded towards the house. 'Is it bad?'

'How would I know? You're usually the expert on everything.'

He laughed shortly. 'You always were awkward,' he said, falling into step with her.

They went in by the back door, Victor's manner altering as he approached his mother, his voice silkily comforting, while his cigarette burned on in the hearth where he had thrown it.

'Mum, Mum. You'll be all right.'

She smiled and touched his cheek. 'I will now you're here. Help me up, Victor.'

He lifted her on to the settee in the front room, the smell of the furniture wax powerfully strong in the cool air. Close to tears, Ron poked the fire and watched the flames redden, his small face turned away.

'We'll get the doctor,' Victor continued.

Zoe watched him and her mother, sensing the feeling between them, the bond which had always been there.

'Get the doctor, Ron!' Victor said, his impatience rising. Slowly, his brother moved to the door. 'And you can go for Father,' Victor continued, turning to Zoe, whose face was impassive, all anger contained. 'Well, go on!'

'Go yourself! I'll stay with Mum,' she snapped, glancing into her mother's face.

Their eyes met, the older woman's faltering, moving away.

'No, you go, like Victor asked you,' she said, her hand clasping her son's. 'Be a good girl now.'

Jane Mellor was admitted to hospital with a

23

suspected heart attack. Victor stayed with her until nine when he made his excuses and left, Zoe and Ron standing guard into the early hours. The ward was half empty, the silence relieved only by the woman snoring softly in a bed by the door. Fitfully, Jane Mellor slept, calling out for Victor, or Alan, or Ron as Zoe sat by the bed and watched her. The previous days had been halcyon, a blessed respite, during which time mother and daughter had gone shopping together without incident or argument, Jane showing interest in Zoe's clothes, suggesting certain items which her daughter agreed, readily, too readily, to purchase. They had even taken a trip to Manchester and eaten at the Kardomah, like normal mothers and daughters.

'You looked well yesterday,' Zoe thought incredulously as she looked into Jane Mellor's sleeping face. 'You fooled me again . . . and now you're ill, and what makes it worse is that you've been kind and I can't hate you.' Zoe shifted in her seat, suddenly afraid that her mother could read her thoughts. 'You fooled me,' she repeated to herself, turning as she heard footsteps behind her.

Her father nodded in greeting. 'How's things?' he asked, his eyes red-rimmed. 'What did the doctor say?'

'They want to do some tests,' Zoe replied.

'Tests? What tests?'

'To see what's the matter.'

'But I thought she was out of danger . . . '

Zoe dropped her voice. 'She is now, but they have to check her out.'

24

'Bloody doctors!' her father replied. 'Your Aunt Frances was all right until the doctors got hold of her.'

'Oh, Dad, you know she wasn't. She was very ill.'

'She would have been here now if it hadn't been for the doctors,' he insisted, scratching his chin. 'I should have shaved.'

'Mum won't notice,' Zoe said gently. 'Ron's there now. You can go in, if you like.'

'You'll wait for me, won't you?'

She nodded. 'Yes, I'll wait.'

Four of them were there when the final diagnosis came through. The heart attack had been brought on by the fall, but there was something else. The doctor paused, watching Victor fiddle with his packet of cigarettes. 'I'm afraid she has cancer.'

The words lost their impact as the door opened and Alan walked in. He seemed colossal in the small waiting room and because he had run all the way from Tom Mellor's he was struggling for breath, his wide face reddened with exertion.

'Where the bloody hell have you been, Alan?'

'Dad — '

'Your mum's been ill,' his father went on, 'but we can take her home now.'

The doctor glanced over to him, surprised. 'Perhaps I didn't make myself clear. I'm afraid that your wife — '

'I don't give a monkeys what you say!' Bernard Mellor replied, getting to his feet. 'She's coming home where we can take care of her.' He swung round to Ron. 'Come on, and get your feet off that table.'

Zoe glanced at the doctor and then moved over to her father. 'Dad, you can't take her home. Mum has to stay here and get treatment, you know that. It's serious.'

He looked into her face, into the wide eyes. 'Does she have to stay? Does she?'

His voice faded, lost its footing, and stopped. Then nodding, he sat down.

The radiotherapy began soon after, Zoe visiting her mother every day twice, before school and after, bringing treats, special foods, underwear. But as the days passed her mother's impatience accelerated; she would not read the notes written for her; would not eat her food; refused to answer phone calls; and lapsed into depression, rejecting all her family, except Victor. And he resented it. From being in the prime position of indulgence and privilege, he was now having to pay off the debt and it rankled on him. His visits became shorter, his tone sharper.

'Have you found a new job yet?' his mother asked, determined that her beloved son would provide the comfort she needed.

Victor shifted in his seat, having spent most of his twenty-six years avoiding work he resented any enquiry into that part of his life. Numerous business ventures had failed, or been replaced by unscrupulous and erratic dealings with low-ranking members of the Manchester underworld. Naturally corrupt, he mixed willingly with petty thieves and failed conmen and his reputation flourished. Before long he

26

became known as 'Slick Vic', his sexual appetite fed by a variety of willing ladies, his greed indulged by playing the horses.

'You'll be out soon, Mum,' he said half-heartedly, his eyes wandering over to a full-breasted nurse. 'You see if you aren't.'

'I'm not well . . . '

Her son sighed. Thinking it a gesture of despair, Jane Mellor's hand moved over his. 'Now, don't take on. I'll be all right.'

Victor glanced away, his eyes lowered, reading the time on his watch.

Touched by such filial piety, his mother said, 'You've always been a comfort to me, always. Not like the others, although Ron's a good lad.'

Here we go, Victor thought, she's as dotty as ever, and as repetitive. Anyway, Ron's a fool. Dumb Ron, the baby of the family, his small, almost feminine face constantly wearing its baffled expression. 'And I always had a soft spot for Alan . . . ' she continued as Victor scratched his nose and thought of his other brother. Fat Alan, sixteen stone of flesh lumbering around the garage at night carving marble like bloody Michelangelo. 'But I could never get on with Zoe. She's too . . . deep.'

Victor blinked at the edge in his mother's voice. She was wrong, he realised, but then she had always been wrong about her daughter. Zoe was sharp-witted and strong, her face dominated by a pair of brown eyes which slanted upwards slightly and gave her an exotic look. Too flaming exotic for Rochdale, Victor thought, smiling. Poor Zoe, out of place as usual.

27

'She's too old for her years,' his mother continued.

'Sssshh.'

'You see,' she insisted, her voice wavering, 'she's not like one of mine.'

Victor groaned inwardly and glanced back into his mother's eyes — and for a moment he was looking at his sister.

★ ★ ★

It had been a bitter night and the street was covered with a fine skimming of ice, making walking difficult. With her head down against the cold, Zoe walked to the corner and caught a bus, swinging into her seat and rubbing her hands together to warm them. Through the window she could see the town centre as they passed, and jumped when someone touched her arm.

'Oh, sorry, love. I was just wondering how your mum is.'

Zoe smiled and moved over in her seat. The bulk of the woman pressed her against the window.

'She's not well at all, Mrs Cheviot. The doctor . . . ' Her voice failed and she swallowed. 'I'm on my way there now. Do you want to give her a message?'

The woman looked at the girl next to her. She's losing weight, her face is getting pinched, she thought. 'Listen, Zoe, why don't you come to our house tomorrow night and have a meal with us? It'll make a change for you.'

She rejected the suggestion quickly. 'I can't,

who'd look after Dad and the boys?'

'All this nursemaiding's too much for you!' the woman said. 'You'll get ill.'

'I won't,' Zoe said quietly, glancing back out of the window, and thinking of the house in Buck's Lane. 'Besides, Mum needs to know I'm there. She relies on me.'

The words sounded phoney in Zoe's ears and she glanced at the woman beside her to see if she had noticed. Mrs Cheviot smiled, her own thoughts running on. Jane Mellor *should* rely on her daughter, but she doesn't, she thought. Instead she hangs on to that son of hers, and everyone knows he's no damn good. Besides, there's been all that trouble with the Clark girl, four months gone and not a sign of Victor Mellor taking on his responsibilities.

The unspoken words tingled in the air between them and made Zoe rise to her feet. 'Excuse me, Mrs Cheviot, I have to get off here.'

The woman smiled and moved her legs so Zoe could pass. 'If you change your mind about tea, love, just turn up, the door's always open.'

At the entrance to the ward Zoe peered through the doors cautiously. Her mother was alone. There was no sign of Victor. Dreading the reception which awaited her, she walked quietly over to the bed and looked down. Jane Mellor was asleep, her face surprisingly high-coloured, the rinse on her dark hair growing out and showing the grey roots at the parting. On top of the covers her hands clenched and unclenched themselves, the thumbs turned in towards the palms.

'Mum?'

The eyes moved under the paper-thin lids, but did not open.

'Mum?'

This time the lids lifted and Zoe flinched and stepped back.

'I'm in pain. Oh God, I hurt.'

Taking her hand, Zoe leaned towards her mother. 'Do you want the doctor?'

'It hurts, it never hurt before,' Jane Mellor continued, oblivious to her daughter's question. 'Am I going to die?'

Startled by the question, Zoe's voice failed her and she merely shook her head, wincing as her mother's nails dug into the flesh of her hand.

'I am! I know I am,' her mother replied to her own question, letting go of her daughter's hand and clasping the blankets around her stomach, pain making her cry out. Her lips were discoloured, stained deep like the juice from the winberry, her breath quick and sour. Zoe looked round for a nurse, but seeing no one, lifted a cup of water to her mother's lips. 'Drink, Mum. It'll do you good.'

Her lips moistened, she swallowed and lay back. Gently, Zoe wiped her mouth. 'There, now you go back to sleep.'

Timidly Zoe stroked her mother's hair, just like she used to stroke her doll's hair years ago. There was no response, but her mother didn't brush her away either. The ward was silent, holding its breath. 'Tell me where the pain is, Mum.' Tell me and I'll take it away, I'll have it for you, she thought. Let me have it, let me prove how much I love you.

'It's in my stomach . . . like something eating me alive,' her mother answered, clutching at the bedclothes, her face distorted, the acrid breath making her ugly, spoiling her. I remember you in that pink suit, your hair loose on your shoulders, Zoe thought. I remember you holding my hand and taking me to the hairdresser's with you. I remember you smiling —

'Get someone!' Jane Mellor shouted suddenly, her head falling back against the pillow.

Hurriedly Zoe got to her feet but her mother grabbed her wrist. 'No, stay, stay with me.' Distressed, she sat down again and leaned towards the dry face. 'You're my little girl, aren't you?'

The words sang in Zoe's head. You're talking to me, she thought, you're talking to me at last. You're loving me.

'You were always pretty . . . pretty eyes,' her mother continued, her face relaxing as the pain passed. 'Strange eyes . . . I was pretty once, like you. Be careful,' she said, leaning towards her daughter. 'You can get on, you're clever and pretty . . . I wanted to, but I was sick.' She smiled, an underwater smile. Unfocused. 'I had devils in my head,' she sighed, as though the explanation exhausted her. 'Sometimes I thought I'd go mad . . . I was cruel to you.'

'No — '

She interrupted her daughter by tugging at her arm. 'I *was* cruel to you . . . I shouted at you . . . I should never have done that.' Her voice altered suddenly as the words broke in the air. Reality

31

was proving too painful.

Recognising the change of mood, Zoe tried to soothe her and preserve the bond between them, however momentary. 'Mum, none of that matters now. None of it,' she said gently. 'I don't remember what you did, it's all in the past . . .' She trailed off, aware that her mother was watching her, her expression cold.

Jane Mellor said stiffly, 'I don't want to talk about it any more. Where's Victor?'

Zoe's face hardened. Love me, hate me, as always.

'Where is he?' her mother continued, her hands in her hair, dragging at the tangled ends, fanning it against the pillow. 'I want him — not that he's any good.' Her eyes moved around restlessly, a secret smile on her face. 'He comes here and looks at his watch when he thinks I don't see him. He pats my hand and can't wait to chat up the nurses.' She laughed suddenly, the sound deep and unreliable. 'I'm his mother, I know him. I know you all, Alan, Ron, Victor and you . . . my little girl. You are my little girl, aren't you?'

Zoe's eyes filled. Don't do this, she thought, not now. Stop hurting me — pulling me to you and then pushing me away. 'I'm your little girl,' she said numbly. 'Of course I am.'

'Of course you are,' she repeated. 'But you must watch out for the top window, won't you? And those dogs in the yard?' Zoe looked at her mother, baffled. 'And the man up George Street.' She stopped and lapsed into silence, then rallied, her thoughts coherent again. 'I dreamt of you

32

last night. You were a long way away.' She squeezed her daughter's hand greedily. 'I never took any photographs of you when you were a baby. Not one. I should have. You were so pretty.' She turned back to Zoe. 'Tell me you'll come tomorrow. Promise.'

Zoe's voice failed her.

'Will you come?'

Sunlight trickled across the pillow as Zoe answered. 'I promise I'll come tomorrow.'

Her mother's face softened. 'Come on your own, then we can talk. Just you and me. Like it should have been . . . We should have had such good times,' she said, suddenly baffled. 'Why didn't we? Why didn't I love you? Why?'

Tears welling up in her eyes, Zoe laid her head on the blanket next to her mother's hand. 'I don't know why. I don't know.' The whole weight of the lost years pressed down on her. 'Oh Mum, why didn't you say all this before? Why didn't you tell me this before?' Zoe asked repeatedly, looking up when there was no response.

Against the wide white pillow her mother's face had lapsed into sleep, the unanswered question circling over her like the clouds skirting the hospital garden outside.

4

'I can't bear to look at her,' Alan said softly, his hands running over the surface of a piece of stone. Carefully he picked at an imaginary flaw. 'Not that she wants to see me at the moment. On, off, on, off — '

'She's confused,' Zoe said automatically, making allowances. Playing fair.

Alan sighed and brushed some chippings on to the floor. They flickered under the garage light. 'She's not confused, she's getting her own back.'

Zoe's head jerked up. It was unusual for Alan to be unkind. 'That's rubbish! She doesn't know what she wants, that's all. She's in pain.'

'They operated,' Alan replied flatly. 'She should be all right now. They said that.'

'It's not so simple. She's been ill, really ill, and she's afraid.'

'So she stays at the hospital when she could come home?'

Zoe looked away from her brother. 'She feels safe there.'

'In hospital? No one feels safe there except doctors.'

Zoe sighed and fell silent. She could not more explain her mother's actions than she could understand them. Four weeks earlier Jane Mellor had undergone surgery; it had been a success and the cancer was removed — at least for the time being. The doctor had said so, just as he

34

had told them all that she could go home. Two weeks ago.

'You are my little girl, aren't you?' she had asked Zoe one afternoon when she visited after school.

'Of course, Mum, always.'

'Then you'll keep a secret.' She looked round quickly. 'I don't want to come home. There's a doctor here who's got a soft spot for me, a real gentleman . . . ' She smiled tenderly, exchanging a confidence with her daughter. Intimate betrayals. 'You won't tell your father?'

'But — '

Her mother's hand shot out and covered Zoe's mouth. A tube snaked out under the bandage, a blood spot flecking it. 'I thought I could trust you, but I was wrong.' Querulously, she closed her eyes. 'I want to see Victor.'

A trolley clanged its way between the beds, steam rising from a tea urn, the ward a distorted reflection on its metal side. Zoe looked away, her head banging. It had been like this for weeks, ever since her mother had first shown her any affection, the love she had withheld for so long now overbrimming. But soon the love had become distorted, its demands exhausting, compulsory.

'Oh, Mum, doctors don't — '

'Don't *what*?' Jane Mellor replied sharply, her mouth narrow with anger.

'They don't . . . you know.' Zoe shuffled in her seat uncomfortably. 'They don't get fond of their patients.'

The silence slapped both of them as a minute

swung past. 'I know that, Zoe!' her mother replied finally, her fingers flicking at the creased ribbon on her bed jacket. 'I meant he felt sorry for me, that's all.'

No you didn't, her daughter thought savagely, you meant to imply something else entirely, and I believed you. I fell into another of your traps. You scared me, and you did it deliberately. You hurt me, and I let you, just as I always do, she thought bitterly. 'Do you still want to see Victor?' she asked, her voice controlled, almost cold.

Jane Mellor studied her daughter for a moment and then shrugged. 'He's a fool,' she said lightly. 'No, I like it just with you and me. I mean to make things up to you, Zoe.'

The words had all the weight of a threat.

★ ★ ★

It was cold in the garage where Zoe was sitting, her legs tucked under her, Alan's donkey jacket around her shoulders. As she had done since she was a child, she sat in silence watching her brother, smiling when he turned and winked at her — an unspoken bond between them. Alan's protection was limited but inviolate on his own turf, the garage proving a sanctuary down the years, the place to which a smaller Zoe had run many times from the threat of the house. Tirelessly sympathetic, Alan would lift her on to the bench, then bend down and polish her shoes until she could see her face in them.

'That's sixpence, or a kiss, Miss Mellor,' he would say, leaning one full cheek towards his

36

sister, knowing that she would kiss him and wrap her arms around his neck, her face pressed into his shoulder. Sometimes, as she grew, the anguish took other forms and his affection, though constant, was less demonstrative. Coming into the garage in tears, Zoe would say nothing, merely walk over to the bench where Alan was working and slip her hand into her brother's. No words were exchanged, Alan understanding that, as Zoe left childhood, her method of self-preservation was to ask for affection whenever she needed it. And he never denied her.

Zoe's thoughts returned to the present as her brother turned round. 'I'm sorry, Alan, what did you say?'

'I asked you what you thought,' he said, holding up his carving.

Her eyes ran over the straight lettering and then down to the simple outline of a book chipped into the stone. 'It's lovely. But why the book?'

Alan shrugged. 'It's something they put on headstones, it's like the Book of Judgement — '

'It's the *Day* of Judgement,' she corrected him. 'So this must be a book of sins,' she continued confidently, 'where all your wrongdoings are listed.'

The garage door opened behind them and Victor walked in. 'You do talk bloody rubbish, Zoe! Why would anyone put something like that on a headstone? It's not fair on the dead,' he continued, gazing off as though reading something. ' 'Here lies George Tatler, who, as you can read from the list which follows, is to be recorded for all eternity as a right bastard.''

Zoe jumped off the work bench. With Alan she could relax, but it never paid to show Victor any weakness. 'I wondered when you'd get back. Your tea's ready.'

Victor leaned against the wall and grinned at Alan. 'I suppose you've eaten?'

'I had a snack when I got home,' his brother replied, discomforted. Victor could always make him feel clumsy, just like his father could. 'Anyway, you shouldn't be eavesdropping.'

Victor raised his eyebrows. 'Is this *your* garage? Is this *your* property? Did *you* buy it?'

'No. But it's not yours either!' Alan retorted, his face scarlet.

'You wouldn't catch me working in a garage — '

'We wouldn't catch you working anywhere!' Zoe responded deftly.

'Alan can answer for himself, little sister,' Victor replied snidely. 'He may be fat, but he's not dumb.'

'Why are you always on at me about being fat?' Alan shrieked, his voice cracking. 'I can't help it. Some people are fat — '

'And some are greedy.'

'And some are spiteful,' Zoe finished, walking past Victor and into the yard outside. 'Do you want your meal, or not? Ron's home and so's Dad, you can eat with them.'

Victor hesitated in the doorway, and then, as Alan turned his back on him, walked out.

The kitchen was hot, the cooker turned on

38

high. From the tiny snug came the sound of the television and Bernard Mellor's snoring. Zoe walked through and looked down at her father. His head was lolling to one side, his breath snorting in and out under the cover of his moustache, which had remained violently black even as his hair greyed. There were few common links between the four men of the family, she thought, although Victor did have the same narrow face as his father, and the same light hazel eyes. Yellow, Zoe used to call them, when she was angry. Fascinated, she sat down on the chair beside her father and scrutinised his face, trying to find some hint, however faint, of the bond between him and his children. But there was no trace of Ron's delicate features, and no hint of Alan's heavy, florid looks. In fact, she decided, there was nothing of herself there either.

Suddenly, he snored loudly and woke himself. 'What the hell!' he snapped, sitting up in the chair and peering at his watch. 'It's bloody freezing in here, what happened to the fire?'

Zoe glanced over to the grate; a sad blaze hiccuped uneasily.

'If you want anything doing, you have to do it yourself,' he grumbled, shaking some coal on to the embers. A wisp of smoke coughed out from the grate. 'Where is everyone anyway? I'm hungry.'

'Ron's in the kitchen and Victor's just got home. We'll be ready to eat when I call Alan in — '

'He's always in that flaming garage! Chipping

away half the ruddy night, I can't think what's got into him. I never thought when I sent him over to Tom's to learn a trade, that he'd end up like this. As if he hadn't enough of it in the day. Headstones, bloody churchyards! It's morbid, that's what it is.' He moved past his daughter into the lobby and then stopped, crouching down on to his haunches. 'Just feel that draught! It's blowing in here like God knows what.' His hand moved along the bottom of the door. 'Fat lot of good having a fire — all the fires of hell couldn't warm this place up.' He looked round. 'Victor! Come here.' His son materialised in the lobby, his hands in his pockets and a look of total indifference on his face. 'We need something for this door,' his father continued, getting to his feet, 'and we need it soon, like tomorrow. I want this place warm when your mother gets home.'

Zoe glanced over to her brother.

'You need some draught excluder,' Victor explained smoothly.

'That is your considered opinion, is it?' his father replied, with a mock smile. 'Well, bloody get it! And get it tomorrow, Mr Mellor, unless you're tied up on some important business.'

'I should be over in Bolton — ' Victor began and then stopped, warned by the look on his father's face. 'All right, I'll get it in the morning.'

'Aye, and get it put on by afternoon. I want it right when I get home,' his father replied, walking past him into the kitchen.

Victor watched him go. 'Old bugger could do it himself.'

'He has to go to work. You don't.'

Victor ignored the barb. 'Alan could do it, or Ron.'

'Alan's up at the stonemason's, and Ron's at school. Besides, he's only thirteen. It's a man's job.'

'I could have done it at thirteen,' Victor continued, his eyes moving to the gap under the door. 'Anyway, it's been like that for years, so why the rush to do something about it now?'

'Because Mum's coming home.'

'That's what he thinks,' Victor said slyly, moving off.

Most of the meal was spent in silence, chairs pushed back afterwards, dishes piled in the sink, Ron's greyhound nosing around the floor underneath the table for crumbs. Changing his clothes, Victor left soon after, his father returning to the snug and turning on the television to announce the start of a new panel game. Tired and cold, Zoe rubbed her eyes and sat down at the table, flicking pieces of broken biscuit for the dog to catch. Unwilling to move, she watched the animal's dark mouth and the long reach of its tongue.

'Hey, you shouldn't feed him biscuits,' Ron said, walking in from the yard. 'I've got proper food here. If you give him junk he'll get fat and never win races.'

'We've had Peter for nearly a year and he hasn't won anything,' Zoe explained patiently, knowing how besotted her brother was with the animal. 'He's not a champion, he's a pet,' she went on, stroking the dog's brindled head, 'so he

41

can eat what he likes.'

Defeated by the argument, Ron sat down next to her at the table and cupped his face in his hands. 'I failed Maths today.'

Zoe sighed inwardly. Ron never passed a Maths exam, he never passed any exam. As finely featured as an angel, Ron's appearance personified class . . . until he opened his mouth. With a gentle movement, Zoe touched his dark blond hair. 'You should work harder.'

'I do!' he responded violently, his face reddening, and making him all the more girlish. 'But I still can't do it.'

'You will, you just have to try a bit harder. Have you done your homework tonight?'

There was no answer. 'Ron?'

'I had to tidy up.'

'Tidy up what?' Zoe asked, astonished.

'The bedroom,' he explained timidly. 'Victor's been up there all day and it was a real mess. I couldn't find anything.'

The sleeping arrangements had been a problem for years. As the only girl, Zoe had her own room, tucked up in the loft, the roof sloping down at a rakish angle. On the first floor her parents had the main bedroom, and for a time Alan, Ron and Victor had shared one big room, until Alan's bulk had effectively squeezed both brothers out. Over a period of nine months some more rooms were built on to the back of the house, a second bathroom being added underneath on the ground floor, the new bedroom for Alan added above.

The way in which Zoe had described it to the

42

girls at school made it sound impressive, whereas, in reality, the extension was built on the cheap by some of Victor's acquaintances and the bathroom was cramped and bitterly cold even in summer.

'Victor should tidy up after himself,' Zoe said hotly. 'You can tell him that when he gets back tonight.'

The look on her brother's face was a study. 'I couldn't, he'd go mad! Anyway . . . ' Ron continued thinly, 'he never listens to me.'

Instinct made Zoe soften her tone. 'Does he bully you?'

'Sometimes . . . sometimes he says I look like a girl . . . you know, soft.'

'Next time he says that tell him' — anger made her incoherent — 'tell him you'd rather look like a girl than have yellow eyes.'

Ron blinked. 'Who's got yellow eyes?'

'Victor has.'

He thought for a moment. 'They're not yellow — '

'They are in some lights! They are so!' Zoe insisted.

Frowning, Ron considered the information. 'Not many people have yellow eyes.'

Zoe leaned forward conspiratorially. 'Exactly! Only cowards have yellow eyes.'

With an expression of complete amazement her brother looked at her. 'Go on!'

She nodded emphatically. 'It's true, for all his talk he's a coward. You can see it in his eyes. So when he starts on at you again, you just look into his eyes and remember what I told you.'

43

With a feeling of triumph Zoe watched as her brother's face relaxed and he smiled.

★ ★ ★

'There really is no reason why your mother should stay in hospital,' Dr Clegg explained. 'Her condition is much improved after the surgery. In fact, the cancer seems to be controlled at the moment.' He smiled and looked at the young girl in front of him. She's fifteen, or sixteen at the most, he thought, but old for her years.

'How long will it be controlled for?'

He weighed the question in his mind. How much should he tell her? How much reality could she cope with? He knew that Zoe was looking after her father and three brothers, just as he knew she was also having to attend school at the same time. It had seemed an unfortunate, but necessary arrangement at first, but now that her mother's prognosis was so uncertain she would need help, especially as Jane Mellor was so mentally unstable, a condition aggravated by the drugs she had to take.

He smiled sympathetically. 'I'm afraid that I don't know how long your mother will live. Really, I don't,' he added quickly when he saw a suspicious look pass over Zoe's face. 'You see, the cancer is controlled for the moment, but her heart is weak, and she can't undergo surgery again so soon.'

Zoe considered the information carefully. 'Will she ever be able to have surgery for her heart?'

44

'I don't know,' he replied honestly. 'That depends on her.'

A plan formed in Zoe's head. 'Then she should come home.'

'She should,' Dr Clegg agreed. 'She would be more comfortable — but we were wondering how you would cope with the situation. You see, she'll need nursing and you can't nurse her, go to school, and look after the family. Is there anyone else in the family who could help?'

'No,' she said emphatically, 'there's no one.' No one else was going to ruin her plan. She would look after her mother herself, and get her better — and then everything would be all right.

'No aunts or uncles?' he persisted.

'There's my uncle, but he's on his own. He couldn't help even if he wanted to.'

Dr Clegg tried to remember what the nursing sister had told him. 'But isn't there an aunt on your mother's side?'

A picture flipped up before Zoe's eyes of her mother's sister: a stocky, wide-faced woman, with an over-tight perm, a pair of thick ankles and a mynah bird. Mildred Cross, the Widow of Salford, married three times and widowed three times. 'Headstones to be provided at a discount from Uncle Tom,' Victor used to joke, 'with the inscription: "To those fallen in battle."'

'She's not close to Mum,' she said.

'They're sisters.'

Zoe panicked. 'My aunt wouldn't like it. She has a life of her own — anyway, she's not even been in to see Mum.'

45

'But if she didn't know your mother was ill — '

'Dad wouldn't like it!' Zoe insisted, interrupting him. 'He hates strangers in the house.'

'Be that as it may, your father may have to come to terms with the situation if he wants his wife home.'

The die, Zoe thought ruefully, was cast. The Widow of Salford would be prevailed upon to help out, with all the attendant chaos that would cause. She closed her eyes, a dull sense of weariness washing over her. I could have coped on my own, she thought — even with Mum.

'Would you like me to have a word with your father?' Dr Clegg asked kindly.

Zoe shrugged and then smiled suddenly, her eyes slanting upwards, her small face transformed, its attraction apparent. Dr Clegg found himself smiling back as she replied.

'No, thank you. I'll sort it all out and let you know what's happening tomorrow.'

He was still warmed by that smile when she left the room.

★   ★   ★

Zoe was not smiling as she walked up Buck's Lane, the February chill keeping the daffodils budded, the birds idle in the bald trees. Pushing back her hair with one hand, she glanced over to the garage thinking of Alan, and then back to the house in front of her. There was no one home — no one could be expected home at three-thirty in the afternoon, except her, and she was only there because she had lied, saying she felt sick after lunch. Knowing how the teachers pitied her, she knew full well that they would let her go and talk about her in the staff room later.

At first she had resented their concern, their polite sympathy. The insecurity which dogged her life had dictated her response to the world and to outsiders she appeared superficial and flip, an impression she did nothing to counteract. Having been swung on an emotional see-saw from childhood, Zoe trusted no one, and never let down her guard except with Alan or Ron. She marvelled that girls of her age had confidantes, that they swapped secrets and opened their hearts. Surely, she reasoned, it was dangerous to confide — a friend one day could be an enemy another. Besides, if love was not to be trusted, what good was friendship?

Safer to love wisely, Zoe decided, and turned more to Alan, knowing that he was not close to his brothers and terrified of his father. It was a wise allegiance. To her brother she was perfect, a mother, sister and girlfriend combined, offering understanding and sympathy, and, most impor-tantly, keeping the world at arm's length — because Alan had no wish to become a part of the world. Always acutely aware of his size, he had been a shy child, and after the trauma of school had slipped gratefully into Tom Mellor's enclosed sphere. Unless he was with Zoe, Alan allowed his work to speak for him, and on the windy bleak tops where many of the cemeteries were sited he would stand, still and silent, his bulky figure dark against the northern sky, thinking.

Zoe glanced up at the dense clouds and frowned; it could snow again and snow meant cold. She remembered Victor's half-hearted attempts to fix the draught excluder. It had fallen off a week later and now they simply pushed a mat against the door, the cold snaking past the edges into the kitchen. Suddenly angry, she sighed and pulled a piece of paper out of her pocket, reading the words and trying to understand the dull statement of her exam results. Fail, fail, fail . . . On and on it went, only the mark in art managing to lift her spirits momentarily.

Angered, she kicked the side of the garage, the tears starting in her eyes. All the excuses in the world didn't excuse failure, she thought bitterly, remembering what her teacher had said.

'My dear, you've had to cope with the worry of your mother's illness and look after your father and brothers. It's a miracle how you've managed, it really is. I don't know anyone else who could have done it as well.'

'But I used to be near the top of the class,' Zoe had explained, 'and now I'm near the bottom and it matters to me.' Her voice lifted. 'It matters because I have to take my exams, *it matters for my future!*'

The teacher had seen how upset she was and tried to comfort her. 'You could have extra coaching — '

'It costs money,' Zoe snapped. 'We don't have that kind of money.'

48

'Well . . . ' The woman trailed off. She felt for the girl, she really did, but although Zoe was bright she was hardly university material. She was attractive, she would get married. After all, she knew how to look after a house and family and precious few other girls did.

'There are other things in life . . . '

But Zoe had stopped listening then, her mind had blanked off like a shutter coming down on a camera. Click, the image taken, preserved — this was how I was. Past tense.

The house stared back at her, defiant: *Look after me*, it said, *and all who live here.* Snow began to fall, flakes masking her dark hair, making it grey, making her old. With resignation Zoe looked at her watch. Three-forty-five — she had only hours left before the Widow of Salford arrived. She didn't know which she dreaded the most — her aunt or her mother. She didn't know whether she truly resented Mildred Cross's intervention or welcomed it. After all, the relationship between her mother and herself had resulted only in disappointment, and worse, embarrassment. But how could she have known that it would turn out that way? Having been rejected from childhood, how could she have possibly supposed that acceptance would have brought as much heartache?

The snow flicked her face and made her hands cold as she turned the paper over and over in her fingers. Fail, fail, fail, she read. God, after all that effort, what's it all for? Work and more work, working for affection, for family, for school, for approval — why? To be disappointed constantly?

To fool herself into believing that things would change? That somehow she would get on in the world? That her mother would love her? That one day she could simply say and do what she wanted without fear of punishment or rejection? She glanced down at her hands, cold and red raw, the nails white, and then smiled, a sphinx smile, the smile which magnetised everyone.

But what was so wrong in fooling people, she thought. If they didn't know her, they could never get close enough to hurt her. If she was clever she could keep everyone guessing for ever. There would be no pain any longer, because Zoe Mellor was safe, hidden away inside. I will make myself a secret place to hide, she thought, and no one will find me. No one. Until one day, when I find myself a home.

Then slowly and carefully she tore up the paper and tossed it, high and weightless, into the terrible sky.

★ ★ ★

'What time's she coming?' Alan asked timorously, wrenching the padlock off the garage door and walking in. 'I haven't seen her since I was a kid. Oh God, I wonder what she's like.'

'Victor said she isn't called the Widow of Salford for nothing and that she poisoned her husbands,' Zoe said, her humour wicked. 'He said she'll poison Mum just so she can marry Dad.'

Alan bent down and lifted a piece of stone on to the bench. His face looked waxy with the

50

exertion. 'I don't believe it.'

'Oh, neither do I — I can't think anyone would want to marry Dad.'

Laughing, Alan glanced through the window towards the house. 'I suppose she will come tonight?'

'Guaranteed. Mum's coming back from hospital tomorrow morning and she insisted that everything had to be perfect before then.'

'But everything *is* perfect, you kept it perfect.'

Touched, Zoe glanced away. 'Ah, but I didn't 'bottom' it, did I?' Alan looked mystified. ' 'Bottoming' means getting right down to it. You know, hoovering under the beds and cleaning all those little parts that no one sees. That's bottoming.' She jumped on to the bench, her legs swinging over the side. 'Apparently anyone who is anyone does a lot of bottoming in Salford.'

A car drew up outside and Alan winced, glancing nervously out of the window.

'Is it her?' Zoe asked avidly.

'I can't see, it's too dark. I think . . . no.' He peered out. 'No, it's Victor.' His relief faded quickly. 'Coming home in a taxi, My God, I bet that cost a packet!'

'Maybe he wants to make a good impression. Show Aunt Mildred how a gentleman behaves.'

The garage door swung open and Victor walked in, wearing a business suit with a camelhair coat clung over his shoulders and his hair newly trimmed. Sliding off the bench, Zoe walked over to him and curtsied. 'Oh forgive us for not coming to greet you, sir, we thought for a moment that it was our polecat of a brother — '

'Cut the cracks. Where is she?'

'Who?' Zoe asked innocently.

'The Widow.'

'She hasn't arrived,' she said, sniffing the air around her brother, 'although possibly that aftershave put her off the track. You could cause a lung collapse with that, Victor.'

He smiled loftily and leaned against the wall. 'My, we are skittish tonight, little sister, what has got into you to cause this sudden flush of high spirits? Possibly the thought of someone to come and lighten your burden? Lift the pressure off those delicate shoulders?'

'Leave her alone,' Alan said bravely.

'Oh, dry up.' Victor jerked his head towards the house. 'Dad home?'

Zoe nodded. 'He's watching TV with Ron. He said that she had to take him as she found him.'

'Starting as he means to go on?'

'Exactly,' Zoe agreed. 'Mind you, I thought she'd be here by now, I gave her very careful directions when she rang.'

'You *spoke* to her?' Alan asked, incredulous.

'I find it's the only way to communicate over a phone,' Zoe replied, winking.

A beam of light suddenly illuminated the window as another car swung into Buck's Lane. Without a word, Victor smoothed down his hair and made for the door.

Zoe turned to Alan. 'He's preparing the ground. He aims to win her affections within minutes, and God help the rest of us.' She paused at the door and shivered. 'Come on,

Alan, we have to say hello.'

Under the garage light her brother stood motionless, his eyes averted. 'I can't. I'll come later.'

For a moment Zoe was irritated, wanting to persuade him to come with her, to force him to do his duty, but the look on his face stopped her and left her silent with pity, his fear palpable. 'I'll go on then, and we'll talk later,' she said gently, the metal door banging behind her as she walked out on to the smudging of snow.

Mildred Cross was in the kitchen, her hands outstretched in front of the fire. Seen from the side, she looked quite attractive, her features firm, her jawline clear. It was only when she turned that the full force of her character struck home. Broadfaced, with a blatant, blue-eyed stare, she scrutinised Ron, Victor, and Bernard Mellor and then, as though satisfied, she placed a large covered object in the very centre of the kitchen table.

'This is Albert,' she said, whipping off the blanket. A large mynah bird blinked under the light and began to whistle.

The master of the house responded immediately. 'I'm not having any bloody animals in here — '

'Oh, really, and what is *that*?' The Widow asked, pointing to Peter, cowering under the table. 'That is a greyhound, and a greyhound is an animal.'

'*Do your coupon! Do your coupon!*' Albert screeched. Four pairs of eyes were fixed on him instantly.

'It talks!'

'It is a mynah bird, Bernard Mellor, and mynah birds are famous for their ability to talk,' the Widow remarked. 'Albert always reminds me to do my pools coupon. I haven't forgotten one yet.'

'Have you ever won anything?' Victor asked slyly.

The Widow's eyes raked up and down his elegant form. 'I may not have won yet, but I may win in the future, thanks to Albert.'

'She'd probably do better if she let the bird do the bloody coupons, and she stuck to the talking,' Bernard muttered under his breath.

'What else does it say?' Ron asked, impervious to the look his father shot him.

Her voice softening marginally, the Widow explained; 'Albert says lots of things, whistles like a kettle, sings several nursery rhymes and can count to thirty.'

Transfixed, Ron leaned towards the cage as the bird regarded him. '*Who's a pretty boy then?*'

'I'm telling you, Mildred, I'm not having a bloody bird in my house, it's dirty.'

'No more than a dog!'

Bernard Mellor's face was livid. 'A dog's a guard. He earns his keep.'

'And a bird is entertainment. Albert lifts the spirits.'

'*Willow, tit willow, tit willow*,' the mynah sang blithely.

With one quick movement, Bernard Mellor snatched up the cage and made for the door, the

54

Widow in hot pursuit. 'I'm not having a bird in my house, and if you can't take no for an answer you can clear off with the bloody thing.'

They were just by the front door when Zoe walked in. She glanced at her father, then at the bird, then at the large, outraged woman by his side, and then at Victor smirking behind them. 'What's the matter?'

'This is Aunt Mildred,' he said silkily. 'Dad's just showing her to her room.'

'*Pop goes the weasel*,' sang the bird.

★ ★ ★

The Widow of Salford was used to her own home, she told them all repeatedly, and the makeshift little bedroom in the loft was not at all what she was accustomed to. Within an hour of her arrival she had organised a bed for Zoe in the front room, while cramming a selection of clothes into the wardrobe and the one drawer Zoe had cleared for her upstairs. When the job was completed she hurled her suitcase under the bed and went downstairs.

Zoe was peeling some potatoes and Ron was doing his homework on the kitchen table, his fair head bent down over the books.

'You'll have to move, young man, I need room to work,' the Widow said, and turning to Zoe, 'and you'll have to tell me where everything is kept.' Frowning, she glanced at the potatoes and picked up a peeling. 'It's good to see you've never been really poor. You're taking off half the potato with the peel. This is how it should be

55

done.' She snatched the peeler and the potato. 'Waste not, want not.'

Behind her Ron sat silent, his eyes fixed on the broad back.

'I can see I'll have my work cut out here,' she said, pushing Zoe aside as she flipped on a gas ring. 'What you children need is good home cooking — '

'Zoe's a good cook,' Ron said gallantly.

The Widow turned. 'I'm sure your sister has done her best,' she said without the slightest conviction, 'but she is a child, and children cannot cook properly. I should really have been called in to help sooner' — Ron's face paled — 'but I was only contacted when things got desperate. It's always the same,' she said, turning back to the potatoes and chopping them firmly, 'people think they can manage and when they can't . . . they come to me.' The full pan clanged on to the gas ring. 'People know I'm strong so they lean on me — just like my husbands.'

Ron shot Zoe a stricken look. For days Victor had been regaling him with tales of the Widow's husbands, describing how she poisoned their food and watched their death agonies. For a boy of only thirteen the image was horribly powerful. Carefully he gathered up his school books, and moved towards the door.

'Where are you going?' the Widow asked.

'Upstairs . . . to do my homework.'

'I'll help you,' Zoe said quickly, following him up the stairs and banging the bedroom door behind them.

56

The room was square, the ceiling low, and apparently divided into two halves as though there were an invisible wall there. The half nearest to the door was Victor's so that the full impact of disorder was immediately apparent. Newspapers, shirts and shoes littered every available inch of floor space, the bed unmade, the small table beside it sporting a radio, a lamp with its shade tilted, and a full ashtray.

By contrast the side of the room by the window was immaculate, the chair empty, the bed neatly made, a poster of Neil Diamond pinned over the bedhead. Under Ron's bed was a selection of games, all stacked, and jigsaws, his current passion. The only jarring note was a photograph on the inside of his wardrobe door of Muhammad Ali in all his regalia, and the legend written under 'Sting Like a Bee'. It mystified Zoe why the delicate, over-sensitive Ron would have chosen such a hero, and on the one occasion when she broached the subject he had blushed and murmured, 'No one would mess with him.' She had to agree. 'Besides I think I'd like to be black.'

She looked into his face, the fine nose, the light skin, the wide-set blue eyes. 'I can't see you black somehow.'

He had shrugged. 'You could if you tried. If I was black I could take up boxing.'

'You want to box?' his sister asked incredulously.

'Not me!' he'd replied quickly. 'But if I was black — then I could box. I could have been Muhummed Ali — if I'd been black.'

Zoe's mind returned to the present as she heard the cooker door being slammed shut in the kitchen downstairs. 'I don't like her,' she said, sitting down on the edge of Ron's bed. 'Mind you, I'd like to see her face when she spots this mess.'

'Victor keeps girlie magazines under his pillow,' Ron said suddenly, apropos of nothing.

'What!' Zoe said, rushing over and pulling back the sheet to reveal a glossy, large-breasted redhead. 'My God! Does Dad know?'

Ron shrugged. 'I doubt it, he never comes in here.'

Zoe's mind raced. While she still had her back to Ron, she tucked the magazine deftly under her school cardigan.

'Victor says the Widow poisoned her husbands,' Ron said bleakly. 'I won't be able to touch that food she's making.'

'Victor is an idiot,' Zoe replied, turning round to face her brother. 'Besides, you should remember what I told you about his eyes. Whenever he starts trying to scare you — look at his eyes.'

Unconvinced, Ron pulled a jigsaw out from under his bed. There was a photograph of a typical English village on the front, with a typically English church, in some typically English county hundreds of miles from Rochdale. Zoe gazed at the picture and imagined what it would be like to live somewhere quiet and tidy, where the roads were white, not like

Rochdale's church and town hall, evil black stone against a murderous sky.

'Who's bringing Mum home tomorrow?'

Zoe's stomach lurched. 'An ambulance, about ten o'clock.'

'Do you think she'll be pleased to be home?'

Who knows, Zoe thought dully, who knows?

Bernard Mellor came in late for dinner, moaned about the food, and left with Victor for the pub at seven. With a look of savage concentration, the Widow set about tidying the house, carrying the Hoover and a bucket of cleaning things into the front room. For twenty minutes she beat the worn cushions, shone the old-fashioned mirror and re-arranged the faded curtains, the furniture glowing back at her as she caught her breath. Zoe had to admit that although it was still the same mean little room it had been before, her efforts had made it a clean mean little room.

Then, without a pause, it was forwards into the snug, a room so crammed with chairs that it was virtually impossible to make it look tidy. But the Widow had plans for it. Totally disregarding Zoe's pleas, she moved Bernard Mellor's chair and re-arranged the seating arrangements, tidying all his smoking things into a cupboard, the dog watching her balefully from in front of a newly lit fire. The kitchen had already been re-organised so she made for the stairs, taking a sharp left into the main bedroom. With burning curiosity, Zoe followed, offering help which was, to her intense relief, speedily dismissed.

With a wrench of the Widow's resolute arms

the bed was dragged forwards and a frenzied Hoovering sucked up the dust. Then back went the bed into position as each wooden surface, mirror, and handle was subjected to a brutal polishing. The Widow's colour altered, her skin deepening to a warm pink, her sleeves rolled up, the admirable arms wringing out a selection of cloths. With a satisfied nod, she left the bedroom and made for Victor's, Zoe watching her expression as she drew back the door.

It was better than she had hoped. With a snort of sheer contempt each scrap of dirty laundry was collected in a pillowcase and hurled downstairs with the toe of her broad fitting shoe to help it on its way. The bed was systematically stripped and remade, the counterpane smoothed over the top, the lampshade straightened and the ashtray's contents flushed down the toilet.

When she had finished the Widow glanced round, and said majestically, 'Pig. Only a pig would live like that.'

Zoe was speechless with admiration.

'My first husband was a pig. Couldn't keep a thing nice around him,' she continued, pushing a duster into the pocket of her apron. 'I thought it'd kill me, all that cleaning. You know, for nearly a year after he died I couldn't look at a can of Pledge in the eye. And he left me nothing, not a damn thing! Never gave me a minute's pleasure, just work.' She turned to Zoe. 'You mark my words, a man who lives like a pig thinks like a pig.'

For a moment Zoe was sorry she had removed the *Playboy* magazine, wondering how vile Victor would have seemed if the Widow had found further examples of his bestiality. But touching her cardigan to check that the magazine was safe and sound, she made her way on to the landing, the older woman following.

'And this is Alan's bedroom,' Zoe said with pride as she opened the door and stood back to let her aunt pass. She knew for a certainty that the Widow would not fail to notice the stack of art books and magazines piled on the bedside chair, and the absence of laundry and cigarette butts. Admittedly the room was not particularly tidy, but it smelt of clean air from the half opened window and the bed sagged comfortably where her brother's weight had moulded it over the years.

'Where is he?' the Widow asked, her duster already aimed at the pile of books.

'He's working.'

'Up at Tom Mellor's at this time of night?'

Zoe stammered an excuse. 'He works in the garage on ideas ... designs.' She stopped, the word sounded grand, important.

'Designs for what?'

'Headstones.'

The Widow sniffed. 'I'm no stranger to those things.' Tact made Zoe remain silent. 'So how long does he work in the evenings?'

'It depends. Until late usually.'

'I still say he could have come in and said hello. It costs nothing to be polite. Nothing at all.'

'He's shy,' Zoe said finally.

The words made her aunt stop dusting as a

detached look came over her face. 'My late husband was shy. Hardly a word to say for himself. Came from down south, a nob.' Her fierce blue eyes defied Zoe to contradict. 'We had a really nice house and a car, holidays every year, Spain the last one. He was bad with his nerves though, being an accountant I suppose.' She considered the thought. 'Worrying about other people's money must make you nervous . . . He died on a bus,' she added finally.

'What about the other one?'

The Widow regarded Zoe coolly. 'What 'other one'?'

'The middle one. Your second husband.'

There was no reply, instead she picked up the Hoover and bucket and made her way resolutely downstairs.

Aware that she had hit a nerve, Zoe tried to make amends.

'What about Albert? Shouldn't he be seen to?'

The suggestion was greeted warmly and the mynah was rescued from the top bedroom. Obviously resenting his exile, Albert was singularly vocal.

'*Ride a Cock Horse to Banbury Cross. Do your coupons! Do your coupons!*'

The Widow's face softened with real affection as she undid his cage and lined it with fresh newspaper. Waste not, want not, Zoe thought wryly.

'You are a lovely boy,' she crooned. The bird put his head on one side, his eyes brilliant. 'You're my treasure, you are.'

'*Bottoms up!*'

The Widow's face stiffened. 'I got him from a publican,' she explained carefully to her niece. 'I'm afraid he reverts to his old habits when he's excited.'

'*Bottoms up! Bottoms up! Here's mud in your eye!*'

Victor eventually sidled in at ten-thirty, his father having decided to stay on out of reach. With mock admiration he glanced round at the kitchen. 'You've done marvels, Aunt Mildred. You really have.'

'No thanks to you.'

The words rocked him. Having always relied on the besotted admiration of the female sex, such animosity was upsetting to say the least. 'I . . . what's the matter?'

'Your room was a disgrace,' the Widow said evenly, her finger pointing to the pillowcase full of washing, her voice ominous. 'I can see why my sister is ill having to cope with the likes of you. You should be ashamed.'

Victor's expression was glassy. 'I don't have time — '

'You have time to visit the pub, drinking beer. So you have time to keep your room tidy.'

This was war.

'What I do is my concern, and has nothing to do with you! At my age — '

'At your age,' the Widow interrupted, 'I was married with responsibilities, and a child.'

'God help him!'

'What did you say?' she roared, leaning across the table. 'My son is the assistant branch manager at a Salford bank now, with — '

'Acne and a mortgage,' Victor snapped.

'My son has perfect skin!'

'Then he ought to stop wearing that Hallowe'en mask!'

'You'll come to no good!' the Widow shouted as Victor made for the door.

Zoe heard his feet pound on the stairs and the bellow as he reached the bedroom. 'What the hell!' The feet pounded downstairs again as he wrenched the kitchen door open. 'What happened to my things?'

'Everything's there — except the dirt.'

A slow realisation dawned on Victor. This was no pushover, this was a female who could make his life difficult. After a second's further consideration he smiled and moved towards her. 'I'm sorry, we started off on the wrong foot, didn't we?'

Don't weaken, Zoe thought frantically as the Widow's expression softened. Remember he's a pig, just like your husband.

'I'm sorry about the mess and in future I'll help you all I can,' Victor continued, turning on the kettle. 'You sit down and I'll fix you a cup of tea. You deserve it.'

With a sense of crushing disappointment Zoe saw the Widow smile and sit down, the kettle humming smugly behind her.

5

Jane Mellor came home to a tidy house. As the ambulance men helped her upstairs to the bedroom, her sister followed behind giving orders and reproaching one man fiercely for knocking the paintwork on the door. The patient was quiet, unusually so, her hair in need of a wash, her face pale so that the straight dark eyebrows showed like smudges on her forehead. When the ambulance men left, Mildred came back upstairs with a cup of tea and two digestive biscuits.

'Here, have this. It'll do you good.' She glanced round the room. 'I tidied up for you. Your girl's done a good job considering her age, but you can't expect a child to do a woman's job.'

'She seemed to be coping,' Jane said half-heartedly, sipping the tea. She felt stronger, much stronger than she had felt in weeks, but strange, out of place back home. Hospital had become her refuge, a place where she was the centre of attention, a release from a tedious husband and the constant family friction. Even her illness had seemed a small price to pay for her change in status. People pitied her now, there were bunches of flowers, telephone messages, a state of grace invoked by suffering.

'I haven't met your Alan yet,' Mildred continued. 'Damn funny I call it, staying in that garage and not even coming in to say hello.'

'He's shy.'

'That's what your girl said. But shy he might be, it's still rude. You know, he must have waited until I'd gone to bed before he came in . . . '

Jane's mind was wandering. She looked around and saw the shabby furniture and the small windows and longed for the activity of the hospital, for the constant checks on her welfare, the attention. Depression curled out from under the bed and smothered her.

'I met Victor though,' Mildred continued, tucking the blanket in tighter at the end of the bed. 'He's charming. I think we've come to an understanding.'

Her sister smiled to herself. Same old Victor, up to his tricks as usual. Even hard-boiled Mildred had fallen for his charms. 'He's a very special boy,' she explained. 'I know mothers aren't supposed to have favourites, but he was always so handsome, and clever — '

'What's his job?'

Jane frowned, it was typical of her sister to think about such things, to look for problems. Irritated, she became suddenly fractious. 'I don't feel too well, I need my tablets.'

Mildred was galvanised into action; she had nursed two husbands and looked upon it as her role in life. She was strong and therefore the right person for the weak to lean upon. 'It's horses for courses' her first husband used to say. 'Have this, love,' she said, passing two tablets and a glass of water. 'You'll soon feel better.'

But Jane Mellor didn't. As the day wore on she

became more and more discontented, her head pulsing with frustration, her voice querulous when she called for drinks or something to eat, the dishes refused almost as soon as they arrived. With an energy remarkable in her condition she lost patience with herself and everything around her, so that when the snow began again and smudged the outside of the bedroom window she turned her face into the pillow and wept.

Bernard Mellor came home from work early, pounding up the stairs two at a time and throwing open the bedroom door just as his wife was struggling with her pillows. He rushed over to her. 'No, no, love, let me. You'll strain yourself.'

Some of her irritation evaporated. At least her husband was being considerate. 'Thank you, Bernard. I find it difficult to get comfortable.'

He sat beside her, flicking on the bedside lamp. The shade was old-fashioned, painted silk, and hung with a weary fringe. It had been a wedding present, Bernard remembered, looking at his wife. He was cruelly aware of the changes in her, the figure which had filled out too much from enforced bed rest and medication, the dryness of her skin when he touched her hands; but the longer he looked at her the easier it was to obliterate reality and see her again as the timorous young woman he'd married.

'Got everything you need, girl?'

Jane nodded, smiled at him and patted her hair. 'I look a mess,' she said, her voice almost flirtatious.

'You look beautiful,' he replied, touching her cheek.

She rested her head against his hand, her anxiety lifting. If Bernard went on fussing her like this it wouldn't be so bad . . .

He sat with her until four o'clock, when Ron rushed in from school, running to his mother and wedging his small face against her chin, his eyes closed, his hair brushing her face. With recovered tenderness she held her son and crooned to him as she had done when he was a child, his body warm against her own. With an unwelcome feeling of embarrassment, Bernard watched them, turning only as the door opened again and Alan walked in.

'What the hell sort of a time d'you call this to come home?'

Alan blushed as he shuffled over to the bed. 'Hello, Mum,' he said. 'We've missed you.'

'What about our Tom? What about my brother?' his father asked impatiently. 'Does he know you've skived off?'

Automatically, Jane Mellor rose to her son's defence. 'Oh, leave him alone — '

'It's no good saying that! I want to know what's going on. He should be at work at this time, what's right is right — '

She moaned suddenly and slumped back against the pillows.

'Oh God, lass, I didn't mean it,' her husband said, his voice close to panic as he pushed Alan out of the way and knelt down next to the bed. 'We mustn't argue, it's not good for you.'

She nodded in response, but she wasn't

looking at him. Instead her eyes were fixed on the dressing-table clock. Half past four, she thought longingly. They would be having tea at the hospital now and a joke. Soon the doctor would be coming round . . .

'You have a little rest, love, and we'll come up and see you later.'

She winced as they turned out the light.

Victor crept in on her later, looking down at her face as she slept. Glancing over to the window, he drew the curtain against the snow flurry. Hoping it would wake her, he turned on the lamp, but she never moved and after a few minutes he left, passing Zoe on the stairs. 'Mum's asleep.'

'That's good.'

He lit up a cigarette. 'Tell her I popped in and that I'll drop in later.'

'You can't go out tonight!' Zoe said, astonished. 'She'll want to see you.'

'Well, everyone else is here, so she's not going to get lonely,' he said, totally unconcerned. 'Just tell her I'll be up later.'

'You're her favourite,' Zoe insisted. 'She's bound to want you with her.'

'In that case, it'll be even more of a treat when I come home.'

'You are a pig, Victor!' she said with real venom, striking out at him.

Grinning, he ducked. 'You missed!' he said, running downstairs and slamming the front door.

Wincing, Zoe continued into her mother's bedroom, relieved to see that she was still asleep.

Silently, she walked over to the window and drew back the curtain to look out. The snow had stopped, but frost glistened on the path and on the rough ground leading to the garage, the moon making each silhouette sharp and deceptively large. At the end of the lane she could make out the figure of Ron, walking with the greyhound by his side, and to her right a dash of light stretched from the garage window.

A movement behind her made her turn. Her mother was waking uneasily, her eyes opening slowly, her lips mumbling.

'Zoe?' she said. 'I meant to ask you yesterday — did you bring back those biscuits from the hospital? They're too expensive to leave for those nurses to eat. It's not that they don't get enough — you wouldn't believe what people bring them.' She pulled herself up against the pillows, the cold air making her shiver. 'It's chilly in here. I'll get cold, and you wouldn't want me to get sick again, would you? I need an electric blanket.'

'They're not safe for someone who's bedridden,' Zoe answered. 'I'll get you a hot-water bottle, Mum.'

'Well mind you wrap a towel round it. I don't want my feet to burn.'

'I'll wrap a towel round it, Mum.'

'Mind you do,' Jane Mellor repeated, watching her daughter leave the room before making her way over to the dressing table, pulling open the top drawer and taking out a large tin box. Safely back in bed, she opened it and began to look at the letters, photographs and old school reports which she had saved for over thirty years. Victor

70

smiled up at her easily, as did Ron, only the photograph of Alan showing a maladjusted child, dreading the camera. There were no pictures of Zoe. Screwing up her eyes she tried to read the writing on an old postcard sent by Victor when he went on a school trip, but irritated and suddenly bored, she pushed the box across the bed and lay back, her arms folded.

'What's the matter?' Zoe asked when she came back with the hot-water bottle.

'You can burn all that rubbish,' her mother said, pointing to the pile on the bed. 'It's all junk, dreams, fairy tales.'

Cautiously, Zoe picked up the box and sat down with it on her knee, turning over the photographs and letters, seeing her father's handwriting and the hesitant printing of children on old papers. At the bottom of the pile was a child's shoe, which Ron had once worn, and a badge with Victor's name scratched on it.

It was a record of the whole family, she realised. Almost. Carefully she replaced everything in the box, well aware that her mother was watching her.

'Get rid of all of it! Throw it out! I don't want all this junk around me,' Jane Mellor continued, turning on her daughter. 'You can think what you like, but I don't want it!'

'You will when you're well again, Mum.'

'I won't be well again!' she shouted.

'You *will*,' Zoe insisted. 'I promise you.'

'What do you know about it? You just want me to get better so you won't have to do all the work! It's no fun, is it, being tied to the house all day, having to look after a family?' Her eyes narrowed. 'Oh no, I don't suppose it's what you'd want, my girl. Well, you don't have to worry now that my sister's here. She can look after me, and she'll do it willingly.'

Zoe's face flamed with anger. Jumping to her feet she stood by the side of the bed and looked down on her mother.

'How could you say that! I've done everything I can for you, and I've done it willingly,' Zoe snapped, finally losing control and hurling the tin box at her mother. Jane Mellor flinched as it fell against her pillow and spilled its contents over the sheet. 'I've always tried to please you, but it was never enough, was it?' Zoe asked, pointing to the clutter of photographs. 'Why is there nothing of me there, Mother? Why?' she shouted, beside herself. 'No photographs, no letters, no records of my childhood, Why is that? I was your child. Why didn't I matter to you?'

Jane Mellor said nothing.

'Damn you! Answer me! You treasured the others — Ron, Alan, Victor — but not me. What did I do to make you ignore me?' Zoe asked, her whole body shaking. 'When did I cease to exist?'

Jane Mellor looked at her daughter for a long moment and then began to refill the box. With no emotion in her voice, she replied, 'You didn't cease to exist, Zoe, as far as I am concerned, you were never born.'

6

The months that followed dragged their heels, the house at the end of Buck's Lane growing warmer, the air musty in the bedroom upstairs where Jane Mellor stayed permanently, her initial forays downstairs curtailed as the effort of recovery proved too much for her, the attraction of invalid status infinitely preferable. And the Widow stayed on. Within weeks of arrival she had organised everyone so well that each of them, except Bernard Mellor, found alternative retreats, spending less and less time at home where the atmosphere was depressive, the air of sickness frightening because it was encouraged.

Victor had long since left, packing up his cases and making a bolt for Manchester, his patience tried by the cloying love of his mother and the affectionate tyranny of the Widow. He phoned home at least a couple of times a week, sending long-distance reassurances that he was working, although no part of his wages ever found its way to the shabby little house. It was easier for Alan, as he had always spent most of his time either at work or in the garage, but Zoe found herself imprisoned and envied Ron who could come in from school, eat his meal and then roam off with Peter, the dog as willing as he to escape the house.

After her outburst, Zoe retreated from her mother, conceding defeat and turning her attention to her schoolwork instead. The disappointment with her results galvanised her and she concentrated all her energies into studying, working late at night in the front room which was still her makeshift bedroom. But the effort was useless, and after her sixteenth birthday she recognised her situation for what it was — she was no academic and had no particular gifts, at least, none which were apparent. It was a Saturday morning when she took stock of herself, locking the door in the bathroom and wiping the condensation off the mirror over the basin to look critically at her reflection.

There was no trace of the child she had been only a year before. Now her figure had rounded and her face matured, becoming especially striking because it was so unusual. Scraping back her hair, Zoe looked at the oblique eyes, the straight nose, and the mouth, and then slowly she smiled, seeing what everyone else saw — the smile of the sphinx which made her unforgettable.

'You're a wonder, Zoe, you really are,' she said to herself, and, satisfied, pushed open the window to look out.

Buck's Lane was muddy, a summer shower making puddles in the earth road, the grass shabby with footprints. She sniffed at the air, suddenly invigorated, watching the clouds and stretching her hand through the open window towards them, her long fingers seeming black against the light. 'I'll prove myself,' she thought. 'I'll be so successful that none of this will hurt any more.' She turned her hand over, the sun nuzzling the skin. 'I'll be successful first, and then loved, and one day,' she whispered, 'I'll come *first* with someone.'

A knock on the door made her jump and catch her arm on the window ledge. Frowning, she looked down at the deep scratch running from her elbow to her wrist.

'Who is it?'

'Your aunt. What are you doing in there?'

'Committing suicide,' Zoe said flippantly, opening the door.

The Widow took one look at her arm and rounded on her. 'You're a bad girl to do something like that!'

Zoe sighed. 'Oh for God's sake, I caught it on the window. I was only joking.'

'Some joke, with your mother lying ill upstairs. You should have more sense.'

'Oh, leave me alone!' she shouted, running past her aunt and out of the house.

As she ran down the lane the bleeding accelerated and in an effort to stop it, Zoe tied her cotton cardigan round her arm tightly while making her way to Tom Mellor's as fast as her legs would carry her. Alan was nowhere in sight when she arrived, and so, after calling out for her brother, she walked round to the yard at the back of the shop. Tom Mellor was working, his head down over a block of marble, his hands tightly gripping the chisel and hammer, dust filling the summer air. Zoe hesitated and then stepped forward, glancing at the array of blank headstones propped against the walls of the yard.

Catching sight of her, Tom Mellor stopped chiselling, pushed up his goggles, and sat down on the crate behind him. His eyes were red-rimmed as usual, his hair white with marble dust. 'How do.'

'Hello,' Zoe said calmly. 'I came to see Alan, is he here?'

'Up at Rochdale cemetery,' Tom replied, wondering what his niece wanted and noticing the cardigan round her arm. 'What's up with your arm then?'

'I cut it.'

'Nasty things, cuts. Get infected if you don't watch out.'

'I don't suppose it would matter,' Zoe said, bitterly. 'No one would take a blind bit of bloody notice.'

Tom Mellor burst out laughing. 'By hell, you're like your father!' he said, sobering up instantly. 'I tell you what, luv, why don't you go inside and get us a cup of tea, then we'll wash that arm and get it bound up good and proper.'

Surprised by the unexpected kindness, Zoe did as he asked, her curiosity overcoming her as she moved indoors.

Tom Mellor had been a widower for nearly twenty years and the house suggested as much. Nothing had changed since his wife's death and the kitchen was as dark and uninviting as it had always been. Heavy paint which had faded to light brown covered the walls, the few cupboards old-fashioned, the only recent acquisition being a small fridge with a dented door. Even the window, although large, was covered with a yellowed net curtain, and on the table a selection of brown envelopes lay unopened.

Zoe filled the kettle and walked through into the front room. An acrid smell pooled out at her from the two large rabbit hutches in the corner, their occupants greedily eating a liberal assortment of greenery, their eyes alert, watching her. Zoe glanced round, noticing the small fifties-style radio and a pile of beer bottles in a black bin liner by the side of an old couch. The impression was one of determined squalor, relieved only by a very large, very new television in the corner, its blank face mercifully silent.

'Got an eyeful then?'

Zoe spun round. 'I wasn't prying . . . I was just looking at the rabbits.'

Her uncle grunted and moved back to the kitchen, pouring them both a cup of tea. From the open back door, the bird song slipped past them, the dust motes making hazy motions in the half light. Sipping his tea, Tom Mellor rubbed his hair with his free hand, white powder puffing around his head like a halo.

'What are you working on?' Zoe asked, knowing full well that if she didn't speak her uncle certainly wouldn't.

'Old man Barrowclough's stone. He made eighty-five — not a bad innings.'

He stopped, the topic exhausted. From the front room Zoe could hear the rabbits scratching against the wooden floors of their cages. 'How long does it take?' He frowned, not understanding the question. 'To make a headstone?'

'You don't make it, you carve it.'

Zoe persisted. 'How long does it take to carve one then?'

'A week's work, unless they're paying you on the cheap like, and then it's less. Two, three days. Depends.'

'On what?'

'On t'weather.' He glanced towards the door. 'It's not the cold I mind, never did. It's the flaming rain. You can't do a damn thing then. I could work indoors, but what with this cough — it's not on.'

Zoe nodded, uncertain how to continue.

'You should do summat about that arm,' Tom said, getting to his feet and wringing out a piece of cloth. 'Let me look.'

Gratefully, Zoe removed the cardigan, surprised by the amount of blood which had dried to a dull brick red and matted the material.

'Well you made a proper job of that,' Tom said brusquely. 'What was it in aid of?'

'I told Aunt Mildred I was trying to commit suicide,' she said, watching as he wiped away most of the dried blood.

Tom Mellor said nothing, even though he was laughing to himself. He had always loathed the Widow of Salford, as he loathed his sister-in-law. In fact, he loathed all women. But not Zoe. No, she wasn't like most of them, sharp and fierce. She was open and she stood up for herself. Trying to commit suicide, he thought, trying not to laugh, I bet that give the old cow a good shaking up.

'How's that feel?' he asked, when he'd finished.

'Better,' Zoe said. 'D'you think it'll leave a scar?'

'What would I know about such things?' he asked impatiently, then relented. 'But I tell you this, when I were only twenty I damn near cut m'leg off with a chisel, sliced through, it were. But it healed.'

'But did it leave a scar?'

'I still got m'leg, haven't I?' he snapped. 'What the hell fire difference does it make if it's scarred? You women want everything!'

Zoe decided tactfully to let the matter rest.

Tom Mellor had been back at work for nearly half an hour when Alan returned whistling as he blundered into the kitchen, his bulk clumsy in the small room.

'Uncle said you were here,' he said kindly. 'He said you'd hurt your arm.'

'Just a scratch,' Zoe replied. 'I came over because I had to get out of the house.' She paused. 'I can't bear it there any more, Alan . . . and I leave school next week. I have to find a job.'

He frowned, and wiped his hands on a soiled tea-towel. 'I don't think there's anything here, love.'

She raised her eyes heavenwards. 'Not here! I just came over to talk to you, that's all.'

Minutes later, Alan was back at work, Zoe leaning against a massive iron bin and watching as her brother brought out a block of stone and placed it against the far wall. There was already a line of writing chiselled into it — 'In Loving Memory' — and the one letter 'M' on the line

79

underneath. With surprising delicacy Alan sorted out his tools and laid them on the small bench next to him, strapping on a leather apron and pulling some goggles down over his eyes.

For the remainder of the afternoon Zoe stayed with them, although there was no conversation, only the steady sound of the tools striking the dull stone. Later, when the sun began to fade, a breeze caught at the dust and blew it on to her arms, the whiteness trapped amongst the fine hairs. Above the noise of the chisels she could hear the occasional dog barking, or a car sounding its horn as it rounded the bend from the hill. Both men toiled on, sweating, their faces chalked around the goggles, their hands working, or brushing the chippings off the carving. By six, the sun had dipped behind the wall of the yard, the light falling towards dusk, as Zoe left, smiling at Alan and tapping Tom Mellor on the shoulder as she passed. He waved and then turned back to the headstone, the patches of sweat under his arms dark on the white shirt, his apron chalked like a blackboard indifferently cleaned.

Reluctant to return home, Zoe walked back through the town centre, Rochdale quiet now that the shops had closed, the town hall a slab of ebony against the changing sky. Aware that her arm was hurting, she hugged it to her, her steps tracing the streets she had known from childhood, past the greengrocer where years earlier there had been a murder, and past the newsagent where John Baxter, the pianist, had been born. She paused only when she came to the school, leaning against the railings and wondering why she had never made any friends there, realising, with a sudden burst of insight, that she hadn't allowed herself to.

The building loomed in front of her, the front doors bolted. In another week she would have left this place, but left it to go where? Uneasily she moved off, and was just passing the traffic lights when she saw a sign in a window. Crossing over, she read, 'Junior wanted. Good wage to learn the trade. Apply inside or tel . . . '

It was with a curious recklessness that Zoe jabbed her index finger on the bell purposefully, the sound ringing mightily behind the shuttered door.

★ ★ ★

'What's a knocker?' Ron asked Victor as he lounged in the chair by the kitchen fire on one of his infrequent visits. 'Is it like a door knocker?'

Victor sighed. 'It's slang for someone who goes round knocking on people's doors and asking if they have anything to sell. Like antiques.'

'Antiques,' the Widow echoed behind them as she pulled some washing out of the machine. 'What sort of antiques may I ask?'

'All sorts. You'd be amazed what people have in their houses.' He paused and lit a cigarette. 'Valuable stuff.'

'Round here?' she asked incredulously.

'Round here, round Oldham, round Salford, round everywhere — '

'And you buy this stuff?' she asked, folding some shirts. 'Sounds risky to me.'

Victor's face was unreadable. 'I buy well.'

'Aye, and cheat every bugger!' Bernard Mellor snapped, walking over to the fire and lighting a taper for his pipe. 'Flaming rogue, you're nothing else. My grandmother had a clock bought by one of these types, only they didn't call them flaming knockers then, they had another word for it.' He drew deeply on the tobacco. 'Three bob they gave her, and it were worth near twenty pound! Robbery, that's what it is.'

'Only if you're dishonest.'

His father looked at his son with open astonishment. 'You were *born* dishonest, Victor. Dishonest and mean. You wouldn't give anyone a cold, and that's a bloody fact — '

'Language,' the Widow admonished.

'Oh, I'm going upstairs!' he said, banging the door behind him.

Totally unconcerned, the Widow turned to Ron. 'Where's Zoe?'

'I don't know.'

'But it's late, and she's never in late,' the Widow persisted, genuinely alarmed by the fact that it was nearly nine and there was no sign of the girl. She turned to Victor who was resting with his eyes closed, his legs stretched towards the fire. 'Go and look for her.'

'Who, me?' he asked.

'Yes, you!' she snapped, and then, pointing to Ron, 'He can't go, he's too young. You'll have to.'

'Oh, give over, she'll be in any time now,' Victor moaned, glancing over to Ron who was watching him avidly. 'And what's the matter with

82

you, you've been staring at me all night. What the hell are you looking at?'

'Your eyes,' the boy stammered.

Victor threw up his hands. 'My eyes! I've heard it all now.'

Ron remained transfixed. In the firelight his brother's eyes *did* look yellow . . . Zoe was right. He was a coward and that's why he wouldn't go out in the dark now. The knowledge made him reckless. 'Your eyes are yellow.'

Victor blinked once and then leaned forward, catching hold of Ron's school jumper, twisting it, and pulling his brother within inches of his face. 'Even if my eyes were yellow, which they're not, what is that supposed to mean, little brother? What does having yellow eyes mean?'

Ron was having difficulty swallowing, but managed finally, in a tiny voice to squeak, 'It means . . . it means . . . that you're brave,' he said, breathing in deeply as Victor let him go. 'Really brave. Honest . . . really brave. The bravest there is.'

7

The two sisters had been running the hairdressing business for the last thirty-six years, their own hairstyles bearing silent witness to their heyday. Marcel-waved, each tinted hair vehemently controlled, the sisters regarded Zoe with amiable eyes.

Miss Ivy, the eldest, was the first to speak. 'How old are you, dear?' she asked, her voice accentless, clean as the shop window.

'Sixteen,' Zoe replied calmly, as she looked at the two women. They were a couple of inches smaller than she was, both round and soft as a cushion, both standing with their hands folded on their stomachs.

'We need a nice young girl to help us out,' Miss Ivy continued, glancing towards her sister who smiled encouragingly. 'Time goes on, and we need a pair of younger legs.'

'To help,' Miss Violet said suddenly, entering the conversation. 'We need help.'

'Yes,' her sister said, nodding. 'Help.'

'I can do that. If you just tell me what you want, I'm sure I can help all you need.'

The sisters exchanged glances. The telepathy was obvious to Zoe.

'Lovely,' Miss Ivy said, Miss Violet smiling in agreement. 'I'm sure we'll all get on very nicely.'

'A hairdresser!' the Widow exclaimed, banging down a pan of cabbage on the gas stove. 'Firstly,

84

my girl, you shouldn't have been out so late, leaving us all running around worried to death about you, and secondly, you never said anything about wanting to be a hairdresser.'

Zoe slumped into the chair by the fire sullenly. She had no desire to be a hairdresser, she just wanted to get out of the house. 'It's a good trade.'

'We should talk about it — '

'Why?' Zoe asked bitterly. 'What's it got to do with you? You're not my mother.'

The Widow blinked and then moved, surprisingly quickly, to the bottom of the stairs, directing her voice up to the next floor. 'Mr Mellor! Mr Mellor! Could I have a word with you?'

Bernard plodded out on to the landing, the light from the bedroom silhouetting him on the landing. 'What the hell is it now?'

'A word please,' the Widow said stiffly.

Jane Mellor's plaintive voice swung out through the doorway. 'What's the matter, Mildred? Bernard was talking to me, can't it wait?'

'It's nothing to worry about, dear,' the Widow continued soothingly. 'I just need a quick word with your husband.'

'It's not that flaming cooker again, is it?' Bernard continued, shouting down from the landing. 'Because if it is we'll have to call in the men again, I can't fix it. Victor said he'd ring — '

'It's not the cooker!' the Widow continued gamely, her voice strained. 'It's . . . '

She was still talking as Zoe slipped out of the

back door and made for the garage.

Alan was peering closely at something on his work bench, and was so involved that he jumped when his sister came in. 'God, you startled me!'

Zoe sighed and leaned against the bench. 'Have you got a cigarette?'

'No,' he said quickly. 'And even if I had, I won't give you one, they're bad for you.'

'Victor always gives me one.'

Alan did not respond. He knew Zoe too well to rise to the bait, just as he knew that she only provoked him when she was upset. Remaining silent, he watched her out of the corner of his eye, seeing her gather a pile of marble chippings in her hands.

'What's up?'

'I'm starting work Monday,' she said flatly.

'Work? Where?'

'At Lady's Pride, the hairdresser's on the High Street. With Miss Violet and Miss Ivy, who are sisters of an indeterminate age who have matching dresses, matching voices and matching hairstyles.' Her voice was light, artificially so.

Alan moved to a table at the back of the garage and turned on an old, weathered kettle. Deep in thought, he opened a tin of biscuits, and offered one to his sister. 'I didn't know you wanted to be a hairdresser.'

'You know, that's just what the Widow said,' Zoe replied, biting into a biscuit and grimacing. 'Arrgh, Jaffa cakes! I *hate* Jaffa cakes.'

Alan ignored her. 'Do you want to be a hairdresser?'

She shrugged. 'I dunno.' She looked at him

squarely. 'No, of course I don't! But I don't know what else to do. I'm not qualified for anything, and I can't see myself typing letters all day. So when I saw the advert for a junior . . . ' She stopped, suddenly aware of the enormity of her decision. 'Stupid, wasn't it?'

'Not if you think you'll be happy there.'

'Well I can't stand being in the house any longer!' she snapped, flinging the chippings on to the floor. 'I can't stand being around all that sickness! Besides, Mum and I hardly speak, and as for the Widow — '

'She's a good help.'

Zoe turned on her brother. 'Sure, she's a good help. But I could have done what she's doing. I *should* have done it. I could have looked after all of you, just like I did before.' Her frustration filled the garage and made Alan flinch. 'It was *my* job, until she came along. I hate the bloody woman!'

'Oh, Zoe.'

'Don't 'Oh, Zoe' me!' she snapped. 'I don't want to hear it. I was cheated. Cheated out of my place here, out of my room, everything!' Alan could hear the hurt in her voice. 'I might have got closer to Mum if we'd been on our own — ' She turned away, her voice breaking. 'God, who am I kidding! Nothing would have changed,' she said with resignation. 'Anyway, I've made my decision now and I might even enjoy hairdressing. I mean, you were forced into working at Tom's and you're really happy there now.'

'I wish the same for you,' Alan said gently.

The kitchen was full of steam when Zoe

87

returned, the window blanked out with condensation, the mynah bird in its cage on the table, whistling. The Widow glanced up, her eyes narrowed, and then turned her attention back to Albert. 'Here's the naughty girl, bold as brass. Not a word of apology, I'll be bound!'

Ron peered round the back of his chair and raised his eyes to his sister as she moved over to the cage. 'Albert looks well.'

The Widow was not about to be appeased so easily. 'No thanks to you! All this upset, it's bad for him.'

'Why?' Ron asked, fascinated, his bravery restored since Victor's departure an hour earlier.

'Upset makes him moult.'

Zoe fixed her eyes on the bird, seeing a sudden image of a bald Albert swinging on the perch.

'How's Mother?' she asked. Having restricted her visits to a minimum, she relied on her aunt's frequent updates to keep her in the picture as to the invalid's health.

'She's a little better. She fancied some dinner,' the Widow said smugly. 'She likes my cooking.'

Ron pulled a face.

'I could pop up and see her — ' Zoe began.

Immediately her aunt interrupted. 'Not just now, dear. She's having a little rest and said to say good night to you.'

★ ★ ★

The summer scorched into a heatwave, temperatures rising early and lingering in the eighties through the listless, lengthy days. In the upstairs

88

bedroom Jane Mellor tossed and turned in her bed, an endless supply of cool face flannels applied by her sister on to her burning forehead, bedpans emptied, sheets changed, the cloying smell of sickness permeating the hot house. Sun poured in through the window and dribbled along the thin carpet, trickling down the stairs and pooling in the boiling kitchen.

The only place which remained cool was the high ground bordering the moors. There a breeze still blew, the clean air of Edenfield thick with colour and insects, the savage blue sky endless, the grass blistered in parts, but cool under the welcome trees. Many times that summer Alan would stride out, making for the high spaces outside Rochdale, away from the thick air and the arguments at home.

Victor visited home when it suited him, his excursions up to the sickroom brief but longed for by his mother, her arms extended towards him like one of Tom Mellor's angels. With a cowardliness which shamed him, Alan avoided his mother and left the comforting to Ron who, not realising the seriousness of her condition, sat with her often, reading. Only Zoe was unwelcome in the sickroom, her visits awkward, her mother's cruelty having resounded in her head until it obliterated all other feelings. With a resourcefulness she had not believed she possessed, Zoe distanced herself, making sure that another member of the family was always present when she saw her mother, never giving Jane Mellor the opportunity to strike out at her again. She learned to protect herself, but in doing so, she changed.

As the summer smouldered on, Lady's Pride offered a welcome respite, although the tiny salon was dizzily hot by eleven in the morning, the heat from the hairdryers making Miss Ivy short-tempered, her skin livid, her hands unusually clumsy as she attended the customers.

'My sister never could bear the heat,' Miss Violet said sympathetically, nodding to someone who was just leaving.

Zoe glanced at the woman next to her, noticing the smooth skin, the perfect hair. Cool as stone. 'But you don't mind it?'

She smiled indulgently. 'I went to Paris once in the middle of a summer like this one,' she confided, the heady temperature of the salon encouraging intimacy. 'With my fiancé.'

Zoe paused, her hands submerged in a bowl of water as she rinsed out the perming rollers. 'Your fiancé?'

Miss Violet smiled impishly, the sunlight making her features even, bleached back into girlhood. 'He was in the Army. He died in the war.' Her eyes gazed past Zoe's shoulder, almost as though he stood there in his uniform in the hot little shop. 'Killed in action.' Zoe shivered. 'I could have been married,' the woman continued, stepping back away from the window, the shadow ageing her again, taking the magic away. 'My sister, poor dear, was never asked . . . So I don't mention him. It would only upset her, and there's no point being unkind, is there?'

But if the sisters offered a quiet haven, the

Widow continued in her usual vehement fashion, her sharp eyes missing nothing, her tongue passing judgement on everyone, her meals prepared without imagination and eaten without enjoyment, Albert's dulcet tones curling down the staircase into the stuffy house as the day began. No one asked how long she would be staying; it seemed to tempt fate, as each of them knew the Widow would remain as long as Jane Mellor did. That while her sister lived, Mildred Cross would live with them all.

Then when Jane Mellor did deteriorate, the suddenness of her failing stunned everyone, her husband incapable of understanding, only Zoe realising that the decline would, like rain down a window, run its inevitable course. And, of course, Victor refused to see the obvious and remained light-hearted, feckless, his attitude unfeeling, his tenderness superficial and on show only when he was with his mother. Cocky and secure in his mother's favours, Victor soon became insufferable. Zoe could have endured it herself, but after he had played a particularly spiteful trick on Ron she decided that he had to be taught a lesson. Running into the back bathroom, she locked the door behind her and sat on the edge of the bath. In a blind rage, Zoe decided to get her own back. But how? She narrowed her eyes and thought . . . and then remembered the *Playboy* magazine.

With a look of pure delight on her face, Zoe pulled it from its hiding place behind the wash-hand basin and, tucking it under her jumper, walked back to the kitchen. The Widow was bent over the table, Albert singing to her from his cage.

'I thought it was Victor's turn to clean the bird out.'

'The bird,' the Widow replied sharply, 'is called Albert. But you're right, it *is* Victor's turn. Give him a shout, it's about time he did something. I have to go down to the shops.' She moved towards the front door and turned. 'He's bone idle, good for nothing. You mind he cleans out my Albert properly — I clean up enough after him.'

Zoe waited until she saw the Widow's bulky figure disappear around the corner of Buck's Lane and then, with a hoot of triumph, proceeded to empty out the soiled newspaper from the bottom of Albert's cage and replace it with the centrefold from her brother's *Playboy* magazine. The bird whistled softly as it swung above the full frontal nude, its bright eyes not unlike Victor's own. The deed completed, Zoe waited in the safety of the front room, hearing Victor's muffled conversation with her mother upstairs, and cringing as she saw the Widow round the bend, returning towards the house. Step by step she advanced, her bare arms swinging the shopping, her face stern. The front door opened and she walked in. Zoe heard the slam of the shopping on the kitchen sideboard and imagined her aunt's delighted face as she saw the clean cage in the middle of the table. She would be walking over to get a closer look now . . . she would peer in . . .

Total silence followed. Complete, total silence.

Not a word. Not a shout. Nothing. Zoe shifted her position and listened. In fact, she was just about to see what was happening when, with undisguised glee, she heard the kitchen door flung back on its hinges and the heavy feet of the Widow moving to the bottom of the stairs.

'Pig!' she bellowed. 'You're nothing but a pig, Victor Mellor! You get down here, and get down here now. I want a word with you!'

'Bottoms up!' cackled Albert behind her.

★ ★ ★

Due to a big wedding that Saturday, Zoe had to stay late at the salon, the heat still burning in through the open doors and windows, the customers fraught and slow to tip. Harrassed, Zoe worked on, Miss Ivy incapacitated and lying down in the flat above, Miss Violet coolly competent, her hands winding up innumerable heads of hair. By six, the last coiffure had been lacquered into an immovable mass, and the till slammed closed for the last time.

Zoe leaned back against the hand basin and looked around. Faded hairstyles from the fifties and early sixties looked down on her, the covers of *Woman's Realm* as aged and yellow as old railway posters. No trace of Vidal Sassoon had ever impinged on the Lady's Pride salon; indeed, no one under fifty ever came in. Fashion was not important; value was. Here hemlines had always remained firmly below the knee, a perm only considered worth its money if each hair remained crimped for months. 'Getting your money's worth' in Rochdale was important, and a hairstyle, like a corset, was expected to last.

Yawning with exhaustion, Zoe stretched and then changed, hanging up her checked overall and pulling on a sleeveless dress. Opening the door on to the warm street, she waved to Mr Riley across the road and turned towards home. The evening was indolent as her feet dragged on the pavement, her head buzzing with tiredness. By the time she reached Buck's Lane it was nearly seven, the sun dipped, the heat releasing its grasp, the house dark against the sated sky.

And quiet. Too quiet. Her steps quickening, Zoe moved towards the front door, opening it just as the Widow walked into the lobby.

She stopped. 'We've been looking for you. Everyone's in the snug.'

Not wanting to face her family then, Zoe moved past her aunt and started to mount the stairs. Each step was soundless, endless, the closed door to her mother's room facing her. It's over, she thought, waiting for the sense of grief, or even relief, but there was nothing.

Slowly she turned the handle and walked in. The curtains were drawn, but because they were unlined they only shaded the room and did not darken it. Standing by the doorway, Zoe's first impression was one of heat and sickliness, and then she became aware of a stillness which was not natural. Stiffly, she turned her head towards the bed and took in her breath sharply when she saw the sheet drawn up over her mother's face.

She was across the room in several quick paces, pulling the sheet away. No one could breathe if their face was covered, she thought stupidly, especially in this heat — then she realised that her mother was dead. She realised it and was instantly afraid, then, disbelieving, bent down towards the still figure. Jane Mellor's eyes were closed, but her mouth was slightly open and looked dark inside, ugly and without life. But that was because there *was* no life, Zoe thought suddenly. Her mother's life was over. Finished. Completed on a hot Saturday, in a room with the windows closed so tightly that not a breath of air could get in to her.

'I was afraid of you,' Zoe said simply, her voice dull, her anger directed at the closed face, 'because you frightened me and you made me unhappy . . . I used to hide from you!' Then, with a vicious gesture, she pinched the cold skin of her mother's arm. 'It doesn't hurt, does it? I don't suppose you can feel anything, can you? How typical of you, Mother, to sneak away before I could even get my own back.' Zoe's breathing was harsh, tight in her chest. 'You were a bitch!' she said bitterly, expecting some response. 'A bitch!' she repeated, pinching her mother's arm again, and then, shocked, she began to cry, rubbing the dead skin to soothe it. 'I don't want to hurt you, but you were cruel to me . . . and now you're dead. Just like that. Gone.' Zoe's sympathy evaporated quickly into bitterness. 'I'll say one thing for you, you went quietly. I expected a scene . . . ' She smiled grimly. 'You fooled me again, didn't you?' she continued, leaning down towards the body. 'I had you at my mercy here, just like you had me

95

at your mercy when I was a child — but I let you off!' She stepped back, away from the bed, tears of frustration burning her cheeks. 'I never punished you — but I will now. Can you see me? Can you? Well, I just want you to know that I'm not crying for you — you're dead and I don't feel anything. That's my revenge on you, Mother, I don't care.'

But she did care and her grief winded her, making her forget the bad memories and recall only the pathetic traces of Jane Mellor which remained — the old pink suit which was still hanging in the wardrobe, and the out of date bottles of hair colour on the bathroom window. She remembered her mother painting her nails for the first time, and lifting her down from the bus when she was still small — and try as she might she could recall nothing of the rejections, the thousand unkindnesses which had been so erratically inflicted. All that remained were the random gestures of affection until she heard, and saw, and remembered only the mother she had wanted — the frail and changing spirit which had ghosted her childhood.

Unable to leave her mother's side, Zoe wandered aimlessly around the room, arranging and rearranging the curtains and then smoothing the sheet. As she did so her foot struck an object lying by the side of the bed, and bending down, Zoe saw the tin box which had been the cause of their final confrontation. Reluctantly she picked it up and held it for a long time, hesitating, wanting to open it and destroy its contents, to tear up each piece of paper and throw each memento into the fire; to punish her mother and revenge herself.

But the impulse passed, and instead of destroying it she laid the box beside her mother's hand. 'It's your family, Mum,' she said, defeated. 'Do you see how I forgive you?'

But the gesture provided no absolution for Zoe. For nearly half an hour the room hummed round her, the open mouth of her mother still a challenge. Unthinkingly cruel. The hundred reminders of her illness crouched on the bedside table — the half empty bottles of medicine which would never be finished and the water warming in its glass.

There is something still to be done, Zoe thought blindly, some way to say goodbye properly. Then, just as the light was fading, she knew what to do. Getting to her feet, Zoe went into her own room and searched through the cupboards before returning minutes later to her mother's bedside.

'I did exist, Mum ... ' she said gently, opening the tin box for the last time and laying amongst its contents a piece of her own baby hair, ' . . . and I *was* born.'

PART TWO

Reality

8

Rochdale
1978

'It's immoral,' Bernard Mellor said for the third time as he read his paper.

Zoe looked up and winked at Alan. 'What is?'

'This test-tube baby. If we were meant to have been born in test-tubes we'd have giant bloody greenhouses, not maternity wards.'

'I don't see anything wrong with it,' Zoe replied evenly. Her brothers exchanged glances. No one, apart from Zoe, ever disagreed with Bernard Mellor. If he had been difficult before their mother died, he was close to impossible now. He missed her, they all knew that, but he never spoke about her. The loss had aged him, his hair completely white now, two years after her death, the black splash of his moustache greying under the sharp nose.

'I still say it's unhealthy!' he insisted, turning his attention to Alan. 'And that's the third piece of toast you've had, you greedy sod!'

The kitchen was tidy, even though the Widow had left a week after Jane Mellor died. Apparently her usefulness had ceased with her sister's death and she needed another outlet. The other outlet turned out to be Edwin Storey, a thin widower with a wart on the end of his nose and a house in Hayfield. Having sighted her prey, the Widow left and from that day on, the only contact the Mellors had with her was a card at Christmas. No one missed her.

Zoe found the business of looking after four men relatively easy. Not overly houseproud, she was concerned only that everyone was fed, housed and watered, her talents lying more in the direction of confidante, than housekeeper. Alan relied on her as much as ever, although Ron's sudden development from a girlishly pretty boy into a six-foot Adonis caught even his sister off guard. No one was prepared for this astonishing creature, whose voice, when it broke at fifteen, was so deep that it was totally at odds with his appearance.

'It's flaming weird,' his father said for the hundredth time. 'It doesn't suit him, it's like he's trying it out for someone else.'

'He's embarrassed by it,' Zoe said sympathetically.

'Embarrassed!' he replied. 'Don't be so damn soft — he'll always get a round in the pub with a voice like that.'

But Ron refused to see the advantages, and for several months was mortified until his body filled out, and his effeminate appearance matured into classical good looks which left Victor disgruntled and not a little jealous.

'He looks like a poof.'

'I don't think so, Victor,' Zoe replied smoothly. 'All the women are in love with him. You should watch out or you'll be losing your girlfriends.'

'Women like brains as well as brawn,' he

102

countered, 'and brains are something Ron is woefully lacking.'

Zoe rose to his defence immediately. 'He doesn't want to be a neurosurgeon. And he's very kind.'

Her brother smiled maliciously. 'He may well be, but he's not going to get on in the world. Not with a peanut for a brain.'

'Oh, I don't know, Victor, you managed it.'

As they all found their feet — Alan content at Tom Mellor's, Victor working as a knocker, or 'dealer' as he would insist on calling himself, and Ron apprenticed at the engineering works — Zoe remained at the salon, hopelessly out of place, and, at eighteen, aware that her future looked bleak. Her mother's death had had a peculiar effect on her, so that long after grief was timely, the loss proved draining. Aware of the hopelessness of her situation, Zoe actively sought to change it, seizing her chance when she spotted a small notice on the back page of the local paper, advertising the local art college, the Holman Hunt, and announcing that the new term would begin the following week. Without any particular idea why she did so, Zoe went along to enrol.

The Holman Hunt College did not live up to the grandeur of its name, being tucked firmly behind the town hall and merely consisting of two draughty studios, an indifferent coffee shop and a staff room firmly off limits to the students. The more promising applicants had already been accepted by the Manchester College of Art, so that only the mediocre remainders found themselves at the Holman Hunt, their portfolios clasped under their arms, their expressions a mixture of embarrassment and defiance. Looking round, Zoe realised she was the only one who had brought nothing with her and for a moment she hesitated.

'Can I help you?'

She turned. The man before her was tall, angular and attractive, his long, pale face topped by a head of thick black hair with a grey streak running from his left temple like a feather. He wore green corduroy trousers, an open-necked shirt and a long woollen scarf twisted rakishly twice around his neck. As he extended a suitably artistic hand in greeting Zoe smiled with relief. This man she could handle — he was too similar to Victor to fool her.

'My name is Foreshaw, Steven Foreshaw,' he said, smiling, his cultured voice at odds with the mean surroundings. 'The tutor for the life class.'

'I'm Zoe Mellor — a would-be student,' she replied easily. 'That is, I *was* going to be a student only I think I've made a mistake.' She leaned towards him. 'I'm a hairdresser actually and no bloody good at that either!'

Steven Foreshaw was captivated. Struggling in his pocket he pulled out a packet of cigarettes and offered her one.

'No thanks.' Zoe looked round and shrugged. 'Unfortunately I don't think this is really the place for me. Everyone looks so serious.'

He followed her gaze, taking in the huddle of students with their portfolios, knowing from grim experience that he would have to go over every dull sketch, one by one. Teaching the unteachable.

'You must have come for a reason,' he persisted, determined that the unusual girl in front of him would not only stay, but provide him with a very welcome diversion. 'You must think that you have some talent.'

Zoe raised her eyebrows. 'Talent?' She seemed genuinely astonished. 'Oh, I didn't realise it was so serious. I thought perhaps people just came for a change . . . you know, as a lark.'

Steven Foreshaw blinked. Art to him was the holy of holies, the reason for his life, his muse, as he was so fond of telling everyone. Not a 'lark'. He smiled grimly and readjusted his scarf. 'I was always taught to believe that art was a serious matter.'

Zoe smiled archly. 'Why? Because you're only talented if you have to work for it, Mr Foreshaw?' He loved the way she said his name. She made it sound teasing, encouraging, familiar.

Fully aware of the effect she was having on the man, Zoe pretended to consider the matter. 'It seems such a lot of effort.' She began to move off, knowing that he would follow her. 'Maybe I don't have the dedication to be a painter.'

'I could help you,' he said deftly, catching her arm.

Zoe raised her eyebrows. 'But you haven't seen my work. I might be hopelessly untalented.'

'I doubt it.'

A long moment passed, Foreshaw holding his breath, Zoe flattered by his interest and her own power over the man. Finally she turned and, smiling her most stunning smile, said simply, 'You're the tutor for the life class?' He nodded, playing the game. 'Well, I suppose I better start living then.'

Bernard Mellor looked at his daughter in total astonishment, while she sat, chewing a piece of bacon, her eyes fixed on her plate. 'An art school! You're cracked, that's what you are! Barmy,' he said sharply. Ron kept his head down, turning only when Victor walked in.

With the benefit of long experience, he summed up the situation immediately. 'What's the matter now?'

Zoe glanced up at her brother. 'I'm going to art school, for lessons.'

'Art school,' he repeated, sitting down. 'I thought you wanted to be a hairdresser.'

'I am a hairdresser,' she replied patiently. 'I will still be a hairdresser, I'll just be taking art lessons in my own time.'

'It's soft,' her father snorted.

Infuriated by his attitude, Zoe dug in her heels. 'I could draw at school. I was good — '

'No one ever made money from painting pictures.'

Victor leaned towards his sister. 'Why?'

'Why what?'

'Why do you want to waste your time doing something like that?'

'Why would it be wasting my time?' she said, laying down her knife and fork, exasperated. 'I'm bored with that hairdresser's. I went there because I didn't know what else to do. It seemed like a good idea at the time. It brought in a wage which we all needed, and it kept me out of the bloody house — '

Her father looked up sharply. 'Hey, less of that!'

'Why?' she snapped. 'I'm sick and tired of it! No one ever asks me what I want! I've got a good brain — '

Her father snorted and she swung round on him. 'All right, so I never said I was an academic, but I've got a brain that's going to waste at a damn hairdresser's. Rolling up people's hair all day. All I get is sore fingers and flaming dandruff! I can't even grow my nails,' she snapped, her irritation taking them all by surprise. Zoe had been easygoing, even flip, since their mother died. 'I don't want to grow old and end up like Miss Violet and Miss Ivy. They're old-fashioned, from another era. This is 1978, for God's sake! 1978! There are women out there burning their bras, liberated, running their own lives, their own men, their own damn businesses.' She breathed in deeply. 'And here am I — stuck in the middle of this ruddy town — '

Her father interrupted. 'Now look here, if it was good enough — '

Zoe was not prepared to let him continue. 'You're going to say that if it was good enough for my mother, and good enough for you, then it's good enough for everyone else. But,' she said, swinging round towards her elder brother, 'it's not good enough for you, is it, Victor? So why, if it's not good enough for him, should it be good enough for me?'

Victor leaned back and folded his arms. He was impressed by her outburst, he liked to see her sticking up for herself, it amused him. 'Well, well, well,' he said. 'That was quite a speech, but what do you intend to do about it? Are art lessons the way to a more fulfilled life?'

Instantly subdued, Zoe sat down again. 'I don't know . . . but it'll be a change. I'll meet new people, get a new outlook on things. Live a bit.'

A bell went off in the back of Victor's head. He had been musing with an idea for a while, and now it seemed that the time had come to broach it. 'I'm going for a walk,' he said, gathering his coat off the back of the chair and glancing at his sister. 'Do you want to come?'

Victor had never extended an invitation to her before, and curiosity made Zoe rise to her feet. 'You'll have to wait until I tidy up — '

Her father interrupted her. 'Oh, don't trouble yourself! I suppose clearing up's too good for you now. I can tidy up myself. God knows, I did it before you were born, and I'll do it after you've gone.'

Zoe sighed. 'Dad . . . '

'No, no!' he said, throwing up his hands. 'Go on, you go out with Victor. You see what two bright sparks like you can do — you can take on the whole damn world for all I care.'

Without another word they both walked out.

They made their way up Buck's Lane, walking towards the lighted street at the end of the alleyway. Neither of them spoke. Victor was half a head taller than Zoe, which meant that she had to look up to him when he spoke. She thought it gave him an advantage, and that irritated her, but she was prepared to listen to what he had to say, even though she realised that Victor was not a person who offered anything to anybody which did not advance him in some way. Kindness in Victor was the equivalent of cruelty in another.

Her thoughts running on, she glanced at her brother out of the corner of her eye. His angular face stared straight ahead as he blew some cigarette smoke out from between his lips. He looked prosperous in a flashy way and sure of himself. 'Slick Vic', she thought wryly, smiling at the nickname. 'So what's all this in aid of?'

He carried on walking. 'All what?'

'All this concern for my welfare. It's not like you, Victor.'

'I was thinking. Isn't the teacher at that art school a wiry bloke with a grey streak in his hair?'

Zoe frowned. 'Yes. Why?'

'Rumour has it that he's a bit of a Jack-the-lad, if you follow my drift. In fact,' Victor continued, 'that grey streak in his hair was the result of one of his sexual encounters.' He took a drag on his cigarette. 'The woman, in the height of ecstatic passion, ripped out a chunk of his locks and it grew back white.'

'Like hell,' Zoe said wryly. 'You made that up.'

He smiled and winked at her. 'Every word is Gospel — '

'Yeah, the Gospel according to Saint Victor.'

'How acid you can be at times, Zoe! I was

merely warning you. Underneath this smooth exterior' — he patted the lapel of his coat — 'beats a kind heart.'

'Underneath that exterior beats a wolf's heart,' Zoe replied smartly. 'What are you up to?'

'I'm thinking about my business,' he said.

'Being a knocker?'

'A dealer!' he corrected her sharply. 'I'm a dealer.'

'OK, OK,' she said, throwing up her hands. 'A dealer then. But what's the difference? You still go around knocking on doors and asking people if they want to flog things.'

'Precisely,' he said. 'But there's a little more to it than that, and, although I don't agree with everything you had to say back at the family hearth, the point you made about being too clever to be a hairdresser was true.'

The unaccustomed flattery almost winded her. 'Go on, Victor.'

'You've got a quick brain, Zoe, and you can suss people out. I've always known it. You're streetwise and you're good at summing up situations . . . you could be useful to me.'

So that's it, she thought. There's the pitch. 'How could I be useful to you, Victor?'

'You could come round with me when I'm buying. Chat up the customers. You know, hunt out the bargains.'

'The bargains,' she repeated, watching as he stubbed out a cigarette with the toe of his shoe.

'Oh, don't act so flaming prim, Zoe, it's strictly kosher! I wouldn't do anyone out of anything.'

'Oh, no,' she said drily. 'Far be it from me to even think such a thing. It would be so out of character.'

The barb struck home and he stopped walking to look at her. 'All right, so you don't like the idea.'

For a second she was worried. She didn't want to lose an opportunity, even though she knew that somewhere, somehow, it would cost her something. She hadn't realised until she made the ludicrous decision to go to art classes, just *how* bored she actually was at the salon. If she went round with Victor, it would be a change. Life was looking up suddenly. She could cope with Lady's Pride if she knew that a couple of nights a week she could have a doodle and a flirt with Jack-the-lad Foreshaw, and a weekend outing with Victor to look forward to. Why not try it? she thought recklessly, it might be a lark.

'You're on.'

Victor turned, his eyes narrowing. 'Good,' he said, and then hesitated. 'Incidentally, until you've proved yourself, there's no money in it.'

Zoe laughed loudly. 'Oh, Victor. I never supposed there would be.'

For once he was as good as his word and the following Saturday they set off for Rochdale town centre. It soon became apparent to Zoe that there were certain areas which her brother assiduously avoided. Perhaps he had caught the wrong person out once too often, but he veered past certain streets with the look of a ferret dodging a terrier. Then in a rush of uncharacteristic thrift, Victor forgot his love of

111

taxis and insisted that they caught the bus to Todmorden, arriving at the village in the midst of a blinding downpour. As Zoe struggled with her umbrella in the middle of the High Street, Victor stood in a nearby doorway, puffing on a cigarette.

'I think we should go down the second turning on the right. I've not tried down there.'

Zoe sniffed into the wet air. 'Whatever you think, just get on with it, for God's sake! I haven't got all day.'

He rounded on her. 'What the hell else were you going to do?'

'I'll think of something,' she said petulantly, rubbing the splashes off the back of her legs. 'Getting a runny nose and chilblains is hardly my idea of a good time.'

Victor was stung by her ingratitude. 'You needn't have come.'

'Oh, leave off! I'm sorry.'

They walked down the High Street, which was virtually deserted because of the weather. Shivering, Zoe pulled her raincoat round her and when Victor hesitated outside a terrace house in a side street, she stopped beside him. He tapped on the door, and waited. A couple of seconds later came the sound of activity from inside, followed by a voice bellowing.

'Who is it?'

Victor smiled at the still closed door. 'Could I have a word?'

Stunned, Zoe looked at her brother. Gone was all trace of his Lancashire accent and in its place was some kind of voice for all seasons. It was the

112

voice, she realised, of that supreme being . . . a salesman.

The door opened a crack and an old man looked out. 'Who is it?'

'I was wondering if — '

'I don't want salesmen here!'

Victor persisted. 'I'm not a salesman. I'm not coming to sell you anything. I may, in fact, be coming to give you money.'

It was a very good ploy anywhere. In Lancashire, it was inspired. The door opened a further inch. 'Give me money? What the hell for? You from Littlewoods?'

Victor sighed softly. 'I'm not from the pools, but I might like to buy some things from you. Bits and pieces which you may not realise are of value.'

The man's eyes narrowed. 'Any bits and pieces of value are staying here, where they've always been! With me!'

Victor remained totally unruffled, his composure impressing Zoe, who stood, fascinated, listening. 'Bits and pieces,' Victor continued, 'I know from experience, can bring you money.'

The old man was weakening. 'What sort of thing?'

'Bric-à-brac, furniture, mirrors — '

'I don't hold with mirrors!'

Victor smiled smoothly. 'Pictures then?'

'Well, I've got a few odds and sods. You know, passed down like.'

'Then perhaps I could — '

The door began to close. This was going to be hard, Zoe thought.

'Steady on! Steady on, young man. I never said you could come in and have a poke around. Ther're some damn funny types around these days. How the hell do I know who you are?'

'I am an antique dealer,' Victor said, with a kind of aplomb which usually comes from a man who has just said 'I am a millionaire'.

The old man looked suspicious. 'Antique dealer, eh? Not one of those robbing bastards from Manchester way?'

Victor looked pained. 'I am a respectable dealer. Accompanied by my sister,' he said, his hand extended towards the soaked figure next to him.

The old man glanced at Zoe. She smiled and he softened. 'Your sister?'

'My sister,' Victor repeated. 'We travel round giving people honest valuations. Now, if you choose not to sell to me, that is your decision. I understand that. I'm not here to pressurise you, that's not my way of doing business. All I'm here to do is to give you a valuation. If you decide then that by selling it to me you could build a new bathroom, or buy yourself a second-hand car — '

The man's eyes bulged almost as much as Zoe's. 'Buy myself a car!' he snapped. 'What the bloody hell would I want with a car at my time of life?'

Victor raised his hands. 'I realise that might have seemed a little excessive. Forgive me . . . besides, that kind of money is only available for something quite remarkable — '

The old man swallowed the bait. 'Well, I might

have something quite remarkable! You can't dismiss my stuff when you've not even looked yet!'

Victor smiled again. They were on the home run. 'Well, if I could just come in . . . ' he said.

And, as with Ali Baba, the door opened before him.

★   ★   ★

For the first few weeks Zoe was not interested in Victor's business. Her whole attention was too taken up by her brother's amazing metamorphosis to concentrate on anything else. She was also struck by the besotted admiration which poured on him from every member of the female population, an admiration as potent as the suspicion which generated from some men. Adept as Victor was with the very young or old, when he came across a contemporary, he was floored.

They resented his cocky confidence and loathed the fact that their wife, girlfriend, mother, aunt or sister, was instantly infatuated by this smooth-talking stranger. It got so bad, in fact, that whenever Victor came across a man of his own age, 'a hard case' as he termed them, he would push Zoe forwards and get her to prepare the ground. His sister did not yet possess his confidence, but she *did* possess a very attractive face and a dazzling smile. Zoe could hardly talk with any kind of authority on people's *objets d'art*, but she could smooth the way, and then, when the victim had been thoroughly charmed,

115

Victor would glide in and make the kill.

But Zoe knew that people in Rochdale are what is known as canny, and are so careful with their money that they are disinclined to throw it around. However, they also like a bargain, and they like to haggle and Zoe soon learned to recognise that if Victor was particularly interested in something he would make a point of ignoring it. He would look at everything else, mutter a lot, compliment people, and generally prowl around, although his eyes would keep flicking back to the desired object in the same way that Jason might have ogled the Golden Fleece. His greed excited, he had to find a way to the prize — and sometimes that could be extremely hazardous.

As it was when they visited a house in Todmorden where a certain gentleman by the name of Gilbert Brewer lived. Mr Brewer was a widower who lived with his spinster daughter, Claire, who was pushing forty and had the kind of mouth which was so criss-crossed with lines it looked like a trawling net. She regarded Victor with a mixture of distrust and longing, and then proceeded to give him a working-over the like of which he had not experienced since the Widow had come to Buck's Lane.

'Why are you interested in that picture?' she asked.

Scenting trouble, Victor looked at the woman in front of him, his eyes sweeping her from head to toe. It was a bad error — what another woman might have considered a compliment, Claire Brewer considered an assault.

'Well?' she queried. 'Has the cat got your tongue?'

Victor's smile went out like a light as he blustered, 'I like the picture.'

Zoe glanced at the painting. It was nice, she thought, the colours good, the figures well executed, but not remarkable, just a pleasant watercolour.

She glanced back to her brother as he continued gamely. 'I could make you a good offer.'

Claire Brewer considered the suggestion. 'You're a knocker, aren't you?'

Victor looked close to collapse. 'I am a d — e — a — l — e — r.'

'Dealer, knocker — same thing! Anyway, if you're prepared to make an offer, here and now, and unless I'm very much mistaken you look keen as mustard, then that means that there'll be someone Manchester way who'll offer me more.'

Victor was unprepared for logic, but he rallied. 'In Manchester you wouldn't get such a good price. They have rents and overheads to pay — '

'Yes. But they also have rich customers. People who want pictures like this, I'll be bound.'

Zoe glanced at her brother. He smiled. Victor, she realised, always smiled when he was in difficulties. 'My dear Miss Brewer, if I am upsetting you in any way, perhaps I ought not to press the matter.' The spinster softened, then melted, as he continued. 'It was just that I thought we could do business. You have a painting which I am prepared to buy — for a handsome fee. However,' he added, 'I quite

117

understand that you don't want to continue — '

Her father, however, thought differently. 'Oh come on now, he seems a respectable lad. If he thinks it's worth having, well, let him buy it. You never liked it anyway, we only brought it in from the back room last month.'

His daughter was not to be persuaded easily, even though her expression was amenable. It wasn't obvious, but Zoe could see it, and so could Victor. 'But Dad, I'm not sure,' she said.

Alerted to the change in her tone, Victor threw out his hands, palms upwards. It was a blessing of sorts. 'Please, please . . . I don't want to press the matter. It was not my intention to annoy you. Besides, I would never argue with . . . a lady.'

The last word had its effect. The small, shabby front room of the terrace house suddenly became something akin to the Orangery of the Versailles Palace, and Claire Brewer underwent the same kind of transformation. She drew herself up to her full height, her eyes brilliant as she looked at Victor with the expression of a woman about to bestow her favours upon a highly desirable suitor.

The moment was electric as, with a generous sweep of her hand, she said, 'Make me an offer.'

9

Steven Foreshaw was sitting in the main studio looking at some drawings. It was an overcast day, the light bad, and with his back against the window he was throwing a shadow over the work. Bored, he pushed the sketch aside and pulled out another drawing from the portfolio. He frowned, sighed, and pulled out yet another, but they were all depressing. The same, the same as the ones last year, and the ones next year. The standard of student which came to the Holman Hunt was not of the highest; he knew that, just as he knew that if he had had real talent he would never have ended up teaching here; he would have been at the Manchester College of Art or the Slade in London.

His mind wandered. The Slade, he repeated to himself longingly — he had had such visions of the place years ago. Then he had believed it possible that he would become a respected society portrait painter, making his name and his fortune. He shrugged. Years ago he could be excused for not having the insight to realise that the days of society painters were numbered. Regrettably, he had not understood the changing trends, being behind the times, as usual.

He lit a cigarette greedily, coughed, and then blew a smoke ring, darting his finger through the hole as it floated upwards. Of course, he could have had a go and tried his luck in London, but how much easier to stay in Rochdale and live the role of the gifted artist who had dropped out of the rat race. He blew another smoke ring and loosened the scarf round his neck, thinking of his ex-wife, with whom he had endured a solidly unhappy marriage for nine years before she left and went to live with a legal executive in Southampton. After her there had been other women, then a few young pupils . . .

He got to his feet and glanced into the Claude Lorraine glass leaning against the shelf, smoothing the streak of white hair with his hand. 'I could have been another David Hockney,' he said, his voice theatrical. 'I could have made it.'

But as he said the words he lost interest. A dream world provided Steven Foreshaw with all he required: in his version, his career was crushed by the indifference of people jealous of his talent. What was a man to do? He couldn't take on the art world single-handed, could he? No, better that he passed on his talents to his pupils and acted as their mentor . . .

He gazed into the mirror and turned his head, admiring himself, his 'arty' manner being taken for sophistication by the Rochdale women. It brought out their baser instincts, he mused, his attention wandering again and his spirits flagging as he considered the possibility that he might spend the rest of his existence as the life class master at the Holman Hunt College where nothing ever happened . . . except for Zoe Mellor.

He conjured up a picture of her face, the slanting eyes, exotic and unusual. Of course, even though he was fascinated by her, he could see she had minimal talent. Her drawings were perfunctory, she bored easily and had no pleasure in her work. It was merely something to fill time, he knew, and although it pained him to admit it, he also knew that she came to the classes to cause havoc and flirt with him. Her attitude made her unpopular with the girls and it made the boys uneasy — they were not used to that kind of bald cheek. They were used to women like their mothers and sisters, who had plenty to say, but lacked Zoe's artfulness. He smiled at the play on words. That was what was so unique about her, he suddenly realised, that playfulness allied to a quick brain.

He knew he wanted to make love to her. He had known that from the instant they met, experiencing a kind of sexual mugging which had left him breathless, his imagination working overtime. In fact, he was hoping that Zoe was as sexually active as her brother, around whom many a tale was woven in the pub. Yet something about her made him doubt it. Streetwise and sharp-witted, she was like a sexy urchin, and although he knew her to be only eighteen, she seemed older, a fact due more to her manner than her appearance. But she was alluring for all her faults, he thought, and in a fit of pique, stubbed out his cigarette and got to his feet.

The studio was cold and silent as he looked around at the rows of easels, the charcoal smudges on the floor and the chalk marks. As usual, during term-time, the walls were covered with drawings and sketches pinned up haphazardly, numerous fingerprints smeared on the doors which had been swinging backwards and forwards for decades. Standing in the centre of the studio like a perpetual understudy, Steven Foreshaw glanced up as it began to rain, the skylight streaked with water and bird droppings.

★ ★ ★

Victor Mellor would have found Foreshaw's yearnings inane as he harboured absolutely no romantic feelings about any woman. To Victor, women should provide sex and amusement. Meaningful relationships were out, and, like a spoilt child, knowing he could have any woman he wanted merely made him despise them all.

He was not stupid, however, and after fouling his own doorstep in Rochdale with the Clark girl, he had no intention of repeating the performance and looked for his sexual diversions further afield. And they were never hard to find. Indeed, he reckoned that he could spot in the first thirty seconds if a woman was going to go to bed with him. He had even laid bets on it, and was seldom wrong. In fact, some fellow drinkers had once been invited to witness a lurid seduction in the back of a Ford van, after which, duly impressed, they had coughed up. He made a few pounds that way, and a few enemies — generally fathers or brothers. But being handy with his fists, Victor was not a man to be intimidated easily, and besides, the odd black eye was hardly likely to make him change his habits.

He was carrying the top of a table through the middle of Salford, thinking these profound thoughts. It was only a small table, and Victor carried it with such panache that it could have become a fashion. Deftly, he shifted it under his other arm, relieved that he had just managed to extract himself from a difficult situation. The woman had *lied* to him, he thought with astonishment. She had said that she wasn't married, but she was — to a docker who sang Country and Western in the Bull and Staff in Moss Side.

Naturally he had to terminate the exciting, but dangerous, affair, and had rung up the woman and told her. She had not taken the news well. In short, she threatened that she was going to get her husband to castrate him, and put the most overworked part of his anatomy in a pickle jar for display in the Public Bar of the Bull and Staff. Unimpressed, Victor told her what to do with the suggestion and rang off. He then bent down and picked up the top half of the table he had bought cheaply from her only the previous night. Business was business, after all.

Another ten minutes saw him at the entrance to a basement, laughingly called an antique market, run by a man called Weiss, a Polish refugee who had fled the Germans in the war. In itself, Weiss was a simple enough name, but coupled with the first name, Ivor, it suffered something in its translation to English. 'I've a vice' became so much of a joke in the neighbourhood, in fact, that he decided to live up to the legend.

He came into the market in the morning and scuttled down to the basement, and then in the evening he locked up and scuttled out again. No one knew much about him, even though he must have had a wife, children, and a home somewhere for whom he worked so slavishly. Yet considering the amount of effort he put in, he did not appear to be overly successful. The market was badly in need of redecoration, the floor covered with bare boards, the windows so grimy that only a vague blur of feet could be seen passing on the street above. But shabby as it was, it was Ivor Weiss's empire, an empire which over the years had extended to include several dank outbuildings.

To Victor's knowledge, no one had ever managed to get into these outbuildings, and many suggestions were bandied about as to what Ivor Weiss kept there. The truth remained hidden, however, as the presence of two underfed Dobermanns discouraged trespassers, and the only out-of-town burglar who had managed to infiltrate the yard had left empty handed, except for a row of teeth marks picked out like tacking stitches across his backside.

Victor and Ivor Weiss went back a long way, and as Victor descended down the uneven stairs with the table top, Ivor rose to his feet behind the counter. 'Good morning, Mr Mellor. And how are we today?'

'Well,' Victor replied easily, putting the table on the counter between them. 'And how are you?'

'Fine, fine,' Ivor replied, looking at the table

top and frowning. He always frowned. He thought it was good business sense and stopped people thinking they had something special. Had Victor Mellor walked in that morning with the Botticelli *Birth of Venus* he would have frowned at it. The top of the table did not escape the ritual. 'So this is the top, eh?'

Victor lit a cigarette. 'Don't act nonchalant, Ivor. This is the top to go with the bottom I brought you last week.'

'So you clinched the deal?' Victor nodded. 'And you got a good price?'

'The lady got more than she bargained for,' Victor said drily.

Ivor Weiss laughed. He knew about Victor's reputation, who didn't? Delicately, he touched the table. His hands were thick, buckled with arthritis even though he went up to the hospital twice a week. It didn't do a damn thing for him, but he liked to think he was getting something out of the National Health Service.

'It'll need restoring.'

Victor had seen this coming. 'Of course it'll need restoring! Everything I ever bring in here needs restoring.' He leaned towards the man. 'You should clean the flaming windows and get some light in here then you could see better. This table's perfect.'

Ivor bristled. 'I have good pieces here! I know quality! You can't fault my stuff,' he said heatedly, turning back to the table top. 'This will need work doing on it, and that costs money.'

Victor glanced round. Indolent sunshine filtered through the open door leading to the yard and fell across one of the dogs as it scratched itself. 'We'll stick to the price we agreed last week,' he said confidently, the matter settled. 'Incidentally, I've got a painting, a landscape. You know the type, a couple of cows and a river. It's good.'

Ivor's eyes lit up. 'Framed?'

'Of course it's framed. You think I've got it rolled up in my pocket?'

'I like a good frame,' Ivor continued wistfully. 'A grand frame can sell a picture. Would it be good enough for a Manchester saleroom?'

Victor's brain went into overdrive. 'I thought you had private buyers. That's why I came to you. I can sell it through a saleroom myself, I don't have to use a middleman.'

Ivor looked astounded. 'I should *cheat* you? You, of all people! Haven't we done business all these years, and never a cross word?'

'Just a minute while I get my handkerchief out,' Victor said sarcastically. 'Listen, you told me that if I brought you pictures you would give me a good price. Can you or can't you? Because if you can't, I can sort myself out.'

Ivor Weiss's face set. Victor Mellor had brought him some good things over the years. Of course he always haggled with him, after all, Victor was hardly a babe in arms . . . Ivor didn't want to lose him now, especially since his sister had been going with him on his trips. The stuff had been improving, the girl had an eye, he thought. Maybe he should work directly with her. Maybe they wouldn't need to use Victor at all.

126

The thought excited him and he glanced back to the man on the other side of the counter, his face repentent. 'Would I cheat you? Would I cheat a friend?'

★   ★   ★

Zoe had to admit that since she had been going around with Victor her life had opened up. She was getting out and about, meeting people. Rochdale, Salford and Manchester were hardly the big time, but she was spreading her wings and learning more about herself. She was clever with people. She could charm them and chat them up — oh, she always knew she could do that with men, but this was different, she was getting more skilful with women and understanding them better. As an enthusiastic listener, she gave people her time willingly, winning their confidence and easing the way for Victor.

But although she agreed to help him, on one thing she was emphatic. Offering to buy people's possessions was fine, but she didn't like it when Victor set about *persuading* them, offering prices which she suspected, although she didn't know for sure, were well below the actual value. He had bought something the previous week from an old lady, and the incident had preyed on Zoe's conscience so much that she had tackled him about it.

'Don't be so damn stupid!' he snapped. 'She'd that damn thing hanging about for years. I gave her forty quid for it.'

'Was it worth forty quid? Or more?'

127

Victor sighed. 'Zoe, this is business — '

'I don't give a damn! You call it business, I call it stealing!'

His expression was one of bewilderment. 'We're in the antique trade, not Help the Aged.'

She realised then that although there were similarities between them, there was a yawning gap between her brother's moral standards and hers. Zoe didn't mind using her charm and capitalising on the talents she had — that was only fair — but she didn't like to see people being used. It upset her because she understood that most people weren't very smart, and that the Victor Mellors of the world preyed on them. She also knew that most of them could afford to lose precious little.

The incident with the old woman made her so uneasy that when the salon closed that Friday she took a bus over to Todmorden and knocked on the door, unannounced.

The woman seemed surprised to see her. 'Is anything wrong?'

Zoe smiled warmly. 'No, I just came over to give you something.' She reached into her bag and took out twenty pounds from her wages. 'My brother asked me to give you this. He said he'd given you the wrong money.' She hesitated. 'Go on, take it. It's yours.'

The old woman frowned and then took the money. 'But — '

'I have to go,' Zoe said quickly, glancing over her shoulder. 'My bus is due.'

'Can't I make you a cup of tea or something?'

She shook her head. 'No, nothing.'

'But I feel I owe you something.'

Zoe paused. 'No. You don't owe me a thing.'

The rich were another matter. In the expensive areas, especially on the outskirts of Manchester, the two of them began to explore further afield, Victor hiring a car for the purpose. As they walked up to the great houses set in their own grounds, Zoe was initially impressed, but as the day wore on and they approached one after the other with no success, she devised the philosophy which she would follow all her life — the weak must be protected, but the strong could be taken for a ride.

The feeling was not one of envy, more of resentment. Zoe's own insecurity made it impossible for her to imagine ever being completely at ease; and she knew by instinct that the seduction offered by opulence would merely cheat her. So she admired the houses and loathed the curt and dismissive owners of the properties. They didn't want hawkers on their doorsteps; they had nothing to sell. No, thank you. Not today. Then bang, the door shut in their faces.

Victor had two words to say on the subject. Either 'cow' or 'bastard', depending on the sex of the person who had answered the door. But Zoe had more insight than her brother and soon understood that in order to infiltrate the middle classes they had to *look* the part. So when they returned to Buck's Lane that night, she tackled Victor on the subject. 'Listen, I think we should smarten up a bit.'

Victor looked down at the sharp suit he was

wearing. 'Smarten up? If I get any smarter than this, they'll be fainting in the streets.'

'That's not smart, that's flashy.'

'Flashy!' he repeated, his pride smarting. 'These clothes cost me a fortune.'

'And that's the point,' she continued. 'You're always overdressed, Victor. You would be overdressed for the Oscar Ceremony in Hollywood — '

'Since when would you know how people dress in Hollywood?'

'I know how they dress in Manchester' — she pointed to his suit — 'and it's not like that,' her voice softened. 'And look at me. I look like a rubbing rag. I should wear a suit, something smart. Classy.'

'And who's going to buy it?'

'You are, Victor,' she replied calmly.

He sat bolt upright. 'Really? How do you make that out?'

'Because I've earned you money, Victor. You made a couple of hundred on those pictures I spotted, and anyway, you said you were going to give me a percentage when I proved myself.' She breathed in. 'Well, I have proved myself, so where's the reward?'

Victor relaxed. 'Well, if I'm going to buy you a dress that'll use up the money.'

She sighed. 'I'll compromise. I'll get the outfit, but you'll give me fifty pounds.'

'What about a small sports car thrown in?'

'Don't be stupid, Victor!'

He leaned forwards in the chair. 'What exactly do you want with fifty pounds?'

'To settle our deal.'

Victor smiled wolfishly. 'And what deal might that be?'

'Our partnership deal.'

He threw up his hands. Bloody women! You give them an inch and they take a bloody yard. '*What* partnership deal?'

'Ours. We could be on to a winner here. I can make you money, Victor,' she said softly. 'Big money.'

And she knew then that she could, that at last she had a value of her own. Her limited skill gave her a price tag, and a tiny tot of power. She had an ability to recognise quality — she didn't know how she did it, only that her senses told her what was worth money. Admittedly, at first she had been convinced that it was merely luck. A couple of good guesses. But luck was luck, after all, and it ran out. Her instinct did not. Within weeks, she joined the library, and repeatedly borrowed Alan's art books, looking at the myriad reproductions and trying to commit them to memory.

But again disappointment dogged her. Zoe had no academic ability. Words were words. Pictures merely pictures. They had no meaning on the page — but in a front room, or on a market stall . . . then they leapt out at her. Buy me, they said, I'll bring you luck, I'll make you money.

And *how* she wanted it — for her own gratification and for the sheer pleasure of cool money in her hand. It gave her a sense of being which she had never experienced before.

But although the revelation was heady, she never deluded herself and realised she had a great deal to learn. Her destiny was not to paint, sculpt, or carve masterpieces — her skill was to *recognise* them. The knowledge gave her an unsteady confidence.

Victor's hunch about his sister was paying off. But he didn't like to be beholden to anyone, and at her sudden show of independence a ghastly turmoil churned up his stomach. He knew what his sister could do and he wanted to profit from her talent, but he didn't want her to get the whip hand.

But then again, he was greedy. 'You're on.'

Zoe was momentarily wrong-footed. 'What?'

He smiled. 'You're on, partner.'

Cautiously, she extended her hand to shake on the deal. She had expected more resistance — just as Victor had anticipated she would. Lulling her into a false feeling of security would keep her happy, he thought, and if she was happy she would willingly do all the hard work and he could enjoy the profits. Women were all alike. 'You get yourself something nice to wear, Zoe,' he said, smiling. 'You've earned it.'

10

'It's really good,' Steven Foreshaw said as he looked over Zoe's shoulder at the drawing. It was more than good, it was an almost perfect copy of an early Turner. Of course it was part of the artistic training that his pupils copied paintings, but although many had the facility to reproduce another's work, few understood and felt the work as the original painter had done.

Impressed, Steven coughed and waved some smoke out of Zoe's way. 'What made you tackle this one?'

She smiled ruefully. 'The principal of this establishment had a word with me. Apparently he did not think my caricatures were amusing.' She laughed, remembering the unflattering portrayals she had sketched, which someone had salvaged from the waste basket and pinned to the notice board: 'In fact, he went so far as to suggest that I might like to go elsewhere to finish my artistic training.'

Steven's heart banged. 'You've been asked to leave?'

Zoe turned to look up at him. 'I begged forgiveness,' she answered, holding her hands together as though in prayer, 'and he gave me another chance.'

With relief, Steven turned back to her drawing. 'So he told you to copy this?'

'And this,' she said, bending down and passing

him another sketch out of her bag. 'Not bad, eh?'

'They're brilliant,' he answered, overjoyed to find some evidence of real talent.

Zoe had been too. For all her nonchalance she had slaved over the pictures, making a space for herself on the end of Alan's bench in the garage and struggling over the work. Numerous attempts were torn and flung into the bin, others were scrumpled up in temper and flung on to the floor, from where Alan picked them up, smoothed them out, and saved them. He knew better than to remonstrate with her, and kept silent, offering encouragement only when his sister finished working and held up the drawing for his aproval.

'That's smashing.'

'It's crap.'

He frowned. 'Zoe!'

She grimaced without remorse. 'I thought it'd be easy, Alan, just a couple of dumb pictures to copy. Any kid could do it. Hah!' she said angrily, pushing the drawing away from her and ramming her paintbrushes into a jam jar. The water clouded like a sky before a thunderstorm. 'I *should* be able to do it. After all, the other pupils do it all the time. A flick of colour here, a brushstroke there, and' — she clicked her fingers — 'there you have it, a Constable.' She sighed with irritation. 'But it's not that simple. You have to get the right colours, sure, that's obvious, but there's a . . . ' she struggled for the word, 'an *atmosphere* to a picture and that's what I can't get.'

'They look good to me,' Alan said softly,

pulling out one of the discarded sketches he had rescued and pushing it over to his sister. 'Go on, try with this one a little longer.' Zoe shook her head. 'Go on! It's nearly there,' he said, pointing to the original in the book before them. 'If you just darken the sky and shadow under those trees . . . ' Zoe scowled, but her temper was fading, enthusiasm taking its place. 'And a bit more white there wouldn't come amiss either . . .'

Feigning indifference, Zoe leaned forwards and rinsed out her brushes. 'It'll still be a bloody mess,' she said defiantly, painting in some shadows as she talked. Alan smiled and watched her, her head bent down, her forehead creased with effort. 'I'll give it five more minutes and that's it.'

But half an hour later she was still labouring, the occasional snort of impatience breaking the silence, her brushes dipping in and out of the water, her head bent down over the tormented drawing, her impatience at odds with her determination to succeed. Finally, at ten o'clock, she leaned back, pushing the painting over to Alan with a questioning look on her face.

'It's champion,' he said simply and her eyes filled.

Steven Foreshaw knew nothing of the effort Zoe had put into the work, only that her sudden promotion to the elitist rank of 'artist' increased his libido to boiling point.

'Fantastic,' he said, laying his hand on her shoulder as he leaned to look at the work. 'You're talented.'

Zoe shook her head. 'No. The people who did the originals were talented, but not me. These are just copies.' She slipped them into her portfolio and rose to her feet. 'Anyway, how are things with you?'

The studio was empty apart from the two of them. Empty and quiet, the only noise coming from the corridor outside. Steven Foreshaw looked at the girl in front of him; she was wearing a maroon wool dress and black stockings, her hair pinned back from her face at the sides, her eyes enlarged by make-up, hypnotic in the still face. Clumsily he took her hand and lifted it to his lips, the gesture romantic, gentle, and almost old-fashioned.

But Zoe didn't laugh. Neither did she laugh when he leaned towards her and kissed her cheek, the faintest impression of her perfume lingering on his lips as he moved away. The overhead light was savage, a penetrating light especially provided so that the students could see clearly. But when Zoe bent her head her hair fell forwards and shadowed her face, changing her. Expertly he laid his hand on her shoulder and then slipped his fingers around the back of her neck and gently pulled her to him. Slowly he kissed her, exploring her lips first, then the inside of her mouth, clasping hold of her more tightly when she responded.

Under the bright light Zoe closed her eyes, her arms around his neck, her breathing accelerating as his did, her mouth in tune with his. Greedily his hands grasped her hair, pulling her head back so that he could look at her face before kissing

136

her again. Aware of an excitement she had never felt before, Zoe leaned against him and moaned softly. Aroused and impatient, Steven's hands slipped away from her hair and began to undo the zip of her dress.

'No,' Zoe said simply, stepping back.

'What the hell!' he stammered. 'I was . . . ' His face altered, passion replaced with irritation.

Zoe blustered, embarrassed and out of her depth. 'I have to go home,' she said.

Sighing extravagantly, he smoothed his hair, the white streak brilliant under the overhead light. 'I don't — '

'I'm sorry,' Zoe said softly, aware that she had infuriated him and anxious to make amends. So this was loving, she thought. It wasn't so different from every other kind of loving, after all. There was the same confusion and anxiety. 'I was — '

'No,' he said suddenly. 'It's not your fault,' he continued, moving away from her, pushing an easel aside. 'I was trying it on.'

But I wanted you to, Zoe thought, and I still want you to. Confusion made her confidence falter and she was suddenly vulnerable. 'Do you still want me to come next week?'

He laughed easily, and then stopped when he saw the look on her face. 'Miss Mellor,' he said, taking her face in his hands and brushing her lips with his tongue, 'I shall . . . ' he kissed her on her left cheek, 'long to . . . ' then kissed the right cheek, 'see you again.'

'Miss me until then,' Zoe said without thinking, the words an emotional order. Long for

me, they said. Want me and think of me. Make
me important in your life. Miss me.

★ ★ ★

'Fake something? Why would I want to fake
something, Victor?' Zoe asked, lowering her
voice as their father walked into the kitchen.

'So what the hell are you two doing then? I
thought you'd be out making a fortune in that
flash car of his.'

Victor looked at his father and then at Zoe.
'We're about to go, I was just having a word with
my sister.'

'Aye, well you're always having a word with
somebody, Victor, and that's a fact. You always
were a good talker. Anyway, what's it all about?'

'Business.'

'Business!' Bernard Mellor repeated know-
ingly. 'It's a funny thing, but with this business
doing so well, Victor, it amazes me that no
bloody money finds its way back here.' He
looked at Zoe. 'Mind you, you've got yourself
dressed up like a May horse, so you must be
earning a bob or two. It can't have come from
that hairdresser's.'

'Victor bought it for me.'

'Victor bought it!' her father said, astonished.
'Well, while the lad's feeling so flush I could do
with something myself. A new carpet, the odd
loaf of bread. And what about my brother?
Freezing his arse off on that bloody hillside half
the time. He could do with a handout. In fact,
we could all do with a handout, Victor.' His son

138

got to his feet, exasperated. 'There's always been a home here for you, no questions asked — '

'We're off now,' Victor said.

'Off! You've been off for bloody years, that's your trouble,' his father shouted, banging his pipe in the ashtray. 'Go on, sod off!'

The door slammed behind them.

They waited until they were at the end of Buck's Lane before Victor tackled the subject again. 'Well, what about it? There's a guy with a pub in Heywood who wants something copying — '

'Faking.'

'Copying! Faking! What's the difference?' he retorted, pushing his hands well down in his pockets. It was October, and the beginning of the winter wind was blowing in from the moors.

'It's illegal,' Zoe said firmly.

'It's not illegal if you don't sign the name of the artist on the copy,' he said with certainty. 'I've looked into it. If you copied a Rembrandt — '

'I couldn't copy a Rembrandt.'

'I was just stating an example,' he sighed. 'If you *did* copy a Rembrandt it wouldn't matter unless you wrote 'Rembrandt' on it and sold it as an original. That's forgery, an attempt to deceive, and then you can be — '

'Jailed.'

'I don't know why you always have to be so serious about everything!' Victor snapped. 'It's just a lark — '

'Which could mean a long stay in a safe place.'

'Listen,' Victor said calmly. 'You do it, sign

your name on the back, and it's above board. He just wants a seascape that looks like a Turner. You can do it, I saw the other things you did — '

She turned round to face him. 'When did you see them? I never showed them to you.'

He had the grace to look embarrassed. 'Well, I looked in your portfolio.'

'God, nothing's sacred, is it? Why didn't you keep your flat on in Manchester and let the rest of us have some peace? I don't know why you had to move back here.'

'When Mother died,' he said, 'I decided that the time had come to return to the fold. Besides, it's cheaper living at home.'

'You can say that again, Victor. You don't contribute any more now than you did years ago, and you can afford it. It's a bit much, Dad was right.'

'OK, OK, I'll give the old man something.'

They walked for a while in silence. The streets were quiet, the first frost edging the pavements.

'So, are you going to do it? It's just a small picture, and besides, he's offering good money.'

Zoe stopped. 'How much?'

'One hundred and fifty quid.'

She narrowed her eyes as she looked at her brother. 'That wouldn't happen to be a lie, would it? It wouldn't actually be more like three hundred, but you're saying a hundred and fifty, which we split, whilst you pocket the difference as well.'

Victor touched his heart with his fingertips. 'I don't know how you could think these things, I really don't,' he said, uncomfortable that she had caught him out. 'Listen, one hundred and fifty quid's not bad for an afternoon's work.'

'It'll take me longer than that,' she said stubbornly.

'Oh, come on, Zoe. You never know what it might lead to.'

'That's exactly what I'm afraid of.'

Zoe did the Turner seascape. It took her nearly a week of effort but it turned out well and she signed her name on the back, writing 'In the style of J. M. Turner, undertaken by Zoe Mellor' and she dated it. It was a lark, after all. In fact, she was so pleased with it that she wanted to show it to Steven, but knew it was impossible, just as she knew that she was falling into the old trap of begging for affection. So resolutely, she blocked the incident in the studio out of her mind, and took comfort in the landlord's praise as he showed the picture to everyone and put it in pride of place above the bar. Besides, seventy-five pounds wasn't bad money and the whole thing gave her a thrill, a buzz of excitement. The painting was good, she could see that, and what if it was only a second-hand talent? It was still talent, and after so many years believing that she was worthless, it was good to be admired.

Her mind turned back to Steven Foreshaw and her impatience flared. Remember what Victor said, she told herself, remember Jack-the-lad Foreshaw and his white streak. Don't make a fool of yourself. Not now, when things are going right for you, she thought. You're clever now, Zoe, so stay clever.

'What is it?'

Alan remained mute.

'Come on, tell me,' Zoe persisted, anxiety marking her voice. Never in all the wide longing of her childhood had Alan denied her anything. Affection had been given willingly whenever she needed it. There was no mystery with *this* brother. Until now. 'You can tell me, can't you?' she urged, kneeling down beside him and taking his hand. 'Alan, tell me what's wrong.'

There was no response, he simply sat, unseeing, gazing straight ahead, his face without expression. He had been like this all day, since he took a diversion from his usual walk to Tom Mellor's and arrived late with no explanation offered. It had been so unlike him that it had unsettled his taciturn uncle, and forced enquiry. But, as with Zoe, no reason was given for Alan's sudden and impenetrable silence.

No explanation was given, but to Zoe, none was needed. She knew, with a complete and deadening understanding, that Alan Mellor had inherited something other than his mother's eyes; that down through the genes, the dark mystery of birth, he had taken on the shape of her illness. With him there would be no violence, no anger, merely a void into which he would pass silently, and linger, and come home, later, when the dark gave him up again.

★ ★ ★

142

'Welcome back,' Steven Foreshaw said easily, greeting Zoe, and then turning back to his other pupils.

Sighing, she pulled out a piece of paper and began to draw the nude in front of her, a Junoesque woman who worked for the Co-Op and who now lounged uncomfortably against the sofa raised on the dias in the centre of the room. The previous week Zoe had thought often of Steven, her mind replaying in her dreams what she refused to dwell on in her waking hours. Previously sex had not been a part of her life. She had been too involved with her mother's illness, the family, the house. Then she had gone to work at the salon, with the two sisters of uncertain age, in whom all passion had long since withered. And by such means she escaped her own sexuality.

It didn't seem a bad way to live. After all, if she opened herself to loving, what might happen? Her only experience of loving had been bewilderment and rejection. She did not want that again, and not with a man, because where would it lead? She had no desire to step over that dark border into the unseen . . . But it was one thing to suppress desire and quite another to deny it.

As she drew the model, Zoe watched Steven move around the class, bending over a pupil, offering advice, or snatching a pencil and sketching in alterations himself. Several girls were fascinated by him, that much was apparent as they leaned towards him, or smiled, or said thank you when he had massacred their work

— the heady attraction he offered potent in the shabby studio. But he kept apart from Zoe, glancing over to her only when he knew she was not looking, remembering the feel of her hair and the vulnerability which had touched him.

The class finished at seven-thirty, the pupils leaving one by one, some hovering, hoping to catch a word with the Master. Unaware of anyone other than Zoe, Steven collected together the drawings and laid them on his desk, thanking the model and rearranging the chairs and easels for the next day's sitting. Stripes of white chalk and black charcoal made snail tracks on the wooden floor and overhead the rain spat on the skylight.

'Wait a minute,' Steven said, catching hold of Zoe's arm as she was about to leave and guiding her back to her seat. 'I think you need a little extra tuition.'

She frowned and then laughed unconvincingly. 'I have to go home,' she said as the caretaker came in.

'Sorry, Mr Foreshaw, but I've got to lock up.'

'I'll do it,' Steven replied, glancing over to Zoe. 'I've got the keys.'

The man hesitated. 'I'm not sure — '

'I'll do it!' Steven snapped. 'Go on, it's all right. After all, we'll be going in a minute too.'

They both knew they would not be going anywhere, and as the caretaker's feet died away on the stairs and the lights were turned out on the landing outside, they both knew that something would change irrevocably that night.

Carefully Steven looked at Zoe's drawing of

144

the nude and then frowned. 'It's not bad, but you could do better.' He pulled up a chair and sat down next to her, his knee touching hers. 'You see, the proportions aren't quite right.'

Zoe nodded, aware of the sexual tension between them. 'I had trouble with the right leg.'

He nodded and then turned to her. 'It looks like it's made out of putty, legs have muscle . . . ' He touched her calf. 'Muscle,' he repeated, looking into her eyes and then turning back to the drawing. 'Feel your own calf.' Obediently Zoe felt her leg. 'You see, it's muscle.' He altered the drawing quickly and confidently, the pencil then poising over the thigh. 'This is wrong too,' he said. 'Feel your own thigh, Zoe,' he said firmly, a master teaching his pupil. 'Well, go on, feel it.'

She did so, transfixed, her fingers running down the length of her leg as he corrected her work. Then, slowly and carefully, he ran his own hand along the line of her calf and thigh. 'Muscle and bone, Zoe,' he said quietly. 'It's all muscle, blood and bone.'

Unable to speak, Zoe watched as his hand stroked her leg. Then he moved and turned to bend over her drawing, scrutinising it for errors, examining every line and curve from the feet to the head.

Finally he looked back at her. 'You don't see things for what they are, Zoe,' he said quietly. 'You see only the outside skin, not the body underneath. You have a lot to learn . . . ' She nodded, her head buzzing. 'These breasts are not real,' he continued, erasing some of her drawing and marking in the full line of the model's bosom, the breasts becoming more lifelike on the page than in reality, the picture taking on a sexuality which was obvious to them both. 'You should feel your own breasts, Zoe . . . ' he said and paused, the forefinger of his hand running down in a line from her throat to her stomach and then back to her left breast. 'Artists have to know their anatomy,' he said, getting up and turning off the light.

In the half dark he led her over to the couch where she lay as he undressed her slowly and then pulled off his own clothes and lay down on top of her, kissing her breasts and whispering her name as she sighed and looked up to the wide skylight. The moon seemed to grin at her, watching, illuminating her as it illuminated the bird droppings on the window. Zoe closed her eyes, but the moonlight kept pouring in and illuminated Steven's naked body and his altered face. It ran along the length of his legs like white chalk and striped Zoe's arms as they pulled him to her. Achingly tender, she kissed him and murmured to him, until, with a sigh, he finally relaxed against her.

'I adore you,' he said simply.

She smiled into the semi-dark.

'I've wanted to make love to you for weeks.' He continued tracing the line of her stomach with his fingertips. 'You are wonderful.'

The words were what she needed to hear, and because it was a form of loving she accepted them, realising as she did so that they were only words, no more.

He looked at her suddenly as though he read her thoughts. 'What is it?'

'Nothing,' she said, smiling automatically.

'It is. Tell me.'

She reached up and touched the white streak in his hair. 'How did you get that?' she asked finally.

'Ask your brother,' was all he said.

11

Harland Goldberg didn't know what he thought about Manchester, even though he had been coming up to the North on and off for forty years. Every time he approached the city his spirits plummeted — even when it wasn't raining, even if there was a high summer sun — the place always seemed unwelcoming. He knew it was a curious thing to feel about a city. Especially the city in which he had been born.

His attention wandered towards the train corridor as he saw a young woman pass. She was darkly attractive, but not remarkable and she held his attention for only a second before his mind passed on to the subject of Myrtle, his wife. He shifted in the seat of the first-class carriage and stretched out his short legs, wincing at the prospect of going into Kendal Milne's to collect the piece of porcelain she had ordered.

'Why couldn't you get it in Harrods? Why should I have to struggle all the way back from Manchester with it?'

His wife's quick hands banged on the dining-room table. 'It's a good buy. I've saved you money, Harland.'

'Why? I didn't ask you to. You could buy the piece anywhere, at any price — '

Myrtle sighed. 'You want I should throw money around? You forget too quickly, Harland. Time was when you would have been careful,

148

when you would have been shrewd.'

He sighed and bit into his toast. He was a rich man, his money made in the art world, his reputation secured by a series of astonishing coups which had been all the more remarkable for their integrity. Harland Goldberg made money . . . but he was an honest man. It made him unique amongst his peers, and a complete schlep in his wife's eyes.

Forty-seven years had not changed her opinion. Physically she had aged, early plumpness shrinking down to a designer size eight, her vanity increasing with the years as her looks decreased. But mentally she was still poor Myrtle Bloom, with a father who spoke no English and three sisters all better-looking than she was. At fourteen she had developed a chip on her shoulder which had increased, not decreased, as her husband became wealthier. To Myrtle, anyone who possessed more than her was lucky. They never worked for it, they were merely luckier than she was. Even a large house in St John's Wood, an apartment in Gstaad, a healthy daughter and a vast allowance, did nothing to lessen her misfortune.

The train shuddered to a halt and Harland got to his feet, pulling on his coat and checking his reflection in the mirror over the seats. A small, dapper man with a good-tempered face framed with a neat black beard looked back. Harland smiled. His beard was his one vanity, still dark though his hair was greying, and styled to give him a look of distinction. Tapping his hat on his head, he stepped out on to the platform. He had come to Manchester to see an exhibition of some lesser known members of the Newlyn School. The show had been given a great deal of hype and he knew that a number of people from the London art world would attend hoping to make a killing, little realising that the Manchester dealers who laid on the exhibition were hardly likely to let the London boys profit.

He caught a taxi from the station and arrived at the gallery, nodding to several London colleagues as he glanced around. The paintings were good, but expensive, and there was nothing he wanted to buy so he wandered off towards another room.

At the door a member of the gallery staff stopped him. 'Excuse me, this isn't the main exhibition.'

'What is it then?'

'It's some of the graduate work from the Blackwell College of Art. The more promising pupils.'

Harland shrugged. 'Can I go in?'

'Certainly, sir, if you wish to.'

Harland Goldberg wished to. There were three rooms hung from floor to ceiling with sketches, paintings, charcoal drawings, and some sculptures in the middle of the floor around which visitors could walk. They were meagrely framed and there was obviously little money spent on the exhibition, but then, as the man had said, it was the students' show, and students had little money. It was simply a way of getting their work to the public — and the critics.

Harland Goldberg walked round very slowly.

He was surprised by the standard of the work. He had, for the last few years, seen a determined deterioration in most of the colleges in London, but he was absolutely stunned by the pure banality of this show. The work was crude, although that was something he knew could be contained as an artist developed his talent. But this was a basic crudeness; the subject matter deliberately shocking, and he had the sneaking suspicion that the paintings were technically suspect. Sighing, he moved his hat to his other hand and unbuttoned his coat. It was stuffy in the gallery as he walked into the second room and found the work there even less inspiring. His gaze came to rest on a sculptured head encased in a leather hood, with a zip for a mouth. The impression was that of cruelty and he turned away, as guilty as a voyeur.

In his haste he stepped back on to someone's foot and spun round to apologise. 'Oh, I do beg your pardon.'

The young woman looked at him and he paused. Something about her was familiar. He remembered her face, the slanted eyes, and realised that she was the girl he had seen on the train.

'It's all right,' Zoe said.

He noticed that her voice had no accent and that she seemed listless.

'Please forgive me,' he continued. 'I was carried away.'

'Which is just what should happen to these paintings,' Zoe said drily.

Harland Goldberg laughed. He liked a woman

with wit. Myrtle didn't have any sense of humour, neither did his daughter, Erica. 'I agree with you. This is one of the worst shows I have seen in some time.'

'That's quite a sweeping statement,' Zoe replied, her spirits momentarily reviving.

'All right, if you think I'm being unfair, point out something which has real talent. I'm always willing to learn.'

Grateful for the diversion, Zoe rose to the challenge. She didn't know who this man was, but she liked him, and besides, anything was better than walking around alone. 'Well,' she said, pointing to a charcoal sketch halfway up a wall. 'This isn't . . . ' She paused. 'Yes, it's absolutely Godawful!'

He laughed again. 'You see, I was right. Have another try.'

Obediently she looked around. 'I concede defeat. There's nothing special here. No individuality.'

His ears pricked up at the word. 'Is that important?'

'Oh yes. You can forgive something for being crude or bad if it's unique. This is just copying, a rehash.' Yes, she thought to herself, she could recognise a copy. After all, she was a pretty good faker herself.

'And you think that's bad?'

'I think it's the death of art,' she said. 'But then,' she added self-consciously, 'I'm not an expert.'

'Really? You seem to love the subject. What do you do?'

She flinched, and then throwing back her head, said, 'I'm a hairdresser.'

He was disappointed, crushingly so. He had hoped for a moment that they had something in common. Not that he made a practice of propositioning young women. In fact, he had only ever had one relationship other than with his wife, and that had been a long-term mistress, a fact which Myrtle conveniently threw in his face at least four times a week. But otherwise, there had been nobody. His interest had been in his work and in his family, and although he had always presumed that if he was a good provider and a loving father affection would follow, it did not. Myrtle and his daughter remained adamantly aloof, and as the girl grew up and inherited most of her mother's personality traits, he found her difficult to know and even more difficult to like. The thought shamed him. He was a caring man and had wished to be protective, believing that women should be idolised and cherished.

'A hairdresser,' he repeated finally.

Zoe nodded. 'Yes. Ghastly, isn't it?'

He shrugged. 'I don't know. Is it?' She nodded. 'Is there nothing else you could do? You seem to know something about art.'

'Oh, I do . . . in a way,' she said eagerly. 'I've read some books and I enjoy exhibitions. Paintings move me.' She stopped, feeling suddenly foolish. What was she talking about? The man must be laughing at her.

'Go on.'

'Well, that's it really. I have no qualifications. I

don't even know what I like!' she said, laughing uneasily. 'But I have a sense of things. I go around with my brother. He's a kn — ' She stopped before the fated word left her lips, ' — a dealer, of sorts.' She lowered her head and looked up at him, smiling. She had charm, he thought, and it was very potent. 'Well, he likes to think he's a dealer,' Zoe continued. 'We go around, buying. We're even branching out now. We started in Rochdale, then Manchester and Liverpool, and now, joy of joys, next weekend we're in Birmingham!'

She laughed, but the sound was strained and brittle. She hoped that the man hadn't noticed.

He had, but it made no difference. 'So do you think you'll go into the business full time?'

'I doubt if I could afford it, especially as Victor seldom sees fit to pay me what I'm due.'

'Your brother?'

'Yes,' she answered wryly. 'Victor is *that* kind of a brother.'

Feeling an unnecessary stab of disloyalty, Zoe moved off, Harland Goldberg falling into step beside her. It surprised her that she didn't resent his attention and actually found his company welcome. He wasn't like her father, who had little conversation with her; he wasn't like Alan who doted on her; or Ron, who admired her because she was his big sister and looked after him; and he wasn't like Victor, who wouldn't give a damn for her if she didn't make him money. And he wasn't like Steven Foreshaw . . .

Unsettled by her train of thought, Zoe walked quickly towards the third gallery and, spotting

154

some miniatures, beckoned to Harland. 'Look, this is a real find!'

Intrigued, he joined her.

'It's good,' she said, pointing to a painting which, although diminutive, had a flicker of spirit.

With a thrill of real interest, Harland pressed her. 'Why is it good?'

'Why?' she repeated, baffled by the question, and quickly diffident. 'Oh, I can't tell you.'

'Yes, you can, Try.'

'It's . . . it's . . . ' She trailed off, wanting to please the man and grateful for his interest. A smart man, obviously up from London, she thought, those clothes must have cost a fortune, they had style, not like Victor's.

'It's complete . . . and the painter felt for the subject.'

The point won, Harland extended his hand to her. 'My name is Harland Goldberg.'

'Zoe Mellor,' she said, taking his hand.

'Miss Zoe Mellor, would you like to have lunch with me?'

She hesitated, and then accepted, smiling.

He took her to the restaurant at the top of Kendal Milne's, stopping on route to pick up the large porcelain rooster Myrtle had wanted. Ordering wine and luncheon for both of them, he chatted, easily and comfortably, without trying to impress her. She found his confidence enormously appealing, and whenever she could she stole glances at him, trying to appraise his age and judging him mid-sixties. As if he knew what she was thinking, he looked up and smiled, his eyes quick, shrewd, and good-humoured. Perfectly at ease, he talked to her about his business and his gallery on Bond Street, explaining how the lucky find of a Richard Dadd painting had got him started. Then he told her how he had built up his clientele, how he had grown to love the business, and because Zoe was such a good listener, he told her more than he had ever told his daughter, sharing something which mattered with a stranger.

Moved by his enthusiasm, Zoe became enthralled, and then, when she was really caught up in it all, thrilled and eager and leaning across the table to take in every syllable and word that this clever little man had to tell her, suddenly her stomach flipped and a dead feeling welled up in her.

'Would you excuse me for just a moment?' she asked, walking into the cloakroom and leaning against the door.

It came back to her with unfair clarity, so much so that she shook her head vigorously. The previous two weeks had been a nightmare, an incubus encroaching into her dreams. It had never occurred to her that she might get pregnant, her naivety making her irresponsible, her disbelief turning to panic. For days she had watched the calendar, checking and rechecking the dates, knowing that if she *was* pregnant she was also afraid of telling Steven. Of course, he might offer to marry her, but that would cement her to Rochdale for ever.

And what if he did *not* offer to marry her? she asked herself. Then her fate might be that of the

Clark girl, her shame looming over Buck's Lane. And she knew suddenly with boiling clarity that she did not even have the courage to tell him. Rejection would be too hard to accept . . . So she had plotted instead, her mind turning to the thought of abortion late one sleepless night. With a sense of agonising relief, she had risen and gone to wake Victor and ask for his help. But his bed was empty, so instead Zoe made her way downstairs, stirring the last mean flames in the kitchen grate into a fire.

The night whirled around her and several times she dozed off, only to wake disoriented and cold, the fire coughing as she poured on some more coal. Thoughts of the pregnancy filtered into her mind and were obliterated quickly, Zoe's whole attention tuned to the sound of her brother's return, and the solution offered by him. She waited impatiently, and with every car that passed, Zoe listened, turning her head and wishing for the blaze of headlights to flash on to the kitchen windows, but still he didn't return. Midnight passed, and only the flushing of the toilet upstairs made any impression on the silence, and by the time two o'clock had hustled in, Zoe was fully awake, her previous impatience replaced with a sense of tingling disbelief.

Dull reason returned. Awkwardly Zoe got to her feet and bent her head down under the kitchen tap, a thin trickle of water filling her mouth, tasting of nothing but smelling of iron. Her thirst quenched, she wiped her mouth and leaned back against the sink, the palms of her hands flat against her stomach. If she was pregnant then she would have the child. The decision was a hard one, and had no comfort in it, only a realisation that duty, however costly, had always to be done.

She was just leaving the room when something made her pause and glance over her shoulder. The kitchen sighed with cold, but by the cooker, for an instant, she thought she had seen her mother standing there, her face the dark mask it had been that Christmas when her childhood ended.

12

Harland was still waiting for her at the table, sipping his wine and marvelling at his companion's sudden change of mood, not realising that at that precise moment Zoe was struggling to compose herself as she remembered the events of the previous morning. Very early, she had woken with stomach cramps, wrapping her arms across her belly and leaning forwards on the bed. She knew from the fierce blooding on the sheet that there would be no decision; no child, no loss of reputation — but she also knew that her relief was for another reason. Now she would not have to tell Steven. The threat of rejection would be avoided, postponed perhaps, to another time. Either way, she would never know . . . It was a safety of sorts.

Harland glanced up as Zoe returned to the table a minute later. 'Are you all right? Can I get you anything?'

'A case of amnesia.'

Harland frowned. 'Pardon?'

'I was being self-pitying,' Zoe said, looking round. 'And I hate that in other people.'

He had the intuition not to pursue the matter and rose to his feet. 'I settled the bill, perhaps we should go.'

Zoe nodded reluctantly. She had known the luncheon would come to an end, but she still resented it, just as she resented having to go back to Rochdale, to the salon, and the work for Victor. In silence, they walked out on to Deansgate, crossing over at the lights and making for St Ann's Square, Harland Goldberg struggling with the porcelain bird under his arm.

'What is that?' Zoe asked, pointing to the parcel.

'A rooster,' Harland said, his face slightly reddened with the effort of carrying it. 'And I have to get it back to London somehow.'

'To the gallery?'

'Not if I want to keep my reputation,' he said, laughing with her.

He knew he should have made his excuses and left; that he should have caught the earlier train back to the capital, but he stayed. Her manner intrigued him, her candour refreshing — as was her shaky knowledge of art — her uncertainty and her desire to learn almost childlike. Besides, even if she wasn't an academic she *did* have enthusiasm for the subject he loved above everything, and enthusiasm was in short supply. Feeling sentimental, he paused at the flower seller by the church to buy her a bunch of violets.

She flushed, genuinely flattered. 'Thank you, no one ever bought me flowers before.'

Her response touched him, and by the time they had walked another few yards he shook off his misgivings, the colour of the flowers hypnotising him, as her eyes did, dragging him into a reckless state of euphoria.

'Do you want a job, Zoe?'

She stopped walking, and, putting her head on

160

one side, looked gravely at him. 'As what?'

'A secretary. *My* secretary,' he continued quickly. 'It's a genuine offer. I need someone who is intelligent and interested in art.' He put the package down on the pavement and opened his coat. The afternoon was warming up, making him hot and flustered — awkward for the first time in many years.

'I don't know . . . ' Zoe answered, trailing off. It was a chance, she realised that. A chance to get away from Rochdale and Steven Foreshaw. Guilt made her pause, did she really want to get away from home and from Steven? And if she did, why now? Because she was afraid that he was not the man she had taken him for, that she suspected weaknesses which were too basic to ignore? Steven might live in a dream world, but Zoe was too wise, too young, to want such a simple escape.

She hesitated. Her ambitions till now had never run along any straight course. Instead, she had tripped into situations, acting on whims, or taking the course of least resistance.

Her lack of courage almost choked her. 'When would you want me to start?'

Harland took a deep breath. Having hoped she would accept, he still felt a certain sense of panic when she did so. What am I doing? he asked himself. What is the *true* reason I offered her the job? Sex? The thought jolted him. No, that would have been simple, he realised. It was worse. He liked her.

The house was quiet when Zoe returned home, except for the noise of the television coming from the snug where her father sat slumped in his chair, snoring. Seeing her pass the doorway, Ron got up and followed her into the kitchen. A sink full of dishes and greasy pans greeted her, as Peter got up from his bed and licked her hand. The room seemed cold, the light unsympathetic, making it worse than it was.

'Did you have a good time?' Ron asked her, settling himself in the chair by the fire. The coals shifted as Zoe looked round, noticing a postcard from one of Victor's girlfriends pushed halfway behind the clock and a few dog hairs on the dark rug.

'I met an art dealer who wants me to work for him in London,' she said, looking for the response on her brother's face.

His eyes widened, the elegant features alarmed. 'Oh no, Zoe! It's not right,' he said in his strong Lancashire accent. 'You musn't!'

'Why not?'

He struggled to answer. 'Well, it might not be . . . you know.'

'What?'

'Above board. Lots of girls go to London and get taken for a ride.'

She laughed at the old-fashioned expression. For someone with a face which could leave a woman gasping, her brother was incredibly naive. 'I'll be working for him, Ron. Nothing else.'

'For who?' her father said, walking in and yawning.

'Harland Goldberg.'

'Harland Goldberg! Is that a name or a

162

flaming disease?' He filled the kettle, turning when Victor walked in. 'Well, now we're all here, we can listen to what Zoe has to say.' He turned on the gas and leaned against the sink, his arms folded. 'She's got a job — although I thought she already had one.'

Zoe sat down at the table, her voice calm. 'It would be a wonderful — '

'Where?' her father asked.

'London. Bond Street.'

The silence was static. 'London,' he said finally, glancing over to Victor who had pulled off his coat and was watching his sister with a mixture of caution and curiosity. 'Well, take a good look at her! This is all your doing.'

'Oh, and how do you make that out?' his son asked, lighting a cigarette, and helping himself to a slab of cheese from the fridge.

'You gave her all these fancy ideas! Bloody London! What's wrong with the North?'

'It has nothing to do with wanting to go down south, Dad. It's just that the gallery's in London.'

Victor's face betrayed nothing, although his mind was working overtime. 'Whose gallery?' he asked evenly.

'Harland Goldberg's. On Bond Street,' Zoe answered, her eyes begging for his support. 'He wants me to be his secretary — '

'Hah!' Bernard Mellor exclaimed. 'If you believe that, you'll believe anything.'

Victor interrupted his father. 'Just a minute — '

'Don't 'just a minute' me, lad! I'm the head of the family, and you'd better not forget it. I told

163

you there'd be trouble if you started putting ideas into your sister's head. All that dressing up! She looked like something that'd fallen off a float the other Sunday — '

'I did not!' Zoe snapped, her temper breaking. 'I was well dressed, that's all. And why shouldn't I be?' She caught Victor's eye and then turned back to her father. 'Oh, Dad, it would be a chance to learn something. A profession — '

'Which profession would we be talking about here?'

No one answered. The kettle whistled suddenly and Bernard Mellor turned away, making himself a mug of tea, his stiff back managing to convey irritation and criticism at the same time. Always unwilling to argue, Ron sat with his head down, his arms crossed, his foot rocking the chair backwards and forwards. To Zoe's irritation, Victor continued to eat his cheese, apparently unconcerned, even though all of them were waiting for him to say something. But Victor was not about to put his thoughts into words; not until he had weighed everything in the balance. If Zoe was working at the Harland Goldberg gallery on Bond Street, he mused, it could be useful. Nonchalantly, he brushed some crumbs from his sleeve and, picking up his half smoked cigarette, looked over to his sister. She had done a good job on that second Turner lookalike and excelled herself with the George Morland fakes. She didn't know he had rubbed off her signature and sold them as originals to Ivor Weiss. What she didn't know wouldn't harm her, he decided. Besides, if she did know she would never have agreed to do them. She was too moral. But how moral was she really? he wondered, looking at her profile and assessing her as he would any other woman. Her face was pale, the eyes lowered, her dark hair falling across her cheek, her small clever hands on the table in front of her. Alerted to his scrutiny, Zoe turned and glanced at him.

So that was it! he thought, that was where the magic lay — in her eyes. Yes, Victor thought, his sister was an exciting woman, and exciting women could go far in the world. The realisation was all he needed to make up his mind.

'I don't see why she shouldn't take the job,' he said blithely as his father swung round. 'Think about it, Dad. She'd be earning a good wage, which you'll need soon when you have to rely on your pension, and if she takes Ron to London with her' — his brother's head shot up — 'she'll be safe.' Victor continued, 'Looking at the size of him most people won't realise he's as soft as shit.'

Ron opened his mouth to speak, but Victor carried on. 'Anyway, I'll be doing a lot of work in London myself, so I can keep an eye on both of them.'

'You working in London? Since when!' his father retorted angrily. 'You've just thought about it, Victor, just so you can all bugger off and leave me with that fat halfwit in the garage.'

'Alan will be company for you,' Victor added generously. 'He's a good worker.'

'And a bloody good eater too!' his father replied, his voice suspicious as he looked at his eldest son. 'You can't fool me, boy. I know you! You're up to something.'

A look of bland indifference washed over Victor's face. 'I was merely trying to find the best solution for — '

'You,' Bernard Mellor concluded, turning to his daughter and frowning. 'You want to look out for yourself in London. And watch him,' he added, pointing to Victor. 'He's after something, and it'll cost you.'

'Can I go, Dad?' she asked softly.

He faltered. He'd never had much to do with his daughter, but she'd done a good job nursing her mother and looking after the house. She had to go sometime, he thought.

'What's the wage like?'

'Oh, it's good, really good. I can send plenty of money home, and when Ron gets a job — ' She turned to her younger brother quickly. 'But Victor never asked you if you wanted to come with us, did he? We just assumed you would.'

Ron looked across to his sister, his face resigned. 'Can we take Peter?' was all he said.

★ ★ ★

'It's broken!' Myrtle wailed as she pulled the rooster out of the box. 'You idiot! I should waste money like this and see how you like it.'

She closed the front door and walked back to the table with a look of irritation on her thin features. Under the strong sunlight pelting down from the landing window, she seemed over made-up, her skin artificially light, her eyelids crêpey, tinted powder blue. Harland Goldberg sighed and walked up the stairs, his wife's voice floating up to him.

'Look at the thing! What did you do to it?'

'I did my best.'

'This is your *best*?' she hollered from the hall. 'Would that I never live to see your worst.'

Harland paused and leaned over the bannister rail. 'Get another one.'

'Another one, he says! It's a waste of money — '

'We have the money, Myrtle.'

'Not for long, if you keep throwing it about!' she shouted, irritably. 'What were you doing to get in such a condition?'

I went out for lunch with a wonderful young woman, he wanted to say, and I offered her a job, and then I dropped the bloody cockerel when she accepted and smiled at me. Because I felt good, he wanted to shout, because I felt happy.

'It was an accident.'

Myrtle eyed the bird's broken wing, her voice a whine. 'It's ruined. What am I supposed to do with it?'

'Ring the RSPCA!' Harland snapped, banging the bedroom door shut behind him.

★　★　★

Zoe stood at the entrance to Harland's gallery and looked in nervously. She saw a long length of polished floor scattered with a selection of Turkish rugs, a mass of paintings mottling each wall, all framed in gold and illuminated by picture lights, a pair of torchères flanking an archway, and a large antique desk by the door. Behind the desk was a woman, watching her. Zoe stepped back, surprised, and then, bolstering up her courage, pushed the door. It remained resolutely closed, and with a look of undisguised impatience, the woman behind the glass gestured wildly and pointed to a button beside the handle. Hugely embarrassed, Zoe pressed the bell and was finally admitted.

'Yes?'

The word rendered her momentarily speechless, as did the woman. Exquisitely overdressed, she was small and inclined to plumpness, her age disguised with skilful makeup and her slick, fiercely blonde hair arranged in a professional chignon.

'I'm Zoe Mellor.'

The woman did not smile, merely gestured for Zoe to sit down. 'Mr Goldberg will be with you presently,' she said, getting to her feet and walking the entire length of the gallery before disappearing through a door at the far end. Zoe breathed in deeply and felt an unfamiliar rush of colour to her face as she stole a glance at her clothes. Her suit was out of fashion, the colour in season several years ago. Humiliated, she crossed her legs and noticed with a cringing feeling of shame, that a fine ladder ran down the length of her calf.

The woman noticed it too as she materialised silently by Zoe's side and said in a patronising voice, 'Miss Mellor, follow me.'

Obediently Zoe stood up, adjusting her skirt as she followed the woman through the archway where she paused and then knocked on a large door marked in gilded letters, 'Harland Goldberg'.

'Come in,' he called easily, rising to his feet when he saw Zoe and gesturing to the woman to leave. 'Do sit down, Miss Mellor, it's so good to see you.'

The room was warm and comfortable, wood-panelled from floor to ceiling, a selection of paintings hanging on the wall while others were propped against the side of the desk where Harland sat watching the girl in front of him. She seemed a good deal smaller than she had been in Manchester, edgy and achingly nervous. Remembering the same feeling from his own early days, he was effortlessly kind.

'Are you all right?'

'I think I've made a mistake,' Zoe said quietly, glancing down at her bag and covering a scratch in the leather with her hand. 'I'm not . . . suitable for the job.'

'I should be the one to decide that,' he said carefully, getting to his feet and closing the door. Mrs Grimaldi always liked to leave his door slightly open, it facilitated her eavesdropping. 'Has she upset you?'

'Who?'

'Mrs Grimaldi,' he replied. 'My receptionist.'

Zoe lied easily. 'No, she was . . . ' She stopped. 'It's not her, it's all of this. I never thought it would be so grand. I can't do the job. I'm sorry.'

'When I first started I was a little Jew with no

contacts,' Harland began, 'and everyone thought I was a creep who would fall flat on his face. All the educated types in the old boy network tried to keep me out. I never got into a golf club, or was invited to be a member of anything,' he laughed. 'I couldn't even get on a charity committee!' He looked evenly at her. 'No one returned my calls, or answered my invitations. It was hard, more on my wife than me. Women need to belong and she felt rejected . . . ' He leaned back in his chair, his eyes bright with mischief. 'But do you know, after I made some good buys and got a few top notch clients, suddenly, like magic' — he clicked his fingers — 'the invitations poured in. It was suddenly 'Harland, be a member of this', 'Harland, come to dinner', 'Harland, meet Lady Bourne'.' He was smiling. 'I was a little Jew when I came to this town and threw up with nerves when I went to my first auction, and I've stayed a little Jew, only now I'm rich and only throw up when I have caviar.'

He paused and tapped the forefinger of his left hand on the desk as he said the next words. 'Don't tell me you can't do it, Zoe, you can. The ones who come up from nothing find it tougher, but hold on to it longer.'

She smiled half-heartedly. 'But I don't know where to start.'

'You already have. You started when you walked through that door.'

★　★　★

There were only two rooms, a bathroom, and a kitchen. The bedroom was Zoe's, Ron making do with the couch in the lounge. Advertised as a des. res. in Notting Hill, it was cramped but convenient, Kensington on one side, Portobello Road on the other. Ron found London terrifying, the noise and the speed of the traffic intimidating him and keeping him indoors for the first few days until Zoe coaxed him out. They were due to go to the cinema and were waiting in the underground for a train, a mess of litter blowing down the black tracks, graffiti smeared like excreta over the tiled walls. Ron glanced round. A woman read a copy of the *Evening Standard* on a bench while the man beside her picked his nose and shouted at a small child who was standing too near the edge of the platform.

'Look at that,' Ron said, nudging his sister and pointing. 'He should watch that kid.'

The train swooped in suddenly and made Ron jump back, his face waxy. A rush of people fled from the opening doors and, losing sight of him, Zoe called out for her brother, the Tannoy exploding over their heads and blotting out every sound. Pushing a few people aside, she struggled against the crush, the crowd pushing for the exits as the train pulled out. The platform was empty, the far-off echo of wheels sounding down the penny whistle tunnels as she looked round for Ron, her mouth dry. Suddenly she spotted him, at the very edge of the platform, flat against the wall only inches from the sign which read 'Passengers must not pass beyond this point'.

That was Ron's first and last venture on to the

London Underground. Since then he had walked everywhere, taking his beloved Peter with him, in fine weather or foul. Within a week of their arrival in London, Ron found himself a job as a waiter in a small café in Frith Street, handing over his wages to his sister without so much as a murmur, the pocket money she gave him spent at the dog track where he went every Tuesday and Thursday. His world was simple and he was happy.

In Rochdale Alan was grieving. Within days he missed Zoe so desperately that he lapsed into virtual silence and his depression returned. Tom Mellor accepted the situation and said nothing to his brother, knowing how impatient he already was with his son. A taciturn man himself, Tom had little desire to talk and so the two of them worked side by side with scant communcation and even less understanding.

'Bring that piece outside for me, Alan,' Tom said, knowing that he could not pick up the headstone, and watching as his nephew heaved it outside and laid it against the wall. A fine spitting of rain smudged the bland marble, then ceased, the weather changing its mind for the day. For the next few hours they worked on, the clouds scuttering across the sky, a sharp catch of wind blowing the chippings across the yard and a later wink of sunshine making the marble luminous.

In silence, Alan laboured until six and then left for home, going to the garage immediately. The house was dark behind him, his father having soon made it a habit to visit the pub every night and thus avoid any ill-fated conversations with his son. Unlocking the garage door, Alan flipped on the light, a feeling of contentment welling up in him as he looked at the sculptured figure at the work bench. But the sensation soon faded as he heard the sound of two girls calling out to each other on the main road, exchanging greetings and laughing. Alan held his breath until they walked on and then, sighing, picked up a chisel and moved towards the figure of a small angel.

Preparing to strike the stone he stopped suddenly, remembering an incident which had happened the previous week. He had been visiting one of the churches outside Bolton, and although it was off his usual beaten track, his attention was soon absorbed by the headstones in the graveyards. It had grown late, and from inside the church he could hear the organ playing and see lights going on. Feeling relaxed there, as he was so seldom anywhere else, Alan listened, his clumsy frame forgotten as the music washed over him. But then it had stopped and soon after someone left by the side door, steps crunching on the shadowed gravel path, the sound of whistling fading as they walked into the distance. Alan paused. Unwilling to go home, and knowing that the church was empty, he moved towards the door, walking in and turning on the lights.

The church was silent as he moved around, reading inscriptions and running his fingers over some of the carving. He was so intrigued that the first murmurs did not disturb him; it was only when he paused to listen that the full impact struck home. His face was burning with shame, he heard the sounds of a couple making love in the vestry, and paralysed, he remained motionless for several minutes, his heart banging with shame and envy.

When he finally left, the night air stung him as he walked home. He felt ugly, fatter than ever, unloved. At twenty-four he had never kissed a girl; had never risked the rejection which was sure to follow. Overly protected by his mother in his youth and despised by his father, Alan was impotent, and without understanding the cause, he had compensated by working, by pouring all his energy and passion into the dead blocks of stone. As they came to life and became his, they were more, much more, than any person could be. His for ever. Even when they were finished and planted into the dark earth he could visit them and touch them. The touching was at first comforting, but later the action moved him emotionally, then sexually, so that every time his hands strayed over the marble Alan would hear the sounds of the couple's lovemaking in the church, the noises tingling down through his fingers and making his heart pump with excitement.

A sense of wracking guilt followed immediately so that when Alan was alone in the garage he found himself reluctant to touch the small angel upon which he was working, his feeling of shame compounded by the fact that this figure was holy and should be worshipped not desired. The same sensation filled him now as he hovered, confused, his hands dropping to his sides, his eyes brimming with misery. Then with infinite longing he leaned forward and pressed his face against the cold stone, his lips burning against the carved leg of the statue. Instantly he remembered the murmured voices from the vestry, his mind playing tricks, so that the statue seemed to embrace him in return, its beauty something terrible and shameful as his own excitement was shaped into the marble for ever.

13

'Who is she?' Myrtle asked her husband when she called into the gallery unannounced.

'My new secretary,' Harland replied firmly, closing the door of his office.

'Since when?'

'Since last Monday.'

Myrtle's eyes narrowed. 'Since last Monday! I don't suppose it occurred to you to tell your wife?' She sat down, crossing her thin legs, the gold chains on her shoes catching the light. The sudden appearance of a young attractive woman had shaken her, she had thought that Harland was too old for sex, after all, it was quite a few years since that débâcle with his mistress . . . She scrutinised him. He might be an old fool, she thought, but he's my old fool, and that girl outside was going to have a fight on her hands if she was going to try and steal him.

'Where did she come from?'

'Manchester.'

'Manchester.'

'Yes, Manchester!' Harland snapped. 'And stop repeating everything I say, it's like having an echo.'

His wife flinched. 'Don't talk to me like that! I have rights. I am your wife, remember that.'

'And Zoe is my secretary. Remember that.'

Preventing further argument, the door opened and Erica walked in. Harland looked at his daughter, noticing the similarity between the two women.

'Who's the new girl out there?' she asked, her voice lazy, indulged.

Myrtle's eyes never left her husband's face. '*That* is your father's mistress.'

Erica's expression was sulky. 'Oh, Mum, come on. You said we were going to Fortnum's for lunch.'

'Your mother's heart broken, and you want to *eat*?' she asked, incredulous. 'That I should be cursed with such a child!'

'Myrtle,' her husband said patiently. 'Zoe is not my mistress — '

'Not yet!'

Bored, Erica walked to the window and looked out, her mind already turning towards the dinner party she was attending that night. 'Mum, you heard what Father said. Stop imagining things and come on. We'll be late.'

Myrtle rose to her feet, a study of injured dignity. 'Don't bother to come crawling round me tonight, Harland Goldberg. You've broken my heart.'

'It'll mend. Go and buy yourself a new outfit, and charge it to me.'

Temporarily mollified, Myrtle left, the indolent Erica following her, passing the reception desk which was now manned by Mona Grimaldi, Zoe having made a discreet visit to the storeroom.

Not a whisper from Bond Street crept in as Mona arranged on the telephone for a business meeting to be conducted that night at Claridges.

Harland liked deals to be made in elegant settings, phenomenal amounts of money exchanged over cigars or dinner, diaries with scribbled figures dipping in and out of expensive pockets of bespoke suits.

The atmosphere in the gallery was one of wealth, taste and power, and one to which Mona Grimaldi had been born and bred. The daughter of a famously wealthy dealer, she had been married at the fairytale age of seventeen to an Italian count, who was regrettably ushered into the next world after missing a bend in the Monte Carlo Rally. 'Out for the Count' as one wag put it. Mona had been distressed and angry, returning home to London just in time to see her father's business crippled and to join him in a hurried departure to America. For the next few years Mona and her father lived on their wits, until his impressive business acumen, and the calling in of several overdue debts, set him back on his feet. The art world regarded him with caution until he began to bring collectors back to London and advise them of the best galleries to frequent, after which he was regarded, quite literally, as the Prodigal Returned.

Mona married again at the age of thirty-five, but this time her father disapproved of her reckless choice and was not open to reason. Result — Mona was disinherited, a fact which did little for her temper, and less for her husband. Exit second spouse, and back went Mona to the nest — which was where she had remained for the last four years, only choosing to work for Harland Goldberg because he paid

178

well, and because she used her position to spy for her father. Harland knew *why* she worked for him, but used *her* for her considerable social contacts, while making sure that all the information she sent back to her father was either common knowledge, or unimportant.

The situation had worked extremely well for both of them. Myrtle being totally uninterested in the business, Mona Grimaldi had been the perfect hostess at Harland's numerous Private Views, and was proficient enough to bid for him at auctions when he was abroad. Her style and ability to speak four languages were appreciated, as was her capacity for gossip, titbits being passed on to Harland in the same way a private passes over a gun for the general to fire. Unfortunately this happy arrangement did not include outsiders and the arrival of Zoe was regarded by Mona as an immediate threat to her position and status. In fact, from the first instant she saw her, Mona Grimaldi loathed her rival, seeing Zoe as a common Northern upstart who was after the boss. It made no difference to Mona that she had always regarded Harland as a common Northern upstart too, her envy still flared at the presence of this younger woman and she immediately began plotting to send Zoe Mellor back to Rochdale.

Zoe was aware of her hostility, but decided to do nothing to inflame the situation. Woefully out of her depth and frequently embarrassed by the gaps in her education and social skills, she walked around the gallery like a waif when Harland was engaged, avoiding the patronising expression in Mona's eyes, and trying to pretend that she couldn't overhear her critical telephone conversations. After all, she was there to learn, and learn she would, even though in the first weeks she was often tempted back to Rochdale and Steven Forshaw.

The impulse was resisted mainly because Zoe was no longer sure of her reception if she did return. Unable to tell him directly, she had written a letter to Steven, explaining inadequately that she had to take the opportunity to make something of her life. She begged him to understand. He didn't, though apparently Miss Ivy and Miss Violet had expected it and took the news calmly, with no rancour, leaving Zoe with the distinct impression that the two years she had spent there were already forgotten. The knowledge wounded her, although it didn't wound her as much as Steven's silence. Daily she expected him to write to her. In fact, she had even told Alan to pass on her new address to him. But he never wrote.

It was not that Steven hadn't attempted to write. Many times, he had put pen to paper and then thrown them to one side in irritation uncertain how to commit his feelings to paper, even though Zoe had seemed willing to believe his amorous outpourings when they made love. Not that she ever said so, it was merely the look in her eyes. Steven lit a cigarette and shouted at a student who put her head round the door, watching with satisfaction as the girl retreated in embarrassment. He liked the art school, it was his little domain, the stage upon which he could play out his 'I could have been a great artist, but chose to be a teacher and pass on my gift to the young instead' act. Here he could fantasise and never actually have to admit to himself that he was afraid . . . He thought of Zoe and the thought rankled. *She had actually gone to London*, packing up her bags and setting off for the big city. Doing the one thing he could never do. Yet despite his bitterness, he could not forget her. Each day he imagined her in front of him; each lesson he saw *her* on the couch, not the model; and when he turned out the studio lights at night he remembered the rainy evening they had spent there and his loneliness scalded him.

★　★　★

Mona was scalding too, especially over the telephone.

'He calls her his secretary.' She glanced out into Bond Street at a passerby stopping to look at his A-Z. 'His secretary, hah!'

Round the corner in Cork Street, the dealer Tobar Manners was listening avidly. 'I heard she was good-looking — '

'She's common!' Mona said quickly. 'An upstart from the North — '

'Like Harland.'

Mona fiddled with her earring. 'Possibly that's the attraction. Birds of a feather flocking together. Perhaps he feels more comfortable with her. Although you should see her clothes. Pure C & A.'

Tobar Manners smiled slyly. He could always

rely on dear Mona to spread the poison. 'Well, I suppose her wardrobe will soon improve . . . '

'Harland wouldn't be such a fool!'

'Oh, I don't know. It's probably his last fling, Mona. You really should have got in when there was no competition.'

Smarting, she changed the subject. 'Are you going to the auction tonight? The Italian Old Masters at Lister's?'

'Yes, I'll be there. Everyone will be,' Tobar said, adding peevishly, 'Will you be coming . . . or the new girl?'

Tobar Manners had been right, everyone *was* there — except Mona Grimaldi, and although Zoe had begged Harland to go alone, he had insisted that she attend the auction with him.

'You'll learn a great deal.'

'I'm not ready,' she insisted awkwardly, by this time fully aware of the rumour which was going the rounds. She had no desire to be pointed out as Harland Goldberg's mistress but she knew that she could never explain the reason for her reluctance to him and was therefore forced into agreement.

So later that evening they walked into the auction room and took their seats at the front. A hum of speculative voices started up behind them, and although Zoe was almost luminous with nerves, her expression was defiant. They could say what they wanted, she didn't care. Let them talk! she thought suddenly, her spirits returning. She knew the truth. Besides, she was safe this way. She didn't belong to him, she never would, she was with him to learn. That was all

. . . Faces peered into hers, assessed the new suit she wore, the stylish shoes, and the flattering hairstyle. The humiliation nearly choked her, although Harland seemed immune, possibly even flattered. Only when the auction began and everyone's attention was diverted, did she relax, unfolding her hands on her lap and fumbling for the catalogue in her bag.

The rumour of their relationship spread like an oil slick, and at the gallery Mona's outrage extended to the other members of staff. It was Leonard Phillips, the restorer, who was the next to attack.

'I'm busy! Too busy to answer fool questions,' he snapped in reply to a query she had made. 'Go and ask your boyfriend.'

Zoe faltered. 'I can't, Steven's in Rochdale,' she said, walking out.

Leonard emerged in the gallery minutes later, looking round before walking in. There was an unspoken rule that none of the workmen were allowed upstairs when there were customers browsing.

'Miss Mellor?' Zoe turned. 'I'm sorry if I spoke out of turn.'

'About what?'

An ex-Guardsman, Leonard Phillips found himself short of words and mortally embarrassed. Dropping his voice, he said, 'About the remark I made . . . oh, you know!' he snapped, irritated.

Zoe raised her eyebrows. 'I shall never forgive you, Leonard — unless you tell me everything you know about restoring.'

Relieved, he agreed. From then on, every lunchtime, after Leonard had hurriedly eaten his sandwiches, Zoe watched as he restored the paintings, his steady fingers cleaning and preparing surfaces, his knowledge of techniques formidable.

'What are you using?' she asked, leaning over the bench as Leonard meticulously restored the background of an Italian landscape.

'Egg tempera.'

She frowned. 'What's that? Tell me.'

Her skill increased as her knowledge did. Before long she knew which paints were chemically stable and which not.

'The yellow paint's fugitive.'

'Fugitive?'

Leonard nodded. 'That means it fades, disappears, so that when the yellow goes, the green turns to blue.' He smiled. 'You look at some of the Reynolds pictures. He used a fugitive red, so that the flesh tones are now chalky white. Some of his sitters look like marble statues.'

She learned about the mediums too. Learned that linseed oil yellowed, McGulp could darken, and bitumen dried black and cracked the paint surface. In fact, she began to make her own experiments, writing up her own discoveries, testing pigments as she began to paint again, her talent limited, her progress slow. Soon the flat was crowded with still lifes and indifferent portraits, all at various stages of completion.

As the months progressed, Harland was as good as his word, passing on information and knowledge which it had taken him a lifetime to accumulate. His fondness for Zoe increased, although he was angered by her shyness and unwillingness to enter conversations.

'Why don't you talk to the buyers, Zoe?' he asked one morning. 'They aren't monsters.'

She found it impossible to explain. 'I would say something wrong, or Mona would say something about me — '

'She's a bitch,' he countered. 'Snap back at her. You could hold your own with Victor, so why don't you have a go at her?'

'Because she's smart. She speaks God knows how many languages, and knows everyone — '

'Only because her father knew everyone first. She never had to do it for herself,' Harland continued, sitting down and flicking on the lamp beside him. 'You're doing very well, Zoe. You're learning the business fast. Don't be fazed by the likes of Mona Grimaldi, she doesn't count.'

'She does, and she's angry because you take me to the auctions now, and not her.'

Harland threw up his hands. 'This is *my* gallery, I take who I want. Not who Mona wants.' Zoe shifted her feet uncomfortably and Harland shook his head. 'I'm sorry. I forget too quickly, don't I?' She looked at him in surprise. 'I should remember how it was for me when I started, I shouldn't expect so much of you, so soon.' He gestured to the seat in front of him. 'Sit down, Zoe, and let's forget Mona and talk about the business instead.'

Harland's talks lasted for hours, and in them he outlined the whole mechanism of the art

185

world. He told her about the corrupt dealers and how they sold a painting twice. First they showed it to one collector, then when they had made the sale, they said it had to be cleaned and relined, and would not be ready for a couple of months. They knew that by that time the collector would have forgotten the niceties of the painting, and besides, most of the patrons had several homes, and the picture would be only one amongst many in a collection. The dealer would then show the same painting to a second collector, who would also buy it. The trick was this — the first collector would eventually get a painting which was similar to the original, but less valuable. The difference in price went into the dealer's pocket.

Zoe frowned. 'But surely the buyer would know it wasn't the same painting — '

'No, because the dealer picks very similar paintings, like Corots, for instance. Besides, if you're very rich but have no real eye for paintings, and if you rely on the dealer, you don't know one from the other.'

'God, it's so immoral.'

Harland smiled. 'That's only one example of the immorality in this business. The list is endless.' He glanced at his watch. 'It's late. Do you want to go home?'

Zoe shook her head. 'No, I'm not tired, tell me more about the dealers.'

Harland leaned back in his seat, the room dark behind him. 'Jimmy van Goyen had a painting once which everyone was after, especially a very greedy, titled lady. She was a tremendous snob, but when he told her that there was one way she could persuade him to sell it to her . . . she was tempted.'

Open-mouthed, Zoe asked, 'What happened?'

'The aforementioned titled lady was duly served in Jimmy van Goyen's office, and when he came out he told his staff that on no account was the painting to be sold to her. In fact, she was banned from his gallery.'

'Oh God,' she said, thoughtfully. 'But how do you know?'

Harland looked at her straight in the eyes. 'Jimmy van Goyen told me. He was very proud.'

The phone beside him buzzed into life. 'Who is it?'

'It's Ahmed, Harland,' the caller said excitedly. 'I'm ringing about that bastard Seymour Bell. He's written another of his bloody demolition pieces.'

At that moment, Seymour Bell was sitting in his office reading the article he was about to submit to the paper for publication the following morning. It was a boiling piece, a direct attack in a painter currently exhibiting at Ahmed Fazir's gallery on Albemarle Street. The attack served two purposes, it satisfied Seymour's naturally peevish steak, and it settled an old score, one which he had nurtured for years. 'People of any breeding take their revenge cold' the proverb went, and in his case, the revenge was positively glacial.

Hardly brushing five feet seven, even with built up shoes, Seymour rose to his feet and went into the private bathroom next to his office, which was separated from the rest of the house. The arrangement had begun thirteen years earlier when Dorothy agreed to segregate a third of the building for Seymour's business, the rest to be used for family occupation. The thought of his wife and son being on the other side of the wall stimulated Seymour and gave his sexual activities a certain piquancy. With mounting excitement, he rinsed out his mouth with Listerine, looking into the mirror. Critical to a fault with others, Seymour looked for flaws in himself, but naturally found none. Before him stood a man who appeared cultivated, Anglicised, his Jewish origins as firmly buried as the rows of dead in Highgate Cemetery up the road from his house, his glasses suspended from a fine chain round his neck, his county clothes marking out the perfect academic family man.

He did not look like a homosexual. In fact, he looked so unlike a homosexual that the thought would never have occurred to Dorothy, even though the frequency with which young men visited her husband's part of the house should have alerted her. At first Seymour had deluded himself, denying his sexual inclinations, the quickening of pulse and heart rate being put down to imagination rather than lust. But after his son was born and he grew bored with his wife, he began to look for his pleasure elsewhere. He tried to make relationships with women, asking a few out for dinner and building up a deep loathing of the female sex when they found his company tedious and his advances laughable. His pomposity did not take rejection well and so he decided to change tack and turned to young men, taking care to seduce only those over whom he had power.

Having trained originally as a painter and having been roundly dismissed as 'trite' and 'unoriginal', Seymour had waited for his revenge and gone abroad to build up a reputation in print, not paint. His success was not immediate, but because he had been original and savage, it took less than a decade for Seymour to become an influential art critic in Paris, moving back to London when his name was known. The few who remembered his ill-fated attempts at artistic immortality were not slow to carp, but after bearing the full brunt of his displeasure when their exhibitions were singled out for ridicule, they were soon silenced. They learned quickly, and soon courted Seymour like a Hollywood gossip columnist, dubbing him 'The W1 Queen'.

Not that Seymour knew of his nickname; he only knew the effect he had on people. It was pleasing to see them squirm, just as it was positively exhilarating to demolish a new artist in a few well-judged paragraphs — the maxim being that where Seymour Bell had failed, everyone else would perish also. But he worked himself up so much during the writing of his column that it always left him sexually excited.

He dabbed his mouth dry with a hand towel before returning to the office. From the other side of the wall he could hear Dorothy's radio blaring out some Erik Satie composition, and his son's car leaving the garage. He could also hear a pair of feet sounding on the steps outside.

Prickling with excitement, Seymour opened the door.

A tall young man with his hands in his pockets stood there. 'Hello, Mr Bell.'

Seymour smiled and stood back to let his visitor enter, noticing how his T-shirt was stretched across his back, the sleeves just covering the top third of his muscular arms.

'Is everything OK? You did tell me to come now.'

Seymour smiled. 'Of course, Michael, everything's fine. Please sit down,' he said, gesturing to the Chesterfield and taking a seat beside the young man. 'As I said, I'm looking for someone to help me with research and I was very pleased with what you did for me the other day at the British Museum.'

'Oh, that was nothing,' Michael said eagerly. After all, the work paid well and he needed the money badly. 'I'm sure I could help you more.'

I'm sure you could, Seymour thought, the naivety of the remark almost making him smile. He liked innocence and found it exciting. Anyway, a man in his position had to be careful, and there was always the threat of disease.

'I would need you to work long hours.'

Michael nodded. Long hours for good pay, so what? He had already been given a ridiculous sum for only an hour's work — Seymour had seen to that.

'Mr Bell, I'm sure I can do whatever you want.'

'Excellent,' Seymour replied eagerly. 'I do need someone who can take orders and do exactly as I say.'

Michael nodded again, moving his leg slightly as Seymour laid his hand on the settee between them.

Seymour was further excited at his reaction. This was going to be a real conquest. 'I thought it might make life easier if you stayed here. There's a spare room . . . ' Seymour saw the young man flinch and played his trump card. 'My wife has made it very comfortable.'

Michael relaxed then, just as Seymour knew he would. Sometimes the young men blustered, obviously embarrassed by their own suspicions, because with a wife in the house, what could happen? The relief even made some lightheaded and over-friendly, as though they were trying to reassure Seymour that they had never suspected him.

'It would make your life easier . . . ' he continued, pouring them both a drink and remembering the critical essay on his desk, a wicked dissection of one of Fazir's favourite artists, which would ensure that the dealers would not buy and any potential collectors would be scared off. Power, real power, was sex in itself. An orgasm on paper.

He turned back to the young man and allowed his thoughts to wander, imagining how he would undress him slowly, and how, later in the dark, cries would filter through the wall to the ignorant Dorothy.

Seymour's voice was unsteady as he stood up

and said, 'Why don't you come and look at your room?'

Rising obediently, the young man laid down his glass and followed his host, Seymour's hand resting lightly on Michael's right buttock as he closed the bedroom door behind them.

★ ★ ★

It was nearly Christmas before Victor visited the gallery. Erica Goldberg had called in to see her father and was just about to leave when he opened the door. She paused, her eyes raking up and down his stylish figure, a slow smile spreading over her sulky features. 'Hello,' she said. A sharp wind blew against their faces from the open door. 'Are you a buyer?'

Victor returned her smile, his voice intimate. 'I could be. It depends.'

'On what?'

'The merchandise,' he replied.

Both played the game with consummate skill. This was something Victor liked about London, the women were as adventurous as he was.

'The merchandise?' she repeated. 'Oh, I think you should talk to my father about that.'

Victor smiled winningly. 'Harland Goldberg is your father?' She nodded. 'He must be very proud to have such a beautiful daughter.'

Erica raised an eyebrow and walked out into the cold street, turning back briefly. 'I hope we meet again, Mr — '

'Mellor.'

She frowned. 'Mellor? But isn't that your — '

'Sister. Yes.' Victor agreed. 'Zoe works for your father.'

Erica considered the information, wondering what she really thought about her father's mistress, and if her opinion would affect any future relationship with Zoe's brother. But her hesitation was only momentary. 'Well, we'll just be one big, happy family then, won't we?' she said.

The door closed behind her and Victor glanced in a large Empire-style mirror to study his reflection. Gone were the sharp clothes and the sideboards, in their place was a well cut mohair suit and a well groomed head of hair, under which his sharp eyes looked less feral. He liked what he saw in the glass and was startled by a voice behind him.

'Do you want to buy it, or were you just admiring the picture?'

'Well, if it isn't my little sister. How are you?'

'I was fine until I saw you,' Zoe replied, relieved that Mona hadn't arrived yet. 'Stay away from Erica, she's out of your league. Besides, she's just got back from Switzerland where she's been having treatment.'

'Whatever it was, it worked.'

Zoe sighed. 'She has a drug problem.'

Victor ignored the remark and walked round the gallery. 'Nice. Very nice,' he said, turning back to her. 'And you look good. That dress must have cost something.'

Zoe bristled. 'I have a clothes allowance.'

'I'm not in the least surprised,' he replied silkily.

'OK, what do you want, Victor?'

'I thought I'd drop in and see how you were getting on. How's London treating you?'

'I'm learning.'

His eyes swept the walls. 'I can see that. Are you getting to be an expert yet? On painting, that is.'

'Harland's a good teacher, and he's very generous.' She caught the look on her brother's face and added, ' . . . with his time.'

Victor lost patience. 'Oh, what the hell, Zoe! I'm no prude. I say you should take the old man for all you can get.'

'I'm not sleeping with him, Victor.'

He stared into his sister's face, baffled. 'You're not?' he asked, and then smiled. 'My God, you are clever! Fancy getting all this on tick!'

Before she had a chance to reply the door opened and two dealers came in. An ill-matched couple, Tobar Manners small and redheaded, his balding colleague, Anthony Sargeant, topping six foot and brimming with misplaced good humour.

'Is Harland in yet?' Manners asked Zoe, his indurative green eyes resting only momentarily on her before skimming over the walls to see what was on offer.

'He said he would be in soon. Can I do anything for you?'

Manners laid down the picture he was carrying and smirked. 'I don't think you're my type, dear.'

His spite winded her momentarily, but she rallied. 'Well, if there's nothing I can do for Mr

Manners, can I help you, Mr Sargeant?'

Uninterested in the young woman in front of him, Anthony Sargeant shook his head and took a seat by the door.

Tobar Manners walked round, undeterred. 'I do loathe Romney, so sentimental.' Zoe ignored him. 'Well, dear lady, what do you think?' he asked, irritated by her lack of response. Behind them, Sargeant burped quietly, indigestion plaguing him from the previous night's dinner, one heavy hand patting his bloated stomach.

Unsettled by the question, and by the presence of her brother, Zoe blustered. 'Romney was gifted — '

'Gifted!' Manners repeated scathingly. 'That means nothing.'

'Oh, leave her alone,' Sargeant said. 'Pick on someone your own size.' He laughed suddenly. 'Come to think of it, she *is* about your size.'

Tobar Manners flinched. Ever sensitive about his lack of height, he resented any reference to it and particularly his nickname, 'The Malevolent Elf'.

'Don't you have some work to do?' he asked Zoe unpleasantly.

'Far more than you have, obviously,' she answered, her voice cold.

But as she moved away the picture on the table caught her eye and she paused. It looked like a Guardi, she thought, remembering how Leonard had restored one only weeks before. It was similar to the picture in front of her, yet . . .

'Is this painting for sale?'

'Why, are you thinking of buying it?' Manners

195

asked her, winking. 'Or perhaps you could find someone to buy it for you.'

His rudeness, allied to the smug look on Victor's face, made her turn on him. 'Is that an offer, Mr Manners?' Zoe asked archly.

Anthony Sargeant burst out laughing. He had to hand it to her, the girl could hold her own. He patted his stomach again, he should find himself a little diversion somewhere. A little amusement. The door opened and interrupted his thoughts as Harland walked in.

Not realising who Victor was, he smiled at Zoe and extended his hand to Tobar Manners. 'So what brings you to see me?' he asked, glancing towards the table and pointing. 'This?'

Sargeant struggled to his feet clumsily. 'What do you think of it?'

Harland studied the painting, Zoe watching him out of the corner of her eye. 'Guardi?' Both dealers nodded their heads. 'It's nice,' Harland said evenly, walking over to the door and peering at the canvas.

'Don't try to make a run for it!' Sargeant joked, his eyes flicking back to Manners, his tongue running over his dry lips.

'I like it,' Harland said finally, walking back to the table and laying the painting down. 'How much?'

Without hesitating, Zoe stepped out from behind the reception desk. 'I'm so sorry to disturb you,' she began, 'but I have to give you an urgent message, Mr Goldberg.' Harland glanced over to her, surprised. Zoe never interrupted him when he was doing business. 'It

196

is very important,' she added.

Excusing himself, he followed her into the back office, closing the door behind him. The walls were stacked with reference books from floor to ceiling, even the window sill obscured by old, bound volumes and faded prints.

Zoe took in a breath. 'There's something wrong with the painting.'

'What?' Harland asked impatiently.

'I . . . I don't know,' she stammered. 'But it's not right somehow . . . it couldn't be a fake, could it?'

His eyes stared into hers for a disbelieving second. What *was* she talking about? A *fake*? How would she know anyway? 'Are you crazy, Zoe?'

'I know how it sounds,' she said, embarrassment creeping up on her, 'but I got such a bad feeling about that picture. Anyway, the dealers are acting so oddly . . . '

'They always act oddly! That doesn't mean the picture's a fake.'

She glanced away from him. 'I know . . . but I watched Leonard restoring a Guardi only the other week and he showed me the pattern of brush marks, and the way the artist painted certain areas on the canvas . . . ' She trailed off. 'There's something different about this one.'

'Guardi was a very prolific artist. There *would* be differences in pictures.'

'But not in the *style* of painting,' Zoe insisted, wondering how she had the nerve to question his judgement. But she had a hunch, and she was determined to follow it. 'Please, Harland, think about it.'

'I've worked in this business for over forty years — '

'It's just a feeling, I know, but if you're wrong, you're out of pocket.'

Harland was tempted to dismiss what she said, but hesitated. He *had* been caught out by fakes before, badly in the 1960s. The memory danced on his nerves. Myrtle had nagged him for months afterwards, the forgeries banished into his basement at St John's Wood, his folly hidden under a stack of dustsheets.

'Are you sure?'

Zoe shrugged apologetically. 'No.'

Shaking his head ruefully, Harland walked back into the gallery. For the next ten minutes he asked about the provenance of the Guardi and cross-examined the two dealers as much as he dared, Zoe keeping out of the way, Victor eavesdropping as he walked around the exhibition.

Tobar Manners's patience faltered quickly. 'What the hell is this all about, Harland? You normally take my word on the provenance of the painting.'

Harland smiled warmly. 'I trust you, Tobar, but I'm worried about this picture, don't ask me why.'

Behind them, Anthony Sargeant burped.

'Oh, For God's sake! Take something for that bloody stomach of yours!' Manners snapped.

'I can't help it,' Sargeant murmured plaintively. 'I'm always the same after garlic.'

198

Harland coughed. 'I don't think I'll take on the painting, Tobar,' he said carefully. 'I just don't feel right about it, that's all.' He walked both dealers to the door. 'I'm sorry, maybe next time.'

Out on Bond Street the traffic was solid, a messenger bike just skirting a taxi as it beat the lights. Manners glanced over to Anthony Sargeant and thrust the painting into his hands. 'Bloody Jew!'

'Don't be like that. Harland usually buys from us.'

Tobar Manners set off down the street, Sargeant lumbering behind him. Why had Harland Goldberg rejected the Guardi? To his knowledge there was nothing wrong with the picture, and even though he hadn't investigated the provenance thoroughly it was supposed to be genuine . . . He stopped at the lights, Sargeant alternately panting and burping beside him. Harland Goldberg! Bloody Jew! he thought maliciously. He must know something about the picture that I don't. But how? They crossed over, a Mercedes pipping Sargeant as it swung round the corner. Tobar Manners didn't even turn round, just carried on towards Old Bond Street, pausing by Asprey's, his pinched face suspicious.

'Think back, Anthony,' he said, as the big man caught up with him. 'What made Goldberg decide against buying the picture?'

Sargeant frowned. The garlic was really taking its toll, and now Tobar was asking him difficult questions. He shifted around uncomfortably, pretending to think, aware of the little man's scrutiny. He hated this kind of thing, even though his late father had told him to ally himself to Tobar Manners and learn from him; even though he realised that his Eton education counted for nothing in the art world mafia.

Sargeant laid the painting against Asprey's wall and patted his stomach again. That was the last time he had garlic, ever.

'He just seemed . . . against the idea.'

'Precisely!' Sargeant sighed with relief as Manners continued. 'He *was* against the idea. But why?' there was no response from Anthony Sargeant. 'Because of the girl!'

'What?'

'The girl. That sly piece in the gallery,' he said, thinking back, his outrage increasing at the thought of a lost sale. 'She put him off it for some reason. Bitch! I thought she looked too good to be true. Those slanting eyes — she's probably a flaming Chink!'

Sargeant winced. Tobar Manners's xenophobia was well known. 'Why should it have anything to do with her?'

'Because until she had a word with him Goldberg was going to buy.'

There *did* seem to be a connection. 'But why?'

Tobar Manners frowned. 'I have no idea — yet! But that interfering bitch has cost me money, and I don't like that,' he said, about to move off. He spotted the painting leaning against the wall. 'Oh, for God's sake, Anthony, pick up that flaming picture! You don't know whose ruddy poodle cocked its leg there.'

It was dangerous for Zoe to make enemies, but

there was little she could do about it. Having been supplanted in Harland's confidence, Mona's vicious tongue rapidly made sure that her contacts knew all about Zoe Mellor. She even embellished the tale, saying that the affair was conducted indiscreetly in the office, humiliating poor Myrtle. Not that anyone cared much for Myrtle Goldberg, but it was easy to fake outrage for a wronged wife. Soon the dealers took sides, those who had lost a sale to Harland, such as Tobar Manners and Anthony Sargeant, were suspicious of Zoe; whereas those who needed his support welcomed her — with reservations.

Unworldly and frequently ill at ease, Zoe learnt to watch every word she said. The gallery was no place for spontaneity. Scrutinising the wealthy women who came in, she learnt how to refine her own image, and toned down her make-up to a smoother, more polished look. She had no Lancashire accent, but her expressions could give her away and so she weighed each syllable she spoke. It slowed down her conversation, but made her appear composed and in command, seemingly unruffled. So while she agonised over her words, others thought her merely cautious.

At times her progress seemed agonisingly slow, her old problem of concentration letting her down when she was faced with books to study. But when Harland was talking to her and describing the dirty side of the business, she remembered everything, and everyone — Jimmy van Goyen and the Greek shipping magnate for whom he found call girls; Ahmed Fazir and his cocaine habit; Seymour Bell and his rent boys; and the suspect Tobar Manners, whose affair with Anthony Sargeant had burnt out when the latter grew fat and flatulent. She learnt very quickly that there were few who could be trusted, and even fewer whom Harland believed to be honourable.

Even though the general belief persisted that Zoe was Harland's mistress, a young dealer called Rupert Courtney-Blye decided that he wanted to know Zoe better. Intimately, in fact. So, with an energy unknown in his father's sculpture gallery where he worked, he set about impressing her. It was an uphill battle. Being very wealthy, he was used to quick conquests; and being very idle, he was soon exhausted by the chase. In a last-ditch attempt, he called at the gallery one afternoon when he knew Goldberg was out.

'My father has a wonderful collection of Giacomettis,' he said, leaning against a plinth and watching as Zoe made some catalogue notes. 'In fact, it's supposed to be the best in London. England actually.'

'Who's Giacometti?' Zoe asked, determined to be unimpressed.

Courtney-Blye faltered, his slightly high-pitched voice rising uncomfortably. 'Giacometti!' He coughed, and adjusted his pitch. 'Giacometti is a very famous sculptor. A genius. His work is very valuable — '

'Is that what makes him a genius?' Zoe asked, her face innocently enquiring.

Courtney-Blye was baffled. 'No . . . no, it's his skill.' Disconcerted, he glanced away from her and changed the subject. 'I know a lovely little watering hole in Holland Park. Would you like to come out for a drink?'

Zoe could see Mona look up from the desk, an expression of malicious curiosity on her face.

'I don't think so,' Zoe replied carefully, mistrusting the man in front of her and remembering Harland telling her of his arrangement with the Royal Irish Linen shop. Every time he had an affair, he ordered the finest sheets and pillowcases with his initials and the initials of his current woman embroidered on them.

Courtney-Blye looked put out, his blond features turning from surprise to something approaching petulance. 'I won't ask you again.'

'I'll try and live with it,' Zoe replied evenly.

★ ★ ★

Gradually, London ceased to intimidate her. Walking down Bond Street at night, she was no longer shocked by the sight of black plastic bags of rubbish left stinking at the top of basement steps, or the soft drink cans scattered along Piccadilly, winking under the lights of the Ritz. Rochdale was dirty, but it was dirt from weather and industry, not human filth, banked high at the end of a day. When she had seen postcards as a child, the capital had looked scrubbed, the buildings of St Paul's, the National Gallery and the Tate, white as sugar. She had imagined people holding their breath as they went into hallowed places like the Royal Academy honoured to be a part of such history. But in reality they stuck gum on the Entrance notices, and after dark, urinated against the railings of Burlington Arcade. Within months the magic curled at the edges, and the myth died under a barrage of wastepaper and condom machines. London was a great lady at times; at others, a slut.

Meanwhile at work Zoe's instinct continued to serve her well, and Harland relied more on her, realising that she did have a genuine eye for quality, an eye which was encouraged by their frequent visits to the salerooms. Although Mona Grimaldi continued to have a great deal of influence with the buyers, her days as Harland's assistant were clearly numbered. Her situation was soon common knowledge and her humiliation inflamed her and made her dangerous.

'Are you coming to the auction on Thursday?' Anthony Sargeant asked her over the phone. He liked Mona, her gossip made him laugh.

'I doubt it.'

Thick-skinned to the last, he continued. 'Why? I don't see you at the sales so often now, what happened?'

Curdling with rage, Mona kept her voice steady. 'I've been busy with other things, and it seemed the least I could do to let our little country cousin see the sights. Zoe needs all the help she can get if she wants to make a career in the business.'

Her ruse was so transparent that even

Sargeant noticed it. 'I thought you didn't like her?'

'It's true she is a little too provincial for my tastes,' Mona continued cuttingly. 'But I feel sorry for her, especially with everyone talking behind her back.'

Sargeant's mind wandered. 'Well, will you be coming to the auction, or not?'

'Not this one, Anthony,' she replied with care, 'but after Thursday, I'll be going to all the others.'

The auction was to be held at eight in the evening, and was being publicised as one of the greatest sales of the decade. The Greeks, Americans and Japanese were expected to be out in force, the pictures mainly Pre-Raphaelites, and therefore highly collectable. For the past two weeks a selection of languid, thick-necked female portraits had found their way up Bond Street to Lister's, the catalogue had been printed, and the myriad invitations sent out. So when Zoe found an invitation on her desk on the afternoon of the sale she was not surprised, although the added footnote with the legend 'Evening Dress' left her somewhat unsettled.

'Evening dress', she repeated to herself, glancing over to Mona who was adjusting the light over a painting. What did that mean exactly? How formal was evening dress? She opened her mouth to ask Mona and then paused; no, better to ask Harland. The she realised that he was away for the remainder of the day seeing to some crisis at home and had told her to meet him at the auction house later.

Worried, Zoe went into her office next to Harland's and looked at the invitation again. Sighing with exasperation, she drummed her fingers on the desk and realised that unless she wanted to let Harland down, a speedy purchase would have to be made.

Mona left at five-thirty that evening. She said nothing, merely reaching for her expensive Lowe coat and, without glancing in her rival's direction, walked out into Bond Street. It was not difficult for Zoe to imagine how she felt, in fact she had tried to persuade Harland to be more tactful in his dealings with her. But he was too devoted to Zoe to listen to reason, and continued to exclude Mona from both his confidence and his business.

Watching her leave, Zoe locked the gallery door and went into her office, picking up the expensive dress she had bought only hours before. It was long dark blue velvet, the neckline shaped to show off her shoulders to their best advantage, the style simple, but stunning. Turning off the light downstairs, Zoe went up to the small flat above the gallery, showered, and then dressed, pulling up the zip with triumph as she stood in front of Harland's mirror. With supreme confidence, she turned, feeling completely at ease for once. The dress was superb. Anyone could see it was first class. Harland would be so proud of her.

She waited until just before the auction was about to start, knowing that all the dealers, the buyers, and the press would be already taking their seats and straining to see the new arrivals.

She waited, almost giddy with excitement, planning her entrance, proud of her composure and her courage in going to the auction unescorted. Harland would be already there, she thought, he would be looking round and wondering where she was.

Pausing for one last look, Zoe took a deep breath and left the gallery, crossing the darkened street and arriving at the auction house. Several well known dealers turned as she walked in. Many buyers glanced up from their gilt chairs, their eyes raking up and down her figure. A few comments were made, and at the front of the auction room, Tobar Manners nudged Jimmy van Goyen and smirked. *Every one of them was in a lounge suit.* Every woman in a business suit, or a day dress. No one wore evening clothes. No one. Not even Harland, who stood looking at Zoe, his face a mixture of embarrassment and sympathy as the whispers increased around her and she ran out, holding up the skirt of her long dress.

Fifteen minutes later the taxi stopped beside Mona Grimaldi's block of flats in Chelsea and Zoe got out, her eyes red-rimmed, her face grey with anger. Pressing all the bells at once, the entrance door was opened by several obliging residents and she walked in. Step by step she took the stairs, up to her rival's flat, her high heels muffled on the carpet.

Beside her, the lighted lift slid by, making patterns on the stairwell as she climbed, the shadow of her figure ominously huge as she reached the door marked 'Grimaldi'. She rang the bell twice. Heard the lock being opened and moved back against the wall, hidden from sight. Disturbed and curious, Mona walked out, dressed in a long white negligée, her face older now that it was free of make-up. From the shadows, Zoe stepped in front of her.

She gasped, then smiled triumphantly as she looked at her rival's dress. 'Well, what do you want?'

'I have a message for you,' Zoe said simply, and raising her hand, struck her full across the face.

14

War was declared. There were no peace pacts, no truces, just unrelenting war. After the fiasco at the auction Zoe altered irrevocably, her suspicion of the art world fuelled by her loathing of the dealers and of Mona Grimaldi. Not one word was ever mentioned about the auction. Harland never referred to it, and after a while Zoe's embarrassment faded under the full weight of her anger. With a determination to succeed which outweighed her mortification, she set about learning the business with formidable energy. Pressing Harland for information she heard how gigantic losses were covered up by sympathetic accountants and sales rigged so that there was never any loss of face, and how it was not unknown for a gallery to buy back its own painting in an auction if it was well published and therefore likely to be an embarrassment if it did not reach its reserve price. She also realised that a gallery could create a demand for an artist out of thin air. Phone calls went along these lines:

'Listen, I have something incredibly special here, and I wanted you to be the first to know. We have an artist who is about to be shown in Europe. This man is a genius, and when he's had his show his work will be fetching thousands . . . even the Royals are interested.'

The bait was swallowed. Most patrons had

more money than discernment, and were terrified of being thought boorish.

'I know how you like to be the first, so I thought I'd give you a ring . . . '

And so it went on, an artificial demand created to pay rent, or to cover unlucky buys — and there were *always* the fakes. It astonished Zoe to see how often the dealers were duped, although some were involved willingly. She knew through Harland that many a customer had been sold a forgery, and even though she knew that he never stooped to such methods, she wondered how many others did.

'But *how* do they do it?' she asked Harland when they were out for dinner one night.

He glanced at her. She seemed altered, almost desperate to learn, her childlike eagerness now rabid curiosity. 'With ivory, it's easy. You get a craftsman to carve something in the Gothic Revival style — that's always very popular — and then they soak it in tea.'

'Tea?'

He nodded and took a sip of his wine. 'Yes. Some of them then cook the ivory in an oven for about half an hour. That cracks it, you see, although leaving it outside on a rainy day can do the same.'

'How much would it fetch at auction?'

'A genuine Anglo-Saxon cross could fetch £200,000. A forgery, anything from £10,000 to £50,000.'

Zoe took in her breath sharply. She could imagine what Victor would think of those figures. 'But if people *know* they're fake — '

'Only the dealers know, and the buyers rely on the dealers not to sell them forgeries.' He shrugged. 'It's been going on for years. People are greedy, you see. A collector wants an early Van Gogh, so the dealer obliges. Some of them even have workshops in Europe working flat out to supply the demand.'

'If the buyers are that greedy, they deserve to get ripped off,' she said phlegmatically. 'I don't much care if someone really wealthy gets caught out, it's not a matter of life or death for them. But for the little people, the people who come down to Bond Street with their pictures hoping that the dealers will buy them, hoping for a lost masterpiece. Well, it *is* life or death for them. And the dealers take advantage, buying things for next to nothing.' She paused, and looked at Harland. 'Those are the people I feel for. They trust the dealers and they accept what they say, never thinking they're going to get ripped off, even though the same painting gets sold for a small fortune the next week ... The kind of small fortune which is someone's retirement fund.'

She stopped and glanced down at her hands. Harland watched her. 'Like your father's?'

'Yes, like his.' Zoe drained her glass, remembering the old woman in Todmorden. 'The rich can look after themselves. The poor have no advocates.'

He was about to answer when Tobar Manners sidled over to their table and, without being invited, sat down. He was dressed well, his tiny frame resplendent in dark worsted. 'Hello,

Harland,' he said, ignoring Zoe. 'There's an auction in New York next week, with an early Poussin on offer, I believe. Are you going?'

Aware of the fact that he had slighted Zoe, Harland made a point of turning to her and asking, 'What do you think?'

Manners was piqued. 'It's for dealers only.'

'Since when?' Harland replied, his voice sharp. 'Since when were auctions solely for dealers? I happen to know that this one is open to the public. Anyone can go — and I want Zoe to come with me.'

Tobar Manners glanced towards the young woman, remembering the night of the auction and what Mona had told him about their lovemaking in the office. 'You're acting like a fool,' he said spitefully. 'Everyone is laughing at you behind your back.'

Harland glanced around Le Gavroche. 'Show me one person who's laughing at me, Tobar.'

'What about Myrtle?' he asked slyly. 'Listen, we've been friends for a long time, a very long time. We've done good business together, we know the same people. Everyone respects you.' He paused to let the words sink in. 'Why jeopardise all that now by fooling around with her?'

Zoe flinched. Harland saw her reaction and leaned across the table towards Manners, dropping his voice, his eyes sharp with anger. 'You are an evil-minded, spiteful gnome of a man.' Manners's fair skin coloured. 'You don't give a damn about my relationship with this lady, you're simply angry because you think she lost you that sale over the Guardi.' He paused, his hand clenched around his crumpled napkin. 'Which I might add, was found later to be a fake. Did you know that, Tobar?'

The man began to speak and then shook his head.

'You didn't? Well, you know now. I have never liked you, I have merely endured you over the years in order to do business with you. But from now on, Tobar, keep your distance, do you hear? And if you ever, I repeat, ever, insult this lady again — you will live to regret it.'

Tobar Manners struggled to his feet, a couple on the next table glancing over to him as he did so. Red-faced, he stammered, 'You've got problems, you old Jew.' The words stung Zoe as he turned and shot a look of undisguised hatred towards her. 'This woman is an embarrassment to you and she'll cause trouble.'

'Only to you, I hope,' Harland replied, turning back to his food.

★　★　★

Summer may well have been blooming in London, but up north the weather was depressing, a dull low sky hanging over the grimed buildings, a spiteful shower tapping against the town hall clock. Ron sighed and waited patiently for Zoe outside Rochdale railway station. His tall frame had filled out since he had been working in the coffee bar on Frith Street, his looks attracting comment, his innocence attracting ridicule — but only from the women. The men would never dare to risk a confrontation with Ron, he was too big to antagonise, and too thick to insult. Dumb Ron, they called him, his devotion to Zoe causing more than a little speculation.

'Do you suppose she really is his sister? I mean, they don't look alike.'

The café owner glanced at his wife impatiently. 'Our son doesn't look like me . . . should I read something into that too?'

Everyone liked Ron, and were impressed by Zoe, well-dressed and courteous when she called in sometimes. She would stay for a while and talk, and although at first they had thought she was uppity, her easy manner soon won people over. Naturally, Ron worshipped her, and after the first few months, he adapted to London, establishing a routine from which he seldom deviated.

In the mornings they would set off together, Ron walking Zoe to work through the park, the journey taking forty minutes. At the door of the gallery he would peck her on the cheek and go on to Frith Street, Peter following behind, and on arrival at the café the greyhound would crawl into a bed under the counter and stay there until lunchtime. Then at two they would both set off for the park, eat some sandwiches, and return an hour later for the afternoon stint, finishing finally at five-thirty. The routine never varied. Ron was happy knowing how his days were mapped out, that he would collect Zoe at six o'clock at the gallery and return to the flat. He was perfectly content as long as he knew what was happening, and when.

Which was why he was getting agitated as he waited for his sister. So agitated, in fact, that he was about to go back and look for her when she tapped him on the shoulder. 'I found it,' she said, opening the magazine and pointing to a photograph of herself with Harland Goldberg. 'Well, what do you think?'

Ron peered at the page. 'It's not good of you.'

Zoe frowned. 'Well, I didn't know it was being taken, did I? I brought it to show Dad,' she said, glancing round at the station forecourt. 'No taxis?'

Ron shook his head and tugged gently on Peter's lead. 'No. Come on, we'll have to get a bus.'

'God,' Zoe said ruefully. 'Nothing changes, does it?'

Buck's Lane was muddy, the garage bolted with a padlock, the house unchanged, although the outside paintwork looked even more faded. For months Zoe had promised to visit home, sending money and writing every week. But she was always busy, and her father never pressed her. All their conversations were short and to the point, no affection extended, no mutual confidences, no gossip. Just duty. The same duty which had brought her home for a long weekend.

'I'll be back on Tuesday,' she explained to Harland, as she tidied away some papers in the back room of the gallery.

'But I thought we were going to look round for some sporting prints. We talked about going to the Lanes in Brighton,' he complained, dreading a whole four days of undiluted Myrtle.

'Oh Harland, we can go any time.'

'No we can't, there's that sale in New York on Thursday.'

She sighed. 'We'll go to Brighton another weekend.'

'If you say so,' he said bitterly.

Zoe paused and locked the desk, keeping her notes safe, her jottings on the dealers' activities secure. The time would come when she could use the information, but not yet. For the present she would stay here. She knew how much Harland Goldberg had come to rely on her, seeing the vindication of her judgement on the fake Guardi as the proof he needed to trust her completely. For all his skill, he did not have the lucky sixth sense which tipped her off to some of the best pictures — and the fakes. At first she had been hesitant to give her opinion, but as time passed she allied her knowledge to her instinct and it seldom failed her.

'I'll miss you,' he said sincerely.

Zoe stiffened and turned away. She did not like any show of emotion, and even though she had adjusted to the fact that everyone, including Myrtle, thought that she was Harland's mistress, she was not about to put the fantasy into effect. It was for them to guess the truth; and for her to know it.

'I really care about you,' he added.

'I have to go — ' Zoe said, moving towards the door.

Harland caught hold of her arm gently. 'I care

so much for you, Zoe. I would like to look after you.'

Two emotions welled up in her in the one instant — revulsion and compassion. Kindly, she patted Harland's hand, but her voice was firm. 'No. Not now, not tomorrow, not ever.'

He blinked, his pride making him angry. Zoe saw this and paused. She needed this man, she knew that, and she owed him a great deal. There was no reason to antagonise her one real ally. No, she reasoned, she must not be stupid, she had been clumsy with Steven Foreshaw — she mustn't be clumsy again. It was love he was offering, and even if she didn't want it, she had no right to hurt him.

'We are the best of friends, Harland,' she said gently. The words had no impact, he felt merely stupid in her presence, and resented the sensation. 'Look at me!' she said firmly. Her tone surprised him and he glanced at her, feeling a jolt of infatuation, a heady attraction without logic. 'I respect you and care for you, Harland. But I don't love you, and it would be wrong for us to jeopardise our relationship for anything less . . . I have to go now, I'll see you on Tuesday,' she said, adding the next words without thinking. 'Miss me.'

He nodded and smiled, and she returned the smile, the smile of the sphinx, the smile which lately had scuttled through his dreams and woken him nightly.

★ ★ ★

'Dad?' Zoe called out as she pushed open the front door. The sound of the television welled out from the snug as she walked in. 'Dad?'

He jumped up, startled. 'Bloody hell! What d'you mean creeping in here like a thief!'

Zoe shrugged, suddenly fourteen again, suddenly stupid and ungainly. 'Sorry if I startled you. I did call out.'

Bernard Mellor breathed in deeply, his anger lifting as he looked at his daughter and then his son. 'You both seem well. You got to be a big sod, our Ron, and no mistake.'

'He's happy now, Dad,' Zoe continued eagerly. 'He likes his job at the café.'

'And d'you like yours?'

She smiled and passed him the magazine, eager for his approval. Carefully he looked at the photograph and after reading the caption said, 'You look like your mother.'

Her voice faltered. 'You can have that copy, Dad.'

'No, I'll not be needing it,' he said, passing it back to her. 'There's not so many folk I'd want to know my business.'

Hurt, Zoe pushed the magazine into her bag and moved into the kitchen, Peter following her. The room was tidy, the fire alight, although the grill on the cooker was thick with grease, the handle twisted. On the mantelpiece was her last letter, the ring of a tea mug on the back of the envelope.

'I've got some bread and cheese, if that's all right.'

Zoe shrugged churlishly and then, turning,

forgot her own anger when she saw her father under the bright kitchen light. His hair and moustache were completely white so that his face had lost its definition and its strength. He also stooped slightly, not from the shoulders, it was more generalised, an ageing which made his movements uneasy.

'Are you coping all right, Dad?'

'Fine. Why shouldn't I?' he barked, slicing some bread and putting the plate on the table with a slab of cheese. 'I get on fine. Go down the pub of a night, you know.'

Zoe nodded and began to set the table. 'What time will Alan be home?'

Her father snorted. 'God knows! He's got to working like a bloody fool. I told him not to go mad, he'd a whole life's work to do, no point trying to fit it all in one week.' He poured some boiling water into the teapot. 'I retire next month.'

Something in the words made Zoe look up, just in time to catch her father's eye. His expression was one of bewilderment, of anxiety and she knew it as clearly as if he had told her. In one month Bernard Mellor would retire from being foreman at the engineering factory; would leave his routine; his friends; his tiny allotment of power. Everything would go, and in its place would be nothing. No wife, no family at home, nothing. Only empty days to fill in an empty house.

'We'll come and visit you every fortnight.'

'Aye, well that'll cost summat, and no mistake.'

Zoe insisted, his panic suddenly her own. 'Not much. Anyway, we'll enjoy it, won't we, Ron?'

Her brother looked up. 'Yes, sure, whatever you say.'

'And we'll bring you things from London,' she went on, tears pricking behind her eyes. 'Loads of things — '

'No need, love.'

She stopped short. 'I want to, Dad.'

He seemed weary suddenly and almost impatient with the well groomed young woman in front of him. 'You've done your bit. You looked after your mother, you don't have to worry about me.'

They faced each other across the table — father and daughter, both trying to put into words everything which had previously been so successfully concealed.

Pity made Zoe bluster. 'You could come down to us — ' she said hopelessly, turning as the door opened and Alan walked in.

Blushing, he hugged Zoe to him and then pulled back to look into her face. 'I've missed you.'

The years rolled back like a window blind.

15

Mike O'Dowd was waiting in the narrow hall of a house in Tite Street, Chelsea. A stocky man wearing a Giorgio Armani suit, he took off the lightly tinted glasses he always wore and began to polish them. Noises came from the back of the house and he looked up, and then, when no one emerged, replaced his glasses and closed his eyes to think. A Dubliner, O'Dowd was a clever man, less academic than worldly, his presence having skirted the perimeters of the international art scene for years. Somewhere between thirty-five and sixty, he knew everyone in every city, his own reputation respected if feared. It was a tribute to his skill that he had made a good living and stayed out of jail, but the upper-class ranks of the London dealers loathed him and he knew it. So he played up the things they despised him for, the Dublic accent and the Irish charm, and covered hundreds of thousands of plane miles every year looking for paintings or sculpture — and dealing in fakes.

Not that the last fact was a secret. Too many dealers had called in O'Dowd to provide a hasty Guercino or a Modigliani, for anyone to deny it. But to admit it was another thing. Uninterested in personal fame, O'Dowd was content to remain in the shadows where he could move around easily, a trans-Atlantic gypsy, his background only guessed at, his family remaining in blissful ignorance in the middle of the marshy Irish countryside.

He sighed and folded his arms across his chest, thinking of Jimmy van Goyen for whom he had done some business. A perfect Tiepolo drawing had found its way into the Dutchman's gallery and been passed on to a wealthy Iranian at considerable profit. Unfortunately van Goyen had seen fit to argue with O'Dowd and withhold his fee. The Irishman had reasoned with him to no avail so he had decided that the time had come for sterner measures. Knowing of van Goyen's passion for aquarium fish, O'Dowd had called round to visit his wife and six-year-old daughter, and, after suggesting to the lady that her husband should pay his debts, he had lifted out a large, highly expensive fish from the tank. The child had had hysterics, the mother watching in horror as O'Dowd made his way to the kitchen. In a final act of savagery, he had then gutted the gasping fish on the chopping board, the bloodied mess congealing amongst the preparations for the child's dinner, the slippery guts mixing with a small mound of diced carrots. The next day, the fee had been paid.

O'Dowd shifted his position in the seat and allowed his mind to wander from van Goyen to Manchester and Ivor Weiss. He had been impressed with the quality of the fakes Weiss had shown him, he had even bought a 'Gainsborough' and sold it on within days to a collector in the United Arab Emirates. He thought at first that Weiss was aware that they were forgeries, but it soon became apparent that the Pole was delightfully ignorant of the fact. Naturally O'Dowd had asked who supplied him, and Weiss had hesitated, although after some money had passed hands, he told him . . . Yes, O'Dowd thought, there were definite possibilities for him in Manchester.

A police car went past on the road outside, its siren blaring. O'Dowd frowned with irritation, his thought turning to Victor Mellor. He had already decided that he didn't like him. In fact, to put it mildly, Mike O'Dowd did not trust Mellor or want anything to do with him. Unfortunately though, it was beginning to look as though he had no choice; the fakes he had purchased through Ivor Weiss came via Mellor, so, for the time being at least, they would have to learn to get on with each other.

'Mr O'Dowd?' He opened his eyes. 'Come through please,' the woman said, walking into an overcrowded drawing room and sitting down at a small walnut table. 'How are you?'

'Fit as a flea,' he replied, the heavy Irish accent accompanied by a wide, capped-toothed smile. 'And how's yourself?'

'Well, thank you,' the woman answered, shuffling the cards and pushing them across the table towards O'Dowd. 'Would you cut them, please.'

Carefully he did so, and then glanced back to the woman. She had hardly changed in twenty-odd years, he thought, or maybe that was just wishful thinking. A Burmese cat rubbed against his leg as he stared at his companion, whose face was as impassively upper class as ever, her accent as expensive as the room in which they sat. She coughed slightly, one liver-spotted hand fluttering against her mouth for an instant, and then said, 'You will have many travels, Mr O'Dowd, and a partner.' She paused, picking up a card and frowning. 'I would be very careful of any partners.' The cat jumped on the chair next to O'Dowd as he listened. 'However, you have a customer in the east, I think?' He nodded. 'Excellent business there,' she said, smiling. 'Money, and plenty of it.'

O'Dowd listened and made notes, just as he had always done. Then twenty minutes later he left, a large fee placed discreetly under the Louis XIV clock on the fireplace.

★ ★ ★

'You're behaving like a fool,' Myrtle snapped. 'Everyone is talking about you. I'm so ashamed.'

Harland began to open his post. He had endured his wife for years in a loveless marriage, but it hadn't mattered, he had been too much occupied with business to mind the loss of any real relationship. Then he had met Zoe, and everything had changed. Nine months ago he was a settled man, a man at peace with his world, successful, respected and rich — a man who had everything he had once longed for as a poor boy in Manchester.

It seemed like light years ago, he thought, although now he felt closer to that boy than he did to the Harland Goldberg he had created. The myth worked for him no longer, he wanted reality . . . realising all too painfully just what it might cost him. Broken nights and interrupted concentration was one thing, but infatuation died — liking and need did not. He needed Zoe because her desire to learn made him useful and gave him a reason to continue working. At sixty-nine, he could have retired, gone to live in Miami or Florida with Myrtle. He shuddered at the thought, his gratitude to Zoe increasing by the second. If she hadn't visited the exhibition that day he would never have met her, he would never have had the chance to love someone . . . He would not live for ever, he knew that, just as he knew that if they had met when he was forty he would have left Myrtle and married her. But for as long as he *did* live she would make sense of his life, and that was more than he had hoped for.

'How can I face everyone at the synagogue?' Myrtle wailed, glancing over to her husband. I remember you when you were a skinny little runt with a permanent cold, she thought bitterly, I stuck with you then, so you owe me something now.

'For years you've nagged me,' Harland snapped, 'and for years I've endured it. You have money and security, what are you complaining about?'

'You've got a mistress, and you ask me what I'm complaining about?'

Harland hesitated, he wished above everything that it was true. Seldom cruel, he looked at his wife and said, 'You can join all the other

225

wronged wives at the synagogue, Myrtle. Not that any of them ever wonder *why* their husbands stray.'

'It's always the same reason!' she countered, angling for pity. 'You all run after someone younger and prettier — '

'And someone who shows an interest.'

Her eyes narrowed. 'Oh, so she shows an interest, but for how long? When she's bled you dry, she'll be off to find her next meal ticket.'

The words enraged him. 'She cares for me!'

'She cares!' Myrtle repeated with a sneer. 'Have you got a bagel for a brain? Have you learned *nothing* all these years? She cares for the gallery, the expensive dinners, the clothes. You're nothing to her,' she said, her voice rising. 'Look at yourself in the mirror, Harland, and you'll see how laughable you really are. You're an old man with a paunch who gets out of breath after walking up a flight of stairs, never mind after — '

'Shut up!' he shouted, turning on her.

Myrtle stood up to him. 'You don't frighten me, you never did. You're still the same common little Jew — '

' — you married!'

'Yes, and the one I intend to *stay* married to!' she shouted as he pushed past her and hurried down the stairs. 'Your little bint is going to be sorry!' she screamed. 'When I've finished with her, she's going to regret ever setting eyes on you.'

★　★　★

226

Victor walked towards Rochester Terrace in West London, whistling under his breath. He had made a sizeable profit on a fake Tissot only that morning and he felt in need of company. Smiling to himself, he thought back. It was only months since he had decided to work alone, circumventing Ivor Weiss and selling the fakes direct to a London dealer. Impressed by the money Zoe's forgeries had fetched, he had found an art student who was sufficiently impoverished not to ask questions, and sufficiently talented to copy anything for which Victor discovered a market. Oh yes, he thought, things were looking up. No more shabby flats for Victor Mellor, no more second-hand cars, at this rate he would soon be good enough to fool anyone, and impress anyone. Especially Erica Goldberg. He smiled, wolf-whistling softly. She was certainly good-looking, and experienced, her manner told him that, and besides, there was a certain humour in the situation. What was sauce for the goose . . . Zoe had set herself up nicely with Harland Goldberg, so why shouldn't her brother benefit from a closer relationship with the family?

He paused by a passageway running between the two rows of faded townhouses and glanced round, smiling as he read a line of scrawled graffiti — DYSLEXIA LURES, KO? — then opened the gate and walked in. The yard smelt of cooking onions and he wrinkled his nose as he knocked on the door.

A young man with protruding teeth opened it. 'Who's there?'

'Victor Mellor.'

The door swung open and he walked through. The smell of onions was even stronger in the cramped room where a gas ring was turned full on, the offending odour coming from a dented metal pan. Against a far wall an easel stood shrouded, the canvas covered with a black bin liner.

Victor glanced over. 'How are you getting on?'

Andrew Coleman shrugged. 'It's difficult — '

'That's why I'm paying you so much,' Victor said, lifting the edge of the bin liner and gesturing to Coleman. 'Turn the light on, will you? I can't see a thing.'

Light flooded the canvas and illuminated a small icon, hardly twelve inches in height, the face of the Christ bland and expressionless. 'It's good,' Victor said, covering it again. 'How long before it's finished?'

'A while. I can't rush it — '

Patience had never been Victor's strong suit. 'Listen, I have a buyer for that. I need it next Wednesday.'

'I can't!' the young man replied, reaching for a packet of cigarettes and lighting one. His hand shook. 'It's delicate work, it can't be hurried.'

'You and I had an agreement,' Victor said coldly, walking towards Coleman. 'I pay you on delivery. No delivery, no money.'

'I could have it for Friday — '

'That's no bloody good to me! The buyer is expecting it Wednesday.' He caught hold of Coleman's jumper and pulled the man towards him. 'I want it by Wednesday, no later. Do you hear me?'

Coleman nodded, terrified. Satisfied, Victor let go of him. 'You disappoint me, you really do. I relied on you.'

The young man did not reply. He had thought at first that doing a few forgeries would be an easy way to pay the rent. After all, he had no buyers for his own paintings and he had always been a skilful copyist, so why not make some money out of it? But the weeks had passed and Victor Mellor had proved to be too hard a taskmaster — lately he had even been violent. Andrew Coleman remembered the previous week and cringed. Being poor wasn't as bad as being owned by Victor Mellor.

'I'll have it ready on Wednesday,' he said finally.

Victor nodded and left.

His bad temper remained with him until he reached Rochdale, when he parked in the middle of the quiet town and smoked a cigarette. Andrew Coleman was unreliable, and unreliability was expensive. Victor needed someone he could depend on utterly. Not losers, because they were a risk. He sighed and, stubbing out the cigarette, pulled away from the kerb into the traffic.

★   ★   ★

Tobar Manners, Anthony Sargeant, Ahmed Fazir and Jimmy van Goyen were having lunch at the Groucho Club. Tobar Manners was relating his argument with Harland and bemoaning the fact that since the emergence of Zoe Mellor, trade with the Goldberg gallery had almost halved.

'The flaming woman's creasing me,' he grumbled. 'Bloody peasant! What the hell does she know about paintings anyway?'

'A damn sight more than she did when she first arrived,' Fazir answered, throwing back a vodka and reordering. 'She's learning fast.'

'Mona's pissed off with her,' Manners went on. 'The damn woman hit her, you know.'

Sargeant smirked at the thought. Having borne the brunt of Mona's tongue more than once he was pleased to hear that she had got her come-uppance.

'She's had her nose pushed out of joint,' Fazir continued.

'I don't think Zoe Mellor hit her that hard, did she?'

Three pairs of eyes looked at Anthony Sargeant before Manners continued. 'She has too much influence with him, and besides, she's not one of us. Mona knows everyone in the business and we could rely on her to let us know what was going on. Now, we hear nothing. Frankly, that Northern tart is costing me money.'

He was putting into words what they were all thinking. Zoe Mellor had to go, but how?

'Mona tried to humiliate her at that auction, but she's so thick-skinned she just brazened it out. Anyone with any breeding would never have shown their face again.'

Fazir nodded ruefully. 'There must be some way to put the pressure on, especially . . . ' he mused ' . . . it it meant that she was discredited in Harland's eyes.'

The four men looked at each other thoughtfully.

★   ★   ★

The garage in Buck's Lane was ablaze with lights as Zoe pushed open the door and walked in. She was surprised by the changes, everything was so orderly, each piece of stone was laid against the wall, the bench cleared, the tools laid out in shiny rows like instruments in an operating theatre. Even the light was different, throwing out brilliant, intense illumination so that everything was clear, defined. Zoe glanced round curiously, noticing that the corner of the garage behind the bench was cordoned off, several sheets of corrugated iron forming a barricade.

'What's behind there?' she asked her brother.

Alan turned. 'Oh, that's just somewhere to keep my bits and pieces. You know, so that the place looks tidy.' She nodded, Alan had always been meticulous. 'How's the job?' he asked.

'I like it. I brought home a magazine for you to see — '

'I did,' Alan said, lifting a block of marble on to the bench. 'That Harland Goldberg looks too old for you.'

'He's not a boyfriend, Alan.'

'But it looks like he is,' he replied carefully.

'I'm not sleeping with him,' Zoe said, seeing her brother's face redden, 'so why should you be worried?'

'But people *think* you are,' he replied shyly, 'and you'll get a reputation.'

231

Zoe laughed. 'You can't put your hand over people's mouths, Alan, and I don't give a damn about what they think. Harland is pleased to have a young woman on his arm — and for my part, I'm learning everything I need to know for the future.'

As she said the words, Zoe's mind was racing. Her father's condition had unsettled her, he was growing older more quickly than she had anticipated, his future bleak and without hope. Because what was there for him to hope *for*? Buck's Lane, innumerable dusty summers, and long, icy winters spent virtually alone? It was a death sentence, and Zoe knew it. Her father would not have any of the luxuries available to Harland Goldberg — no winter holidays, not even a decent home. He would be scratching to get by on a pension and the money she could afford to send home. Frustration welled up inside her. She had to do something to help him, but what? Reputations in the art world took years to build, there was no overnight success to speed up a flagging income.

Zoe was still preoccupied when the garage door opened fifteen minutes later and Victor walked in.

He nodded to a surprised Alan and walked over to his sister. 'I didn't think you were coming home until tomorrow. You caught me off guard.'

She glanced up. 'Like hell! God couldn't catch you off guard, Victor. What are you doing here?'

'I thought I'd drop in. I'm doing some business Manchester way.'

Zoe looked at her brother carefully. He

seemed cocky as usual, unconcerned. 'I'm worried about Dad.'

Victor lit a cigarette. 'Why?'

'He's not well.' Alan glanced up. 'It's OK, he's not really ill, just getting old. He's retiring next month ... ' She trailed off, both brothers watching her. It was impossible to try and explain the situation to Ron, and her misgivings would have been incomprehensible to Alan.

Instead, she confided in Victor, the person least interested, but most able to help. 'If we could make his life more comfortable. You know what I mean, smarten the house up, get someone in to help.' Her patience snapped. 'Oh, stop staring at me, Victor! You know what I'm talking about.'

'It'll cost money.'

'Yes,' she said softly. 'I send home what I can, so does Ron, and Alan's generous — how much are you contributing?'

Victor's eyebrows rose. 'As much as I can.'

'But we're not likely to find out?' she asked sarcastically.

'Some things are sacred.'

Annoyed, Zoe glanced back to the bench. Alan was watching her closely, as usual waiting to follow her lead. 'Is Dad really ill?'

'No, but he's old, Alan. He needs something to look forward to. He's lonely because he's no company.' She thought back to her mother. 'He misses Mum.'

'She's dead.'

'We know that, moron!' Victor snapped, watching Alan's face colour up. 'If you can't say anything useful, dry up. Zoe and I have things to discuss.'

Zoe turned round, surprised and curious, and then followed Victor's retreating figure as he moved out into Buck's Lane.

It was a brainwave on his part — benefiting everyone, himself, his father, and even Zoe. Simple, as all Victor's schemes were, it did, however, carry a higher penalty than most. If they were caught they could be fined, or jailed. But on the other hand, if they *weren't* caught . . .

'It's dangerous.'

Victor inhaled deeply. 'It's dangerous if we have to rely on people outside the family. You and I can trust each other, and that gives us the edge.' He looked into his sister's worried face. 'For God's sake! You've been bleating about the dealers for ages now. You told me about Tobar Manners and the Guardi, about Jimmy van Goyen — all of them. You know how corrupt they are.'

The hair prickled on the back of Zoe's neck. 'And what do you know?'

He smiled. In the dim light inside the car he looked smooth, even elegant. Age and money were refining Victor. On the outside. 'I've been dealing with fakes for years.' She widened her eyes. 'And for the last six months I've been on my own, relying on some buck-toothed toerag in West London.' He ground out his cigarette and wound down the car window an inch. 'But he's useless. In fact, I was only thinking about the old days on the way up today. When we worked together.'

Zoe shrugged. 'That was different. I was just doing pictures in the style of certain artists, not faking them.'

Victor's laugh startled her. 'God, you are an innocent. Do you think I sold them like that? I sold them as originals.'

Zoe could feel her hands grow cold. 'You did *what?*'

'I sold them originals. And no one suspected a thing.' He leaned towards her, his narrow face only inches from her own. 'Your work's good, Zoe, really good, even if you are painfully slow. We could make a killing. We could take all those rich bastards for a ride, up the bloody river without a paddle.' He laughed. 'Rob them blind! All those public school shits would be at our mercy. Say you'll do it. Please. We could make money.'

Her face was incredulous. Here she was, sitting in a car in the middle of Rochdale talking about fakes; talking about duping the London art market. She almost laughed.

'Have you no idea what the dealers are like? These aren't kids in some little Northern town. This isn't Todmorden, Victor!' she snapped, her temper rising. 'The London auction houses would spot a fake like that.' She snapped her fingers.

'Not yours. You're too careful, and besides, you've been practising.'

She glanced over to him, wondering how he knew about the stacks of drawings and paintings she had been working on over the months. 'I've been trying out techniques, that's all.'

'Like hell, Zoe. I can read you like a book. You're putting aside a little nest egg.'

235

'I was just experimenting,' she repeated coldly. 'I'm having a rough ride at the gallery, Victor, I don't want to do anything to jeopardise my job. We need the money too much.'

'But if you did a few fakes we would have the money to really look after Dad, *and* have the last laugh on those poxy sods.'

Zoe glanced away. The thought stimulated her imagination, and spiked her feelings of revenge. Oh, the dealers had certainly made her suffer over the last couple of years, they had kept her in her place well and truly. But taking revenge was one thing, taking on the London art world was quite another. Yet she was tempted. Yes, she thought, I'd like to get my own back on the likes of Tobar Manners and Anthony Sargeant; I'd like to relieve them of some of their inheritance; redistribute the wealth a little more evenly.

'Forget it.'

Victor frowned. 'Why?'

'Because I say so,' she said, her heart banging. Forgery was a criminal offence, punishable by imprisonment. To be caught would mean disgrace, to be an outcast, cut off from society.

'Zoe, think about it.'

'No!' she snapped, finally. 'I want to be successful and rich, Victor, but I don't want to end up with an institution haircut.'

'Listen, it's them and us. They'll never accept you as one of them.' He sighed, angered with her obstinacy. 'You should see life as it is, Zoe. You could stay at the gallery for ever, but you'll never belong.'

The words slapped her.

The following Tuesday Zoe was in the gallery alone, Mona having gone out for lunch and Harland having been called back to St John's Wood. Apparently Myrtle was determined to keep him away from Zoe physically, if not mentally, and would, on the slightest pretext, insist that he return home. Having attended to several browsing customers, Zoe was reading a book on technique when Rupert Courtney-Blye walked in.

'Hello,' he said, glancing round. 'Where's Mona?'

'Out to lunch.'

'Never mind,' he said shrugging. 'It was you I came to see. Harland's just phoned and asked if you could find that tiny Epstein head for me. I have to show it to Seymour Bell tonight.' He grimaced. 'Do you know him?'

'I know Mr Bell,' she said carefully, on her guard and unwilling to say anything which could be misinterpreted.

'So can you get hold of the Epstein for me?'

Laying down her pen, Zoe rose to her feet. 'Of course, I just wonder why Harland didn't phone me direct.'

Rupert looked pained. 'He was ringing from home . . . '

'Oh, I see,' she said, walking towards the storeroom.

Rupert fell into step beside her. 'This is the address,' he said, handing her a piece of paper.

Zoe had never been attracted to this man, but he was something of a loner and her sympathies were aroused. 'Don't you want me to get it now? It would only take a few minutes.'

'No, I can't hang around. I've got to meet someone,' he said hurriedly. 'Harland said you wouldn't mind helping me out. All you have to do is to deliver the sculpture, after all.'

'It's all right. I never said I wouldn't do it.'

He smiled gratefully. 'Thanks. Just drop it by tonight around seven and I'll be in your debt for ever.'

The address was an avenue off Phillimore Gardens in Kensington. A butler answered the door as Zoe stood with the small sculpture in her hands, the rain beating down around the porch where she sheltered.

'Come in, Miss,' the man said, standing aside for her as she entered the hall, her feet making patterns on the marble floor. A high ceiling reached out overhead and from her left came the muffled sound of music.

'I just came to deliver this,' she said, handing over the parcel.

The valet smiled. 'Mr Courtney-Blye is expecting you.'

She frowned. 'But I thought . . . is this *his* house?'

'Yes, Miss,' the man replied, walking off.

A moment later Rupert emerged. 'Thank you so much, Zoe,' he said, genuinely grateful. 'You saved my life.'

'Why didn't you tell me that it was your address?' she asked, suspicion in her voice.

He heard the tone and turned to her. 'Would you have come?'

She paused. 'No.'

'So now you know why I didn't tell you.'

A mixture of emotions welled up in Zoe. At first she felt only a sense of being cheated, then the familiar sensation of uncertainty — but both were closely followed by flattered amusement. 'Well . . . ' she said. 'I have to go now.'

'No, not so soon,' he said guilelessly. 'Just have a drink with me,' he said, putting up his hands. 'I promise not to jump on you.'

She smiled uncertainly, painfully aware that she appeared naive in his eyes. He took her wet coat from her and led her into the drawing room, watching with satisfaction as she looked around the magnificent room. Heavy crimson damask hung from the ceiling to the floor, the sofas covered in similar rich material, a wide fire blazing from the hearth and a scattering of ornaments, photographs, and books covering every table top. Against the bleak night the curtains were drawn, and on an impressive Georgian table stood a bowl of gardenias.

'What a fabulous scent,' Zoe said, leaning over the white flower, the perfume indolently seductive.

'They're my favourite,' Rupert said, passing her a glass of brandy and raising his in a toast. 'Here's to Zoe Mellor, may she prosper.'

The room was intoxicatingly warm, the scent from the gardenias almost overpowering as she sat with her eyes fixed on the fire in front of her, the flames curling up the chimney.

'You are very lovely,' he said finally, and she smiled, shifting her position as he sat down beside her. The brandy made her more relaxed than usual, the little Epstein statue blinking in the firelight on the table in front of them. Glancing at Rupert, she was surprised to find that she was attracted to him and actually wanted him to touch her.

As though they had communicated by telepathy, he slid his arm around her shoulder gently. 'There, that's not so bad, is it?'

She smiled and almost moved away, but changed her mind and leaned towards him instead. The gardenias pulled her into their scent, the fire sapping the coldness out of her body. Softly, he kissed her on the cheek, but when his lips moved over her mouth she tried to sit up, the brandy swinging in her glass as she moved. 'I don't think this is a good idea — '

'Why not? Or is it that you only fancy old Jews?'

She had no chance to respond to the shock of his words before the door was pushed open and Tobar Manners, Anthony Sargeant, Ahmed Fazir and Harland stood there, all watching her. Quickly Rupert got to his feet, Zoe struggling to rise, the brandy spilling over her dress.

'Oh, I'm so sorry,' Manners said idly, as Sargeant glanced over to Harland.

'It's not what you think!' Zoe began, looking at him and seeing the expression in his eyes. 'You told me to bring the sculpture over here.'

He said nothing, merely frowned.

'You told me to bring it . . . ' Zoe repeated,

turning to see Fazir's smug face and hear Sargeant laughing. 'No . . . I don't believe it,' she said simply. 'It was a trick, wasn't it?'

Manners was the first to speak. 'My dear lady, whatever you're thinking, I can assure you that we're all here for a meeting.' He smiled apologetically. 'And we're mortified to think we interrupted your little rendezvous.'

The smell of the gardenias sickened Zoe suddenly and without saying another word, she rushed past the men and out into the street beyond. The rain pelted down on her as she walked blindly on. Without her coat she was soon saturated, her feet and legs running with water, her face wet as she hurried towards the main road in the hope of hailing a taxi.

Footsteps sounded behind her and she quickened her pace, but within seconds Harland caught up with her. 'Zoe! Wait!'

Her eyes were burning as she turned to face him. 'However it looks, it wasn't what you think.'

'I know,' he said simply.

'*What* do you know!' she snapped, her temper breaking in the chilled air. 'Do you know that I'm an embarrassment? That every time I think I've got somewhere, some bastard pulls me down again? Don't you think I see myself in their eyes, some pathetic little kid from the sticks trying to make it?' She shook off his hand, the rain lashing down on both of them. 'I'm pathetic, Harland! Bloody useless. I couldn't even see the trap — I just walked into it, like the fool I am.' She stopped, sobbing, remembered the feeling of comfort and the open fire. Love me, hate me.

241

'Get away from me, Harland! I'm a flop, a failure. Whatever you did I'd be nothing but an embarrassment . . . ' She stopped, her hands covering her face, tears wracking her whole body.

He leaned towards her and rested his face against hers, his beard wet with rain.

'No, don't forgive me! I'm not worth it,' she said, pulling away. 'I should have gone back to Rochdale a long time ago. I should have realised I would never make it — '

The words struck out at Harland and he grabbed her arms, shaking her. 'How *dare* you!' he shouted. 'How *dare* you give up and let me down! Those men aren't worth a damn, Zoe. They're shits, every one of them.' He shook her again and she flinched. 'Have some pride in yourself! If you go back to Rochdale now you've let them win, and I'll despise you for it.' Zoe stopped crying, her eyes fixed on Harland's. 'Where are your guts? Don't bloody cry, fight back.' He pushed her away, and she stumbled, falling on to one knee. 'You're beaten, are you? Well, stay down there then. Go on, *stay there!*'

Breathing heavily, Harland turned and began to walk away, his feet echoing on the wet street, his head bent down against the rain. When he had walked ten feet he turned round and shouted, 'You're right, you *are* a loser, Zoe. Like all the rest. You're *not* special . . . That's what you wanted to believe, isn't it? That's what your mother told you, all those years ago.' His voice rose in the empty street. 'Well, she was right! You're a nothing, a no one — '

Zoe was on her feet before he finished the

sentence, running towards him, her face ashen as she faced him. 'I *am* someone!'

'Hah!' he said, turning away.

She caught hold of his arm and pulled him round. 'I *am* someone . . . ' she repeated, fighting for words. 'I'm Zoe Mellor.'

'Who's she?'

'She's a winner,' Zoe said, her confidence rising, 'and she's going to pay them all back. She's going to make them remember her. She exists.' The words sounded in both their heads as she added finally. '*I* exist.'

Gently, Harland touched her cheek, his own eyes filling. 'In that case, welcome back. I thought I'd lost you.'

16

'You're on,' Zoe said flatly.

Victor turned over in bed, cradling the telephone, grimacing at the sleeping woman beside him. 'What's bloody on?'

'Your little idea about the fakes.'

He blinked, fully awake. 'Why the change of heart?'

'I've been thinking, and now I think it's a good idea,' Zoe answered. 'But I must be certain of one thing, Victor, that we keep it in the family. This arrangement is between you and me, no one else. I have to be safe.'

'Sure, sure,' he agreed readily. 'We'll keep it in the family. Relax, you can trust me.'

'Now let's not be silly,' she replied, ringing off.

The flat in Notting Hill was not really a suitable studio. It had been cramped before with Zoe, Ron and Peter all huddled together, now it was almost impossible to move without nudging an easel or bumping into a table cluttered with drawings. In an attempt to make more space, Zoe erected some shelves, stacking materials and paints there, although they soon became overloaded, brushes slipping off in the middle of the night and waking Ron. The work was difficult too. Knowing that Victor would go elsewhere unless she kept up with him, Zoe kept as close an eye as she could on her recalcitrant brother. In general, he called one night a week to collect her work, wrapping whatever fakes Zoe had completed in corrugated brown paper and carrying them out to the car.

'Listen, I can do the drawings quite quickly,' Zoe said, thinking of the tiny Burne-Jones fake she had just completed, 'but the paintings take longer. I have to stick with the Pre-Raphaelites at the moment because I'm certain of the materials they used. Anything else I wouldn't be that confident about tackling yet, Victor.'

They would also take longer because she had to find canvases which corresponded to the time of the 'original'. It was no good putting a Reynolds sketch on to a nineteenth-century canvas, or using twentieth-century acrylic-primed canvas for a Rossetti portrait. Innumerable visits to jumble sales and auctions had resulted in a stock of canvases on to which Zoe painted directly, or which she used to line one of her fakes, thereby covering a new canvas. Such care was necessary, because any dealer suspecting a fake would check the back of the painting first. Zoe knew the pitfalls — just as they did.

'Well, you'll have to hurry up. I think I've got a buyer for a Greuze.'

Zoe raised her eyes heavenwards. 'This isn't a supermarket, Victor! Every artist has his own method and style, he's unique.' She thought of all the different types of paint and media with which she had been practising, night after night, her eyes itchy with tiredness. One mistake could give the game away. 'If I rush, the results won't fool anyone.'

'I've a good contact,' he replied, thinking of

Mike O'Dowd. 'We can shift any amount of stuff if you get a move on.'

'And get caught, just because we were greedy?' Zoe replied warningly.

Ron had taken Peter for a walk, something he always did when he knew his brother was coming because he now resented Victor more than he had ever done. No longer physically afraid of him, he was, however, completely unable to defend himself against Victor's sarcastic remarks. Ron was also worried about Zoe. Whatever she chose to do was all right by him, even working on those daft paintings and leaving them all over the place, but he hated it when she got overtired and jumpy. Ron frowned, realisation dawning. Zoe had been all right before she began working with Victor. It was all his brother's fault! he thought, stopping in his tracks, his mind whirling. At that moment Peter began to bark at a passing cat and Ron's attention wandered. By the time he had calmed the greyhound down again he had forgotten his anxiety about Zoe and, whistling, set off for the dog track.

Zoe had no idea of what was going through Ron's mind, but she could guess at the thoughts in Victor's head as he arrived the following week at the flat. Gesturing to a chair, she asked him to sit down.

'This place is a dump,' he said generously.

'It's all we can afford,' Zoe replied, making them both a coffee and walking back into the lounge which smelt strongly of turpentine, a palette half covered with paint lying on the table in front of them. 'I need more room to work.'

'Perhaps your gentleman friend could help out.'

'No!'

'It was only a suggestion.'

Zoe sipped her coffee. 'When I finish this next painting, I have to take a break — '

'What!'

'A break, Victor,' she repeated adamantly. 'I'm tired. After all, I've got a job too. I have to do the fakes in the evenings or the weekend.' She leaned her head back against the chair. 'I get tired, and when I'm tired I make mistakes.'

She knew the last words would have the desired effect. Aware that his sister's carelessness might end with him behind bars, Victor was all sympathy. 'You take your time, Zoe. I don't want you to get ill. We'll slow down a little — unless you want to give up your job.'

'Oh yes, why not?' she replied sarcastically. 'Then what would we live on? And what about Dad?'

'If we did more fakes — '

'No! You can't swamp the market overnight, it would look too suspicious and they'd be on to us like a shot. They aren't fools, Victor,' she snapped. 'Besides, I don't intend to give up my job. I like it and I'm learning the trade there. Anyway, being at the gallery means that I get to hear what's going on.' She paused, remembering something her brother had said earlier. 'Anyway, who's your good contact?'

Victor smiled enigmatically. 'You don't need to know.'

'No, I just get all the work and you get all the

money,' she replied, putting her head on one side. 'Incidentally, Victor, you owe me for that last drawing.'

With profuse apologies, he opened his wallet and counted out £150, handing it to Zoe with a mock bow.

'You don't mind my asking?' she queried mockingly. 'It's just that I don't like to think of you weighed down with all that money. You could pull a muscle that way.'

Victor looked wounded. 'That's not fair, I always give you the money willingly.'

Zoe smiled. 'Victor, getting money from you is about as easy as shaving an egg.'

The days pooled into weeks, and weeks into months as she toiled over her work. Evenings yawned into early mornings as Zoe sat hunched over a makeshift drawing-board, the picture in front of her drawn almost exactly from an original colour reproduction. Almost, but not quite. Artists frequently made several depictions of a scene or sitter so it was much safer to make minor adjustments rather than slavishly copy something which could be spotted too easily. It was demanding work, but the fakes consumed Zoe, providing the only means of revenge she had at her disposal, and she never forgot it. Sometimes she was irritable, her weariness making her careless, but she only had to think of Rupert Courtney-Blye and she would bend her head down again and continue.

'Come on, Zoe, it's late,' Ron said one evening, waking up to find her still working at two in the morning.

'I have to finish this.'

'Tonight?' he asked, yawning. 'Why?'

'Because I have to!' she snapped, throwing down her brushes and pointing to the picture. 'Look, I've ruined that now, just because you can't mind your own bloody business!'

Stung, Ron responded sharply. 'It's not my fault, you're too tired to know what you're doing half the time. You should tell Victor to get someone else to do his dirty work — '

'I *want* to do this!' she shouted. 'It's *my* work. Mine.'

Without saying another word Ron dressed and left the flat, slamming the door behind him. The sound echoing in her ears, Zoe sat down and sighed, looking at her hands. Green and yellow paint stained her fingers, her nail polish chipped, the blue overall she wore spattered with what looked like dried blood. Aching with tiredness, she rested her head against the back of the chair, her gaze directed upwards. The ceiling was dingy, the paint yellowed, the light bulb bare because she had taken off the shade so she could see more clearly. Her eyes moved along a crack which ran from one side of the room to the other and descended the wall to the door. The whole flat seemed suddenly sordid, the rented furniture past its best, the curtains over the windows thin with use.

'Sorry,' Ron said, pushing open the door ten minutes later and walking over to his sister.

Zoe merely extended her hand as her brother sat down next to her. '*I'm* sorry, I was a bitch.'

'You're tired.'

'No,' she said, 'that's no excuse.' Her eyes moved back to the crack in the ceiling. 'Look at that, Ron. When I was a little girl at home there was a crack in my bedroom ceiling and when things got bad I used to imagine that I could squeeze into it and hide.' She turned to him, but the words obviously made no sense so she got to her feet. 'Just one more hour, Ron, and then I stop work for the night.'

He was already yawning. 'Just one hour then. 'Night.'

But it was never just one hour, and the work became addictive to Zoe, so that her only respite were her visits to Rochdale or travels with Harland, which were now undertaken more frequently, Mona Grimaldi left in temporary charge of the London gallery. Paris, Milan, and Rome all became familiar to Zoe, her passport well used, her composure masking any remaining anxiety.

Aware of the change in her after the episode at Courtney-Blye's, Harland was admiring but protective, understanding her insecurity without ever referring to it. In fact, when they went to New York to attend a large auction on Madison Avenue he was prepared for her last-minute nerves, but they never came — Zoe had learnt the hard way not to show her feelings, and no one would guess that the elegant young woman with Harland Goldberg was unhappy and horribly aware that she was seen as nothing other than an old man's travelling companion.

The auction in New York was an important one with many valuable Italian sixteenth-century paintings on show, all of which were expected to fetch record prices, a recently rediscovered Zuccaro attracting great interest with the Arab collectors. The humidity when they arrived was suffocating, the steaming streets momentarily wetted with a quick shower, the windows reflecting the cabs, cars, buses, pedestrians and the boiling blue sky. Quickly Zoe got out of an air-conditioned cab and made a bolt for the foyer of the Waldorf, Harland following behind, immune to the heat.

'It's amazing,' Zoe said, as they entered the lift. 'How the temperature doesn't affect you.'

'Good blood,' he said, smiling.

Returning the smile, she waited until they reached their floor and stepped out. A black maid saw her and glanced away, pushing a laundry basket towards the exit, the doors swinging back far enough to allow a glimpse of stairs. For a second Zoe wanted to make a run for it, the city terrifying her, the miles of Atlantic yawning between her and Rochdale, Ron, the flat, security. *Take me home*, she thought as the bellboy opened her bedroom door and stepped back, the insolent expression on his face reminding her of a boy at school who used to swing on the railings by the town hall . . .

'I'll see you later,' Harland said, bringing Zoe's attention back to the present. 'Dinner in half an hour?'

'Half an hour,' she repeated, closing the door behind her.

The hotel bedroom was sumptuously indifferent, the paper wrapper round the toilet seat, the inevitable basket of fruit on the table, the grapes pendulous, almost vulgar. Formidable drapes guarded the netted windows and muffled the sound of a police siren outside, whilst above, a few silenced birds flew through the blank Manhattan air. The single bed was smooth as ice, the pale green silk cold to Zoe's touch as she lay down with her arms extended, her hands dangling over the sides. Falling quickly to sleep, she found herself back in her mother's bedroom, the tin box of mementoes lying next to the corpse of Jane Mellor. Then the dream altered, the box taking the place of her body under the sheet. In slow motion, Zoe moved over to the bed and pulled back the covering, the lid of the box flipping open as she did so, a series of playing cards spiraling out on to the bedspread in front of her. Cautiously she picked one up, the Queen's face turning into her own, then Mona Grimaldi's, then her mother's — the card becoming heavier in her hand until she realised that she was in fact holding her mother's head.

Screaming, she awoke and the phone rang.

'Miss Mellor?'

'Yes. What is it?'

'Could you come down to Room 114? Mr Goldberg has had a heart attack.'

17

He was taken on a stretcher down the back stairs, the management thinking it bad taste for a stretcher case to leave by the main entrance. In the alleyway Zoe clambered into the ambulance and sat next to him, clasping his hand as the doors were slammed shut. They pulled out into the traffic, passing Central Park, the siren screaming, cars moving over to let them past, the night suddenly full of motor horns, flashing lights, and shrieking noise. Harland's face was coated with a misting of sweat, his eyes closed, his mouth covered by an oxygen mask, his shirt undone, the skin of his chest as waxen as his face. He seemed smaller, his personality closed off, his breathing steadied by an injection.

Zoe touched his forehead, the clammy skin cold under her hand. 'Hurry, please hurry,' she begged, glancing out through the windows and seeing the wide strip of the road and the lights on 'Stop' ahead of them. They passed through, the ambulance light whipping round and round into the black night.

Everything happened quickly as they pulled into the hospital emergency entrance, the ambulance doors snatched open, the stretcher pulled out and lowered on to a gurney. Zoe ran to keep up with them, her eyes fixed on Harland, panic making her breathless. But as she moved towards the entrance to Intensive Care, a nurse blocked her way. 'You can't go in.'

Zoe stared at the woman. 'I must! You don't understand.'

'You can't go in there,' she repeated, leading Zoe towards the reception desk and picking up a pen. 'What is the patient's name?'

Zoe was too confused to answer. What was this woman asking such stupid questions for? she thought blindly. Harland was *dying* and she was asking what his name was! The realisation punched her. Oh God, she thought, what if he did die? She remembered her dream and said firmly, 'I *have* to go in. He needs me.'

'He needs a doctor more,' the nurse replied, laying her hand gently on Zoe's arm. 'What's his name?'

'Harland Goldberg,' she answered dumbly, remembering how he had introduced himself that day in the gallery, extending his hand to her . . .

'Age?'

'What?'

'How old is he?'

Zoe thought for a moment. 'Sixty-nine.'

'Address?'

Oh God, Zoe thought, what was his address? 'Twelve, Littleton Crescent, St John's Wood.'

'New York State?' the nurse queried.

'No, London. We're from London.'

'Are you his daughter?'

The question shook Zoe. With a dull feeling in her stomach she looked at the nurse and said quietly, 'No, I'm just a friend.'

They stabilised him within an hour, although

the doctor told Zoe that he was seriously ill and would have to be kept in for observation.

'Who's his next of kin?' he asked Zoe.

'His wife is his next of kin,' Zoe answered, looking up, the full force of her eyes catching the man off guard. She knew what they had been saying about her and was already on the defensive. 'I've given the address and phone number to the nurse. Can I go in and see him now?'

'He's asleep.'

'Then I won't be disturbing him, will I?'

She sat with him throughout the night, her hands over his, her head nodding as she fought sleep. Attached to an ECG machine, Harland Goldberg's heart beeped on, the green line zig-zagging across the dark screen, his breath coming in sighs at times, as though he was wakening. But he didn't wake. He staggered through the night, separated from Zoe in some eclipsed cradle of illness, his spirit rocking, his eyes flickering under his eyelids, his fingers jerking under her own.

Four o'clock found him restless and muttering. Zoe leaned towards him and listened, but she could not understand what he said and rang for the nurse. Pulses were taken, injections administered, charts read and written on, the corridors outside quiet, all patients asleep except for Harland, and he was already slipping back, dipping away from consciousness.

'Fight, Harland!' she willed him when they were alone again. 'Come on, you made me fight, you wouldn't let me give up.' His eyes remained closed. 'Please don't die,' she pleaded, 'please, not you . . . not you.'

It was six o'clock when Zoe finally fell asleep, her head resting on the bed by his hand, her face shadowed by the dark fall of her hair. But exhausted as she was, it was only minutes before she woke again and glanced over to Harland.

Awake, he tried to smile at her, his eyes following hers, his mouth moving without speech.

Quickly, Zoe leaned towards him. 'Harland?'

He pushed the oxygen mask off his face, his hands clumsy. 'Zoe . . . thank you.'

She smiled, close to tears. 'What for? You fight for me, and I fight for you,' she said, picking up his hand and laying it against her face. 'I thought you were going to die.'

He shook his head and smiled, his breathing laboured. 'I wouldn't leave you, Zoe . . . only when you don't need me any more . . . I'll die when you're safe.'

★ ★ ★

Myrtle took the first flight out of Heathrow the next morning, Erica making an excuse to stay at home while her mother flew to New York. Unused to travelling alone, Myrtle was demanding and impatient, begging for assistance from everyone. It was nearly twelve o'clock when she reached the hospital after leaving her luggage at the Waldorf.

'I'm Mrs Goldberg,' she said sharply to the nurse on the reception desk. 'My husband was

256

admitted last night.'

The nurse looked at the admittance chart. 'Room 761,' she said simply.

Her face set into the lines of a grieving wife, Myrtle stalked down the corridor, her thin legs moving like a marionette, her skirt creased from the long flight. Pausing only to check the room number, she walked in, just in time to see Zoe bend and brush the top of her husband's forehead with her lips.

★   ★   ★

Victor was already halfway down his third vodka when he got off the bar stool and went over to the phone. Pushing in some coins, he waited as it rang out.

'Hello?'

'Ron?' he asked, relieved. 'Where's Zoe? I called round last night and there was no one at the flat.'

'I was walking Peter.'

Victor breathed in deeply. 'Good . . . but where's Zoe?'

'New York.'

He frowned. 'But she was supposed to be back days ago. Why's she still there?'

'Her boss had a heart attack.'

'A what?'

'A heart attack,' Ron repeated blandly. 'She's stayed on with him.'

This was bad news for Victor; he needed Zoe in London. He needed the fakes she had promised him. Damn Harland Goldberg! The bastard had no right to mess up his arrangements like this.

'When's she coming back?'

'I dunno.'

'But she must have said *something*.'

Ron was annoyed by the tone in his brother's voice. He wasn't stupid, he just didn't know.

'She sent her love.'

Victor was almost incoherent. 'You've been a big help. Thank you.'

'Oh, that's OK,' Ron replied, mildly flattered. 'You can ring any time.'

Back at the bar, Victor downed the remainder of the vodka in one gulp and looked round. Perhaps there was someone who could take his mind off things, someone with whom he could while away the evening. His predatory eyes swept round the room and came to rest on a small-featured face, framed with a mass of ash-blond hair. The eyes caught his and an understanding smile curved the narrow mouth. With a jolt of embarrassment Victor looked away.

'Can I get you a drink?'

Victor turned round on the stool and faced the questioner, outraged. 'Get lost!'

Unperturbed, the stranger slipped on to the stool next to him. 'You shouldn't jump to conclusions — '

'Neither should you!' Victor hissed. 'Bugger off.'

'I thought you were interested.'

The words galvanised Victor into action. He was getting more outraged by the minute, his masculine pride threatened, his whole reputation in jeopardy. 'I don't want to offend you, jerk, but I like women.'

The small face seemed baffled. 'But I was told — '

'I don't care *what* you were told!' Victor snapped, grasping hold of the man's arm and twisting it. 'I don't like queers.'

Squirming, he persisted. 'But I was told to — '

The blow struck the man on the side of the jaw, sending him plummeting back off the bar stool and on to the floor.

Victor towered over him. 'Don't you ever come near me again, scum.'

The man rubbed his jaw with a weak hand, his eyes hard with malice. 'Suit yourself, Mellor. But Mike O'Dowd sent me.'

It turned out that O'Dowd had discovered a forger working in Wandsworth called Lino Candadas, an Italian who had been forced to leave Florence and set up business in London.

'So who the hell are you?' Victor asked suspiciously.

'Noilly.'

'Noilly?' Victor repeated unpleasantly. 'As in 'Prat', I suppose?'

Bemused, the man frowned. 'I'm Austrian.'

'Well, it's quite a little United Nations, isn't it?' Victor said drily, beckoning for another drink. 'You won't mind if I don't buy you one, will you? It would be bad for my image.'

Noilly ignored the remark. 'Mr O'Dowd wanted me to introduce you to Lino, he said you should meet him.'

'Do you work for O'Dowd?'

'I've worked for him for years. We go back a long time.'

'Oh, I see.'

'I doubt it.'

An ungenerous silence followed.

'Well?' Noilly asked finally. 'Shall we go?'

Lino Candadas worked in a deserted Methodist church in Wandsworth. Having told the minister he was an impoverished artist who concentrated on religious work, the churchman had offered him the use of the building in return for various odd jobs done in the parish. Candadas had agreed, knowing that he would be left to his own devices, the church of no interest to its neighbours, the myriad hiding places invaluable to ensure that if there was a break-in, no one would find anything.

The church loomed up in front of Victor as they paused at the end of the street. There were no lights on at the front, only one burning round the back. Clambering over a broken wall, Victor stumbled. 'God above!'

A door swung open and a man stood back to let him pass. 'That's blasphemy, Mr Mellor — '

'And that's bloody dangerous!' Victor snapped, walking in and glancing at the man in front of him. Lino Candadas was about forty, his hard face dominated by a heavy, pendulous nose, his chin marked by a deep cleft, his hair worn long over his ears.

'Please, come through,' he said, his voice still carrying a strong Italian accent.

Victor followed him down a dim corridor and into the body of the church. The pews were covered with dust, chairs piled high, old pieces of carpet and boxes stacked haphazardly, a mouse darting out as they passed. Only the altar was cleared, two candlesticks at either end, both sporting lighted candles. 'Your idea?' Victor asked.

'To the glory of God,' Candadas replied ironically, moving off into the vestry. Three easels were in use, two supporting canvases, the third holding a tiny ivory cross, on which some carving had been begun.

'So you're a sculptor too?'

Candadas touched the cross. 'As you see, Mr Mellor, I turn my hands to most things. It would seem to be the will of God.'

Victor lit a cigarette and inhaled deeply. 'Some people believe that religion is a substitute for sex,' he said smoothly, glancing at Noilly. 'But perhaps in your case, it's merely an accompaniment — like the organ.'

Candadas smiled. 'If there is a God, He will be the one to judge me.'

'Well, let's hope for your sake that He's an art lover,' Victor replied, changing the subject. 'Your girlfriend said you worked with O'Dowd.'

Candadas turned away from Victor and gestured for Noilly to leave. When the door closed, he turned back to him. 'He's too talkative — '

'Especially with strange men in bars.'

'Oh, he's faithful to me,' Candadas said briskly. 'He's just young, that's all.'

Victor shrugged. 'Why did O'Dowd want us all to get together?'

'He thought you had some trouble meeting

the demand,' Candadas explained. 'He thought I could help you.'

Feigning indifference, Victor listened. After all, Zoe was in New York. She had let him down badly. He could hardly be expected to lose trade.

He glanced at Candadas, sized him up, and then said, 'I have a collector who wants to buy a Guido Reni — '

'It will take time.'

'How much time?'

'Two months.'

Victor thought for a moment. 'No sooner?'

'Not if you want it to look genuine,' Candadas replied evenly. 'Mind you, if it had been going into an auction or a museum it would take longer. I have to use the right paints and the right mediums. These take a long time to dry out, and then they have to be aged — '

'One hour on Gas Mark 7?' Victor quipped.

'To begin with,' Candadas agreed. 'But there's more to it than that.'

'Such as?'

'Those are my secrets.'

Victor grinned. 'Oh, secrets. I see. Perhaps you could let me into the *secret* about your charges.'

'A thousand pounds for the Reni.'

'A thousand pounds! Are you mad?' Victor asked, stubbing out his cigarette and moving towards the door.

'Mr Mellor,' Candadas began. 'This game can be dangerous. An amateur does an amateur job. If you want to make money you have to use the best, and that costs money. Don't risk your reputation, or your freedom, by being overhasty.'

Victor thought for a moment. 'Two months for the Guido Reni?'

Candadas nodded. 'Two months.'

'OK. I'll try you out. But you'd better be worth the money.'

'No one's ever come back to complain,' Candadas said drily.

★   ★   ★

'Get away from my husband!' Myrtle screeched, rushing over to the bed and pushing Zoe away. 'Get away, you bitch, unless you want I should kill you!'

Zoe stepped back, glancing over to the sleeping Harland and lowering her voice. 'I didn't know you were coming.'

'Maybe I should have sent you an itinerary!' Myrtle replied, pouring herself some water from Harland's jug and drinking it quickly. 'Get out of here. This is no place for . . . a slut.'

Zoe expression never changed. After all, the woman was Harland's wife, she had a right to be angry in the circumstances. 'It's all right, I'll go now.'

'You should do me such a favour! If he'd been at home with me, this would never have happened. You've killed him!'

Zoe was about to retort when the doctor walked in. He glanced at both women and asked, 'Who is the next of kin?'

'I am!' Myrtle shouted triumphantly. 'I am his wife.'

'And you?' he asked, turning to Zoe.

'She's nothing! A cheap little piece who's trying to take my husband away from me,' Myrtle replied with a catch in her voice. She could see how seriously ill Harland was, but her initial pity faded almost instantly, her resentment turning her thoughts to his will, the vast accumulation of money which might now be left to his mistress, not his wife. 'She's not welcome here,' she continued, pointing to Zoe, 'and I want her to leave.'

The doctor hesitated and turned to the young woman standing beside the bed. 'Perhaps you — ?'

' — would go?' she finished for him. 'Yes, I'll go,' she said, walking out, the door closing with a dull sound behind her. Harland Goldberg is now with his wife, she thought bitterly, and all's well with the world.

Throughout the long afternoon Myrtle sat with her husband, making long-distance phone calls to Erica when he slept, and when he awoke, admonishing him for his lack of thought.

'You should never have come here,' she said, dabbing her face with a handkerchief. 'I told you it would end in tears. That you could do this, after all Erica's trouble.' She shrugged. Her daughter's drug problem had been a bitter blow, her addiction almost as embarrassing to her mother as the existence of her father's mistress. 'Now this! That Mellor girl is bad for you, she's brought you bad luck.'

'Don't pretend to care about me,' Harland replied quietly. 'You're only worried about the money — '

'What a thing to say to your wife!' she snapped, slamming down her powder compact on the bedside table and looking round. 'This place must cost a fortune.'

Closing his eyes, Harland tried unsuccessfully to sleep.

* * *

New York was already humming with dealers when the news of Harland's illness leaked out. In various hotel bars the story was traded and embellished until little trace of the truth remained.

'He had a heart attack while he was in bed with that Northern piece . . . '

Or ' . . . the management had to lift him off her . . . ' The garish details sniggered over and passed on like a dirty book in the back of a classroom.

Zoe knew what was going on even before she walked into Hampton's auction house so she was at least prepared for the rabid curiosity which greeted her. The afternoon of the sale was a humid one and after the air conditioning temporarily broke down the temperature was soon making clothes hang heavy, the men irritably mopping the perspiration off their foreheads, the conversation limp with heat. In direct contrast to Lister's in London, Hampton's was decorated in a pseudo-English style, the effect being one of a gigantic country house with too many gossiping foreign guests.

The entrance was almost deserted as people

passed through into the main gallery, the major dealers and the most important collectors finding their seats, the obligatory hand waves and nodding of heads ascertaining the pecking order. Zoe looked straight ahead as she walked in wearing an expensive Joseph suit, her presence causing a small scuttle of interest amongst the London dealers. With a mock salute in her direction, Rupert Courtney-Blye smiled and turned to Seymour Bell beside him.

'Harland's little spy has arrived.'

The critic's face was expressionless. 'How is he?'

'In a bad way.'

'Shame,' Seymour Bell said, his interest turning back to his catalogue. 'Well, let's see which ignorant Yank buys the Bellini, shall we?'

The auction began slowly, building into a series of healthy sales, but only spinning off into the incredible when an early Giorgione tripled its reserve price, and kept climbing. The audience was enthralled, leaning forward in their seats, each face a study of anticipation. One by one the bidders dropped out, until only two remained, a pugnacious American and a Japanese dealer bidding over the telephone. For over three minutes in the suffocating heat they fought it out, the American unwilling to be defeated, the Japanese dealer matching every bid. The atmosphere had altered from autocratic dignity to a bull fight, all eyes on the bidder, all ears waiting for the response coming over the phone.

The painting stood in front of all of them, aloof, poised, the sensuous lines of the woman's naked figure inviting admiration not desire. Then suddenly the American faltered at the last bid, and throwing up his arms, dropped out of the auction. A collective sigh went round the gallery, native New Yorkers feeling disappointment for the bidder, others wanting only to know the identity of the Japanese dealer. Zoe marked the page next to the Giorgione and added the price, her attention diverted away from the hall. Yet someone was watching *her*. A stocky Irishman, his tinted glasses catching the light as he moved his head in her direction, his arms folded. He watched her and remembered what someone had told him in Rome about Harland Goldberg's young mistress, Zoe Mellor . . . The name rang a bell loudly in his head, making him frown and then laugh silently to himself. Victor Mellor . . . Zoe Mellor . . . no, it couldn't be, could it?

Blithely unaware of O'Dowd's scrutiny, Zoe stayed to see the sale of the remaining lots and then left, pausing on the kerb to hail a taxi. The sun was liquid, the smells from the exhausts and the heat waves undulating over the cars making her unsteady. Suddenly her arm was grasped and she turned. 'What the — '

'Zoe,' the man said gleefully. 'I thought you were about to plunge headlong into the traffic. Are things so bleak?'

Leon Graves lived up to his nickname 'the Bracelet' as his fingers encircled Zoe's arm, the brown skin of his hand almost luminous under the hot daylight. It was his trademark, this grasping of people, his way of making immediate contact with men or women. He leaned towards

Zoe, his face with its overlarge ears inquisitive, the good-humoured mouth grinning over the heavy jaw.

'Hello, Leon,' she said easily, pleased to see one of the few men who treated her with respect, even though she realised that he could be dangerous to her and knew more about the underbelly of the art world than anyone else. If Harland knew everything about trade above board, Leon knew everything at sewer level. Kind and amusing, his appearance fooled everyone as he tracked down forgers with the same zeal Simon Wiesenthal used to trace Nazis. In short, he was the stumbling block of every fake's progress.

'You look well, but what about Harland?' he continued.

'Poor soul, he should rest more. Running around like that in the middle of a New York summer! It's enough to harden anyone's arteries.' He smiled hugely. 'Still, I called in at the hospital a little while ago and he seemed much improved now that Myrtle has been summoned back home, no doubt to find her daughter walking around two feet off the ground.'

Zoe grimaced. 'She has a real problem, Leon — '

'Yes, one which she keeps stuffing up her nostrils.'

Mentally conceding defeat, Zoe changed the subject. 'What are you doing here anyway?'

'On the track of the demon daub,' he said. 'Fakes popping up like mushrooms here, and our dear trans-Atlantic cousins can't recognise them. All money and no taste.' He shifted his grasp of her arm, but did not let go. 'They can't tell one of Rubens's pink round bottoms from a Jordaens rump! Incredible! No one paints cellulite like Rubens. A thigh man, like me!'

'Taxi!' Zoe called out, then shrugged as it passed.

'Oh, come on, walk with me,' Leon insisted.

'You must be mad. It's too hot for that,' she replied, laughing, his good humour infectious.

'Nonsense! It's all in the mind,' he said, starting off and pulling her with him. 'Think *cool*, cool as a Poussin, cool as Picasso's blue period — '

'I don't like Picasso.'

'All right, cool as — '

'Millais's *Ophelia*?'

He raised his eyebrows. 'Oh no! That's not cool, that's waterlogged. The silly bitch asked for it anyway, picking all those wild flowers. Talk about conservation!'

'How's your garden?' Zoe asked, knowing that it was the chief passion in his life — after catching forgers.

'Blooming. All violet, red, gold and cerise — like an oil slick without the gunge,' he answered, screwing his eyes up against the sun. 'Did you see Mike O'Dowd at the auction?'

Zoe shrugged. 'Who's he?'

'The Irishman who was watching you with such avid curiosity,' he replied. 'Really, you are unobservant! People get mugged here for being so myopic.'

Zoe smiled. 'OK, so who is he anyway?'

Leon's grip tightened slightly. 'He's a very clever, very adept, very ruthless handler.'

'Handler?'

'Yes, of everything. Fake sculpture, paintings, icons, statues, parts of Greek temples, fakes of Chinese door stops, Egyptian toilet roll covers — everything. He's clever, really clever, and dangerous.' He glanced at her. 'You must have heard about Malta.' She shook her head. 'You didn't know about the forger who arrived in Malta with ten digits and retired soon after with six?'

'Very funny, Leon.'

His face was serious. 'I'm not joking. I don't have enough proof yet, but O'Dowd used to run a group of forgers there, and one got greedy. The Irishman taught him a lesson with a carving knife.'

'Personally?' Zoe asked, shivering as a breeze sighed down from the towering buildings and chilled her.

'Oh yes, that's the part he enjoys. He started as a boxer in Dublin, then decided to use his brains instead and went into the art business. I can't prove that he's killed anyone, but he's certainly been responsible for a number of sickening incidents and it's more than likely that he's into blackmail — '

'So why hasn't he been stopped?'

'No proof. Yet.' Zoe noticed the change in his voice, the hard edge which reminded her that underneath the joviality was a very determined man. A man who was out to break the fake trade. An enemy. 'I can't catch him,' he repeated, glancing over to Zoe.

'But you will, Leon,' she replied evenly. 'You will.'

The conversation with Leon Graves played on Zoe's mind, a timely reminder of the kind of people she was up against. The Bracelet was no fool, and neither was the Irishman, but where they differed was that Graves played fair and O'Dowd was a dirty fighter.

'Harland,' she said later when she visited him. 'What do you know about Leon Graves?'

'The Bracelet?' he asked. 'I've known him for over twenty years. Why?'

'He said he was in New York because of some fakes.'

'He's anywhere and everwhere 'because of some fakes',' Harland replied, coughing slightly before continuing. 'He was a brilliant art historian, you know. Studied at Cambridge, got a first, lectured there and then abroad, building up his reputation. No one on earth knows more about Italian or French art. No one.'

'What happened?'

'He married a French girl in the sixties. She came from a very wealthy family, the typical old aristocracy. They weren't thrilled about the match, but when she became pregnant they rallied and accepted Leon.' Harland sipped some water from the glass Zoe held for him. 'He was working in Paris at a well-known gallery then. That way he could earn far more than when he was lecturing, and in his spare time he wrote articles. The gallery owner was called . . . ' he paused, 'Louvaine, and he was believed to be dabbling in fakes. Because he was greedy and clumsy, people quickly became suspicious of him and of his associate, Zanetti. They were about to be exposed when Zanetti conveniently drowned while staying at Louvaine's country house. They tried to make it look like suicide, but the rumours kept flying around, and suspicion conveniently fell on the man who was last seen with Zanetti . . . and that was Leon.'

'No!' Zoe said sharply. 'I don't believe that he would do anything like that.'

'Neither did anyone else. But he was a foreigner and he was blamed for Zanetti's death *and* the forgeries. He hadn't a leg to stand on, and he knew it. Leon was the scapegoat for Louvaine, who had actually killed two birds with one stone. First, he got rid of the indiscreet Zanetti, and then he cleared his own reputation by blaming the forgery business on Leon Graves.'

'What happened then?'

'The matter was hushed up because Leon agreed to leave France in disgrace. What else could he do? But his wife's family never forgave him and Leon's wife and child remained with them. He never saw them again.'

Harland paused and sipped at his water, his eyes never leaving Zoe's face. Why was she so interested in Leon? he thought. Why him?

'Is that why he started to track down forgers?' she asked finally.

Harland nodded. 'Leon never gave a damn about what people thought; besides, no one believed the story over here. He could have gone back into the academic world, but he wanted revenge, and he wanted a crusade. So he set about tracking down and exposing every forger he could discover, and the dealers involved, then he brought them to justice — just as Louvaine never was.'

'But how does it work? Do people hire him?'

Harland shook his head. 'No one knows how Leon supports himself, because no one has ever admitted to me that they've employed him. It seems that he hears about some forgeries going the rounds and then sets about discovering who's at the bottom of it. When he finds the culprits he passes them over to the police.'

'But what about his expenses? He can't go around the world on his own money.'

'I don't know how it works. Honestly,' Harland said, looking at Zoe carefully. 'I imagine that dealers or private collectors who have been duped reward him in some way.'

'You mean paintings?'

'No, Leon has no possessions and he travels too much to have a real home, although he keeps a small cottage with a magnificent garden somewhere near Cambridge. You see, Leon can't afford to settle anywhere.'

Zoe was mystified. 'Why not?'

'Firstly, he'll never settle down because he's a wanderer; secondly, he can't stay in one place because there are too many people after him.'

A sense of fear washed over Zoe. ' 'After him'? God, Harland, don't be so dramatic!'

'The art world looks glossy and faintly silly from the outside,' Harland explained carefully.

'But it's a rich world and where there's money there's crime. Don't underestimate the villains, Zoe, because they feed off the dealers and the collectors, and they have too much to lose to be scrupulous.' He stared at her levelly. 'Be wary of them — and be wary of Leon.'

Zoe frowned. 'But he seems so guileless.'

Harland shook his head. 'Never be fooled by him. He is the *most* dangerous man I have ever met.' Zoe glanced at him in astonishment. 'You find that hard to believe, don't you?' She nodded. 'Well, so does everyone else. But I know him, and have done for a long time. Leon Graves was not capable of killing Zanetti then, but now . . . now I would not be too sure.'

'Oh, Harland, I can't believe — '

He raised his hands. 'No, don't interrupt. Listen to me and *remember*. A man is capable of love when it is offered, but if he loses that love through injustice he learns to hate, and such hate festers. Leon does a great service to the art world — he scrapes off the scum and tries to keep the real villains powerless. But such actions have their price, and one day they may cost him his life.' He paused. 'Leon knows that . . . but because he lost the family he loved, he has nothing left to lose. Beware of people who have nothing to lose, Zoe. They can drag you into hell with them.'

★　★　★

'I'm surprised you could tear yourself away from New York,' Victor said drily when Zoe answered the door of the flat the following week.

'I've just got in about fifteen minutes ago,' she said wearily. 'It was a hell of a flight — '

He interrupted her impatiently. 'Did you do that Blake watercolour?'

'Oh sure. I finished it on the plane, although I had a little trouble with the signature when someone kept nudging my arm!' she replied, exasperated. 'For God's sake, Victor, there's a limit.'

With a sigh of irritation he slipped off his overcoat and sat on the arm of a chair. Ron had gone to the dog track with Peter again, leaving the flat in an appalling state. A filming of dust skimmed every surface, a plate of half eaten dog food lay by the television and several pieces of clothing had been left haphazardly on the settee.

Victor looked round. 'What a tip!'

'Ron's old enough to clear up for himself. I can't do everything.'

The subject bored Victor immediately and he changed tack. 'I've been thinking while you've been away. If it's a struggle for you to keep up with the demand, why don't we get someone else to help with the fakes?'

'Like *who* for instance?' Zoe asked suspiciously, her instinct warning her.

'I met someone the other day — '

'You don't say!'

'There's no need to be snide, Zoe,' he said. 'I can't neglect the business while you travel the world.'

'I've spent most of my time in hospital with Harland!' Zoe shouted. 'He wasn't in there for a

275

haircut, he'd had a heart attack.'

'I was pretty close to one myself when you didn't come back,' Victor replied coolly, lighting up a cigarette and inhaling deeply. 'Lino Candadas is very good — '

'*No!*' she snapped. 'We agreed that we were going to keep it in the family — '

'We would have, if the family had been more reliable.'

'OK, I've got the point, Victor!' she said angrily, pushing Ron's clothes off the settee and sitting down. 'I let you down. Sorry about that, brother, but it doesn't change anything. I don't want anyone else in on this. Who the hell is Lino Candadas?'

'He's an Italian who works in Wandsworth. A painter and a sculptor, and his fakes are really good. The best.'

'Well you always did have an eye for the best things in life,' she replied, a sense of betrayal making her voice hard. 'How did you find him?'

'Through a friend of a friend.'

'Who has no name, I suppose?'

'None that you need to know.'

'No, I'm just supposed to follow behind you, aren't I, Victor? 'Zoe do this, Zoe do that — ''

'Oh, dry up! You get paid — '

'No money is worth it! I'm not putting myself at risk by dealing with a stranger.' She looked at her brother's face and read his thoughts. It was simple, as it always was with Victor. If she didn't play along with him, he would go elsewhere. Gone would be her revenge. Goodbye. 'I want to meet this Candadas.'

He smiled at her warmly. 'Oh, so you shall.'

The following evening Victor collected Zoe outside the gallery and drove through the heavy traffic, humming under his breath. Arriving at Wandsworth, he parked the car and got out, stopping to talk to a young coloured boy as he did so.

'You see this car?' he said, pointing to the Jaguar. The child was sullenly dumb. 'If anything happens to it while I'm away I'll hold you personally responsible — '

'Piss off,' the boy said defiantly.

Victor smiled and showed him a five pound note. 'Watch the car, like a good little lad, and you'll get this when I come out. Although if anything should happen to it you'll get this instead,' he said, bunching his fist and tapping the boy on the chin with it. 'Savvy?'

'You're going to make some lucky little kid a fine daddy one day,' Zoe said as she followed her brother round to the back of the church. A light burned out from a high window, illuminating the crippled branches of a tree which leaned against the church wall, its branches scratching the stained glass figure of St Peter.

Victor turned to Zoe and whispered, 'Follow my lead and don't tell him anything about our business.'

Nerves paralysed Zoe as she stood shivering outside the abandoned church. She was suddenly a child again, threatened and unsafe, and she panicked. 'I don't like it here.'

'Jesus Christ!' Victor snapped. 'You're the one who wanted to come in the first place.' He caught hold of her arm and yanked her towards the door. 'Get a bloody grip on yourself.'

The sky was darkening, an angry red smouldering into indigo behind the black mass of the church as Victor knocked on the door loudly. Lino Candadas opened it on the third rap. He hesitated when he saw Zoe and then stood back, his wide face vaguely amused. 'Follow me, please.'

The temperature was below fifty, the walls keeping the summer evening out, the damp stone barricading them in as they followed Candadas down the corridor towards the main body of the church where he paused, pushing open a heavy wooden door. Their footsteps echoed in the darkening church, the altar candles making little impression on the gloom, the changing sky nuzzling up against the arched windows. Shadows stretched up the aisle and crouched round the deserted pews, and as they moved towards the vestry one of the candles sputtered in the damp air.

'Cosy, isn't it?' Zoe whispered, nervousness making her flip.

Frowning, Victor followed her into the vestry and closed the door behind him.

The room had changed immeasurably since his last visit. Before there had been signs of some industry, but now the arched stone walls were almost covered with a variety of paintings in various stages of completion. Pontormos rubbed shoulders with Guardis, Guercinos with Monets and on the easel the medieval cross was almost finished. Two bright light bulbs provided good illumination, and a couple of anglepoise lamps on the window ledge and on the top of a cupboard obliterated any shadows on the canvases. A noise behind them made Zoe turn sharply.

Noilly stood with his arms folded, his thin face curious under the aureola of pale hair. 'Who are you?' he asked, then, turning to Victor continued, 'We don't want girlfriends here.'

'She's my sister,' he responded impatiently.

'Sister,' Noilly repeated, walking over to Zoe and looking her up and down.

'Are you just browsing, or would you like to make an offer?' she asked finally.

Lino Candadas laughed, the sound huge and mellifluous in the cold vestry. 'Come now, let's not fight, I thought we could all be friends,' he said, pointing to a sculpture resting on a small oak table under the window. 'Look at this, Miss Mellor, and tell me what you think.'

Zoe studied it carefully. It was a delicate statue of a Cupid, in the Renaissance style, and although she knew it had been finished only recently, it looked weathered and aged. She scrutinised it inch by inch, noticing how the stone was marked and uneven in patches, the surface worn by age. Well maybe not age, she thought, more likely lime or acid, or . . .

'Urine?' she queried, turning back to the Italian.

Again Lino Candadas laughed. 'As you say, urine.'

Victor was baffled. 'What the hell are you two talking about?'

Zoe turned to her brother, her confidence returning. 'Urine ages stone, it makes it look old, and pretty quickly too. There was a case of some fakes in Europe being left under a urinal for several months to give them a genuinely authentic appearance of age. Urine does that to stone.' She put her head on one side. 'You're not getting squeamish, are you?'

Victor smiled. 'No, I was just thinking that it was the first time anyone'd been pissed on and enjoyed it.'

'As delicately put as ever,' Zoe replied, turning back to the sculpture. 'It's a wonderful piece of work.'

Pleased, Lino Candadas motioned to Noilly. Reluctantly he opened the side door of what appeared to be a large closet, and brought out several bronze sculptures of animals.

'In the eighteenth-century French style,' Candadas explained, handing one to Zoe, pride singing in his voice. It was an almost perfect copy which could have fooled all but the most scrupulous dealer, she knew as she turned it over in her hands. Victor was right, Candadas was extremely gifted.

The threat of potential danger swamped her as she said, without thinking, 'Have you sold many?'

The atmosphere changed immediately. Candadas snatched the sculpture out of Zoe's hands and passed it to Noilly who locked it away with the others, tucking the key into his trouser pocket. Victor was no longer lounging against the table, but alert, his instinct warning him of impending trouble.

280

Candadas's face was cold, his accented voice brusque. 'Why do you want to know?'

'It was an innocent question,' Zoe said quickly, glancing over to Noilly who moved behind her, his shadow thrown high on the stone wall. The damp air trickled over her and chilled her, creeping along the concrete floor and crawling across the easels.

'Don't get so dramatic,' Victor said, grinding out his cigarette and running his forefinger down the side of the cross. In an attempt to forestall trouble, he kept his tone nonchalant and unconcerned. 'I know a really greedy dealer who asks no questions, who could find a buyer for this tomorrow.'

But Candadas's eyes were fixed on Zoe. He mistrusted her and overreacted. Maybe she wasn't Victor Mellor's sister after all, she could be anyone, a dealer or a collector . . . even the police. The lights above them flickered for an instant and then went out, flashing on again almost immediately. Caught under the glare, Zoe panicked and looked over to Victor, who had risen to his feet and seemed suddenly nervous.

'Victor!' she shouted, seeing Noilly move away from Candadas and head towards the main body of the church — just as the lights faded completely and the darkness swamped them.

18

Myrtle could hardly conceal her delight. 'I told you she'd let you down one day.'

'I don't understand it. Zoe told me she'd be here this morning,' Harland Goldberg said wearily to Myrtle over the phone. 'She's usually so reliable — '

'It's over, my dear,' his wife replied, glowing with delight. It was about time too! That bloody girl had been ruining her sleep. 'You shouldn't be at the gallery anyway. It's too much for you.'

'I only called in — '

'To see her!' Myrtle snapped. Damn him, she thought, she had promised not to upset herself, and now, here he was, irritating her again. Her tone mellowed suddenly. 'You should come home and let me look after you. Forget Zoe Mellor.'

'I'll be along soon,' he replied with a slight shudder. Myrtle had been loving since his heart attack, her affection forced and unreciprocated. His thoughts turned back to Zoe. She'll be here, she *will* be here, he repeated to himself, any moment now the door will open and she'll walk in, all brimful of chat, and she'll kiss my cheek and smile . . .

'You know what the doctor said. You can only stay at the gallery for a couple of hours. So what time are you coming home?'

Harland sighed. 'Soon,' he snapped, changing

282

the subject. 'I've got some work to do on a sale which will mean a lot of money. I should stay here and sort it out.'

Myrtle hesitated. Maybe it was good for him to take an interest. Besides, men get bored at home all day. 'You do what you think is right, my dear. I'll see you later.'

Harland put down the phone and rose to his feet. Having made a steady recovery, he was unprepared for the weakness he was now experiencing. It was exhausting to be back at the gallery and he found himself weary after only an hour, leaning against the desk for support. For days he had longed to touch the walls and relish the paintings, to feel the rush of pure excitement, tinged as he was with the realisation that he might never have seen these things again . . .

'Welcome back,' Mona said abruptly, walking in and laying her handbag on the desk. Glancing round, her mouth curled into a smile when there was no trace of Zoe. 'I spoke to Myrtle early on and she said you were tired. How are you feeling now?'

'Fine,' Harland said automatically. So she had been talking to Myrtle, had she? No doubt they had been in constant touch for months, their mutual dislike of Zoe making them unlikely comrades. 'Is there anything urgent?' he asked, turning away from the woman's poisonous concern.

'Nothing that won't wait,' she said deftly.

Oh, but there was, Harland thought to himself. Some things couldn't wait . . . like wanting to see Zoe.

283

She had returned to London a week before him. Finally convinced that he was on the way to recovery, she had flown back from New York to prepare for the latest exhibition at the gallery, phoning him several times to say that everything was running along smoothly and that she would be there to welcome him on Thursday morning.

But it was Thursday morning now and there was no sign of her. Profoundly lonely, Harland sat down on a seat by the door, his hand resting on one velvet-coloured arm, his head leaned back against the cushions, his gaze travelling across the ornate white and gold ceiling. The pale walls of the gallery surrounded him, painting after painting in their gilt frames providing the audience to his misery. He sighed, remembering how he had loved this place, how the soft thump of the door closing had made his heart lift, how the wide deep front window with its dark crimson lining had displayed his good taste. 'Never exhibit more than one painting at a time,' he had said. 'One painting is enough for passers-by to appreciate.' So many pictures had been displayed, famous and infamous, portraits of titled heads, landscapes, allegorical scenes, all chosen carefully, all in exquisite taste, and at night, under the soft window lights, each came into its own and smiled out into Bond Street, catching the eye of a road sweeper or a Sloane Ranger on her lonely way home. What a reputation, he thought, how people had envied him, Tobar Manners, Anthony Sargeant, Courtney-Blye, Jimmy van Goyen — all of them wanted his advice, his skill, his status.

He sighed. The gallery was warm and only the faintest hum of the angry traffic smudged under the heavy glass door. He wondered where Zoe was, and if she would come back, or if she had finally gone. Maybe he was expecting too much to presume that she would stay — she was clever and lovely and the world was always ready to be conquered. But they had a special feeling, he thought with a rush of real despair, there was a real affection between them. Wasn't there? Sighing, he signalled to Mona to ring for the chauffeur to take him home, and as he waited he kept looking around him. All this is mine, he thought, all my achievements are here. Everything I ever wanted, everything . . . except her.

★   ★   ★

In New York a private view for an exhibition of contemporary American sculpture was being held on East 67th Street. Outside the wide double glass doors were two large potted palms, and just inside the entrance a couple of nubile young women in bronze-coloured body stockings were handing out catalogues. The passing public peered in at the windows to get a better look, the young women in question turning two well shaped rears towards their onlookers.

The private view was well attended. Many serious collectors were there, as were a number of minor members of the European aristocracy all vying with each other to be snapped by a strolling press photographer for the society page. Each piece of sculpture was exhibited on a plinth, mostly at eye level, except for the larger pieces which were free-standing. The gallery itself was high-ceilinged and bare-floored, the minimalist look in full flow, the only concession to comfort a large buffet and innumerable glasses of champagne. However, as there were no seats provided, the guests were encouraged to gorge on foot, the principle being that continual movement made for sales. Indolent chit-chat on comfy chaise longues, did not.

Indolent chit-chat however, was far more absorbing than contemporary sculpture. 'It's something to do with alternative medicine and it's called colonic irrigation,' Tobar Manners said, leaning towards Jimmy van Goyen. 'They shove a piece of piping up your backside . . . '

'What?' Ahmed Fazir said, turning his head to catch the conversation. '*Who* puts what up *whose* backside?'

'It's supposed to leave you feeling wonderful . . . '

'I can imagine,' van Goyen replied drily, glancing round and flinching as he saw Mike O'Dowd across the room. 'What's he doing here?'

'You can get it done off Oxford Street somewhere . . . ' Manners droned on, 'and I was wondering if we ought to mention it to Seymour . . . '

Unaware of the Dutchman's intense scrutiny, Mike O'Dowd had just knocked into somebody behind him and sent a rush of champagne down his expensively clad leg. 'Oh, damn and blast!' he snapped, his Dublin accent even stronger in his irritation.

286

A hand came down and clamped his left arm. 'Well, hello, Mr O'Dowd,' Leon Graves said easily. 'You didn't spill any of that wondrous champagne over these lovely exhibits, did you?'

The Irishman smiled, his eyes alert behind the tinted glasses. So the Bracelet was in town, he thought. I better mind my step. 'How well you look,' he said, scrutinising Graves's ingenuous face and the English country gentleman tweed. Such a clever disguise, anyone would think the man was an idiot. 'It seems ages since we talked.'

'I was only thinking of you the other day,' Leon continued, his public school accent as precise as ever. 'You know, wondering how you were getting on.'

'I survive. I make a living,' O'Dowd replied, lighting up a cigarette.

'You shouldn't smoke though, it could kill you.'

The Irishman smiled, then put out his hand and with a deft movement palmed the lighted cigarette. An instant later, he flicked it back between his fingers and inhaled.

'How dreadfully clever, you must be a magician,' Leon said admiringly. 'But don't tell me you have a couple of little white bunnies lurking under your jacket.'

'I don't like wildlife.'

'You're not too keen on fish either, I hear,' Leon replied.

O'Dowd said nothing and jerked his head towards the dealers. 'Look at that, a Dutchman, an Egyptian and . . . an American,' he added, seeing a tall man join the group. 'He's a detective, you know, called Larry Hands. Interesting, don't you think?'

'Could be,' Leon replied, sipping at his drink.

'I won't run away.'

'Pardon?'

O'Dowd looked down at Leon's hand which still encircled his left wrist. 'I said I won't run away.'

'Sorry,' Leon replied, releasing his grip. 'Force of habit.'

'Why do you do that anyway?'

Leon's reply was tongue in cheek. 'It's the result of a bad upbringing, and public school insecurity.'

O'Dowd grinned. 'Seymour Bell went to public school too, didn't he?'

'Ah, but he suffers from the spanking syndrome.'

The Irishman's curiosity was alerted. 'The what?'

'The spanking syndrome. At public school, if you do something wrong you're spanked. Only they tell you that you'll be spanked in a week's time — giving you all that time to dread it. It builds up the fear level. So when the spanking actually happens it's a relief. Ergo,' he concluded easily, 'spanking becomes synonymous with relief and, because we poor Englishmen are so sexually retarded, as we get older that physical relief turns into sexual relief and spanking becomes a highly desirable form of activity. It intrigues foreigners.'

'You sound like an enthusiast yourself.'

'Oh no, I'm more into ball games,' Leon replied innocently. 'Tennis, you know.'

O'Dowd laughed and turned his attention back to the group. But although his eyes remained on the Dutchman he was wondering about Leon Graves. Too many times he had been pursued by the indomitable Englishman; too many times he had been hounded out of Italy or Spain, moving lucrative businesses, hiding forgers, paying people to spread false trails. Leon Graves had cost him a great deal of money over the years, and a great deal of irritation. The Irishman smiled to himself — irritation and money were one thing, but being caught was another, and Leon Graves hadn't caught him yet.

The champagne tasted good against his tongue as he drank. He would have to be careful now that he was using new people like Victor Mellor. New people, he realised, could be dangerous. He swallowed, the coolness of the liquid stroking his throat. Yes, he must be careful. The Bracelet was back.

'Just boys?'

'What?'

O'Dowd repeated the question. 'I asked if Seymour Bell was just interested in boys?'

'From what I hear it's just young men, which is fortunate.'

'How come?'

'It makes him vulnerable,' Leon replied, his gaze resting on O'Dowd's suit. 'You really do dress fearfully well. I find it so difficult to get suits to fit. I have them made, like my shirts.' He tugged at his cuff. 'Beauchamp and Treeves on St James's, they make the best collars and cuffs in London. So good for long, lanky, English limbs.'

O'Dowd smiled. 'I wear Giorgio Armani myself. The material's first rate, and the cut's perfect. They fit like a dream.'

Leon's eyes raked down Mike O'Dowd's exquisite suit, and then, with devastating innocence, he said, 'How fascinating. I do so long to see you in one.'

★ ★ ★

Ron was slumped in a chair when the phone rang. Slowly he got to his feet and answered. 'Yes?'

'It's Zoe,' she replied, her voice steady although the events of the previous evening had alarmed her so much that she had spent the whole day trying to understand what had happened and to map out her future. 'I'll be home in ten minutes. Hide that painting on the easel, will you?'

'Do you want me to come and meet you?'

Zoe smiled down the phone. 'No. Just put the kettle on and I'll be there before the water boils.'

Zoe had no sooner arrived and taken off her coat than the doorbell rang and Victor walked in. His face was livid, his voice dropped low with pent-up fury. Ron took one look at him and disappeared into the bedroom. Peter crouched under the table.

'Where the bloody hell have you been, you stupid bitch?'

Zoe rounded on him. 'How dare you talk to

me like that!' she shouted. 'I'm the one who should be angry. How could you take me to a place like that? Those men were criminals, you stupid sod!'

'Stupid!' he repeated, raking his hands through his hair. 'Who's the bloody fool who said, 'Have you sold many?''

'I wasn't thinking — '

'That much was obvious!' Victor snapped. 'You're just a snivelling kid. I gave you a chance — '

'*You* gave *me* a chance?' she repeated incredulously. '*I'm* the one who does the fakes, *I'm* the one who's making the money for us!'

'But I'm the one with all the contacts,' he shouted back, pointing his finger at her. 'You're a bloody menace. You need some sense knocking into you — '

'Don't touch her!' Ron shouted, walking into the room and standing protectively in front of Zoe.

Victor was unimpressed. 'She's a dead loss!' he snapped, trying to push him aside.

With an impatient gesture, Ron grabbed hold of Victor's jacket and jerked his brother towards him. Taken by surprise, Victor tried to shake him off, his fist pounding into his stomach. Ron winced, but still managed to swing his fist upwards into his brother's jaw. Victor lost his balance and crashed back into the table, brushes, paints and paper falling on top of him. With blood pouring from his face, he struggled to his feet, anger making him ugly as he lunged towards Ron again, his hands grabbing his brother round the neck as they both fell on to the floor.

'Stop it!' Zoe shouted, trying to pull them apart. 'For God's sake, stop it.'

Victor's eyes were blank, his hands fixed round his brother's throat, Ron's face reddening as he fought for air. In desperation, Zoe pulled viciously at Victor's hair, jerking his head back and giving Ron the chance to throw him off.

Shaken, he struggled to his feet and gasped for breath. 'Don't ever touch her,' he said hoarsely, his face tight with fury. 'You do, and I'll kill you.'

'Do me a favour!' Victor sneered, wiping the blood off his face with a handkerchief. 'You fight like a bleeding ponce.'

'If you touch Zoe I'll kill you,' Ron repeated, rubbing the red weals on his neck and sitting down heavily on the settee. 'I will, I swear it!' he shouted.

A loud banging started from the flat next door. 'We've woken the neighbours,' Zoe said wearily.

The banging started up again and Victor swung round, slamming his fists against the walls angrily. 'Shut up, you bastards!'

'No, you shut up,' Zoe snapped. 'We have to live here.' She dropped her voice and added calmly, 'I'll get us all some coffee.'

Minutes later she returned to find Ron and Victor sitting opposite each other in silence, the threat of violence palpable in the shabby room. 'I don't want us to fight. We're family, we should work together.'

'That's what the whole bloody argument's

about,' Victor said sourly.

Zoe kept her temper as she replied. 'I'll say it once more — I work with *you*, and not anyone else. Certainly not with Candadas.'

'You didn't keep to your side of the bargain — '

'I did! But I had to stay in New York, I couldn't leave Harland.'

'He's not a bloody kid, Zoe. You should have come back to finish off the work here.'

She struggled to keep her patience. 'We're doing very well, Victor, but we must take things slowly. I've told you, if you drench the art market too soon we'll be found out.'

'I have contacts abroad, not just in London — '

'Contacts which you never told me about!' she shouted, and then lowered her voice. 'I don't feel safe with you, Victor. You're greedy, and you're only in it for the money — '

'You want money too!'

'Yes, but not for the same reasons,' she explained wearily. 'I want the money for Dad and for . . . my own satisfaction. Don't look at me like that, Victor! I know I'm doing something illegal, but I certainly don't want to get caught because you're being reckless. Frankly, the whole business is beginning to scare me.'

'I don't want to get caught either,' Victor hissed, dabbing at his face and turning to Ron. 'I'm still bleeding, you bastard,' he said, eyeing his brother warily as he got up and left the room.

'You nearly blew it the other night with Candadas, Zoe — '

'I'm glad. I want nothing to do with them,' she said coldly. 'When the lights went out I was terrified. And don't try and fool me, Victor, you were looking none too comfy yourself.'

'Whatever you say, Candadas is a good forger,' he replied.

'I agree, but we don't know if he's reliable or not.' She paused. 'How *did* you get to know him?'

'That's my business.'

'Oh no, Victor, not any more!' Zoe replied sharply. 'I know you use bent dealers to sell the fakes, but *who* are they? And *where* are they, Victor? I'm the one who's forging the pictures, I'm the one who could be jailed, I'm the one who's most at risk. Not you!'

What she said made sense, but Victor was too arrogant to lose face and refused to back down. 'We can still use Candadas — '

'NO! We won't use him!' Zoe replied hotly. 'Or I'll stop working with you.'

Victor blinked, the words smarting. He needed Zoe and he knew it. The knowledge made him bitter and in an attempt to conceal his feelings, he tried to frighten her. 'You're in no position to dictate terms to me. I only have to expose you and you would be finished for ever.'

Zoe faltered, thinking she had misheard. 'You wouldn't give me away, Victor,' she said disbelievingly. 'We're family, doesn't that count for anything?'

'No.'

The man in front of her was no longer Victor, he was an imposter, more closely related to the likes of Mike O'Dowd than the Mellor family. She had known she could never trust her brother, even from childhood she had been wary of him. But this was something more, a betrayal of blood. Love me, hate me.

'You wouldn't do that to me?' she asked, her voice dropping to a whisper. 'No, you couldn't . . . could you?'

'Not if you toe the line, Zoe. But if you don't, I'll ruin you. By God, I will.'

'But I'm your sister,' she repeated, bewildered.

The words faded on her lips. There was no security anywhere, she realised. There were promises, hopes, but no real safety. Just as her mother had deceived and rejected her, so her brother was prepared to abandon her. I am only welcomed and loved for my usefulness, she thought, not for my own self.

Victor's anger was dispersing fast. He had seen Zoe's expression, and heard how her voice had changed. She knew her place now, he thought, she was under his thumb again and he could afford to relax. Taking in a deep breath he leaned across and tapped her on the knee. 'Just keep on working as you are doing, and we'll be fine. No trouble.'

She hesitated. 'If I agree to carry on, will you drop Candadas?'

Victor smiled, his eyes yellow in the lamplight. 'I'll drop Candadas,' he agreed, 'and we'll keep it all in the family.'

19

Two years passed. Zoe continued to work with Harland Goldberg and to make forgeries for Victor. After their argument a form of uneasy peace settled on them both and a peculiar form of confidence grew in Zoe with the knowledge that her fakes were being bought and sold by the very people who dismissed her as nothing other than a rich man's mistress. It amused her to know that a picture she had worked on in the cramped surroundings of the flat would be exhibited in Jimmy van Goyen's gallery, the blond Dutchman lauding it to the skies as he sold it on to a collector. The feeling of power left her almost euphoric and, as Victor was arranging all the deals, she began to feel divorced from the situation, and dangerously safe.

Yet she continued to resent the control which Victor exercised over her. Loyal to a fault, she had previously made allowances for her brother, but his threat had changed her attitude. If Victor wanted to play dirty, she reasoned, then she had to be in a position to defend herself. So she devised a plan of action — and swore that from now on, Zoe Mellor was going to protect herself.

Harland's infatuation was constant. Aware that she was never going to be his mistress, he nevertheless loved and encouraged her, seeing in her a continuation of his life's work. Above all he knew she needed his protection, that her vulnerability made her lonely just as her loyalty kept her running backwards and forwards to Rochdale. In him she found a reliability she had never experienced before, and clung to him as a child might.

He had no knowledge of the fakes however. That was Zoe's compulsive secret, the shadow side of her personality. She needed the security Harland provided, but she also needed the sordid side of life which Victor represented. As a child she had never known in which mood her mother would greet her; her world had been a series of uncertainties, which, as she grew, formed the pattern of her life, the insecurity becoming finally addictive. Zoe Mellor found her true self only when swinging from one extreme to another, the alternating stimulus of security and danger providing the extension of her childhood experience.

But even if she agreed to play the game to his rules, she was not prepared to let Victor have it all his own way. Within weeks of their argument, she began to trade for herself, placing a simple 'George Frederic Watts' sketch in a small auction and entering it under the name of Mrs Belinda Noble. The 'history' of the drawing was simple: Mrs B. Noble had been left the sketch by her grandmother and now wanted to sell it. The auction house saw nothing suspicious and accepted the details of Mrs Noble's bank account in Manchester, which Zoe had opened the previous month. When the Watts was sold as an original, a cheque winged its way to the bank and Zoe split the money with Ron, opening a savings account for his half and sending hers to her father.

In the year that the Pope was shot and Prince Charles married Lady Diana Spencer, Zoe began to expand her talents. Long hours were spent perfecting the fakes, using only the correct inks and paints, and drying out each layer thoroughly before continuing. Various coats of varnish were applied, some too quickly, so that the previous layer of oil paint would crack. Others were left to dry and then varnished, heated in the oven in the kitchen, and then rubbed over with soot to get grime into the cracks. This way they looked genuine, as did the backs of the forgeries where the old canvas showed. Meticulous as ever, Zoe also used old, worn stretchers, some even slightly buckled, as supports for the paintings. It gave the air of authenticity to use such antique stretchers, although Ron had to spend much of his weekends searching junk shops and flea markets for worthless paintings just so Zoe could use the canvas or the stretchers. Every painting was a work of art in itself, and when she spent longer than was strictly necessary on some pieces, she was amazed to find Victor pliant.

'You see, they must be right, then no one suspects anything, and we won't be found out.'

Victor smiled, agreeable to a fault.

It was several weeks later that Zoe was working on a Bonington watercolour fake, struggling over the washes, her fringe falling over her eyes as she leaned towards the special handmade paper. Irritated, she tied her hair back with a piece of string and bent down again over the picture. A seascape looked up at her, a fishing boat and two small figures sketched in as Zoe's eyes flicked from the open book beside her back to the paper. But it wasn't gelling together, the colours were too bland, the drawing amateurish. Glancing at the clock, Zoe saw that it was only seven, hours before Ron would be home from the dog track. She tried again, but gave up, yawned, and went into the kitchen to rinse our her paintbrushes.

The water hissed into the sink, the colours melting into the whirlpool as it swept down the drain, the brushes spreading their fine hair like wet fans, the shiny ferules spotted with spray. Mesmerised, she watched, unaware that some-one had come in and was standing behind her. A touch on her shoulder made her turn sharply, her heart banging.

'Sorry! I didn't mean to frighten you!'

She looked at Steven Foreshaw in disbelief. 'I . . . '

'It's good to see you.'

'How did you get in?' she asked, glancing round. 'And how did you know where I lived?'

'Alan told me,' he answered, looking at Zoe avidly. She was quite different from the girl he had made love to in the studio. Her face was tired, the make-up worn off, and her hair was pulled back, but she had a poise which hurt him. Zoe Mellor was a city girl, no trace of Rochdale left. The thought made him hostile. He had hoped to find her unsure of herself. Instead, he was the one who felt unsure.

'You look good, Zoe.'

'You too,' she said fatuously, turning back to the brushes. He seemed taller than she remembered, his hair sporting its dramatic streak, his clothes proclaiming the legend 'artist'. But for all of that, she found his presence disturbing, her mind slipping back to their love-making, her loneliness suddenly dragging at her. Flicking the excess water off her brushes, Zoe was about to walk back into the lounge when she remembered the fake lying fully exposed on the table only feet from where Steven stood.

'I thought . . . ' she began, hesitating and looking towards the table.

Steven followed her gaze and in an effort to distract him, Zoe leaned forward to kiss his cheek. He responded to her immediately, his lips pressed against her mouth as he gripped her, the old desire momentarily obliterating the bitterness.

Zoe pulled away. 'Hey, I was just welcoming you,' she said lightly, walking into the lounge.

Her attitude puzzled him and he followed her. 'So you're still painting?' he said, spotting the picture and moving towards it.

Zoe was there first and grabbed the paper, holding it to her chest. 'No! Don't look! It's so amateur — and you're so talented,' she blustered idiotically. But it was the right thing to say to Steven.

His confidence restored, he put his arms around her. 'I was always a good teacher,' he said, trying to pull the painting from her. Zoe hung on. Steven tugged. 'For God's sake, you'll

300

rip it!' he said finally, letting go. 'Don't show me, if it bothers you so much.' He sat down and stretched his legs out in front of him. 'Come and sit down instead.'

Still gripping the picture, Zoe hesitated, wanting the intimacy he offered, but holding back. Then he held out his hand to her, and by the gesture he somehow obliterated the years and experiences which had slid between them. Quickly he pulled her down on to the settee, his eyes fixed on her unblinkingly. His attention was so distracted, in fact, that he never noticed the painting slip from Zoe's fingers, her left foot pushing it under the couch out of sight.

'I've missed you,' he said thickly, catching hold of her, his hands undoing the string which tied back her hair, his tongue prising her lips apart.

She moved against him, trying to pull away and then relaxing as she realised that she wanted him. Having denied herself any kind of sexual relationship for two long years, she responded without thinking, her hands exploring his body, her lips tracing the line of his throat and chest as she unbuttoned his shirt. Whispering urgently in her ear, Steven unzipped her dress, his hands searching each part of her, his fingers warm against her flesh.

'Tell me what you want,' he said, his eyes dark.

Zoe smiled. 'I want you.'

He rolled on top of her and bent to kiss the rise of her stomach. 'No, tell me exactly what you want.'

The excitement hummed inside her as she replied, 'I want you to make love to me.'

He kissed her. 'Say please.'

She frowned. 'What?'

Roughly Steven caught hold of her wrists and lowered his weight on top of her, his face altered. 'I told you, say please.'

'Steven — '

His hands clenched her wrists more tightly, his fingernails tearing into the skin. Zoe struggled and then relaxed, her mouth opening obediently to say the magic words to take her to oblivion.

*　*　*

Zoe was in the bath when Steven finished dressing and lit himself a cigarette thoughtfully. He had come down to London to see Zoe because he couldn't forget her. But even making love to her he could not forget that she had left him, humiliated him . . . and he could not forgive her.

He waited to hear the water running and then leaned over and pulled out the painting from under the settee. Frowning, he pored over it and wondered why Zoe would spend her time faking a Bonington and then take the trouble to hide it. She was obviously doing well in London and had a good job, so why was she doing this? He was still trying to understand it when Zoe slipped out of the bath and peered through the half open bathroom door. For a minute she watched him and then slipped back, unheard.

*　*　*

Ahmed Fazir was back in London, his Rolls Royce depositing him at his gallery on the Old Brompton Road, his large form hustling through the rain into the entrance. He paused and passed his coat to his manageress, Minnie Simmonds. 'What weather! It's sunny in New York.'

She returned the smile mechanically, looking into Fazir's dark-complexioned face and noticing that good living had increased his jowls and made the skin puffy round his eyes. 'Dr Beaumont is coming in to see you at eleven, sir,' she said evenly, her schoolmarm appearance and voice providing an invincible shield against any kind of familiarity. 'Did you have a good flight?'

'Not bad,' Fazir responded, picking up his mail and beckoning for a coffee before continuing into his office. The room was crowded, Persian carpets on the floor and on the side walls, a variety of busts and statues covering the mantelpiece and window sills. Behind his desk a glassed area was walled off, a plethora of exotic plants growing behind, their fleshy leaves illuminated by spotlights. It looked wonderful from a distance, Minnie Simmonds repeatedly said to her mother, but the place was full of dead flies and it was murder to water the plants. Not that Ahmed Fazir ever thought about things like that, she grumbled.

Heavily he lowered himself into a chair and went through his mail, throwing half of it in the waste-paper bin and jamming a forefinger on the buzzer.

Minnie appeared immediately. 'Yes, sir?'

'This letter from Harland Goldberg — ring up

and make an appointment for me to go over and see him this afternoon, will you?'

She nodded. 'Anything else?'

Fazir looked up. God, the woman was a dragon, and she looked like his first wife. He smiled insincerely. 'No, that's it, thank you.'

Closing the door behind her, Minnie Simmonds turned and with a childish gesture put out her tongue.

Harland Goldberg was not pleased to see Ahmed Fazir, having never forgiven him for the indelicate incident at Courtney-Blye's all that time ago. Repeated protestations that he had merely been attending a meeting there had not convinced Harland, but the Egyptian was too important a dealer to dismiss — besides, a scandal was only a scandal for so long. And after all he had the upper hand: the plot had failed on two counts, Zoe was still in London, and several dealers now owed him a considerable favour.

He greeted the Arab with his hand extended as Fazir towered over him, smiling. 'How's the heart?'

'Still going. How's yours?'

Fazir frowned. 'I had it broken in Paris, mended in Cannes, and removed by some bitch in Cairo.'

'You love your reputation,' Harland said, sitting down, Fazir beside him. 'I have my suspicions that you're actually celibate.'

Fazir frowned. 'If all else fails, I'll consider it.'

'So what are you interested in today?'

'The big Reynolds portrait,' Fazir answered, leaning back and taking out some snuff.

'Snuff now?' Harland asked, his tone cold.

'It's better than cocaine — it doesn't rot your nose.' He pointed to Harland's generous beak. 'Mind you, both of us could do with a little less.'

'Big noses mean money,' Harland replied, his mind turning back to the Reynolds. 'Do you want to see the painting?'

Fazir nodded and the picture was brought up from the storeroom, supported by two gallery hands, and displayed in front of Fazir for his approval. He sniffed and peered at it, leaning forward on the couch. 'Nice.'

'It's more than nice, and it's in good condition. You know how Reynolds fooled around with his materials? Well, there's no bitumen in this paint, so there's no cracking. It's beautiful.'

Fazir sniffed again. 'What about the provenance?'

Harland turned to Mona. 'Ask Miss Mellor to bring the provenance will you?'

Zoe materialised a few moments later and with a look of complete disdain, passed the papers to Fazir. She was wearing a fine wool dress which accentuated her slimness, silk stockings which showed her legs to advantage, and her face was impassively lovely under the dark surround of hair.

'You're as beautiful as ever, Miss Mellor,' the Egyptian said without a hint of embarrassment.

Harland sighed. 'I could get a fortune for this painting at auction, Ahmed. What do you say? Do you want it?'

Fazir's attention returned to the picture. He

liked it very much and he knew that portraits of consumptive Englishwomen sold well in New York. 'How much?'

Harland pointed to the figure on the bottom of the provenance.

Fazir sniffed. 'Expensive.'

'You have customers who would pay that without blinking. Incidentally, there was a very interesting little tidbit of gossip I heard the other day,' Harland said lightly. 'There were no names mentioned, naturally, but apparently one of the dealers sold a very valuable picture and the temp who was working in his gallery let the buyer take it home, thinking they were a regular customer.' Fazir's face was impassive, but his eyes were alert. 'Of course they had no address to bill so the dealer lost over forty thousand pounds . . . until he hit on a little scheme to recover his costs. Do you know something? He had three copies of the bill drawn up for forty thousand pounds, and had them sent off to three of his wealthiest Middle Eastern customers, knowing that it would be paid without question by their accountants.' Fazir took in his breath as Harland continued. 'And he was right, all three paid! So he made a profit of eighty thousand pounds just like that.' Harland smiled warmly. 'It's amazing what people get away with, isn't it?'

'It's a good painting — that Reynolds of yours,' Fazir said finally. 'I think we can come to some arrangement.'

20

She came out of the mist like a ghost or an island of the dead, her buildings pooled in the water, the boat drawing closer, the bells of St Mark's chiming the hour. Under a fierce February sky Venice was shrouded, the misted windows overhanging the dark, fathomless water, shutters closed, the decay evident in the face of the crusted plaster-work and the dank smudge of the lapping tide. Arranged in rows, the gondolas knocked against their flaking, barley-sugar posts, the vast silent square before them scattered with snow, although as the boat reached the steps, the snow shifted suddenly, and a hundred pigeons took flight and winged themselves into the grudging mist above.

From windows, a few lights burned into the gloomy afternoon, while a cat scurried across a bridge, water rats searching an underground realm of their own and coming up for breath in dense alleyways, or by the edges of the blank, foul-smelling canals. Carefully, Zoe climbed out of the boat and walked up the few steps to the square, the railing cold to her touch, a fine rain making the paving stones treacherous underfoot.

Harland followed her and she watched him and thought back to what he had told her the previous day. 'I have an old friend in Venice, Marcella Rimimi, the Marchesa Marcella Rimimi, a lady with a vast fortune left to her by her husband.' A stab of envy had pricked Zoe as she listened. 'Even though she's wealthy, now and again she needs to raise funds quickly and *discreetly* and asks me to sell something for her.' He had smiled and glanced away, remembering. Remembering what? Zoe had thought.

'I thought we would get ourselves settled at the hotel and then call on Marcella this afternoon,' Harland said, dragging Zoe's attention back to the present and opening an umbrella over their heads. 'You'll like her.'

No, Zoe thought, I will hate her. I will hate anyone who takes you away from me.

Afraid that he had somehow read her thoughts, she turned to look at him, but Harland was gazing away, his eyes searching the plaintive stretch of old stone buildings filled with memories. The rain pelted down on them as they walked, for once not in unison, Zoe feeling a sense of loneliness which rendered her silent, the plaintive sound of a cheap radio echoing sadly on the rain-damp stone. They walked on over muted bridges, the water slapping at the cold buildings, wooden archways rotting, the tide marks striping the narrow streets where people squeezed past them without acknowledgement. It was obvious that the Carnival was about to begin as many shop windows were hung with masks, face after face proving an audience to the onlooker, each of them hanging on tired strings under the dull afternoon light. They registered in the hotel and unpacked, each in their separate rooms, and later they met in the foyer, ill at ease with each other.

The villa of the Marchesa Marcella Rimimi stood at the head of a short street, its plaster painted façade weathered to a faded azure, its doors natural dark wood, the windows glowering under the Venetian sky. On arrival, they were shown into a drawing room in which a fire burned, the mantelpiece surrounding it shaped into the form of two nudes, the firelight making the marble yellow as it crept over it, along the silk carpet and under the gilded chairs. Due to the overcast sky the room was already gloomy, and the impression of sombre darkness was aided by a series of oppressive murals which covered every inch of the walls. Zoe glanced round, and then turned at the sound of the Marchesa's feet behind her.

Luminous white skin framed indigo eyes, her ivory hair tied back in a dense coil at the base of her neck. A silk suit lingered against her long legs as she moved, the fabric swinging from her fine shoulders and framing the delicate neck. As she approached Harland she smiled, kissing his cheeks, and then she moved towards Zoe, one manicured hand extended. The Marchesa Marcella Rimimi was as fabulous as her city and possibly eighty years of age. 'Dear child,' she said, with unaffected warmth. 'You are welcome to my home.'

Ashamed of her previous envy, Zoe sat down and glanced towards Harland who was scrutinising Marcella unashamedly. 'You look wonderful. Younger than ever.'

She smiled and squeezed his hand, affection apparent. 'But you have been ill,' she said, frowning. 'You should take more rest.'

'I'm busy.'

'Too busy to live?' she teased him, ringing for some tea to be brought in to them. Her voice was playful, intimate, her attitude confident and almost seductive. Zoe watched her, fascinated. 'I asked you here for a favour.' The Marchesa glanced over to Zoe. 'I know I can trust you. Anyone Harland trusts is my confidante also.'

Zoe smiled. The afternoon shadows lengthened, the fire yawning with warmth.

'You know how committed I am to the Venice in Peril fund?' the Marchesa continued. He nodded. It was the passion of Marcella's life. 'Well, they need funds, and as you know, my money is now largely in trust for my grandchildren and my son.' She turned to Zoe. 'He is a fine boy, a lawyer. He's done well, but although he looks after my affairs, sometimes he leaves me a little . . . ' she struggled for the word '. . . financially embarrassed. So that's when I call for Harland!'

The door opened and a maid came in with tea, laying down the tray on the low table between them. The Marchesa waited until the door closed before she returned to her original theme.

'So I had a brilliant idea,' she enthused, her eyes luminous with delight. 'The Venice Carnival begins the day after tomorrow and I've organised an auction to be held here on Saturday.' Harland

310

raised his eyebrows. 'It's for my friends, some Italian dealers, and some useful contacts.' She smiled again. 'The works have been given by wealthy families or interested organisations, and all money from the auction will go to the fund . . . You see, it's the only possible way I can donate.'

Harland frowned. 'But you could have come to me.'

She shook her head. 'I'm always coming to you and asking you to buy paintings — and he always does.' She turned to Zoe. 'Even when he doesn't want them! No, Harland, this time I've arranged everything to suit myself, and everyone will still think of me as a splendid benefactress.' She paused. 'I just thought that if there was anything in the auction you *really* wanted then you could buy it more cheaply from me beforehand.'

Harland sipped his tea and glanced over to Zoe. It was a clever ploy and it amused him. This way the Marchesa would raise money at the sale *and* from a secret deal with him. The Italian aristocracy, he mused, was still marvellously adept at politics.

'I would love to see the paintings,' he said smoothly, 'when we've had our tea and you've told me your news.'

The villa was immense, room after glowering room crowded with dark antiques, all stretching out from an arched colonnade, any daylight making little impression on the shadowed walls. Zoe walked behind her companions, lingering over the Marchesa's impressive collection of oil

311

paintings, each lit by ornate picture lights.

'Do you like this one?' The Marchesa asked, beckoning for Zoe to come and look. 'This is a Correggio.'

Zoe stared at the face of the young girl depicted. 'Correggio?'

The Marchesa nodded, but behind her Harland frowned and shook his head. Taking her cue, Zoe moved on.

The paintings for the auction were locked away behind the carved double doors of the library, the Marchesa unfastening the lock and standing back for her guests to enter. The room seemed compact as it was virtually square in shape, the walls lined with books, light coming in from a bank of high windows and striking two massive globes which were planted firmly on the polished terracotta floor.

The Marchesa pulled the doors closed behind her and gestured to the pictures. 'Well, what is your opinion, Harland? Some works have not arrived yet and some will come tomorrow, but most are here.'

Harland moved across the room, past the globes and into the shadow. 'I need some more light, please, Marcella.'

She flicked on the switch and the paintings came into view more clearly, the colours glowing against the faded murals on the walls behind.

He smiled, crouching down for a better look. 'Andrea del Sarto,' he said happily. 'I love his work, Marcella. I always have.'

She walked over to him and glanced down. 'I know you have, Harland,' she said, without pursuing the point. 'But what do you think about these?'

He glanced towards the far wall where a Tintoretto, a tiny Rubens and a Berchem were stacked in a row. 'Ah, Nicolaes Berchem,' he said confidentially. 'This is a fine landscape.'

Zoe watched both of them, but remained silent. Her attention was fixed on the Marchesa, on her gestures, the way she smiled, a sudden, almost wearying response which made her seem anxious. Harland continued to scrutinise the paintings, his enthusiasm immense. After another minute, he stood up and looked around. 'It's a long time since I was in here,' he said, 'but this room never changes.' He walked towards the library shelves and counted along the third row. 'One, two, three, four . . . ah . . . ' Carefully he took down a book and turned the pages, his hands hardly brushing the leaves. 'Dante . . . '

'Dante,' the Marchesa reponded, her voice low. 'You remembered?'

Harland glanced over to her, his eyes fixed on the woman whose hand now rested on one of the huge globes. Her fingers almost obliterated Italy, her thumb curling towards England.

'I never forgot . . . ' he said, then, suddenly embarrassed, he replaced the book and turned back to the Andrea del Sarto painting. 'Tell me how much you want, and I'll buy it.'

Zoe expected some response, some rush of gratitude, but when she turned to look at the Marchesa there was only an expression of unutterable regret on her face, a loneliness which

313

reached across the ancient shadowed room and moved her so much that she lowered her eyes.

★ ★ ★

They were walking across the Bridge of Sighs an hour or so later when Harland turned to Zoe. 'Did you know that the Doge of Venice built this bridge between his palace and the state prison, so that his enemies could be taken across it after sentencing?'

'Hence the name?'

He nodded, changing the subject. 'I've known Marcella for many years.'

'I was jealous of her before I came,' Zoe said quietly.

Harland stopped walking and looked at her. 'What?'

'I was jealous of the Marchesa,' she repeated, glancing down into the dark water.

'Oh, Zoe . . . ' he said gently.

She shrugged, embarrassment making her vulnerable. 'I thought you loved her,' she explained, glancing away to watch a woman brush the high water off some stone steps.

'I love *you*,' Harland said, continuing quickly, 'Marcella is a very old friend. She was spectacularly beautiful when young, but when her husband died she never remarried, instead she devoted herself to her son and then to her grandchildren, and the Venice in Peril fund.' He gestured to the buildings which surrounded them. 'She raises money to keep this city restored, to try and stop the damage that the sea

314

does yearly. It's an impossible task, and she knows it.'

'But it's worthwhile.'

'I'm not sure. Venice always makes me feel old.'

Zoe nudged him gently with her elbow, affection restored. 'That's the kind of thing I say. You're supposed to be the romantic.'

'Too romantic for my own good,' he said, slipping his arm through hers. 'You noticed the Correggio, didn't you?'

'Is it a fake?'

He nodded. 'Yes . . . but she doesn't know and I don't intend to tell her.'

Zoe changed the subject tactfully. 'I've got the most incredible costume for the auction.'

His spirits lifted immediately. 'What's it like?'

Flirtatiously, she moved away and then said over her shoulder, 'I shan't tell you! It will be a surprise. You are wearing fancy dress, aren't you?'

'I shall wear my costume with pride,' he said, bowing, 'and escort the most beautiful woman in Venice.'

Zoe remembered the Marchesa and glowed at the compliment. 'I shall make you proud.'

'You always do,' he said softly. 'You always do.'

It had been arranged as an auction, but Marcella's reputation was such that everyone knew a party would follow. Guests were to arrive at the villa around eight, the auction would be held at nine. Sumptuous menus had been drawn up, wines personally selected, the villa decorated with exotic flowers and immense swags of fruit, no detail overlooked. Harland had called on Marcella the previous day to find her excited and full of the auction, her fine hands tossing the bunch of acceptances towards Harland.

'Are all the paintings here now?' he asked.

'All but a few,' she replied, clasping her hands together and leaning towards him. 'Have you a costume?'

'Of course, not that I want to wear it.'

'You have to! Half the fun of the auction is that no one will know *who* is buying.' The thought excited her. 'You won't know who's standing next to you!'

Harland grimaced. 'How many are coming?'

'Oh, it's nothing grand, about a hundred people, that's all.'

'I remember the party you threw when I first came here,' he said and then paused, watching her face alter, the memory creeping up on both of them.

★   ★   ★

Harland did not like his costume. He said so repeatedly, pulling the cape around his shoulders, the material slipping between his fingers and making him irritable. 'I can't wear this blasted thing,' he snapped. 'I look like a fool.'

Zoe sighed and, ignoring his bad temper, leaned over the balcony of the hotel room. A man paused on the dark street below, turned his masked face up to the window, smiled, and walked on.

'Well, I'm going to get ready,' she said, leaving

316

Harland, her spirits lifting as she went back into her room. Her own costume lay on the bed, a black taffeta gown edged in gold, the matching mask beside it, large enough to conceal most of her face. For some inexplicable reason, her thoughts wandered back to Rochdale as she changed, drawing the dress over her body, fastening the waist and fluffing out the wide skirt. Carefully, she piled her dark hair on top of her head and paused, looking at her reflection and remembering her mother. In the same instant other memories crowded in on her, the smell of the hot kitchen returned vividly, as did the sound of Peter barking in the yard outside and the sight of her mother's hand extended through the railings to wave goodbye on her first day at school. Leaning towards the mirror, Zoe studied her reflection, seeing traces of Jane Mellor and then, suddenly alarmed, she tied the mask over her face and left.

Harland opened his door on the third knock, saw her, and paused. There was no hint of the girl he had met in Manchester, no uncertainty, only a beautiful enigma.

She moved him immensely. 'You look . . . '

'Like an ass?'

He laughed and walked out into the corridor with her.

The villa was ablaze with lights when they arrived, the strains of music playing over the deep night water, the dark sky brilliant with fireworks. In their sumptuous costumes, men and women mingled, some masked only across the eyes, others hooded and cloaked, their faces

317

totally hidden. The atmosphere of decadence was palpable, the guests already behaving with the familiarity anonymity afforded them, straying hands passing scribbled notes for reckless meetings, couples fondling each other and leaning against the raised dais in the ballroom where the auction was to be held.

'It's the Carnival atmosphere that makes everyone act like this,' Harland explained, passing Zoe a glass of champagne. 'If the sale's a success Marcella will make a fortune tonight.'

As the music grew louder, voices rose over the strains of Prokofiev amidst bubbles of indulgent laughter as the next fireworks were ignited, the white trail of fire feathering the indigo night, the smell of burnt powder mixed with winter flowering jasmine intoxicating. Pushing forward into the garden for a better view, the guests shrieked with excitement, bare backs exposed in exotic dresses, some hands exploring and grasping, others extended for glasses or adjusting masks. It was all pretence — and picturesque decadence.

'Ladies and gentlemen,' a voice announced over the speaker. 'The auction is about to commence.'

In a rush to get the best seats, everyone hurried back into the ballroom, the hum of voices raised in admiration as the Marchesa ascended the dais. She stood, head erect, her features uncovered — hers was the triumph and had to be recognised as such. Under the bright lights her costume shone faultlessly silver, the bodice high around her long neck, the sleeves almost covering her fine hands. Glowing, she announced the opening of the auction and welcomed the auction-eer on to the stage as she left it.

He began slowly, his Italian indecipherable to Zoe, who glanced at the first paintings and then turned her attention back to the guests, her eyes searching the crush of bodies around her. There was no one there she knew. At least, no one she could recognise. But then the auction was select, and one which only a few of the dealers would attend. A buzz went up around the ballroom as the Rubens was brought out supported by two of the Marchesa's staff. The bidding began and then escalated violently, Harland catching hold of Zoe's arm and pulling her nearer to the front where he could see more clearly. One by one the pictures arrived, Italian exchanged violently, bids thrown up and matched, or beaten, the atmo-sphere frenetic. The ballroom grew warmer, the voices more loud-pitched in excitement. Speak-ing Italian, Harland had the advantage over Zoe and even entered the bidding when the Nicolaes Berchem was brought out, his voice loud and clear as he became more and more elated, bid-ding against a man in a harlequin's costume.

Then with a shake of his head he dropped out. 'I've got the Andrea del Sarto,' he whispered to Zoe. 'I wasn't prepared to pay a stupid price for the Berchem.'

'It's in a good cause,' Zoe replied.

'Venice in Peril?' Harland asked, smiling. 'More like Harland in Peril if I'd spent all that on a landscape.'

She laughed and turned her eyes back to the stage and the penultimate lot, and froze. Before

319

her, displayed for all and sundry to see, was one of Lino Candadas's fakes in the manner of Bernadino Luini. The shock stunned her for a moment and she took a quick gulp of champagne to steady herself.

His interest aroused again, Harland began to bid. Without thinking, Zoe shook her head vigorously. 'Why not?' he asked, puzzled.

She opened her mouth to speak then stopped. How could she tell him it was a fake? He would ask her how she knew, and how could she explain that? How could she tell him that her brother had dealings with the forger? That she had met him herself? That the painting for which he was now bidding was a fake that she had seen in the vestry of a Methodist church in Wandsworth. She took another drink of champagne and then wondered how the fake got into the auction. It was only a small sale, not open to the public . . .

Beside her, Harland continued to bid blindly, squeezing her hand to reassure her as Zoe's head began to swim, her eyes travelling round the room in sheer panic. Then, with a dread feeling, she recognised the man standing by the entrance. Dressed in black, a large hat covering his head and a full face mask hiding his features. But she knew who it was. His gestures, the way he turned his head, the shape of his hand on the door. She recognised each action, each movement known from childhood. It could be no one else, it had to be him.

'Victor,' she said blindly.

'What?'

'Nothing,' Zoe said, smiling half-heartedly at Harland and trying to gather her thoughts. What was her brother doing there? The answer became obvious as she looked back towards the painting on the stage. Lino Candadas's fake — and Victor. So he had been double dealing, she thought, dully. How *could* he have been so stupid, and so greedy. And how could *she* have been so naive as not to have realised that he had been selling her fakes *and* Candadas's; that he had been risking the whole set-up, ignoring her advice and jeopardising her reputation and her safety. Damn him! she thought blindly. Damn him! Her hands slipped against the glass as she struggled to hold it, listening as Harland continued to bid for the fake, her panic rising, her eyes never leaving Victor whose own face was unreadable behind the mask. Had he seen her? Had he recognised her?

Up and up went the bids, whirling into the warm night, up into the lights, into the painted ceiling as Zoe stood transfixed. She couldn't hear the bidding any longer, her heart was pounding loudly enough to block out every other sound. She was going to lose everything. Money . . . success . . . safety. The words rushed round and round in her head. Money . . . success . . . safety . . .

A touch on her hand startled her and she jumped. Harland's face was strained and she swallowed, unable to speak. 'I lost it!' he said angrily. 'Damn! I wanted that painting, it was a beauty.'

Weak with relief, Zoe leaned against him and

he caught hold of her anxiously. 'Are you all right?'

'I'm hot . . . ' she stammered as he helped her towards the door.

People pushed against them, hands grasping as they fought to escape. Agonisingly slowly, they made their way through the crowd, Zoe pushing frantically against people as she fought her way to the door. When she got there the man turned, the mask impassive, no expression. Only the eyes were Victor's, and they saw her. They flickered, and although Zoe could not be sure, she was certain that after his initial shock, he smiled at her.

'Let us through!' Harland snapped, pushing past Victor, completely unaware of who he was. 'This lady is going to faint.'

Amused, Victor watched them pass. He had never expected Zoe to attend such a small auction, especially with big shot Goldberg in tow. Not that it wouldn't teach her a lesson, he thought slyly; dear Zoe would now realise that she wasn't the only good forger. She had competition, and besides, she had to realise that she couldn't boss him around. No one could, he thought, adjusting the brim of his hat and smiling hugely behind the blank mask. No one could tell Victor Mellor what to do.

His smile faded suddenly. Across the ballroom a man stared at him, his stocky figure in its clown's outfit deceptively harmless. Victor watched carefully, then some instinct warned him and he moved, spinning round and heading out of the door towards the dark streets.

'Are you all right?' Harland asked, his concern obvious.

'I'm fine,' Zoe answered, wanting to be alone to think. 'You go back in.'

'No, I'll — '

'Please,' she begged, 'I'm all right. I hate a fuss.'

Harland smiled. 'I'll be back in a minute then.'

She nodded and just as he walked away she saw Victor pass him in the entrance hall and rush for the door. Startled, she moved behind a pillar and watched her brother's departure, a sense of danger welling up in her. An instant later she saw the man in the clown's outfit follow her brother. Without a moment's hesitation, she moved into the dark night, her slippered feet silent on the street.

Victor was crossing a moonlit church square, his tall figure silhouetted clearly on the stone pavement. The clown followed, his heavier build making him slower, his feet sounding loudly on the cobbles as they crossed into the alleyway. Zoe followed both of them, her breath coming in gasps as she ran, the heavy dress slowing her progress. Blindly they raced across alleyways punctuated by church squares, bumping into masked revellers in the narrow streets, the gaudy shop lights striking them as they passed. With a frantic burst of acceleration, Victor managed to pull away, his long strides running past St Mark's as the clock boomed eleven, his masked face fixed on the street in front of him, his breath rasping in his chest.

And the clown kept coming, his steps beginning to falter, but persistent, his eyes never leaving the running figure in front of him. Zoe slipped, but righted herself, bunching up her dress in her hands, her slippers tearing on the cobbles. Victor was in danger, she knew it, her brother was in real danger. Terror kept her running, without a thought for her own safety, running down the alleyway where Victor had passed, the clown following him.

Suddenly she had lost them both and stopped running, standing alone, listening. The dark walls of the passageway surrounded her, an unearthly silence replacing the frantic sounds of running feet. She caught her breath, walked to the end of the alley and stepped out on to the bridge, looking around her, the water lapping beneath her feet, her reflection luminous. Unreal. Silence crept out from every stone, each shadow taking shape, each movement making her heart pound as she leaned heavily against the bridge and tried to get her bearings. She thought of Victor and tried to calm herself, forcing her mind to remember the layout of the streets, the shadowed buildings looming around her, unrecognisable in the dark.

Then she heard something. Not close, a little way off, the sound of feet. Only they weren't running this time, the clown wasn't chasing Victor any longer. No, she thought, her hair rising on the back of her neck — he was coming for her. Catching her breath, Zoe moved silently towards the alleyway, step by step. The bridge was too exposed, anyone could see her on the bridge, she had to get into the dark. Her feet made no sound as she edged towards the dark mouth of the passage, turning round repeatedly to see if anyone was behind her. She was almost there when suddenly a shadow moved, lurching out from the stone archway and seizing her arm.

Zoe screamed and struck out, her right hand catching the clown on the side of the head and making him reel backwards.

'Oh God, no! No!' she screamed, running in blind terror back across the bridge, a firework from the villa exploding overhead and illuminating the man who was chasing her, the clown's outfit with its white face terrifying in the moonlight.

'Help, someone help me!' she shouted, her voice echoing down the deserted streets. 'Help! Oh God . . . help,' she repeated, her voice fading as she struggled for breath, crossing another bridge and frantically looking down into the water for some other means of escape. If she could just find a boat . . .

He caught up with her before she had a chance to move and hit her where she stood, a firework blazing overhead, a streak of red bleeding against the blackness. Others followed, colours bursting into the dark, the orchestra striking up again from the villa, the music pounding down the deserted streets and stroking the dark well of the water.

The noise drowned out Zoe's cries as the clown slid his arm around her throat, his mouth so close to her ear that she could hear him panting for breath as she began to lose consciousness. Her strength was leaving her and her chest was bursting when he suddenly released her, stepping back to allow her body to drop heavily on to the bridge.

For several moments Zoe did not move, then agonisingly slowly she lifted her head and looked round. There was no sign of the clown. With a massive effort of will, she pulled herself upright and began to walk, gasping for air, her breathing rapid as she moved off the bridge; her eyes straining to see any sign of movement, just as her ears listened for any sound. Slowly, painfully, she began to run again, repeatedly glancing behind her as the fireworks exploded overhead, the noise roaring past her as she fled down alleyways and passages, looking. Intuition made her backtrack suddenly, retracing her steps for a whim, a second sense which drew her back to St Mark's. Crying out for her brother, Zoe's feet pounded on the cobbles of the alleyway which led her back, her skin crawling with terror, her eyes fixed on the light at the mouth of the exit.

As she entered the moonlit square, her whole body went rigid with fear and she turned. A low moaning came from a shape slumped against the wall behind her, the heavy fall of shadow making its outline indecipherable.

'Victor,' she said simply.

He was still masked, his body huddled into his costume as Zoe helped him to his feet, his tall figure leaning against her, his breathing coming in irregular gasps. Not a sound came from the square and there was no sign of the clown.

Nothing, only silence.

'Mike O'Dowd,' he whispered to her and then slumped suddenly, Zoe stumbling as her brother's weight dragged her down on to the pavement with him.

Landing awkwardly, Zoe pulled his arm from around her neck and touched his face. He felt chillingly cold. The moonlight shone down on the deserted square, picking them out, and illuminating Zoe's bare shoulders and upper breast. With a feeling of growing horror she lifted her hand and touched the wet smear which was streaked across her skin. It was dark, without colour, but it was obviously blood; even though it seemed black in the moonlight, it was obviously Victor's blood.

21

Ten minutes passed. In desperation, Zoe tried to lift Victor but he remained stubbornly immobile, his hat falling off as she moved him, one arm twisted under his body. She was still struggling when she heard footsteps, and with a futile desire to shield him, she shrank against her brother with her arms outstretched. Under the moonlight she seemed almost childlike, a small figure hunched against a creature which had no shape.

With a feeling of intense relief, Harland ran towards her. 'She's here!' he shouted to the two men who ran behind him. 'Give me a hand.'

'He's hurt,' Zoe said dully. 'My brother's been hurt.'

Kneeling down, Harland felt for the pulse in Victor's neck. 'It's all right. He's alive.'

Zoe's face was expressionless.

'It's going to be all right,' Harland repeated slowly, seeing that she was in shock.

The words made little sense to Zoe, all she knew was a dead sense of fear and the realisation that she was in danger. I've been such a fool, she thought disbelievingly. I thought it was a game, a harmless game . . .

The two men tried to move Victor and she turned quickly. 'Leave him alone!'

'They're friends,' Harland explained, astonished by her reaction. 'They won't hurt him, Zoe.'

She frowned at him and then nodded, struggling to her feet and walked beside the unconscious Victor as they carried him back across the square towards the villa.

'He'll have the best of care. Don't worry,' Harland said, trying to reassure her. 'I didn't know he was here, did you?' Zoe shook her head, but said nothing. 'Marcella's doctor will look after him.'

He could have been killed, she thought blindly. *I* could have been killed. Her hand moved up to her throat and she winced, glancing at Harland suspiciously. I should confide in him, she thought, dismissing the idea immediately as he turned to her, his face concerned. 'I love you' he had said earlier . . . She flinched suddenly, and remembered the clown. Mike O'Dowd, she thought, trying to recall what she had heard. What *was* it that Leon Graves had said about him?

'You're in shock,' Harland said gently, putting his arm around her. She leaned against him, his words distant, disorientated. I'm afraid, she realised hopelessly.

'Are you hurt, Zoe?'

'No.'

'Did you see what happened?' he asked.

The lie was already on her lips. One, two, buckle my shoe. 'Victor was attacked . . . by two men.'

'Why?'

'I think they were drunk.'

A firework burst overhead and Zoe jumped.

Tightly, Harland held on to her. 'You're safe, I

won't let anything happen to you. I promise.'

Marcella insisted that they all stay at the villa overnight, and hurriedly organised the rooms. If she was surprised by the turn of events she did not say so, merely ushered Zoe into a guest bedroom, drawing the curtains against the night outside.

'Drunkards!' she said disapprovingly. 'What can you expect?'

The first shock had lifted, and instead of dull blankness there was only an immediate urgency. 'Where's Victor?' Zoe asked. 'I have to see him.'

'You rest a little — ' the Marchesa began.

'I don't want to rest! I want my brother!' Zoe wrenched open the door and followed Marcella to a bedroom down the hallway. Below, the party was still in full flight, the noise of revellers travelling up the stairs, a few masked faces peering up through the bannisters. They could be anyone, Zoe thought bitterly as she walked over to the bed and glanced down at Victor. He was still unconscious, his chest naked except for the bandages which covered the upper portion. He breathed irregularly and his eyes flickered under the lids.

'The doctor says that because he is young and fit he will recover soon,' the Marchesa said quietly, 'but he has lost a lot of blood and needs looking after.'

Zoe touched her brother's shoulder; the skin was clammy. 'I must take him home.'

'He cannot be moved for a few days,' Marcella said adamantly. 'He's not fit enough for travel. Besides, you are both welcome to stay here with me. I have plenty of room.'

She expected a show of gratitude but Zoe's thoughts had already turned back to Mike O'Dowd. She wondered if it had been a warning or a real murder attempt. *I want to go home*, she thought blindly. I want to go home.

'The doctor will come and see him tomorrow,' the Marchesa continued, and when there was no response, shrugged and walked out.

In the drawing room, Harland was grey-faced with shock. 'Is she all right?'

The Marchesa raised her eyebrows. 'Do you love her?'

'Only with all my heart.'

'Oh,' she said simply, picking up two glasses of champagne and leading him out to the balcony outside. The fireworks had finished, the sky now silent, the moon savage against the uncertain stars. 'Is she your mistress?'

'No,' Harland replied, pulling off his mask and leaning against the balustrades.

'She's too young for you.'

'I know, Marcella, I know.'

'And too pretty.'

'Yes, I know that too,' he said, smiling ruefully. 'She's clever as well, and getting to know the business inside out.'

Marcella changed the subject quickly. 'Did you know her brother was coming to the auction?'

Harland frowned. 'No. Did you?'

She drained her glass before answering. 'I have never seen Victor Mellor before in my life.'

It didn't surprise Harland that Victor had

managed to infiltrate the auction — it seemed that he could infiltrate anything he set his mind to — but he wondered about Zoe. *Had* she known he was coming? After all she had seemed uneasy during the auction . . .

'How's Myrtle?'

Harland shrugged. 'Don't try and make me feel guilty, Marcella. I have no stomach for that any more.'

A trace of anger flashed across her face and then she smiled. 'I'm glad you remembered the Dante, but so you remember this: '*Nessum maggior dolore, che ricordarsi del tempo felice nella miseria*'?'

'No greater sorrow than to recall in our misery the time when we were happy,'' Harland translated. 'But I'm not in misery, Marcella.'

'I am,' she said, glancing away from him. 'I'm lonely.'

He took her hand. 'You could have married again.'

'No. I loved my husband and when he died . . . well, no one else came close.' Her face altered. 'Be careful of Zoe, she is very young and very insecure. She might rely on you.'

He smiled, a small man in a ludicrous costume. 'That's all I expect, Marcella.'

'Then we are both fools,' she said, walking back into the villa with him.

★ ★ ★

Zoe could not sleep. The night taunted her and each sound woke her, every detail of the attack

332

playing over and over in her head until she could bear it no longer and got out of bed. It was three in the morning by then, the guests had gone and the villa was silent, the entrance hall lit by the unkind moonlight, the debris of the party much in evidence. Quietly Zoe made her way along the corridor, listening outside Victor's room for any sign that he was awake. There was none.

The silence was absolute as she made her way downstairs, and when she couldn't find the light switch in the drawing room she picked up a silver candelabra and lit the four candles before making her way over to the stage where the auction had taken place. Shivering with cold, she glanced round, but the fire had died and there was no comfort there. In a concerted attempt to marshal her thoughts, Zoe reran the events of the previous evening, sitting on the edge of the dais, the candles flickering beside her. She now knew why Victor had been there — he had been selling Lino Candadas's fakes without her knowledge, pocketing the proceeds and risking her safety and his own. But why had Mike O'Dowd attacked them?

Slowly and carefully she thought back, remembering her brother, remembering the way *he* thought. Slick Vic, they called him: 'Too bloody clever for his own good,' their father used to say, 'too bloody clever . . . ' She remembered the photographs in the tin box: Victor as a boy with his hands in his pockets; Victor smirking into the camera lens; Victor, wily and clever, smiling for his mother.

'Smile, love, hold it. Good boy.'

Victor Mellor, always one step ahead of the game. Zoe frowned, the answer coming to her suddenly. Of course, that was the reason for the attack — Victor had tried to be too clever with the wrong person, someone tougher than he was. He had double-crossed Mike O'Dowd and had paid for it. The moonlight scuttered along the floor as Zoe thought back to Leon Graves in New York and remembered his words: 'Mike O'Dowd is a dangerous man.'

Dangerous men do not like to be cheated, Zoe thought, weariness dragging on her. *Why* had Victor been so greedy when they had been doing so well, she wondered. Not one breath of scandal, not a suspicion had been raised. Her fakes had been unquestioned, her position at the gallery secure. But no longer. Now her brother had jeopardised everything, and now Mike O'Dowd knew about her . . .

'I never meant it to go this far,' she whispered, pushing her hair back with her hands, her fingers pressed against her closed eyes. The world was rocking under her, even the city seemed unsteady, an island unanchored on a drowning sea. I'm alone, she realised suddenly, alone. I can't confide in Steven because I don't trust him. I can't go to Harland for help — and there is no one else to turn to. The thought frightened her and made her whimper softly as she curled up on the dais, her face shaded in the dying light.

Unknown to her, Harland had woken and followed her downstairs. He had watched her in the ballroom, seen her distress and remembered her unease at the auction. He also remembered the hundred little nuances, the myriad hints and hesitations over the previous four years. Victor Mellor, Zoe Mellor . . . He turned the names over in his mind endlessly, repeating them again and again while he watched the huddled figure of Zoe in the dim candlelight . . . and wondered.

PART THREE

Revenge

22

Victor awoke early the following morning to find Zoe dozing in a chair beside his bed. He turned and winced, clutching at his side, and then slumped back against the pillows. Heavy drapes blanketed the windows and barred the daylight, the indifferent fire still burning in the grate providing the only illumination in the dimmed room. Trying to focus clearly he could just make out the shapes of several paintings and two marble busts which flanked the fireplace. He winced again, an involuntary gasp coming from his lips.

Zoe awoke immediately. 'Are you OK?' she asked, flicking on the lamp by his bed. He grunted incoherently and closed his eyes, playing for time. 'Victor, you've got to tell me what happened.'

'I cut myself shaving,' he said drily.

'Well next time aim higher!' Zoe snapped, pulling her chair round to face him. 'You could have been killed, *I* could have been killed.' He sighed dramatically as she continued. 'I don't know why I give a damn, after what you did to me.'

Victor's head buzzed. He could remember little of the previous night after he had been knifed, and he had no recollection of what he had told her . . .

'You told me it was Mike O'Dowd,' Zoe said,

as though she had read his mind. 'You're such a fool, Victor, trying to double-cross someone like that.' He blinked. Had he told her about O'Dowd? God, it was worse than he thought. 'You cheated me and you cheated O'Dowd, and look where it got you. Why did you have to be so greedy? We were doing so well on our own — '

'I don't feel well.'

Zoe was not about to fall for any of her brother's ploys. 'Don't try and kid me! We talk this out, here and now. I'm not going to leave this room until everything's sorted out.'

Victor looked at her through half-closed eyes. The dim light made it impossible to see more than a hazy image of her. It was almost like dreaming. 'Weren't you following me last night?'

She nodded. 'I ran after you and O'Dowd. I didn't know what was going on, Victor, I thought you were in danger.'

He smiled wryly. 'You were right there, the bugger nearly killed me.' He touched his side gingerly. 'I never thought — '

' — that something like that would happen?' she asked. 'No, neither did I. I thought it was all a big laugh, a way to cock a snook at the dealers and make money.' As Zoe leaned forwards in her chair, the lamplight struck her face and clarified her features. 'But it's so dangerous, Victor. That man attacked me last night.' She waited for his response, but there was none. 'You *have* to stop dealing with Candadas and just deal with me. *No one else.* It's the only way we can be safe.'

'And if I don't agree?'

'Then that's it. We're finished. I won't work

340

with you any longer.'

Victor sank back against the pillows. He had been lucky, and he knew it. For several months he had been developing his activities in Monte Carlo, Cannes and Geneva, trading with the Irishman and leaving a trail of fakes across Europe. He had made an arrangement with O'Dowd that he would work with him — and no one else. Every fake that Victor obtained was to be handed on to O'Dowd for him to sell.

'Don't ever think of going into business for yourself, Mellor,' the Irishman had said. 'You work for me, and me alone, do you understand that?'

Victor smiled blandly. 'You're asking a lot.'

'And you're getting paid a lot,' O'Dowd replied. 'I have contacts all over the world. Every fake I get from you I can sell on for twice or even three times the amount you would get at auction or in a gallery. The people I deal with are greedy and don't ask questions, so it's safe — if you do it my way. Work with me and we'll both get rich, try to double-cross me and I'll ruin you.'

Victor had agreed willingly, knowing that for every fake he passed to O'Dowd, another was sold through his own contacts. Work solely for Mike O'Dowd! he had thought. Fat chance! This was much better, this way he was making his own fortune and getting O'Dowd to work for *him*. All he had to do was to continue selling privately and at the small auctions and the Irishman would be none the wiser . . .

Well, no one should have been any the wiser, Victor thought wryly, touching the bandages

341

with his fingers and raging against O'Dowd inwardly, a fierce desire for revenge seething in him. 'Are you suggesting that we cut back?'

Zoe nodded. 'For the time being. Who are you using apart from Candadas?'

Contrary to his usual policy, Victor was truthful. 'Only him. I needed more pictures than you could provide. Anyway, he's a sculptor too, and I had so many dealers wanting stuff.' His eyes misted over at the memory. 'Sculptors sell so bloody well.'

Zoe considered the information. The night had been a long one, but after experiencing a bewildering sense of terror and panic, she now felt only anger, and much of that anger was directed towards Victor. There was no going back for her, she knew that; things could never be the same. As with so many things in her life, the decision had been made for her. She glanced at her brother. His treachery was not surprising, but his stupidity was.

'We have no choice, Victor, we have to restrict our dealings to paintings and drawings.'

He groaned with sheer aggravation. 'I was making a fortune with those sculptors — '

'Which you kept to yourself,' Zoe said bitterly. 'I don't suppose one pound found its way back to Dad, did it?'

'OH, TAKE THE FLAMING MONEY!' he snapped.

Zoe glanced round, laying her fingers against her brother's lips. 'Shut up! You'll wake everyone.'

Victor's eyes fixed on hers, and then his hand

covered her own and his lips kissed her fingers gently. 'What would I do without you? You're my guardian angel, Zoe.'

She hesitated and then withdrew her hand. 'We're going home today. The doctor's coming to see you and then we're off.' She pushed back her chair and stood up. 'You can recover in Rochdale. It might give you time to realise how lucky you've been.' She moved towards the door and then turned back. 'I'll still work with you and stand by you because that's the way *I* want it. But don't ever threaten me again, Victor, because we need each other. If one of us falls, the other falls too . . . remember that.'

★ ★ ★

Rochdale was deep into winter when they returned, Zoe making her excuses to Harland and begging a few days to secure her brother's recovery.

'Do you need anything?'

She shook her head, but kept her eyes averted. He had noticed her withdrawal and an unfamiliar discomfort hung between them.

'Well, if you do, just give me a ring,' he said. 'It was a terrible thing to happen, but I still think Victor should have reported it to the police.'

'For what? It was a drunken attack, nothing more. Victor was in the wrong place at the wrong time. It could just as easily have happened in London or New York.'

'I suppose you're right. But I still think there's more to it than that,' Harland continued easily.

343

'If it was an attack, why wasn't he robbed?'

Zoe took a deep breath. 'Oh, but he was . . . he had quite a lot of money taken.'

Harland nodded, apparently satisfied, and when the boat came to take Zoe and her brother to the mainland he stood, grim faced, waving in the windy rain. But when they had passed out of sight on the angry water, he thought back and remembered what Victor had told him.

' . . . *it was such a bloody stupid attack. I didn't even have any money to make it worth their while . . .* '

★ ★ ★

'Stabbed!' Bernard Mellor said as Ron lifted his brother out of the car and into the snug at Buck's Lane. 'I'm not surprised, I always said he'd come to a bad end.'

Zoe followed behind them, carrying Victor's coat and a travelling rug which she slipped over his shoulders when he was settled in an armchair.

'This isn't a bloody hospital!' their father continued, his eyes betraying the fact that he was secretly delighted by the drama. 'I can't wet nurse this stupid great lummox.'

'I'll do it, Dad,' Zoe explained. 'It's just until he gets on his feet again.'

'On his feet! I'd keep him off his bloody feet, he'll get into less bother that way.' He moved towards Victor and prodded his chest. 'Who did it?'

'I told you, Dad, a couple of drunks in Venice.'

Bernard Mellor was thoughtful. 'Bloody foreigners. You should have stayed home. You can get stabbed in Moss Side any night, you don't have to travel all that way for it.'

It was as though time had run backwards for Zoe. By late afternoon she was making them all a meal, although Alan had not returned yet from Tom Mellor's. The same cooking smells came from the kitchen, even Peter was back under the table, and a mean fire sputtered into the damp air. Venice was a dream. She had faded within hours, evaporating as the grim reality of Buck's Lane pushed the water city away. Zoe was an ignorant girl again, every pan told her so. Every dish she picked up and laid on the scratched table reminded her of her beginnings. Even the calendar on the wall took her back, a photograph of the high moors calling and stamping their memory on her. There was no magic, no costume, no masks any longer . . . just a young woman in a kitchen cooking. The realisation picked at her nerve ends.

She was just about to draw the curtains when she saw the light go on in the garage. Holding a tea towel over her head to keep off the rain, she ran outside. Pushing the garage door open she saw Alan jump and then turn, his broad face glowing with pleasure.

'Oh, Alan,' she said, running towards him. 'It's so good to see you.'

He held on to her, his deep laugh bouncing off the thin walls of the garage, and felt her in his arms as though she was a child again. She was home, he thought wonderingly, Zoe was home.

345

'I've missed you,' he said finally, letting go of her and putting on the kettle. 'Things get quiet round here.'

Her guilt nearly choked her. 'I've neglected you, haven't I?'

'You've been busy,' Alan replied, unable to lay any blame at her door. 'We get your postcards and the money.'

'I'm sorry, really sorry,' Zoe said, taking the mug of tea from her brother and glancing round. The bench was empty, but Alan had built several shelves along the back wall, stacking his art books on them until there were dozens, all well thumbed and used. 'What are you working on?'

Alan's face flushed and he turned away.

'Alan?' Zoe questioned. 'What's the matter?'

He nodded, unable to speak for an instant. 'I've got something,' he said finally, going behind his makeshift cupboard and pulling out a small object covered in sacking. 'It's for you.'

Zoe laid down the mug and gently pulled away the cloth. A life size putti looked up at her, its face androgynous, a soft welcoming smile on its lips. Without saying a word, she tore away the sacking quickly and then turned the sculpture round and round on the bench. The body was supple, living, the arms inviting, the whole creation breathing with life and something more, a deep sensuality which was so compelling that it consumed every inch of the marble and bled through the stone.

'Did you do this?' she asked finally.

Alan blushed, and turned away, wondering if she had guessed his secret. But she must have, he realised, it was so obvious. Surely it was there for anyone to see? Standing in front of the statue, Zoe's remained motionless while her brother moved away and bent over the bench. She *had* guessed, he thought wretchedly, and now she would be disgusted with him. She wouldn't understand, how could she?

The statue stared back at Zoe, its knowing expression amused. Her mind raced. Victor had made a fortune from sculpture, he told her so. It had been so profitable that he had taken chances and worked with the likes of Lino Candadas. She had told him to stop, insisting that they keep the business within the family . . . and all those years, under their very noses, Alan had been carving works like this. The putti smiled at her. In on the joke.

'Have you any more?' she asked her brother, her voice sounding high-pitched in her ears.

Alan hesitated. 'Well, some. But they're copies like. From books.'

'Copies?' Zoe repeated disbelievingly. 'What did you copy?'

'Photographs,' Alan replied, embarrassment making him diffident. Was she angry with him? Had he done wrong?

'Let me see, please. Please, Alan.'

Reluctantly he pulled back the corrugated sheeting and drew out three sculptures wrapped in sacking. One by one he laid them on the bench and then stood back, his hands deep in his overall pockets, his face burning crimson. Zoe unwrapped them with shaking hands. A Madonna and Child looked up at her; then an angel with one arm extended; then a replica of the *Dying Gaul* — all faultless, the copies meticulous. She felt her mouth dry as she fingered them. Night after night while she had been working on the fakes in London, Alan had been labouring up here, his shyness providing the perfect cover; his loneliness well known. No one came to see Alan, no one visited the fat man who worked at the stonemason's, no woman missed him, no man pressed for his company at the pub. Alan Mellor was of no importance to a world which had dismissed him . . . was sweet revenge.

Zoe looked at her brother carefully. 'Would you like to be rich, Alan?' she asked.

Victor was watching the television, a tray of half-eaten sandwiches on the table beside him, a can of beer in his hand. He looked comfortable and perfectly at ease, turning when Zoe came in. 'This is rubbish,' he said, switching off the set with the hand control and taking a long drink out of the can. 'Where have you been?'

'Talking to Alan.'

He grunted. 'He's not been in to see me,' he said pathetically. 'I don't think he'd give a stuff if I'd been killed.'

'He's been working hard and I think you should have a look at what he's done.'

'In that garage? It's freezing,' he said, outraged. 'Do you want me to catch my bloody death?'

'Oh, I think it might well prove to be worth catching cold for.'

Something in her voice made him curious and

348

he struggled to his feet, pulling on a coat and wincing as he touched his chest. 'Bastard,' he said reflectively.

Buck's Lane was cold and hard underfoot, frost making the earth stone, the air catching their breaths. The lights blazed out from the garage windows, illuminating the path, and when Zoe pushed against the doors, the metal felt cold under her hands. Victor followed her in, banging his feet on the floor and walking over to a small electric fire in the corner by the kettle.

'God above, it's perishing,' he said, turning to Alan. 'So what's new?'

His brother shuffled around the bench. ''Lo, Victor. Sorry about your . . . accident.'

'I was knifed,' Victor said dramatically. 'I could have been killed.'

Alan hesitated. 'Sorry . . . yes, well . . . sorry.'

Victor raised his eyes heavenwards. 'What did you want to show me, Zoe?'

Winking at Alan, she uncovered the sculptures on the bench, flicking on an angelpoise lamp and turning its full illumination on the figures. 'Look, Victor.'

His eyes registered surprise and then disbelief and he touched the marble and ran his fingers along the carved limbs, his expression altering as a slow smile of realisation spread over his face. Finally, he turned to his sister. 'Alan's?'

She nodded. 'What do you think?'

Alan waited for his response, as she did. But Victor was too transfixed to reply, his thoughts centred on the sculptures. He could almost see the money pouring off them, and he could also see a way of getting his revenge on Mike O'Dowd. Suddenly he knew he was free again. If he used Zoe and Alan he was safe, it was in the family. Safe as houses.

'Well?'

Victor extended his hand towards his brother. Alan hesitated, wiping his own palm on his overalls before taking Victor's hand.

'They're wonderful.'

'You think so?' Alan asked, his face colouring up with pleasure.

'Wonderful,' Victor repeated enthusiastically, flinging his arm around his brother's shoulder, his face wreathed in smiles. 'We'll make a fortune,' he continued wildly, grabbing hold of Zoe and pulling his sister and brother towards him. 'We're going to be rich!'

Zoe was cleaning the floor the following evening when there was a knock on the door. She turned round and looked towards the snug, but although she could see the back of Victor and Ron's heads, and that of her father, no one moved. Irritated, she wiped her hands on her apron and opened the door. A stocky man wearing tinted glasses and a very expensive suit looked back at her. 'Zoe Mellor, what a pleasure.'

Startled, she leaned against the door to close it, but Mike O'Dowd had already put his foot inside. Pushing hard he opened it and walked in. 'How's your brother?' he asked, passing her and moving into the kitchen. His glasses steamed up and he removed them, polishing each lens on a white handkerchief. 'I asked how your brother was.'

Nervously Zoe glanced towards the snug door. O'Dowd smiled, satisfied to see the effect his presence was having on her and then leaned forwards, lifting the edge of her apron and fingering the material. 'Last time I saw you, you were in velvet. In only a week you have fallen a long way, Cinderella.'

Zoe pulled the apron from his hand. 'What do you want, O'Dowd?'

'Oh, so you know my name,' he said, gratified, leaning across the table and taking half a biscuit off a chipped plate. 'It's pleasing to see that I'm so well known. Mind you, we did meet only the other night. Venice, wasn't it?' he asked. 'It's a romantic city . . . and so full of surprises.'

Zoe ignored him, trying to keep her voice steady. 'What do you want?'

O'Dowd bit into the biscuit, chewed and swallowed slowly, his eyes malignant behind the tinted glasses. 'Nice dog,' he said, nodding his head towards Peter under the table. 'Not much of a guard though.' He leaned towards the greyhound, holding out a piece of biscuit. 'There's a good boy,' he said softly as he took it. 'Well it's good to see that not everyone in this family bites the hand that feeds him.'

'What do you want here?' Zoe repeated, taking in a deep breath when she saw Victor walk in from the snug.

'Like she said, O'Dowd, what the bloody hell do you want?' he asked.

'There's really no cause for bad feelings,' the

Irishman replied, facing him squarely. 'You asked for it.'

'How the hell was I to know you would be attending that auction? It was supposed to be private,' Victor said, baiting him.

O'Dowd's face was set hard. He had expected to see a cringing Victor brought to his knees, not this cocksure bastard. 'I'll ruin you if you step out of line again!'

'Like hell you will! You know my stuff's the best, that's why you're here. This little scratch,' Victor said, his voice a sneer, 'was just a way of trying to keep me in line. It wasn't meant to be serious. You need me, O'Dowd.'

The Irishman smiled. 'Maybe I do at that,' he said, turning to glance at Zoe, 'but I also need her.'

'Why her?' Victor asked, his voice thick with suspicion.

Mike O'Dowd sat down at the table, his fingers drumming on the cloth. 'You see, I got to thinking about *where* you got your fakes. I knew about Candadas, after all I'd introduced you two, but where were you getting the others from?'

He paused and Zoe swallowed. She had presumed that he already knew about her, but apparently he didn't. Or hadn't until now.

'So I thought and thought and,' O'Dowd paused for effect, 'came up with this little lady. You see, Victor, I have a great many contacts. I built them up over twenty odd years. You're a novice by comparison.' He leaned over and took another biscuit, his mouth opening to take a bite as Bernard Mellor and Ron walked in.

'Who the hell are you?'

'This is Mr Lambert,' Zoe said quickly as she turned towards her father.

O'Dowd smiled, taking her cue. 'And how's yourself, Mr Mellor?'

'I never heard anyone called Lambert talk like that!' he said flatly.

'I got the name from m' father,' O'Dowd explained, 'and the brogue from m' mother.'

Bernard Mellor was unimpressed and turned back to Zoe. 'Get me a cuppa, will you? I want to watch *Coronation Street*.'

She nodded, then as she turned towards the kettle she noticed that Ron was standing behind his father. As always, they communicated by telepathy and, immediately understanding what she meant, he whistled for Peter. 'Come on, lad, we're off for a walk.'

The ruse mystified Bernard Mellor. 'You want to watch out, Ron, you'll walk that greyhound once too often and end up with a bloody corgi!' He moved back to the snug door. 'Hurry up, Zoe, I can hear the programme starting.'

O'Dowd watched the old man leave the room and calmly finished his biscuit, waiting. The wall clock ticked between the two men, the hum of the washer filling the cramped kitchen, the windows steamed up with moisture. When Zoe returned she leaned against the sink with her arms folded, an expression of loathing on her face.

'You were saying?'

'That I got thinking about the fakes and did a

little digging and my spies told me that *you*,' he turned to Zoe, 'were doing them.'

She laughed. 'Me? Do me a favour!'

'Oh, now there's no reason to deny it. I know it for a fact,' O'Dowd replied. 'So I would watch my step if I were you.' He turned to Victor. 'And as for you, I need you for the moment, but I won't tolerate any more pissing about. You provide me with the fakes I want, *when* I want them, and stop any independent dealing.'

Victor's expression was disturbingly bland. 'OK, you win. But I don't know why you're so bloody het up, Zoe can only do the drawings and the paintings, she can't do sculpture, Candadas is the only one who can do that.'

Zoe held her breath. She could see the trap and watched avidly as O'Dowd fell into it.

'Agreed. That'll be the way we do business, Mellor. Your sister continues to supply the paintings and Lino Candadas will supply the sculpture.' He rose to his feet. 'You see how easy it is really?'

Victor pretended to be cowed. 'Listen . . . I'm sorry for what happened . . . I was stupid.'

Mike O'Dowd was in an expansive mood. 'Forget it, we all make mistakes,' he said, opening the door and walking towards his BMW. 'But don't try and get clever with me again, Mellor, or I'll kill you.' He paused and leaned towards Zoe. 'You're a good forger. Very good,' he said smoothly. 'And you're clever to hold that job down at the gallery, even if it means sleeping with the old Jew.' She drew in her breath as he slid into the driver's seat. 'But you're a scrubber really, and your brother's a lying thief. Just remember that.' He turned on the ignition. 'Oh, and one more thing, if you feel inclined to try your luck on your own again, spare a thought for your dear old Dad — '

'What the hell is that supposed to mean?' Victor snapped, the words blanked out as the Irishman's car roared into life, the threat left swinging in the Northern air.

Zoe watched him drive off and then sucked in her breath. 'That pig — '

' — is going to be sorry,' Victor finished for her, lighting a cigarette and blowing smoke into the sky. 'Oh yes, that nasty little toerag is going to come a cropper.'

Zoe turned and looked at the house, at the mean house on Buck's Lane where her father had lived for years; where all of them had grown up. At that moment Bernard Mellor was watching television, an old man ageing rapidly, relying on his children for his security. He wasn't so quick any more, not able to defend himself the way he used to when he was younger. In fact only the other night Zoe had said that he shouldn't walk home late when it was dark. It might not be safe, she had said, without realising that *she* was the one who had brought danger to her father's door.

'Oh God, what have I done?' she said despairingly. 'What have I done?'

23

Revenge bound brother and sister together far more effectively than love could have done, and in the months which followed Victor and Zoe were almost inseparable. He recovered quickly on a diet of cigarettes and beer, slipping back easily to his Rochdale roots, his voice even taking on the old Lancastrian accent. But when he returned to London with Zoe and Ron, he changed like a chameleon overnight and became Victor Mellor the dealer, the same dealer who had seduced the likes of Erica Goldberg, the same dealer who knew his way across Europe. It was common knowledge that Victor had a shady reputation, but he also had a reputation for quality and that gave him an entrée to the buyers, even though it didn't make him popular. So while he returned to his old ways, Zoe returned to the gallery where Harland welcomed her, his protective instinct to the fore. He did not know *what* she had done; he knew only that she had lied to him. That was a surprise in itself — she had always been honest with him before — yet if she had lied, Harland decided, there must be a good reason, and that reason was probably bound up with her family. He knew how closely tied Zoe was to each of her brothers, and he knew how much the family meant to her and how deeply she still felt her mother's rejection and her father's early indifference. In fact, Zoe was sister, mother, and almost a wife to each of the men in her life . . . but there was no one to love her.

Harland sighed. Oh, he adored her, but it wasn't the kind of love she needed, it wasn't love from a man of her own age, a lover in the proper sense. That was something she appeared to avoid. Instead, she had become committed to her family, knowing that they all needed her and that they all took more than they gave. *He* was guilty too; he took her glamour, the kudos which her presence gave him. Certainly he had taught her and protected her, but he had still got the most from the arrangement . . . The truth pricked him and he shrugged. He would have given her more — money, a flat, anything — but she wouldn't take it. No, he thought, if I really loved her I would force her to find someone else.

Then he pictured some man making love to her and his jealousy raged, and he realised that there was no point in conning himself because he would keep Zoe Mellor as long as she would stay. Disgruntled, he pushed some papers away and rubbed his eyes. His protection was proof positive of his love. Whatever she was involved in, whether directly or indirectly, he would watch over her. It was his pledge, an unspoken oath. He had moulded and taught her and set her on her way, but it could be a bitter way, and Harland Goldberg knew in his heart of hearts, although he couldn't say the words, that somewhere, somehow, Zoe was risking herself.

★   ★   ★

She was at that moment having a conversation with Ahmed Fazir in his gallery in the Old Brompton Road. His hand repeatedly strayed around her shoulders and each time Zoe moved away, but on the last occasion her temper snapped.

'I don't like being mauled,' she said, her eyes burning into the Egyptian's dark face.

He bowed; mock apology. 'I'm sorry, but you are a very attractive woman.'

'Yes,' Zoe said coolly, 'that's the usual excuse. But I still don't like it.'

He shrugged and stepped back. Enormously gratified, Minnie Simmonds watched from her desk. She hated his big hands and the way he said her name — 'Meanie' he pronounced it — just wait until she told her mother about this . . .

'My heart's broken to think I've insulted you,' Fazir went on smoothly, his eyes assessing her legs as she stood looking it one of his paintings. Having originally dismissed her as a bimbo, he had been surprised to see her steady climb into respectability, her intelligence marking her out from the myriad women who flocked around the peripheries of the art world. In fact she was even forcing the dealers to take her seriously now, buying well and employing an almost supernatural ability to spot fakes. It was all very surprising, he thought admiringly, soon she might even be able to give the likes of New York's infamous Suzie Laye a run for her money.

'So what do you think of the Modigliani?'

Zoe shrugged. 'What I always think — he's overrated.'

He smiled. 'Why don't we discuss it over dinner?'

'I wouldn't discuss it over a wall, Mr Fazir.'

He was still laughing when she left the gallery.

Outside it was raining as Zoe walked towards Harrods, pushing open the glass doors and catching sight of herself in a mirror. Dressed in a fitted suede suit, her hair loose, she looked confident and self-possessed, just as she had hoped to look when she had first arrived in London all those years ago. Zoe winced, her embarrassment almost too painful to remember, and moved on thinking of Fazir. At least she had the gratification of knowing that he had bought her Bonington fake only the other week. He had even brought it over to show Harland, his face positively glowing as he lumbered in with the picture under his arm.

'Well, Harland, what do you say to this?' he asked, luminous with confidence. 'I bet Tobar would give his eye teeth for it.'

Zoe bit her lip.

'It's very nice,' Harland said pleasantly.

' 'Very nice'?' Fazir repeated, reaching into his pocket for his snuff box. His eyes were bloodshot, his face unnaturally pale. 'It's a beauty.'

Excusing herself suddenly, Zoe moved off into the back room, savouring her revenge. She closed the door and smiled widely, hugging the secret to herself as a child might. People's attitudes were finally changing, she realised, and she was finally making a reputation. Even Mona was forced to review her opinion, recognising that Zoe Mellor was here to stay — and she herself might not be. Most importantly, Zoe had her bank balance to encourage her. It was swelling nicely, she had even managed to persuade her father to have the house redecorated at Buck's Lane. She wanted to do more, to rebuild the back and have the woodwork painted — but he wouldn't hear of it.

'I like it as it is. It's my bloody home and if it was good enough for your mother, it's good enough for me.'

'But Dad — '

'Don't 'but Dad' me! You want a palace, then buy yourself one down south. I like it the way it is,' he said, hurling her kindness into her face.

Meanwhile, Victor was being a lamb. Zoe spent many an hour wondering what he was working on that might either rob her or ruin her. But apparently he was still getting too much satisfaction out of the situation with O'Dowd to want to be occupied elsewhere, continuing to provide the Irishman with pictures while he was busily selling Alan's fakes all around the world.

Temporarily free from the threat of depression, Alan had surprised them all. They knew he was a hard worker, he always had been, but they hadn't realised just how much work he could undertake. Certainly he was physically strong, but it was more than that; their interest in him had given him a driving force, his life suddenly had value, meaning. For years he had grappled with his loneliness, and now, to be needed and flattered . . . it was all Alan Mellor required to keep him working day and night. Not that he liked Victor any more now than he had done as a child, but he would have done anything for his Zoe. So he studied his art books and memorised the sculpture, noticing the differences from century to century and country to country, and he took notes of the different methods of execution. He was studying Romanesque portal figures when Zoe called in to see him one Friday night.

'Be careful with those, Alan, we have to be sure they're convincing before we float any at auction. They *have* to be right.'

'They'll be right,' he said quietly, his voice firm, his face burning red. 'I promise you, they'll be right.'

But whilst Zoe trusted one brother, she kept an eye on the other one, and knew that in the background was Ron. Poor dumb Ron. The eternal gofor. The 'fetch me', 'carry me', 'do me', 'Ron lift me this', 'Ron get me that', 'Ron carry this'. Ron who painted the flat; Ron who mended the front door in Rochdale; Ron who wrapped the paintings, wrote the labels, fixed the broken frames. Always Ron . . . and he never let her down, even sitting up with her when Zoe was painting late at night, Peter curled up by his feet, the greyhound now going grey round the muzzle. They both watched over her, and when she stretched her stiff arms and looked up, Ron smiled at her.

He was her companion, as consistently faithful to Zoe as Peter was to him. His only interest was the dog track, the twice weekly visits longed for, even though he lost more money than he ever won. He liked the smell of the place, the high floodlights over the track, the bookies, and the sound of the traps snapping open as the dogs were let free. Shouting for his favourite, he would lean over the railings, his fists clenched as the dogs passed, the betting slip torn up afterwards while he drank a cold beer in the public bar.

Uncomplicated and loving, Ron offered his sister the warmth she needed, keeping an eye on Victor and his mouth firmly shut about the fakes — even though he knew that one day his sister would be caught. Yet strangely, the longer she continued, the more Zoe believed that she would *not* be found out. It was not bravado or foolhardiness, she simply *knew* she would get away with it, and amazingly, she continued to do so, the only thing to threaten her peace of mind being her relationship with Steven Foreshaw. He had changed, becoming too petulant for comfort, his demands on her excessive.

'Why didn't you ring me yesterday?'

'I was busy,' she snapped. 'It's ridiculous anyway, trying to keep a relationship going long distance.'

'Then don't hold it long distance. Move back up North.'

She looked at him with undisguised impatience. 'Oh, Steven, you're not serious!'

'Why not?'

'Because you're trying to make me give up everything, and I won't. Besides it's what you wanted once, so why shouldn't I have it?' She shook her head. 'It's not fair, and if you cared about me, you wouldn't even ask me to return.'

He pulled her down beside him on the settee in the flat in Kensington. 'You know I care about you. You're my life, you're everything to me.'

'Yes,' she replied sadly. 'But everything's not enough.'

Many times she phoned him to cancel their arrangements; many times she was out when he made the long trip down South. She hated herself for being a coward, but didn't know how else to reject him as words were never enough. It seemed that the only way she could break the ties was to distance herself, to travel, and become part of another world. But he clung on rigidly. Once she had even seen him outside Jimmy van Goyen's gallery, watching her, and yet when she walked out he had disappeared into the crowd.

He had been standing at the window, peering in. An outsider, hopelessly out of place in battered cord trousers, the inevitable scarf round his neck. Losing weight and smoking too much, his bitterness had obliterated every part of the sexual attraction which had first tied her to him, and left him almost violently envious.

'Our relationship's no good,' she said to him one day as they walked round the zoo in Regent's Park. She had chosen a busy place to meet to avoid a confrontation.

'No good!' he exclaimed.

'I don't . . . have the time,' Zoe said, 'and I don't care enough to make time.'

The words were brutal and rode the high sky between them.

'You don't *care* enough?' he asked bitterly. 'Well, what *do* you care about?'

The phrase repeated itself in her head — *what do you care about?* 'I care about my family,' she said finally.

'Your family . . . Is that enough?'

'They need looking after,' she persisted.

'No, they don't! They're fully grown and they can all fend for themselves. You act as though you're in love with them.'

Zoe threw her hands up in exasperation. 'You can't be in love with a family, for God's sake!'

He banged his hands on the railing. A startled penguin dived under the water away from him. 'But you *are*. Every one of them. Ron, Alan, Victor, although he treats you like shit, even your father — '

'That's enough!' she warned him.

'No, it isn't!' he shouted. Angrily, she moved away and he followed her. 'It's the truth, Zoe.'

'No, it isn't!' she said vehemently. 'But you want an argument, so I'll give you one.' She paused, her hands clenched. 'I care for my family and I *choose* to make them my first concern.'

'So they're more important than any man could be?' he asked, grabbing hold of her hands.

She shook them free. This affair has gone on too long, she thought. Why hadn't she stopped it before? Why hadn't she walked away that first time when she realised she wasn't pregnant? 'Steven,' she said gently, 'it's over.'

'No! I don't believe it, it's not over!' he said,

grabbing hold of her and kissing her roughly on the mouth. She pulled away, seeing a group of schoolchildren turn to watch them, the girls giggling and nudging each other.

'I don't want to argue in public!' she snapped. 'And sex isn't the answer.'

'You're everything to me. You changed my life!' he continued blindly. 'You have no *right* to do this.'

'I changed your life?' Zoe repeated with deadly calm. 'Well, I didn't mean to. I didn't set out to hurt you, and I took nothing from you. I only gave to you, Steven.'

'You only *gave* to me! Gave me what, your virginity? God, that was noble,' he said, making a mock bow. 'I'm honoured, although if it hadn't been me no doubt it would have been someone else. You hardly needed persuading.' He stopped. The look on Zoe's face was one of loathing. 'Oh God, I didn't mean to say that. I *love* you.'

'I didn't ask you to!' she shouted, turning on her heel and walking away.

He ran behind her. 'No, you didn't ask me to love you, but it was convenient, wasn't it? It didn't take up too much of your time — a long-distance devotion from a faithful lapdog.' His voice was hard edged. 'You were OK as long as you knew you had good old Steven stuck up North to dance attendance. I suppose it fanned your ego while you swanned round the world being the big shot.' He paused before delivering the final blow. 'Oh yes, you've done well for yourself, very well indeed. You've got a job and a rich provider.'

Zoe turned on him. 'Never say that again! Or even suggest it! I've told you the truth about that relationship, so don't you ever try and make it sound dirty!'

He cowered in front of her. 'I didn't mean it! Oh God, I didn't mean it! Say you forgive me.'

'I don't have to forgive you.' Zoe said, her voice cold. 'But it's over.'

He was beyond reason. 'No. Let's go back to the flat, Zoe, come on. We can talk there, we can make love . . . Without you my life is meaningless.'

'Don't be melodramatic.'

'If you leave me I'll kill myself.'

The threat winded Zoe momentarily. 'I'm going to pretend you never said that.'

She put her hands over her ears to blot out his words, but he pulled them away and faced her. 'Listen to me! There is nothing in my life without you. If you leave me, I'll kill myself.'

'You have no right to threaten me!' Zoe said sharply. 'No right at all. You said my family used me, well what are you doing, Steven? If you loved me you'd never do this. You don't love me at all.'

The words had no effect. 'I'm warning you, if you leave me — '

'I heard you!' she snapped, looking into his face. He was older and thinner, his charm fading under the midday sun.

'Well, what do you say?' he asked again.

'I say we should go and have a look in the Reptile House,' Zoe said woodenly.

'For Christ's sake, answer the question!' he

bellowed. 'Will you leave me? Or will you see me next week?'

A child ran past, scattering a flock of pigeons into the insensible sky. Their wings battered the still air.

'Yes . . . I'll meet you, Steven. I'll meet you.'

★ ★ ★

Victor had the cooker installed in the garage the following week to assist their faking activities. It caused no comment whatsoever because Alan was well known as an eater and putting in a cooker merely implied that he now preferred his food hot rather than cold.

'A bloody cooker!' his father said when he heard. 'I don't know why he doesn't set up a restaurant in there.'

Zoe rallied to his defence. 'Oh, Dad, come on. He works long hours — '

'He *eats* long hours,' he said irritably. 'Anyway, what does he find to do in there?'

Zoe hesitated. 'He makes things, you know . . . carves things.'

'Is that why you and Victor are always hanging around?'

She smiled, knowing how to put her father off the scent. 'Well the stuff's so good we sell some of it in London. Alan's very talented, you could come and have a look if you like — '

The suggestion had the desired effect. 'I'm not bloody interested! Anyway, he carves things all day long up at Tom's, so God knows why he has to work half the night as well.'

'What else has he got to do?' Zoe asked sharply.

'You can take that tone out of your voice! Remember who's boss here!' her father snapped. 'I can't bear lip from a kid.'

So the cooker was duly installed, and a small fridge was also put in. It became quite a home from home, and Alan learnt the business quickly. Astoundingly so. He had no power of reasoning, but if he was told something he never forgot it, and despite his vast bulk he was meticulous with his tools and materials. Having found a supplier, Victor provided the stone and the marble. It would have looked suspicious if Alan began to buy large quantities from Tom Mellor, so Victor would bring some up at the weekends. He would stagger in, prop the material behind the bench, and then brush the dust off his clothes with a pained look on his face.

'How soon can you have that last piece finished?' he asked, pointing to a half finished frieze which he wanted for a buyer in France.

'Give me five days.'

Zoe frowned. 'You don't have to work day and night.'

'No, no!' Alan said eagerly. 'It's my pleasure.'

'I know it is, but you don't have to kill yourself.'

'Listen,' Victor said impatiently. 'If he wants to do it, let him.'

'He's doing it because he feels he should,' Zoe said hotly, turning back to Alan. 'As I said, don't kill yourself.'

He smiled warmly. 'I won't. Besides, I love it.'

And he did, especially on the long dark nights, when it was cold and he turned on the battered electric fire and pulled on his overalls. The winter evenings crept round the garage and nudged against the windows where he had hung blinds to keep out prying eyes. But no one came near; no one ever came near Alan Mellor. So he chipped away and turned on his radio and whistled to the music, until Victor, in a rush of uncharacteristic gratitude, bought him a cheap cassette player. Then Alan's life was transformed. Within days he had bought himself three tapes, one of Barbra Streisand's, another of Vivaldi's *Four Seasons* and the third of Christmas carols. He knew each of the tapes by heart, and sang the words or whistled while the music played to the sound of chisel striking stone, and everything came into focus for him and made sense. The bodies he made, the hands, the breasts, the thighs, all began to pulse like real flesh and blood, as though under the marble there was life and all Alan's sexual longings became a part of his work. Hour after hour passed in a kind of erotic euphoria, until, dizzy with desire, he would lock and door and wrap his arms around his creations, skin to stone . . . the night unravelling itself outside.

Victor was no slouch either and was busy extending his interests even further afield. He learnt that one way of making a successful forgery was to graft new parts on to the body of an original. Consequently he set off for the French and Italian countryside, visiting tiny chapels and churches where the artefacts and statues were in a deplorable state, many crumbling, their hands and feet missing. Spotting something worthwhile, Victor would then offer to buy the statue, and because the priest was usually amazed that anyone should want the piece, and because he generally needed the money for a new roof, he would agree to sell. The transaction completed to everyone's satisfaction, the priest would then help Victor lift the broken statue into the boot of his car, raising his hand in blessing as he drove off.

Victor never had any problems getting his trophies back into England either. Having devised several methods of concealment, such as hiding the sculptures under fruit or in a consignment of children's toys, he made sure that he did business with the kind of people who were notorious for their lack of curiosity. Backhanders frequently oiled the wheels, and a threat often succeeded when someone was impervious to reason. When the concealed statues arrived in England, they were picked up at the Liverpool or London docks by either Victor or Ron. The system worked perfectly. They took risks, but they were mixing with the kind of people who made a living out of taking risks, so few questions were asked. Then when the sculptures finally reached the garage in Rochdale, Alan would examine them and run his hands over them, sometimes even talking to them.

'He's flipped,' Victor said to Zoe, as he tried to get his breath back.

'You're in bad condition,' she replied. 'You

only carried that piece from the car.'

'It weighs a bloody ton!'

'Ron could have done it without hyperventilating. He's fit,' she said, baiting him.

'Ron's brawn makes up for his lack of brain.' Victor lit up a cigarette.

'You shouldn't smoke, the smell clings to your clothes.'

'Like the women,' he replied smartly.

Without paying either of them any attention, Alan had been thumbing through his art books, checking on a detail and smiling when he found a statue which corresponded well with the headless saint on the workbench. 'She's lovely.'

Victor's eyebrows rose. 'Isn't there something missing?'

Alan was immune to sarcasm. 'Oh, I'll fix that,' he said, glancing at the picture of the thirteenth-century French sculpture and making a mental note of the facial expression. With perfect confidence he understood immediately how to set about rebuilding the statue and faking the missing parts. It was easy for him to rebuild an arm, or replace a missing Christ child, and then, after grinding down part of the stone from the back of the original sculpture, he would mix it with cement and use it to fill in the cracks between the original sculpture and the additions. That way, even an expert could hardly tell if the joins indicated forgery or simply the wear and tear of the ages.

Alan was gifted, and more, he was committed. When he finished one of his fakes he stood it on the workbench and looked at it keenly, assessing just how it would appear to another pair of eyes. Then with a ruthlessness which surprised even Zoe, he set about ageing it, hacking at the feet, digging away pieces of the drapery, roughening areas with his file, and grinding away pieces of stone to take away the perfection and add an appearance of age. Afterwards he might rub the sculpture over with soot, and sometimes with acid, which ate into the stone and gave it a pockmarked surface, which usually only weather and time achieved.

He never asked what the statues were for, although he had his suspicions and knew that faking was illegal. All that was really important to him was that someone, for whatever reason, wanted one of his works. It didn't matter that it was a copy, that it was partly his and partly someone else's — it was part of him and it was going out into the world in which he never ventured. The secrecy thrilled him, but like Ron Alan Mellor did not want to know any details, and when they began to make really big money he was baffled. 'What do I do with it?'

Victor snorted. 'Spend it.'

'On what?'

Zoe stepped in. She could see Alan's bemusement and knew what Victor was about to suggest. 'Don't even think it, Victor.'

He was all innocence. 'I was just going to suggest that I invest it for him.'

She ignored him and turned back to Alan. 'Do you want me to look after it for you?'

He nodded gratefully.

But if Ron and Alan found their money a

burden, Victor relished his and spent it on a flat in Swiss Cottage, trading in the second-hand Jaguar for a new Daimler. Zoe, on the other hand, kept her money hidden and her mouth shut. There was no outward show of affluence, because even though she dressed well, she did not drive and, apart from moving into a larger flat by Kensington Gardens with Ron, there was little change in her lifestyle.

Her frugality fascinated Victor. 'What are you going to do with all the bloody cash?'

'That,' she said drily, 'is for me to know and you to guess. Besides, I don't believe in conspicuous consumption, it would make people suspicious.'

'Well, I spend enough, and no one's said anything to me.'

'That's different, everyone knows you're a crook.'

Victor bristled, but he was not about to drop the topic. 'You must be putting away thousands — '

'And I shall continue to.' Zoe picked up a small drawing and laid it on the easel.

'But *where* are you putting it?'

'Under the mattress,' she snapped. 'Where else?'

'All right,' he said plaintively. 'Don't tell me, if you don't trust me.'

'Victor, to trust you would be like hitting a tiger with a mallet and expecting it not to tear your head off.'

In fact she never told anyone, although they all benefited from her generosity, especially her father. But after a while there was little more she could do for him. After all, at his age, what did Bernard Mellor need from life? He had dreaded loneliness after his retirement, years stretching before him with nothing to fill the time, the remainder of his life alone, with only the distant companionship of Alan in the garage. But when his children started visiting regularly, every few weeks in fact, it was enough for him. Indeed, if they came more often he got annoyed.

So he adjusted and if he suspected that there was some monkey business going on, he said nothing. Well, nothing directly. 'What the hell were you lifting out of the back of that car of yours the other night?'

'I can't remember . . . ' Victor said. 'I think it was a tool for Alan.'

'Well unless he's building another Manchester Ship Canal in there, it were a bloody big tool.'

'Oh, I remember now,' Victor said warmly. 'It was — ' Zoe watched him, breathlessly waiting for the explanation — 'some food for Alan.'

'Food?' his father repeated. 'Wrapped in a blanket? I suppose it was all tucked up so as not to catch cold.'

Victor stuck to his guns. 'Yes, it was fruit. From Italy.' He smiled engagingly. 'You know, melons, apples.'

'And he ate it?'

'Yes, he ate it.'

Bernard Mellor was outraged. 'The great, greedy bastard! I never laid my hands on so much as a bloody Granny Smith, not a ruddy pip passed my lips.'

American collectors proved to be amongst the most gullible. With considerable funds at their disposal and a desperate desire to possess anything over two hundred years old, Victor was seen placing Romanesque portals, Anglo-Saxon crosses, and numerous saints throughout the USA, depositing a trail of fake twelfth-century religious statues on an unexpected pilgrimage across Reagan's America. Besides, as Victor well knew, their museums and galleries were not as adept at spotting fakes as they were in Europe, and as for the private collectors . . . Easy game, he told Zoe. They had all the money and none of the sense, and before long Palm Springs matrons were vying with each other for the latest garden statuary. Victor's powers of persuasion did not go amiss either. If a man hesitated, his wife soon convinced him. He flourished, loving the game, the travel, the danger, the sex which was readily available, and it was only Zoe's steadying influence which prevented him from losing all restraint. But he wasn't stupid, and by selling mainly to private collectors Victor avoided an unhappy recurrence of the Venetian auction. Discreet deals in vulgar homes were safe, selling on the wide open market invited suspicion. So he kept Mike O'Dowd supplied with Zoe's paintings and sold Alan's sculpture wherever the Irishman was least likely to venture.

It worked throughout another year, Zoe's personal reputation rising steadily as she gained ground in the art world. After a long discussion with Harland, she decided to work as a consultant.

'It's demanding work,' he said, noticing how she had matured, the girl replaced by a sleek, glossy, brunette.

'I know it is, Harland, but it would be a challenge, and although I love working with you — '

'You want to spread your wings.'

She nodded.

He had expected it for a while, but now that she had finally said the words it still hurt, still scratched at his peace of mind. 'Ahmed Fazir wants you to go out to Cairo and see his new purchases. He wants some advice.'

Zoe laughed. 'Not on the paintings.'

'If you can keep him at arm's length he could be useful.'

'I'm not sure . . . '

Harland sighed deeply. 'Think about it. He has a fine collection and he buys well. You could learn from him.' He changed the subject. 'Anyway, Marcella was hoping we might visit her in Venice again.'

'Is she short of funds?'

Harland smiled. 'I imagine so. Do you want to go?'

Zoe hesitated. She had spent much of the previous year distancing herself from Harland — not professionally, just personally. Without being obvious, she had tried to bury the reputation which dogged her, knowing that although people no longer talked about her being Harland Goldberg's mistress, they remembered it every time they were seen together.

'Well . . . I'm busy at the moment.'

His face set as he looked away.

'Maybe in September,' Zoe said hurriedly, cursing herself for her weakness, just as she cursed herself for her continued association with Steven Foreshaw.

'Do I embarrass you?' Harland asked suddenly.

'Embarrass me?' Zoe replied. 'How *could* you embarrass me?'

'I'm old,' he said, without self-pity. 'And I don't want you to feel committed to me.'

Oh, but I do, Zoe thought, I feel committed to all of you, and I can't break free. Whenever I try, one of you calls me back.

'We'll go to Venice in September,' she said lightly, pushing aside her misgivings. 'I promise you, we'll go then.'

Harland's face altered immediately, the look of rejection lifting as he turned away and sorted through some papers. 'There's a baronet in Sussex who wants his paintings valued and I suggested you,' he said generously.

'Thanks, Harland. What else is new?'

'I heard from Anthony Sargeant this morning. You know how weak he is. He's no idea how to run that gallery now that his father's died. Well apparently he's been taken for a ride and sold a number of fakes. Unfortunately he made the purchases himself, and he doesn't dare to tell Tobar Manners because he usually advises him on everything.' Harland smiled. 'What makes it all the more interesting is the fact that Tobar Manners told me a similar story last week! He said he'd been duped and swore me to secrecy.' He stopped talking and laughed out loud. 'They're all running around like headless chickens, and no one's admitting to the other that he's been had.'

The news was gratifying to Zoe. 'Who's doing the fakes?'

'God knows,' Harland replied. 'Half the time they never catch the forgers, although whoever it is had better watch out — the Bracelet's back.'

Zoe was more than a little alarmed by the news. 'Leon Graves is in London?'

Harland picked up the notepad in front of him. 'Yes, he's staying at the Hyatt Carlton. I thought you and I could have lunch with him. I like him, and besides, he seemed to want to talk.'

Suspicion made her flinch. 'About what?'

'How would I know? Forgeries? His garden?'

With a smile of welcome, Leon Graves rose to his feet as Zoe walked into the restaurant an hour later, clasping her wrist with his familiar salutation. Naturally observant, he noticed a difference in her, a slight hesitation of manner which made her seem nervous, her vivacity forced.

'How lovely you do look, Zoe.'

'Thank you, Leon. It's good to see you too.' Her arm tightened under his grasp and he released her. She's twitchy, he thought.

'We haven't seen you for a long time. Where have you been?'

'In Italy, then France, then Mexico.' He

clicked his fingers. 'A disgusting armpit of a country. And the dogs . . . ' He trailed off, taking a drink of his wine. The liquid had frosted the outside of the glass and his hand left a print when he returned it to the table. 'I found a young woman, not much older than you, Zoe, faking masks.'

She was listening intently, her attention fixed. Was he trying to tell her something? 'Oh really, what happened to her?'

'I frightened her away from the ways of sin and directed her on to the ways of righteousness.'

'And her accomplices?'

Leon's eyes fixed on Zoe. 'How did you know she had accomplices?'

'They all do, don't they?' she asked, as though the matter was merely light-hearted conversation. 'Last time we met you told me about an Irishman . . . ' She paused, as though she was trying to remember his name.

'Mike O'Dowd.'

'Yes, that was it. You said he was a handler — so I presumed this young lady had a handler too.'

'You're too clever for me!' the Bracelet said generously. 'What a memory!'

Zoe leaned back in her seat, her expression relaxed, her mind racing.

'Mr O'Dowd certainly gets around,' Leon continued, taking another sip from his glass. 'In fact, it's strange that you should mention him as I was only talking about him the other day.' He paused. 'The police in France had just picked up a very unpleasant oddity called Noilly. We thought he was one of O'Dowd's cronies, but we couldn't prove it.'

Zoe caught her breath, watching Leon Graves intently. Thank God Victor was no longer working with Candadas. Instinct had told her that it was dangerous, and she had been right.

'What happened to him?'

Leon looked up from his soup. 'To Noilly?' She nodded. 'We let him slip back into the mire. For the time being he'll be left alone.' He emptied his soup bowl and then wiped his mouth with his serviette. 'Don't worry, I'll get Mike O'Dowd in the end.'

'You and your Irishman!' Harland said, laughing. 'I think it's a contest between the two of you, a clash of the gladiators.'

Leon smiled but his eyes moved back to Zoe. 'Well, we English always like our games. It's a throwback to the rugby field, a way of getting revenge in the name of good clean fun. Like hunting and shooting.' His smile faded instantly as his hand pointed straight between Zoe's eyes. 'Bang, bang — you're dead.'

She jumped, just as he meant her to.

★ ★ ★

Jimmy van Goyen was standing by the door of Anthony Sargeant's gallery, leaning against the wall. Frowning, he shifted his position to ease the strain on his bad back, the result of a riding accident, and looked out into Bond Street. A selection of people passed, wealthy women in fur coats, carrying Hermés bags, a group of dealers deep in talk coming out of Sotheby's and a small crowd of Japanese. 'The Vuitton Run' he thought, smiling half-heartedly. Every day in the summer there were scores of Japanese crossing at the lights and making for the luggage shop, buying dozens of pieces to sell later at a profit back home. He sighed and shifted his gaze, his hazel eyes raking the street for interest.

Round the corner from Bruton Street came Tobar Manners, one finger poking his ear, his tiny form moving in and out of the tourists like a wasp, his hand extended quickly to hail a passing taxi. Van Goyen sighed and smoothed back the thick blond hair which he wore in a short pigtail, and then rearranged the watch chain which hung across his waistcoat. His attention was alerted suddenly as he saw one of his favoured clients, a Greek heiress, slipping out of Courtney-Blye's gallery. Bitch, he thought idly, noting her thick ankles and wondering why plastic surgery hadn't been employed to reshape them. After all, everything else she had had been taken in or lifted up.

He moved position again, his mind working overtime wondering if the woman had bought from Courtney-Blye. Damn it! he thought. The Greek bitch was one of his best customers, and business had been slow lately, hindered by a rash of fakes which had caught him out. A taxi stopped in front of the gallery and Seymour Bell stepped on to the pavement, his glasses swinging from the chain round his neck as he paid the driver.

Van Goyen's curiosity was alerted and he smiled as the critic walked in. 'Hello, Seymour,' he said. 'You look well. What brings you to Anthony's gallery?'

Seymour Bell gave him a long look and then glanced round. 'The exhibition, Jimmy, what else? He has some interesting things.'

The Dutchman smiled manfully. 'I've got some lovely Dirck van Buburen's — '

'I'm more interested in English art just at the moment.'

Van Goyen winced, then fell into step with Bell as he walked around. Much as he might detest the man, he needed a good review urgently to increase his business. 'How's Dorothy?'

'Very well. She's away in Portugal at present.'

Portugal, van Goyen thought spitefully, that was lucky. It left the bastard more time for his boys. 'Next month I'm holding a new show,' he persisted, stopping as Bell lifted his hands in a priggish gesture.

'You don't listen, Jimmy. I'm not interested in Dutch art at the moment,' he said, pleased to read the look of resentment in van Goyen's eyes. 'I'll be in touch.'

Trying hard to keep his temper, van Goyen left the gallery and walked down Hay Hill towards Berkeley Square, knocking a backpacking tourist off the pavement as he hurried along. Bloody Bell, he raged inwardly, bloody Courtney-Blye! Bloody town, he thought viciously, and then stopped, looking down.

'Jesus wept!' he said out loud, pausing to

382

scrape some dog dirt off the sole of his Gucci shoes.

It wasn't just the Dutchman who was suffering. Within weeks the situation had escalated quickly and dangerously: rumours circulated around Bond Street, Madison Avenue and the Cote d'Azur, with dealers of every nationality, religion, and political persuasion out for blood. Victor soon heard the mutterings and, knowing that the Bracelet was back in London, put two and two together and disappeared, leaving a hurried message on Zoe's answerphone.

He would have warned her, had she been there at the time. Unfortunately, she was at that moment at the delapidated ancestral home of a baronet, deep in the Sussex countryside. The titled gentleman had provided her with light lunch and heavy conversation, his middle-aged eyes alternately flicking from her to the paintings which covered the walls.

'My family fought in the Civil War . . . ' Flick went his eyes and fastened on a Van Dyke. 'Later we were rewarded by Charles II . . . ' The eyes hovered and then landed on a dowdy portrait of the king.

'You're very fortunate to own such works,' Zoe said automatically as the baronet turned to face her. The collar of his shirt was royally frayed, his jacket leather-patched at the elbows, his cravat a national treasure.

'But having things like this is such a responsibility . . . it's a life's work,' he replied, sighing expansively.

It beats having to earn your living, Zoe

thought ungenerously. 'So you would like me to value your paintings and have them cleaned for you?'

His eyes dragged themselves away from a Canaletto. 'I thought it would be a good idea . . . but you seem very young to do such a responsible job.' Zoe smiled, and his reserve staggered momentarily. 'I meant no disrespect. You certainly came highly recommended.' Zoe kept smiling. 'I respect Harland Goldberg's opinion.'

The baronet rose to his feet, followed quickly by a bad-tempered Pekinese leaping up from under the table and barking hysterically. 'You see — '

'Pardon?' Zoe said.

The baronet raised his voice, and the Pekinese raised its own. 'I realise they do need cleaning.' Zoe nodded. 'The place will seem so bleak without them. I suppose you'll have to take them away?' The dog hurled itself against the baronet's legs, its bark rising to a crescendo as its owner moved across the room.

'Oh, you must have it done, sir,' Zoe continued, her voice a shout, her eyes fixed on the malevolent Peke. 'They will be so much better afterwards. You must take care of your collection.'

The baronet hesitated and then, with a deft movement prodded the Peke in the ribs with the toe of his riding boot. The animal howled twice and returned to its spot under the table. 'Do you really think it will improve the collection, Miss Mellor?'

'It certainly will,' Zoe responded, smiling brightly. 'When they come back you won't believe they're the same pictures.'

★   ★   ★

' . . . I think they're on to us.'

With those words the message finished ominously on the answerphone. Zoe flicked off the switch and sat down, her bag falling on to the floor next to her. So Victor had gone to ground, leaving her to fend for herself, she thought blindly. The dealers were on to her . . . they knew. Her stomach turned, the September sunlight pouring into the hallway and making her warm, then hot, then uncomfortable. Too hot to handle, she thought, rousing herself and hurrying into the bedroom, pulling out a suitcase and piling in some clothes. The case was almost full when, in a fit of exasperation, she tipped the contents out on to the bed. Running away would be useless, where could she go? Besides, even if they were on to her, what could they do?

The memory of Venice came back with savage clarity and answered her — she could be injured, or worse. She shook her head — this was England, for God's sake. Nothing could happen to her here. Besides, she had allies . . . or did she? The phone stared at her from the bedside table. Just pick me up and dial, it said, call Harland and you'll be safe. Zoe's hand hovered over the instrument, and then dropped to her side. If she told Harland it would ruin everything. She would lose the one real friend she had, and anyway Victor could be wrong.

The front door of the flat opened suddenly and Ron walked in. 'Hello,' he said. 'What's up? You look awful.' He bent down and stroked the dog's head.

'There's been some trouble. That is, there *might* be trouble for us,' Zoe trailed off, miserably uncommunicative.

'What trouble?'

'Victor left a message on the answerphone to say that they know about the fakes, he's done a bunk.'

'Who's they?'

She turned on him. 'Who the hell do you think? Anthony Sargeant, Rupert Courtney-Blye, Tobar Manners,' she counted them off on her fingers. 'And Ahmed Fazir. Oh God,' she said slumping on to the bed. 'Fazir! He bought that portal in June. He must know!'

Her hands reached out for her clothes and she began to throw them into the suitcase again. Ron watched her, mesmerised. 'But what will they do?'

'I DON'T KNOW!' Zoe shouted, badly frightened.

'But — '

'Stop asking questions, Ron, just get some things together. We've got to get out of here,' Zoe said, slamming the case shut.

'Why?'

His stupidity rocked her. 'Why? Because they're out for blood.' She pointed to her chest. 'Preferably mine.'

'I'd kill them if they hurt you.'

She softened momentarily. 'It's not that simple — '

But Ron ignored her, his own thoughts running on. 'D'you remember what Mr Potts used to say?'

Zoe raised her eyes heavenwards. 'Who is Mr Potts, Ron?'

'My old Headmaster,' he continued calmly. 'He used to say that running away meant you were guilty — '

'We *are* guilty!' she snapped.

'But if we run away everyone else will know that too,' he said simply. Brother and sister faced each other, Zoe's eyes fixed on her brother as he folded his arms across his chest.

'You know, that's smart,' Zoe said finally, her panic subsiding. 'Really smart.'

Ron was glowing with pride. 'So we'll stay here, bold as brass.' He thought of Victor and his confidence swelled. 'Only cowards run.'

The next day Bond Street hummed with scandal, intrigue, gossip and injured pride. Harland came in around nine to be faced by the only calm gallery in London, his staff apparently untouched by the furore outside, although when Mona Grimaldi arrived at eleven she seemed excited and almost flirtatious with him. Alerted to her high spirits, Zoe glanced up from her papers and passed Harland a pile of catalogue notes. She seemed perfectly composed, her dark hair full around her face, the long eyes unfathomable.

Harland accepted the notes and glanced around. The gallery was empty, no browsers, no dealers, no one. The large ormolu clock over the archway chimed the quarter hour. 'Have there been any messages for me?'

'Nothing,' Zoe replied, getting to her feet and moving over to adjust one of the spotlights in the window. 'It's very quiet.'

'Which is remarkable, considering everyone else is in a panic.'

'Really. Why?' Zoe asked, turning to Harland, her face showing undisguised astonishment.

'Because of the fakes!' he replied shortly. 'Everyone's up in arms, and they've all been meeting up to try to work out how much they've lost. God knows what's going to happen, I've never known so many dealers get taken in by fakes. Apparently the provenances of the pictures were as convincing as the paintings themselves.'

Zoe turned back to the light. 'How many dealers are involved?'

'Most of the ones we know round here,' he answered, looking towards the phone. 'I can't understand why no one's been in, or rung. It seems damned odd.'

'Maybe they're all preoccupied.'

'Maybe,' Harland replied, his tone implying something other than agreement. Zoe's attitude was irritating him, and that was surprising in itself as she had never annoyed him before. Harland watched her as she fiddled with the light. Her composure wasn't totally convincing, and only the other day she had behaved very oddly with Leon Graves. What the hell was happening to everyone?

'I'm usually the first person they run to when things go wrong,' he persisted.

'That's true,' Mona said suddenly, breaking into the conversation.

Harland turned to look at her, mystified by the smug look on her face. 'Have you heard anything?'

'My father said they know who the forger is,' she replied, tying a label on to a Raeburn portrait. 'Apparently they've given him enough rope to hang himself.' She smiled. 'Jimmy van Goyen and I had a long chat this morning about it.'

The words whistled past Zoe as she kept her face averted, Harland shrugging and going into his office. Between the two women the atmosphere was leaden, just as it had been all morning.

Minutes later, Harland materialised carrying his notebook. 'How did you get on with the baronet?'

Zoe had no time to reply before Mona said lightly, 'It looks as though you might have a visitor after all.'

All three of them glanced over to see Tobar Manners hovering outside the door. Instinctively, Harland raised his hand in greeting, then lost his temper when Manners walked on without acknowledging him.

'What the hell's the matter!' he snapped angrily. 'I'm going to have a word with that little creep and sort this out.'

Zoe took in her breath. 'I wouldn't.'

'Really? Why not?'

'You might not like what you hear,' she said slowly, knowing that the game was up. She had

389

gambled and now she had lost. Mona glanced up from her desk, a look of real delight playing over the well-bred features.

'Zoe, what *is* this all about?' Harland asked, noticing Mona out of the corner of his eye and dropping his voice.

Zoe hesitated, experiencing a real sense of sorrow. She had betrayed him and now all she had to do was admit it and she would lose the one true friend she had. Harland would never recover from such treachery, his disappointment would age him, her deceit making a mockery out of their relationship. You took me on when I needed help, she thought, and I rewarded you like this. The words of confession were on her tongue as she turned to face him, but at that moment the gallery door opened and Anthony Sargeant, Rupert Courtney-Blye, Tobar Manners, Jimmy van Goyen and Ahmed Fazir walked in. All of them seemed ill at ease, Anthony Sargeant's dull face reddened with the exertion of walking quickly from Cork Street, Tobar Manners holding a collection of papers in his hand.

Harland regarded all five men evenly. 'Good morning, gentlemen, what can I do for you?'

'It's not what you can do, it's what your assistant can,' Manners said, glancing slyly over to Mona, who was sitting chewing the end of her pen and thinking of the tale she would tell her girlfriends that night. 'We would like to talk to Miss Mellor.'

A sense of foreboding washed over Harland and he instinctively moved to block her, his body

390

shielding her from the men. Silent and pale, Zoe watched them and said nothing. It was all over, soon Harland would know, soon she would be facing prosecution, imprisonment.

'Why do you want to talk to her?'

'It's important!' Manners said sharply. 'For God's sake, Harland! Don't you know about these fakes? We've all — '

' — lost a fortune,' Fazir finished for him.

Zoe felt her legs weaken and swallowed, keeping her eyes on Harland's back.

'I don't understand. Why do you want to talk to Zoe?' Harland persisted. 'She can't help you.'

Oh but I can, Harland, she thought bitterly. I can come clean, tell these nice gentlemen which of their purchases are fakes and promise never to do it again. Then I can be taken off the scene so that they won't be embarrassed any more and start a new career in Holloway.

'We need to talk to her!' Fazir shouted.

'Don't raise your voice in my gallery,' Harland said coldly. 'I won't have bad manners here. Say what you want and we'll sort it out somehow. I know you're all upset, but we can still behave like gentlemen. After all, it's only money.'

'Only money!' Courtney-Blye howled, his voice vibrant with indignation. 'I've lost over a hundred and fifty thousand pounds.'

Harland blinked.

'And I've lost over sixty thousand,' Manners said.

Anthony Sargeant smiled idiotically. 'Really? I only lost about fifteen — '

'Shut up!' Manners snapped.

391

Harland was watching Ahmed Fazir carefully. 'How much did you lose?'

'Quarter of a million.'

So much! Zoe thought, her fear lifting for an instant. Victor must have stung him for that portal.

'Quarter of a million! Dear God, Ahmed, I had no idea.'

The Egyptian nodded his head and then turned to Zoe, his eyes dark and unsympathetic. She stared back, refusing to be intimidated. Remember what they did to you, she thought, remember the private view and the night at Courtney-Blye's. Get on with it, she thought, do your worst. You'll never get the money back, and anyway, it was almost worth getting caught just to see your face now.

Surprised by the look of defiance in her eyes, Fazir hesitated. 'Miss Mellor,' he said coldly, 'I would like to speak to you alone.'

Zoe smiled without humour. 'No. Say what you've got to say now. I want Harland to hear it.'

He sighed. 'You know about all these fakes?' Zoe said nothing. 'You know we've lost a fortune and we've been made to look a laughing stock. Well, I want revenge.' Her heart began to pound in her chest but Zoe's face remained composed, fearless. 'I want to get my own back on the forgers. I want to pay them back for every pound they took from me.' She flinched inwardly and saw Harland watching her out of the corner of his eye. 'They have been very clever, very clever indeed, but all good things come to an end. And this *is* the end.'

'And?' Zoe asked, her mouth dry.

Fazir paused, the words were difficult for him. 'You know this business and you've proved many times that you know how to spot a fake . . . ' Embarrassed, he rushed on. 'Will you join forces with us and help us to find the forgers? We would all appreciate it so much.'

24

Alan's version of Barbra Streisand's 'Evergreen' would have offended anyone's ears if they had been sober. As it was, Zoe and Victor were happily inebriated and Alan was mindlessly, childishly drunk. With his arms stretched out to his sides and his round, red face tipped up under the light in the garage, his voice peeled upwards and outwards in the cool Rochdale air.

' . . . *love, soft as an easy chair* . . . ' he sang, as Zoe and Victor sat on two deckchairs, like a first night audience. '*Love, soft as the morning air* . . . '

'Not bad,' Victor murmured, his eyes glassy, his voice thick with a mixture of champagne and relief.

'It's awful. He can't sing,' Zoe replied, passing her glass over to her brother to be refilled, and nearly toppling over in her deckchair as she did so.

' . . . *love soft as an easy chair* . . . '

'You've already sung that bit!' she called out, good-naturedly. She had escaped, she was home free.

Alan continued, unperturbed, as she turned back to Victor. 'I thought we were done for yesterday. I was really frightened.'

'Nah!' Victor said easily, sipping at his glass.

'Well, *you* thought we were! Mind you, we'd been so lucky for so long, I suppose it was inevitable, even though I don't understand how everyone found out about the fakes at the same time.' She sipped the champagne thoughtfully. 'We must have been putting too many out on the market. You'll have to watch that, Victor, and monitor it more carefully.'

'I know what I'm doing,' he replied impatiently.

'Oh really? So why the panic — you were the one who ran off,' Zoe snapped, remembering how he had deserted her. 'I could have ended up carrying the can for you.'

'Nah.'

She focused her eyes on her brother as he slumped further down the deckchair, his jacket riding up behind him, his pale eyes half shut. 'I could!'

'Nah.'

Infuriated, Zoe punched him so sharply in the chest that he spilt some of his drink. 'Bloody hell! Mind the jacket.'

'*One love, that is shared by two . . .* ' Alan continued happily as his brother and sister began to quarrel.

'I could have ended up in jail,' Zoe wailed. 'In jail.'

'Regular food and a roof over your head, what more could you want?' Victor asked wickedly.

'You rotten sod!' Zoe snapped, struggling to get up out of the deckchair, the champagne spilling over her skirt.

'*Ageless and ever . . . ever . . . green . . .* ' caroled Alan.

Her hair disordered and her clothes stained,

Zoe managed to get to her feet. 'We were lucky. *You* were lucky, and it's all thanks to me, Victor.' He raised his glass in a mock toast. 'And you needn't be so patronising. *I* was the one who insisted we keep it in the family, and I was right. Remember what Leon Graves told me only the other day about Noilly?' She pointed an accusing finger at her brother. 'You would have carried on working with him and that pervert Candadas. Besides, the Bracelet would have found out and put two and two together . . . ' A real sense of foreboding washed over her. 'We must learn our lesson from this, take things slowly and *always* keep the business in the family. Always.'

'I agree,' Victor said, yawning widely. 'You were right all along about that.'

'Yeah . . . well, I was,' Zoe finished, surprised by her brother's capitulation.

'Anyway, stop worrying. We're safe and sound,' Victor continued affably, turning to his brother. 'Let's have another couple of verses, Alan — for the road.'

At the same time as they were celebrating in Rochdale, Ron was walking Peter down Great Portland Street, his shoulders hunched against a sudden shower. He could have gone to Rochdale with Zoe but he had made an excuse, for once drawing back from her, his disappointment apparent. She could have been in real trouble, he thought ruefully, hurrying to keep up with Peter as he pulled on the lead. She could have been put in jail. He blinked, the rain dripping off his hair and running down his face — Zoe in jail, Zoe taken away. What would he do without her?

He crossed at the lights and moved towards the shelter of some buildings to keep the rain off them, although Peter seemed not to notice it, his coat shiny, his eyes alert, scanning the pedestrians in front of him. Ron shook his head in astonishment — Zoe had gone back home and was *celebrating* with Victor. Victor! Who had run off like a coward and left her. He stopped suddenly, his mouth set into a thin line. He would never have left her. Never. They would have had to kill him first. A car passed by and threw up a shower of dirty water from the gutter, missing Ron, but drenching Peter. With an irritated shake, the greyhound soaked his master and then strained at the lead to continue his walk. Reluctantly Ron moved on, Victor was no good, he thought, no good at all. He had left Zoe when she needed him.

If only *he* was smarter, if only he could do all those things his brother could do, then they wouldn't need Victor. Ron smiled grimly. He would like to see how his brother fared without Zoe and her paintings, and Alan and his sculptures. Not that Victor could manage without him either, Ron thought, no, he needed him to deliver and collect and lift and carry, and all the other things Ron did to help keep the business running smoothly. Smarting with a previously unknown fury, his whole body was racked with jealousy and anger. Poor Ron, too dumb to come in from the rain, walking through the dark London streets, thinking.

✱ ✱ ✱

'It must be very sweet revenge,' Harland said, smiling, 'to think that they had to come to you for help.'

Zoe shrugged and bent down to pick up a small painting which was propped against the reception desk. 'Revenge doesn't come into it.'

Harland thought otherwise, but wasn't about to press the matter. Maybe she was being magnanimous, he thought, and then again, maybe she was lying. 'I like that,' he said, watching as she unwrapped a small Corot landscape. 'I've always liked his work, even though there's a saying that Corot painted a thousand pictures, fifteen hundred of which are in America.'

Zoe laughed and stepped back to admire the landscape. 'Real or fake?'

'You're asking me?' Harland said in astonishment.

With a rush of warmth, Zoe slipped her arm through Harland's and leaned towards him. His head buzzed uncomfortably as it always did when she showed him any affection. 'But tell me what *you* think.'

'I think . . . I think, it's genuine.'

She squeezed his arm. 'You see! You can do it when you try.'

Harland looked into her face and noticed the wide, luminous eyes, the faint flush of colour on her cheeks. She was light-hearted, almost childish, he realised, and then with a stab of real distress, wondered if she was in love.

'You seem happy.'

'I am, Harland,' she replied without releasing

his arm. 'I'm very happy.'

'Zoe, is there someone — '

Harland's question was interrupted as her attention wandered. At the gallery door, Ron's tall form suddenly appeared, his hand waving to her self-consciously. Mystified, Zoe walked outside to find her brother leaning against the gallery window, Peter by his side. 'There's no trouble is there?'

He shook his head miserably. 'I was fed up, that's all.'

The words puzzled Zoe. Ron seldom moaned about anything. It was out of character, just as it had been out of character for him to stay in London while she had gone up to Rochdale to celebrate.

'What are you fed up about?'

'Things.' He shrugged, his eyes flicking from his sister to Peter, his mouth drawn into a tight line.

'Tell me, Ron, or I can't help, can I?' Her sympathy did nothing to help. 'Do you want to go for a walk?'

Ron's initial sulkiness was taking shape as they walked towards Piccadilly and had set hard by the time they entered Hyde Park. An equally sullen sun brushed the full trees and fell on the park benches liberally carved with initials, a page of the *Evening Standard* blowing against an overflowing litter bin. Ron was walking with his head down, his hands deep in his pockets, Peter sniffing the grass behind him. The sunlight chalked the top of his hair and made it artificially blond.

'So, what's the matter?'

'Did you have a good time up home?' he asked flatly, his voice pugnacious, his broad Lancashire accent defiant under the southern trees.

'You could have come,' Zoe replied, shading her eyes with one hand and looking up at her brother. 'I asked you to.'

'I was busy.'

She stopped walking. 'Busy! Doing what?'

'I have my own life!' he snapped in temper. 'I've got a girl now. I have my own life and my own things. I can do as I like.'

'Of course,' Zoe said, shocked by the outburst. 'I never said — '

'I'm nothing but a flaming,' he struggled for the word 'errand boy'. 'Go for this, do that, get me the other.' It makes me sick!'

The attack winded her momentarily. 'Ron, don't say things like that. You know how I rely on you.'

'Why? You've got Victor,' he answered, turning to face her. 'And we all know what a big shot he is — running off like a bloody soft girl.'

His jealousy caught her off guard and left her speechless. Embarrassed, Ron shuffled his feet and glanced round. He hadn't wanted to be angry with her, but it seemed wrong that she should trust Victor. 'Who works with us? I mean, in the business?'

Unprepared for such a question, Zoe hesitated. 'You've never been interested in the business before.'

'I knew you didn't trust me!' he snapped, whistling for Peter and moving off towards the Serpentine.

Zoe ran after him. 'What is this all about?'

'You think I'm thick,' he said, twisting the dog lead round the fingers of his left hand. The sunlight made him achingly handsome. 'Well, I'm not smart, I know, but I can think.' He turned to her defiantly. 'I know what you all say behind my back — thick Ron, all brown and no brain.'

'It's 'all *brawn* and no brain' actually,' Zoe replied, smiling slightly.

He refused to be humoured. 'Whatever it is, it's not true. I could be a good help.'

'You *are* a good help,' she replied, taking hold of the other end of the dog lead and tugging it slightly as they sat down. 'I could never manage without you. You know that.'

'But who's in the business?'

Realising that her brother would not be content until he knew, Zoe explained. 'You mustn't tell anyone, Ron, otherwise we will all be in danger.' He nodded his head in impatient agreement. 'Victor does the deals, Alan does the sculpture, and I do the paintings and drawings.'

'Who else?'

She was shaken by his stubbornness. 'That's a stupid question! You know we keep it in the family now. So that's it.'

'That's it?' he repeated dumbly. 'But Victor must . . . talk to people.'

'Naturally, he has to organise the sales.'

'Who with?'

Zoe was suddenly impatient. Apart from Mike O'Dowd, she knew nothing more herself. 'I don't know,' she replied, and then, seeing the look in her brother's eyes, confided, 'There's a man he deals with called Mike O'Dowd. He's the only one I know about.'

Ron nodded, almost pacified. 'What does he look like?'

'Why? Are you going in for portrait painting?' she snapped, folding her arms and leaning back against the bench. A cocky pigeon strutted in front of her, Peter's eyes tracking the bird avidly.

'Please . . . Tell me what he looks like.'

Zoe paused and thought for a moment, remembering the Irishman with reluctance. 'Five foot ten, nondescript face, tinted glasses — and sharp suits. You must remember, Ron. He came up to Rochdale . . . just after Victor was stabbed.' She glanced over to him. Ron was frowning. 'Now are you any the wiser?'

This was not what he had been expecting, and his brain staggered on the information. With slow reasoning, Ron built up a picture of Mike O'Dowd and then shook his head. 'I'm off back to work,' he said flatly.

'Well, we must do this again some time,' Zoe said, amused, and dropping into step beside him. 'It's good for us to have a chat, Ron, that way we know what we're both thinking.' She stopped and tugged at his shirt. 'But I *don't* know what you're thinking, do I? For the first time in my life I don't know what's going on in your head.'

Looking down on his sister, Ron smiled, his good humour fully restored as he patted Zoe affectionately on the head. Just like Peter. 'Nothing to worry 'bout. I was just mad at Victor, that's all.'

'Are you sure?'

Ron's face was bland. 'Oh sure, I'll leave the business to you two — you're the clever ones.'

He walked off under the trees as Zoe called out after him, 'Who's your girlfriend, Ron?'

The shadows hid him for an instant and as he came back under the sunlight, he smiled without answering.

★   ★   ★

Wandsworth was dark, half of the street lamps smashed or not working, a skip filled with rubbish blocking the pavement, an old carpet left propped against a wall. At ten o'clock the only people about were an old woman walking a terrier and a couple necking behind a van. Ron Mellor looked round, his foot tapping to the sound of rock music coming from a house across the road, one window boarded up, the others hung with sheets making improvised curtains. Sniffing, Ron pulled up the collar of his jacket and glanced round as the gate creaked uneasily in the wind.

For the fiftieth time in half an hour, Ron looked towards the church and then, disappointed, dug into his pocket and pulled out a Mars bar. Slowly, he bit into it and began to chew, leaning back against the wall and breaking off a piece at a time. He had been hiding there for over an hour, Ron realised, sniffing again and huddling further into his jacket. If someone didn't come out soon, he'd freeze to death. Almost on cue, an outside light illuminated the church door and, swallowing a lump of unchewed Mars bar, Ron moved back into the shadows and watched as the door opened. The first man was small and weedy, pitifully so, Ron thought, craning his neck forwards to see the second man, who was fat with long hair, appear. Ron frowned, puzzled. That wasn't right, he thought. He wasn't Mike O'Dowd. This guy had no glasses for a start, and he sounded — Ron listened carefully — he sounded foreign.

Mystified, Ron would have moved then, but did not dare risk being spotted and kept his eyes on the door instead. There were no prizes for guessing who the third man was. Tall and lean as ever, well dressed and sharp as a new penknife, Victor stood in the church doorway, his hand raised to say goodbye, the fingers spread out against the light in a blessing of sorts. Ron waited for a couple of minutes until Victor's glossy car disappeared down the shabby little street, and the light went out over the church door. Finishing off the Mars bar, he shivered again and turned his feet homewards.

★ ★ ★

Across London, Erica Goldberg was waking up slowly, turning over in bed and reaching out for Victor. The sheet was cold to her touch as she opened her eyes quickly and looked round the bedroom, calling out for him. Silence . . . Disappointed, she reached out for her handbag and rummaged in it for a bottle of pills, taking a couple of amphetamines with the stale water which had been by the bedside all day, then sighing, she leaned back against the pillows.

It had been like this ever since she had fallen in love with Victor Mellor. For weeks he pursued her and then when they had finally made love his interest had waned and he had started to make excuses. Erica closed her eyes, waiting for the tablets to take effect. She had been off booze and cocaine since her trip to the clinic, taking regular classes to keep herself in shape and even getting on better with her mother. Then Victor had come along and spoiled everything. The depth of her feelings astounded her as she found herself unable to stop thinking of him, her every thought and action remembered so that it could be related back to him later. Yes, she certainly made him laugh, she thought, and she satisfied him in bed but then again he liked to make love several times a night and sometimes she didn't feel like it. Besides she wanted to get closer to him, to understand him, not simply have sex with him.

'You won't like me afterwards,' he had said the first night he had taken her back to his flat. 'I'll make you do things you won't like,' he continued, sliding his hand under her skirt. 'You'll feel used.'

She had moaned and longed for him to continue. Sure of her, he had slipped her forefinger into his mouth, his tongue running over it, his eyes fixed on hers. Finally he pulled it out slowly, his lips sucking it. 'And that's only a finger, Erica,' he said, pushing her back on to the bed.

The memory upset her so much that she kicked off the bed sheets and was about to get to her feet when she looked down at her stomach. There was a huge 'V' printed on her skin, drawn in her own red lipstick, the point of the 'V' directed towards her pubic hair. 'V' for Victor, she thought, angrily rubbing the lurid mark off her skin. To the Victor the spoils.

★ ★ ★

'He should be castrated like a cat!' Myrtle said violently, her right hand hovering over the outstretched fingers of her left hand. The nail varnish was vermilion. 'He should be maimed,' she continued, jabbing a blood-red smear on to her left thumb. 'I've always been unlucky. No mother had so much to bear — '

'Erica is involved with Victor Mellor, she isn't dead — '

'Is that meant to console me?' Myrtle snapped, screwing the top on the nail polish. 'Such a comfort!'

Raising her eyes heavenwards, Harland glanced into the dressing-table mirror behind his wife. His beard needed trimming, he thought, moving into the bathroom and picking up his scissors.

'How *can* you do that?' Myrtle asked, leaning against the door frame, her fingers, with their wet nails, spread out before her. 'How can you trim that ridiculous thing when I want to talk?'

Harland's eyes focused on an unruly hair and he snipped at it waspishly. 'What good is talking? What do you want me to do?'

'Do what any father would! Find her a husband.'

'How can I do that? She doesn't like the men we suggest — '

'You should be firm! There are hundreds of suitable men. What's wrong with Laurence Templeton?'

'He's an accountant with halitosis.'

'So? No one's perfect,' Myrtle said phlegmatically. 'She should be married! Like everyone else's daughter! That this should happen to me!' Myrtle wailed, trailing into the bathroom after her husband, her hands still extended out before her like a robot's. 'We don't even know what he does for a living.'

'He's a dealer,' Harland muttered without moving his mouth, his eyes fixed on the mirror.

'A what!'

'A dealer.' Harland snapped, the scissors closing viciously on his beard, a jagged edge appearing before his horrified eyes. Slamming back the shaving mirror, he peered into the main glass over the wash-hand basin. He'd ruined it! Now he'd have to trim the whole beard to make it look right. 'My God, look what I've done!' he said, turning to his wife, his face pale, his index finger pointing to the damage.

'So what! It's only hair. If you were a real man you'd take those scissors and cut something off Victor Mellor which would never grow again.'

★　★　★

'Things are settling down in London,' Fazir said to Harland a month later. The trees were turning, the premature cold snap biting many leaves off with a bitter frost. Inside the gallery the heating was turned up, the window sporting a large Orpen portrait, the basement humming with activity as Leonard Phillips restored several paintings from the famous collection of the Guido brothers. To all intents and purposes, things were back to normal, although the art world was jittery and very easily spooked.

'Everyone needed to calm down after all that trouble,' Harland agreed, pouring them both a brandy and returning to his seat. 'You lost a great deal of money.'

'I can afford it, but I don't like to be duped,' Fazir replied, sipping his drink. 'And I'm not alone. There are a great many angry dealers baying for blood.'

Idly Harland fingered his mutilated beard. The room was warm and he was tired, too tired to think deeply about anything. 'Zoe did her best to help all of you, and it looks as though her enquiries succeeded in scaring him off. But the forger's gone to ground somewhere, Ahmed, just as they always do. You should put it behind you and just be grateful that he's moved on — '

Zoe walked in at the same instant, saw Fazir and nodded her head stiffly in acknowledgement, before turning to Harland.

'Leonard wants to see you about one of the Guido paintings.'

'Now?'

She smiled. 'I'm afraid so. Unless you want me — '

Harland struggled to his feet. He was getting older and resented the stiffness of his joints.

'I'll be back in a moment,' he said, adding guilelessly, 'Would you keep Ahmed company for me?'

The carpet muffled the sounds of her footsteps as Zoe moved forward to tidy Harland's desk. Several daily papers were spread out, each turned to the Arts page, a couple marked extravagantly in red, circling something which had caught his eye. The rich aroma of a cigar wafted in front of her as she glanced at Fazir and passed him an ashtray.

'I haven't found out any more about the forger, although naturally I'll keep trying. That is, if you all want me to.'

'You've earned your money,' Fazir said. 'At least he's moved his little business out of London.'

'Perhaps he took the hint,' Zoe added.

The conversation was peculiar and disjointed, as there were in fact three levels of communication going on between them. The persistent and heady sexuality which Fazir exuded, the complicated web of duplicity in which Zoe was embroiled, and the electric tension of knowing that one wrong move, or word, could give her away.

'He's in Malta,' Fazir said suddenly.

'The forger?' she asked, attempting to keep the surprise out of her voice. 'How do you know?'

'I have my spies too.'

Zoe refused to appear intimidated. 'Well, in that case, maybe we should get together and catch him *en masse*?'

He smiled but continued to watch her as she

gathered the newspapers together, her mind racing. What the hell was going on? she thought uneasily. The forger's in Malta, she repeated to herself, flicking on a picture light over another large Orpen portrait. Fazir must be trying to trick her into giving herself away. She shook her head, no, that couldn't be it. The dealers would never have hired her unless they thought she was completely honest — unless it was a double bluff.

Excusing herself, Zoe walked out into the gallery, passing Mona talking on the phone, and looked out on to Bond Street. For three months she and Victor had only sold the fakes on the Italian and French markets, steering clear of London and New York, where the Bracelet was currently active. Not one fake drawing, sculpture or painting had been sold in England. Unsettled, she closed her eyes and tried to think. She remembered Leon Graves's remarks about O'Dowd having a set-up on Malta. He would never be stupid enough to stay, she thought, the Irishman would have moved on as soon as he knew he was suspected. There was only one solution — there was another forger at work. Her relief was only temporary. If there *was* another forger she would already have heard about it, either from the dealers or Victor. A dull sense of unease nudged at her, unsettling her so much that after another minute Zoe snatched up her coat and left, slamming the gallery door behind her.

As had been her habit over the years, Zoe did what she always did when she was frightened and rang home. 'Hi, Dad. How are things?'

'Same as usual. How's things with you?'

She smiled half-heartedly. 'OK. We're busy. How's Alan?'

Bernard Mellor was not about to be fooled by anyone — least of all his daughter. 'The same as he was last weekend, when you saw him. What's all this about?'

I miss you, she thought. No, that's no true, that wasn't it, she realised. She didn't miss her father, instead she missed Lancashire, Buck's Lane, the draughty hallway, the moors, the familiarity of it all. I miss my childhood, she thought longingly, I even miss Steven. I miss it all because I want to be safe.

'Hello! Hello! Oh, bloody hell — '

'I'm still here, Dad. I just rang to say that we'd be up on Friday night.'

'Again?'

She shuddered at the tone in his voice. God, she thought bitterly, why don't you want to see me? Why can't you miss me?

'Yes, again, Dad. Is that all right?'

'You'll do your own, whatever I say,' her father replied. 'D'you want a word with that fat brother of yours?'

'No . . . send him my love and tell him I'll see him Friday.'

She was about to put the phone down, when he called out to her. Eagerly, Zoe answered him. 'Yes, Dad, what is it?'

'I said, don't forget to ask Victor if he'll bring those cigarettes he promised, will you?' Her heart ached with disappointment as he continued. 'He

411

gets 'em off the plane, so I don't see why I shouldn't get the benefit, after all, he's got the money, and he's bloody mean enough as a rule . . . Zoe, Zoe? Are you still there?'

★ ★ ★

The newspaper headline concerned some talks in Washington, the politicians' photographs carefully inserted into the type, the weather forecast below spelling out a period of unexpectedly warm weather. Zoe turned over the page. The piece which caught her eye had been circled in red by Harland so she wouldn't miss it. There wasn't much to read:

> . . . an unknown Italian, believed to be in his thirties, and to have been involved in a series of forgeries which have fooled the European art world throughout the summer, was found dead in Malta yesterday morning, his body . . . '

Zoe swung round as the door of the office opened and Harland walked in, his face serious. 'Have you seen it?'

'The piece in the paper?' He nodded. 'I was just reading it,' Zoe said, turning back to the desk. 'It's terrible. Who could have — '

'Murdered him?'

Zoe blinked, but kept her eyes averted. 'Murder? Did it say murder? I haven't read all the article yet.'

Harland moved round the desk and lifted the

412

paper to read it for her. 'Murder is suspected . . . ' he finished adamantly. 'Not that it could have been anything else. The man was hanged from a tree.'

'What kind?'

Harland's face was incredulous. 'What kind of tree?'

'No!' Zoe snapped impatiently. 'I meant what kind of forgery was he involved in?'

'The illegal kind, I suppose. The dangerous kind, certainly,' Harland continued, his instincts jangling again. After the dealers had employed Zoe to find the forger he had dismissed all his stupid and unfounded suspicions, but now he wasn't so certain. Zoe looked upset, frightened even. 'Forgery is not for amateurs. Remember what I told you about Leon — '

'I should have found the forger!' Zoe cried out suddenly, her mind working quickly. She had to excuse her obvious distress and convince Harland that it was simply professional pique. He would understand that; he would even expect it. 'Damn it, Harland, I was hired to do a job.'

'You did your best.'

She snatched the paper from his hands. 'My best! What good was that? I should have got this man.' She read the piece again and crumbled the paper in disgust. 'Why did they kill him?'

'That's the way forgers usually end up,' Harland said, relieved now that his fears had been allayed. She was angry because she had failed; nothing more. 'Thank God you didn't get involved too deeply.'

The words swam in Zoe's head and she sat

down heavily. 'You think *I* could have been hurt?' she asked, playing out her role to the full. Convincing him.

Harland nodded. 'I never thought it would come to this, or I would never have allowed you to become involved.' He put his arm around her shoulder. 'Leave such things to men like Leon Graves, who can handle them.' Zoe nodded dumbly as Harland continued. 'At least Fazir will be pleased to know that his Gainsborough forger has been stopped. He was badly stung on a portrait only three months ago.' She knew, she had painted it. 'I imagine it will please him to read about this over breakfast.' It could have been me, Zoe thought dully, it could have been me. 'After all, that Ramsay cost him a packet too . . .'

Zoe stiffened. What was Harland talking about? She had never faked a Ramsay. 'Which Ramsay?'

Harland threw up his hands. 'I was sworn to secrecy. Fazir thought it would make him look a complete fool in your eyes if I told you. The one which was supposed to be a painting of Kitty Fisher, the courtesan. She was dressed . . .'

In blue, with a straw hat, Zoe thought ruefully, seeing the same portrait in her mind's eye. The same portrait which had hung on the cold, high wall of the Methodist church in Wandsworth. The same portrait which Lino Candadas had painted, and which Victor had sold behind her back. She sighed. So he was trading without her again, was he?

Suddenly everything made perfect sense.

Victor had got greedy again. He had been selling her paintings, Alan's sculptures . . . and Candadas's works. And unless she was much mistaken, Leon Graves probably knew about it. He was certainly on to Mike O'Dowd and Noilly. After all, hadn't he told her as much? But did he know about Victor yet? And, more importantly, did he know about her?

'I've just got to look something up for a customer,' Zoe said to Harland, walking into the library and closing the door behind her. She forced herself to be calm and sat down. Victor had the upper hand again, she thought ruefully, as ever. There was no way to outsmart Victor. He never learnt his lesson, even Mike O'Dowd had failed to keep tabs on him. Or maybe, Zoe thought suddenly, maybe the two of them were working together and making a stooge out of her. Her anger smouldered dangerously. Revenge had bound brother and sister together very successfully for a while, and that revenge should have been vented on O'Dowd, or the art world in general, not on each other. Frustration welled up in her. They *could* have succeeded. But she hadn't allowed for her brother's temperament, the duplicity from which they had all suffered. Childhood had been bad enough, Zoe seeing Victor absorb all their mother's love and then reject it — the same love she had longed for and had never enjoyed. That had hurt deeply, but now he was risking her safety. And for what? Did he hate her? *Why?* she asked herself repeatedly. Why did he care so little for her?

For that was what hurt her the most: she had

been betrayed and endangered by her own brother. The truth savaged her and made her angry — so angry that the object of her revenge altered from that moment. From then on her whole rage settled on Victor, the man who had taken every scrap of affection for himself; the man who had used her, and cheated her, the man who had always beaten her. Yet Victor was her brother, her blood — she of all people knew him. She smiled inwardly at the Biblical connotation, and as she wondered how to repay him, the words played repeatedly in her head: Know Thine Enemy.

25

The pub next to the dog track was named The Merry Fiddler, its red brick front displaying a selection of posters advertising the forthcoming attractions — 'George Evans sings Country and Western' and the following Thursday, 'Jerry Flack — hard rock'. The images of the entertainers were black and white mug shots, Jerry Flack bearing an unfortunate crease across his forehead like a slash wound. Zoe paused and then walked in looking for Ron. A thick smog pooled round the bar, the crush of bodies filling the few tables or leaning against the bar, others playing pool in what had once been the snug, the irregular click of balls straying through the open door. The light was dim, red-hued from a row of cheap imitation coach lamps, a series of gaudy fairy lights strung haphazardly over the bar.

Quickly Zoe walked past several tables ignoring the comments of the drinkers, having spotted Ron waiting alone by a wan electric fire, Peter lying on the floor next to him.

This is a great place to meet,' she said, sitting beside him and watching as a young woman came in and began to work the bar.

'Gimme something, just the odd pound — it's for the babby,' she said, pointing to the child she was carrying, its body wrapped in a blanket, its face a white smudge. 'God bless you, sir,' she said to the landlord, turning to a group of young men leaning by the door. 'Give us something for the babby — '

'Bugger off!' came back the reply from one of the drinkers, his friends egging him on. 'Get a bloody job and work for it like the rest of us!'

'Zoe?' Ron said, dragging his sister's attention away from the woman. 'Thanks for coming. You want a drink?'

'Yes, get me a lager, thanks,' she said, watching as the woman moved towards her brother as he made his way to the bar. Without hesitating, Ron dipped into his back pocket and gave her a selection of coins.

'Here you are, Zoe,' he said, returning to the table. 'Thanks for coming — '

'You've already said that,' she replied, glancing round. 'This is a dump.'

'I've got mates here.'

'You'd probably need them,' she said drily. 'What did you want to see me about?'

'I've been thinking. After what you told me about that guy in Malta, I got worried. It's not safe, is it?' he asked, dropping his voice, Zoe straining to hear him over the noise of the fruit machines. 'You could be caught, couldn't you?' She said nothing as he continued. 'Why don't you stop forging and just continue at the gallery. After all, we don't need the money — '

'I enjoy it,' Zoe interrupted him.

But you've been like a cat on hot bricks for months and you were impossible to live with when you thought they'd found you out — '

'I was worried.'

'So why do you do it?' he persisted. 'What's it

for, if it's not the money?'

'I like the excitement,' Zoe snapped, shrugging her shoulders and taking a sip of her drink. 'I like to think that I'm getting away with it and that the dealers are paying fortunes for *my* work.'

'They could catch you out. Through Victor.'

The name snapped at her. Frowning, Zoe took another drink, watching Ron over the rim of her glass.

'You told me that he only dealt with your paintings and Alan's fakes,' he went on, 'but it's not true. He uses other people as well.'

She flinched, but kept her voice even. 'How do you know?'

'I followed him.'

'Followed Victor?' Zoe replied incredulously. 'But you don't drive, so how could you?'

Ron grinned self-consciously. 'I asked Sally, a girl who comes into the café, to lend me her motorbike and I also asked her to look after Peter for me while I was gone ... ' He paused, his thoughts drifting. 'Sally's been teaching me on the bike for a while, on the quiet like. It was going to be a surprise for you.' One of many, Zoe thought wryly. 'Anyway, I followed Victor to Wandsworth and saw him go to some church off the main road. A wreck of a place. He came out about two hours later.'

Zoe's face hardened. 'Then where did he go?'

'Give me something for the babby,' the woman said, interrupting them and holding out her hand, the dirty palm turned upwards. Absent-mindedly, Zoe began to dig in her handbag for her purse.

419

'He's only six weeks old,' the woman went on, 'and he's hungry.'

'There you are,' she said, turning back to Ron.

But the woman hung on, turning the money over in her hand. 'Just a little more . . . for the babby. You could end up in my situation one day.'

Zoe turned to her in irritation. 'I have no more — '

'Come on, that's enough!' the barmaid said, moving over and taking the woman's arm. 'Don't bother the customers, there's a good girl.'

'Bother them!' the woman shouted. 'Just look at her clothes and then look at mine.' Zoe rose to her feet quickly as the woman was pushed out of the door, screaming. 'You don't know what it's like to be poor, you bloody cow!'

Zoe sat down again, her hand shaking as she picked up her glass. 'Go on, Ron.'

'Well I had to return the bike and pick Peter up, so I couldn't follow Victor to find out where he went afterwards . . . ' Ron trailed off, palpably embarrassed.

'Oh,' Zoe said simply, draining her glass and holding it out to Ron for a refill.

'But that's not all!' Ron said eagerly. 'The next day Victor went back to the church and I asked Sally if I could keep the bike a bit longer. She was bad-tempered about it, and started saying something about — '

'Ron, get back to the point,' Zoe said impatiently. 'No — get me another drink first.'

Obediently he did so, and then continued. 'This time I followed Victor from his flat, down to a place called Saltdean.'

She frowned. 'Saltdean? Where's that?'

'Near Brighton.'

'Near Brighton . . . why would he go there?'

Ron's face glowed under the cheap lights. 'To see the same men. They came out when he arrived and started loading some things into his car from the back of a . . . oh, what do you call those little houses? They're like proper houses, but only half a house.'

'A bungalow.'

'Yeah, that's it. It was a bungalow by the sea, and they were piling some stuff into the car boot and after a while Victor drove off back to London.'

'Is that it?' Zoe asked finally.

There was a roar of applause behind them as a middle-aged man wearing jeans began to sing, the microphone swelling the sound to a deafening level. Around them, the drinkers turned to watch the show, Zoe picking up her glass and nodding to Ron.

'Well, go on, continue.'

He thought back to the previous night. It had been raining, in fact, every time he had followed Victor it had either been raining or blowing a gale. Not that it stopped him; he had still tracked his brother from his flat to Wandsworth, waiting until he saw Victor go into the church before stopping the bike and looking for a place to hide. This time he had decided to explore the yard behind the church, skirting the black walls and creeping over the broken paving stones until he could look in through a window. The church was deserted, and he could see only the dim vestry, and a few boxes, already packed. Carefully, Ron crept round the building, his fear of dark graveyards at eleven o'clock at night making him sweat. Steadily, and quietly for such a big man, he moved towards the nearest window and looked in.

In the dim light, a man looked back at him and he ducked, catching his breath, waiting for shouts and for someone to rush out and catch him. But no one did, and after another instant, he risked looking in again. The room was divided into two portions, the first, facing him, was in semi-darkness, the 'man' being a portrait on an easel. Sighing with relief, Ron peered into the further portion of the room and saw the back of Noilly and the unmistakable figure of Victor talking to the fat Italian. Craning his head to one side, Ron tried to hear what was being said, but the conversation was muffled and indistinct. The memory was so fresh in his mind that he remembered the feel of the damp church wall, and the hoot of an owl as he crouched in the rainy night, listening.

'Go on, tell me what happened,' Zoe said, her voice expressionless.

'Victor turned on the light in the bit of the room nearest to me and I ducked down,' Ron paused, reliving the moment. 'I could hear them better then, and make out what they said. There was something about a man called Crowbar — '

'Crowbar?'

He shrugged. 'Well, it was something like that.'

Zoe thought for a minute. 'Could it have been

Tobar? Tobar Manners?'

'Yes, that's it! And then Victor said something about an auction in New York.'

The two words made her heart begin to thump. 'New York? Are you sure, Ron?'

'That's what he said, 'New York',' Ron replied firmly. 'Er . . . then he said that he'd had enough of you,' he pressed on, glancing away from from the look on his sister's face, knowing that he had to tell her, otherwise she would go on trusting Victor, and Victor was not to be trusted. 'He said you were a pain, and besides, you were holding him back when he could be making a real killing.' Zoe swallowed the remainder of her drink. 'He said you were too scared to be of any use any more, and he said you were too — ' Ron hesitated. 'Shall I go on?'

'Please,' she said, turning to the singer and watching him, her thoughts elsewhere. 'You must tell me everything.'

'He said he was going to retire after this sale.'

Zoe smiled grimly. 'What else?'

'That he was going to plant one of Alan's fake sculptures — and then uncover it at the sale.' Zoe sucked in her breath. 'He said he wasn't going to tell on you, but it would scare you off the forging and make you drop out of the business.' Ron paused. 'I heard him say he would be back tomorrow night . . . Listen, I'm sorry if I hurt you.'

'Get me another drink, will you, Ron?'

'That's your third.'

'I don't need you to keep tabs on everything,' she snapped, pushing the glass towards him.

She was more angry than she had ever been in her life, so angry that for an instant she found breathing difficult. 'Thank you,' she said coldly when he returned to the table.

Ron was baffled by her reaction. 'I didn't mean to hurt you, but you had to know — '

'Oh yes, one should always know the worst. I'm used to that.' She gulped at her drink. 'Up and down, isn't it? Always up and down . . . '

'What?'

'You don't understand, Ron, and why should you?' she said, her hand reaching out towards his, the pain in her chest tightening even though the lagers were making her head muzzy. 'You did very well, Ron, and I'll tell you why. Next week there's a sale in New York. It's been organised by the Guido brothers and it is *very* important.' She spread the fingers of both hands on her knees, talking slowly as she began to feel more lightheaded. 'I talked to Victor about it only last weekend and he said that we weren't putting any of our fakes into the sale because it would be too dangerous.' The memory scalded her. 'Too dangerous. Hah! You see, Ron, he just wanted to keep the pitch clear for himself and use it as a chance to expose me . . . '

'But he can't now, not now that we know — '

Her frustration flared. 'But why would Victor do this to me?' she said, then drained her glass, her voice so soft he had to strain to hear it. 'You're his brother, you must have some idea how he thinks.'

'I can't really say,' he blundered. 'Only that — '

'Oh, what, for God's sake.'

He told me once that he hated the way Mum used to cling to him . . . he said he hated the smell of her when she was ill, and that all women had the same kind of smell, a kind of unhealthy odour on their skin. He said it stayed on his clothes afterwards . . . '

Zoe tried to make sense of the words, but her head was beginning to spin and she felt nauseous in the smoky atmosphere. 'What does that mean?' The pub hummed round her, the singer's voice rising and falling. 'Tell me what it means.'

Again Ron hesitated. His sister's face was flushed, her voice slightly unsteady. He should never have told her, he thought stupidly, he should never have said anything. 'I think . . . I think he hates women, all of them especially the ones who are cleverer than he is. I think he hated our mother — and I know he hates you.'

The floor slipped away from under Zoe's feet, her voice now merely a whisper. 'Why?'

'Because you're what he wants to be.'

★ ★ ★

It all came back to love, she realised. Her yearning for love; Victor's distortion of love; Ron's loyalty and love. They all spun around each other and for a while it had helped them together — but no longer. Love blinded me, Zoe thought grimly, but not any more. Quickly, she slammed the drawer of her desk closed and turned the key, slipping it into her pocket just as Harland walked in. 'I think we should go to the

425

Guido sale in New York,' she said, even before he had time to wish her good morning.

'Why?'

She smoothed her skirt as she stood up. The day was overcast, grey like the velvet suit she wore, and the high heeled suede court shoes. Even her earrings were grey pearls, a present from Harland for her last birthday. Love in another form. Constant.

'I think it would be interesting,' she said, moving towards him, and leaning over to pick some non-existent fluff off the collar of his mohair suit. Time slipped back for her momentarily, back to the studio of the Holman Hunt art college, and the collar of Steven's corduroy jacket. 'I think it would be a change too.'

Harland swallowed, the smell of Zoe's perfume intoxicating him, her nearness making him ache for her. Rashly he curled his arms around her, but she moved away, smiling.

'I'm talking about business, Harland. We could learn something in New York,' she said, thinking of Ron's words. 'Let's go. Please.'

He would never deny her anything, she knew that. Just as she knew that by lunchtime they would have the airline tickets booked and two rooms organised at the Waldorf. It was so simple.

'I don't feel the same affection for New York that I used to have,' Harland said, tapping his chest. 'I'm not sure about San Francisco, but I think I left my heart somewhere in Manhattan.'

'Then we'll have to see if we can pick up the pieces, won't we?'

426

★   ★   ★

Mike O'Dowd was looking forward to New York too, although at that moment he was in the lounge of a stately townhouse in Tite Street, his hands shuffling a pack of Tarot cards. Across the table, the woman waited for him to pass the pack back to her, and then, carefully, she laid them out in five rows. The pictures on the cards were faded, the edges worn, and in parts the paper was broken and peeling. At the head of the spread lay the Hanged Man, and beside it the Chariot. She coughed discreetly, one hand lifted towards her mouth, the other tapping the second card.

'This is good . . . but this . . . ' her eyes moved to the bottom of the spread and Mike O'Dowd listened intently as a Burmese cat rubbed against one leg of his expensive suit, ' . . . is not so good. If you are thinking of going to America, I would be careful.'

'Why?'

The woman raised her white eyebrows in surprise. 'It would be better for you to stay away at present, that's all.'

Her voice was slightly impatient and clashed with the impassive face.

'But I have to go on business.'

'Then you must be very careful, and you mustn't take risks.'

O'Dowd was discomforted. The Guido brothers sale was coming up and he wanted to be there. Besides, he had to keep an eye on Victor Mellor. He was getting cocky again, and

427

although O'Dowd wasn't sure if he was actually double-crossing him, he was astute enough to know that something was brewing in the Englishman's mind — and it was certainly something which wouldn't benefit him. The woman talked on as O'Dowd shifted his position in the ornate gilded chair and adjusted his glasses. His thoughts drifted off as he glanced at the pack of cards in front of him. Leon Graves was in New York, he mused, and had been for a while, ever since he had had Noilly arrested for questioning. Everything seemed suddenly to be revolving around that city, and everything seemed suddenly to be coming to a head . . .

'That's all I can tell you today, Mr O'Dowd.'

His attention snapped back to the present. 'Oh, sure. That's fine then,' he said, the brogue as thick as ever, his eyes unreadable behind the glasses. 'I'll call by when I'm back in London,' he said, rising to his feet and walking towards the mantelpiece. A large ormolu clock chimed four as he slipped a small wedge of money behind it. Then automatically he checked his reflection in the mirror and saw the woman gathering up the cards on the table, her hands marble white against the green baize cloth.

★　★　★

'So you're coming back to New York,' Leon Graves said, his tone one of delight and expectation. 'How splendid, Harland. And is the lovely Zoe coming too?'

'Yes. She particularly wanted to attend this

auction,' Harland explained, his voice rising over the hazy transatlantic line. 'I think she's got a hunch.'

'A hunch?' Leon repeated, his intuition sharpening on the word. 'About fakes? Or about a good buy?'

Harland shrugged. 'Who knows? She's being mysterious, and very — '

'Very what?'

The word escaped him, and he hesitated. 'She has mood swings. One day she's light-hearted, almost giddy, and the next she's low.'

Leon's attention was alerted. Zoe Mellor was a fascinating woman, he had thought so from the start, fascinating and clever. But it didn't do to ask too many questions. Not yet, anyway.

'How's Myrtle?' he asked suddenly, changing the subject.

The cold draught of reality poured over Harland like a bucket of ice water. 'She wants to move house. She says the place is too gloomy and she doesn't like the neighbours any more.'

'Is Erica still with you?'

Harland poured himself a glass of Evian water and took a sip. The bubbles fizzed against the roof of his mouth as he swallowed. 'I have a feeling that my daughter is going to remain with us for a very long time,' Harland replied, sighing. 'Myrtle likes her there, because this way she has company, and besides, she thrives on the trauma — '

'Erica's having trouble with men again?' Leon asked, vastly amused. 'What a ghastly waste of energy. I have a theory that everyone should be

429

given a little pill when they reach twenty-five, which would depress their sexual inclinations. Squash them to a pulp, like dropping a rock on a slug. All that romance and angst would then be over . . . but they would at least have a few memories to treasure. One doesn't want to be cruel.'

Harland smiled wryly. 'Love is important to some people.'

'If love had been abolished, someone would have found a cure for cancer by now. Instead, there's a brilliant scientist spending his time trying to get a woman into bed, instead of saving lives.'

'You're being deliberately cynical,' Harland replied, 'and I don't believe a word you say.'

'You should,' Leon replied, his voice serious. 'Love is merely self-indulgence.' He was speaking from the heart, having no time for affairs any longer; no time and no inclination. 'I don't suppose your daughter would agree with me however.'

Harland hesitated, wondering if Leon knew about Erica's involvement with Victor Mellor. He had never alluded to it directly, and neither had Leon, but as he knew about every liaison in the art world, it seemed unlikely that he would be unaware of this one.

'She's involved with Zoe's brother.'

A long laugh swung down the line. It tickled Leon's imagination, this affair between Erica and the appalling Victor Mellor; just as Harland's relationship with Zoe delighted him.

'He would make an ideal husband, Harland

430

— for Lucretia Borgia.'

'Myrtle hates him too.'

'Myrtle has such admirable passion. And what about you?'

Harland paused. 'I think he's a creep.'

'A scumball, as I believe the Americans would say,' Leon responded. 'I heard that he's doing well, that he's even managed to seduce Suzie Laye, or Easy Lay, as she's known over here.'

'Suzie Laye!' Harland repeated with considerable interest. The woman was in her early forties, and had inherited one of the largest and most influential galleries in New York. Tall, statuesque, and with a deceptively lazy way of talking, she was good in business and, so the story went, even better in bed. 'I can't see Victor Mellor with Suzie Laye. And if they are having an affair, I can't see it lasting.'

'Certainly not if Erica finds out. I'd lock up the kitchen knives if she ever does, Harland,' Leon said smoothly, shifting topics. 'Let's meet up for dinner next week. It would be nice to see Zoe again.'

'I'll tell her. She'll be thrilled.'

'Oh, I wouldn't go that far,' Leon replied languidly.

★ ★ ★

'We could kidnap him.'

Zoe swivelled round to look at her brother and smiled indulgently. 'Don't be crazy, we can't hold Victor hostage — even the Mafia wouldn't try that.'

Ron smiled sheepishly and picked up the drawing Zoe had just finished. 'The tree's wrong.'

She put her head on one side and screwed up her eyes to focus. 'That's the way it was painted in the original.'

'But it's still wrong.'

'So take it up with Gauguin.' Zoe snatched it from him and changed the subject. 'There must be a way to outsmart him,' she continued, carefully unlocking the trunk where she hid the fakes and laying the drawing on the top of several others. 'He wanted to get me out of the business, so it's only fair I should return the compliment.' She smoothed some tissue on top of the board. 'There must be a way.'

'We've only got tomorrow left to do something.'

'I know Ron, I know,' she said wearily, curling her legs under her as she sat down next to him. 'Victor will be at the auction waiting to expose the fake,' she said, thinking aloud, 'thereby making himself look a hundred per cent genuine dealer, and a hero to boot.'

Ron stroked the top of Peter's head as the greyhound regarded him thoughtfully. 'We could tell everyone the truth — '

'Oh yes, and spend all our money on plastic surgery so the dealers wouldn't catch up with us. Do be reasonable, Ron!' she snapped, looking away, her eyes alighting on the photograph of a sculpture which Harland had just bought. It was a small head and shoulders of a woman, with her hair dressed in the Neo-Classic style. 'Double bluff . . .'

Ron was baffled. 'What did you say?'

'I've got it,' Zoe said, hauling her brother to his feet. 'We've got to go out now. What time is it?'

'Half past ten.'

With a smile on her face, Zoe moved to the phone and dialled Harland's number.

It was answered on the fourth ring. 'Is Mr Goldberg there?'

'Who wants to know?' Myrtle asked, her voice like an out of tune violin.

'I would just like a word, please.'

'How dare you!' she howled. 'How dare you phone my home.' There was a commotion over the line, and the sound of Harland's voice behind her. The line went dead.

A minute later the phone rang just as Zoe was pulling on her coat. 'Is that you, Zoe?'

'Listen, Harland, I'm sorry I had to ring you at home, but — '

'It doesn't matter. Are you all right?'

'I've got an idea,' Zoe said brightly. 'I think we should put that Lord Leighton marble bust in the Guido brothers sale.'

'Why?'

'We'd get a good price for it.'

He hesitated. 'I'm not sure.'

'Well, OK, Harland, I just thought . . . you usually trust my judgement.'

Half an hour later, unbeknown to Harland, the Leighton sculpture was being transported in the back of a black London taxi, squeezed between Zoe and Ron. The journey from W1 to Wandsworth was uneventful, the cold November

433

streets empty except for a few wet cats and the odd pedestrian spilling out from a pub doorway. Otherwise the cold snap was keeping people indoors, and when the taxi pulled up outside the Methodist church, there was only one faint light burning over the door.

'You religious freaks or something?' the cabbie asked, jerking his head towards the church. 'I didn't know they had services at this time of night.'

Zoe passed the money towards him. 'Oh, we've not come for the regular service, we've come for the Black Mass.'

The cabbie was unimpressed. 'Like hell!'

'Yes, exactly like,' Zoe replied.

There was no sign of Victor's car, so they made their way around the church to the back window, Ron clutching the marble bust in his arms, and Zoe feeling her way along the damp walls. The darkness was so intense that it was difficult to see anything, and she moved slowly, her eyes straining into the black night, her feet already wet from the puddles. The window was blank and unlit, the whole church eerily quiet and unwelcoming.

Zoe paused to fasten the collar of her coat and then ducked down, startled, as a light came on. Ron ducked down with her, his eyes fixed on his sister as she raised a finger to her lips. Noises followed, the sound of a door banging and a radio being turned on, the strains of 'I'll Be Watching You' floating out on the night air. It was a nice touch, Zoe thought wryly, it was just a shame that Victor couldn't appreciate the joke.

For one uncomfortable, nervous hour they crouched under the window, until the sounds of a familiar voice seeped through the church walls.

'Is everything ready?'

'Everything. Stop worrying,' Candadas replied.

'I just want to be sure,' Victor said brusquely, his voice fading off as a series of tappings followed. They were nailing down the box, Zoe thought.

'I won't bother coming tomorrow,' Victor continued, when the tapping stopped. 'But I'll see you at the weekend. Make sure it's delivered as we planned.'

'Stop worrying. Noilly's going to New York with it.'

'Good,' Victor said finally.

Seconds later, the side door opened and they heard their brother's quick footsteps walk away, followed soon after by Candadas's slow, ponderous steps. In silence, they waited for another few minutes and then Zoe tapped Ron on the arm.

'Come on. Now.'

With admirable agility Ron pulled himself up on to the window ledge and worked on the lock, Zoe glancing round her for any sign of movement outside, or of Victor's return. After a few more seconds, the lock gave and Ron pushed open the window, jumping in and then helping Zoe over the sill. Cautiously, she flicked on the light and then turned it off, switching on her torch instead.

'I can't see,' Ron whispered.

'Yes, you can, your eyes will get adjusted,' she

said quietly. 'If we turn on the light someone might see it from the road, and it's not worth the risk.' She moved away, scanning the walls with the torchlight. A stone putti flashed before her, then the pale features of a mock Bernini. 'I hate to admit it, but Candadas is good,' she said grudgingly, directing the torch towards the far wall, where its beam fell on a packing case, newly labelled. 'That's it!'

Both of them moved at the same time, Ron laying down the Leighton bust on the floor and peering at the top of the case. 'I'll have to do it very carefully, or they'll see it's been got at.' He turned to his sister. 'Hold that light steady for me, will you?'

For the next five minutes Ron loosened every nail painstakingly, lifting each out carefully, almost noiselessly, and putting them into his pocket. There was no sound except from the noise of water from a faulty drainpipe dripping against the dank outside wall. When the last nail came out, Ron glanced over to his sister and smiled. She looked small in the darkness, and scared, her face only half illuminated as she watched him bend down into the case, lift out the packing straw, and then the sculpture.

It was one of Alan's best, a nude male, rising as white and glowing as the moon out of the box. Both of them sucked in their breath and Zoe watched as Ron laid it carefully on the floor.

'Ready?' Ron asked.

For some reason, Zoe laughed suddenly. 'This is ridiculous! Creeping around like this in the dark.' A noise outside made her jump and she froze, waiting for several seconds before speaking again. 'Hurry up, I want to get out of here.'

With great care, Ron lowered the Leighton bust into the case, tucking the packing straw around it as tenderly as a mother settling her child down to sleep. Suddenly he paused and with a gesture which was infinitely gentle, he patted the marble head with his hand before obliterating all trace of it under the remaining straw. Then he carefully tapped every nail back into every hole, so that when he had finished no one would have known that the case had been tampered with.

26

Buck's Lane
Rochdale

'Alan?'

When he answered his voice was remote, the words spiralling up from Rochdale over the dark sea. ''Lo Zoe! I thought you were in New York.'

'I am,' she said, sitting down on the hotel bed. The room was sulkily silent, all action suspended behind the double-glazed windows. 'I just wanted to phone you, that's all.'

He beamed with pleasure. The snug at Buck's Lane was desolate, the fire having gone out, the curtains undrawn so that the night glowered in, hard and unfriendly. The first frost had come the previous week, November wicked as ever, trailing winter down from the moors.

'Dad's at the pub,' Alan said, tugging up the collar of his shirt as he talked. 'Is Victor there?'

Zoe winced. 'I'm not sure if he is yet. But I heard he was coming.'

The door of the kitchen banged behind Alan and made him jump. 'Dad's back. D'you want a word?'

Zoe frowned. 'No, just tell him I'll see you both soon.' She paused. 'Oh, and Alan . . .'

'Yes?'

'Take care of yourself.'

Bernard Mellor walked in just in time to see

438

Alan put down the phone and turn, smiling sheepishly. That boy gets fatter, he thought bitterly, and he's got an arse on him like a bloody elephant, especially in those overalls. He nodded towards his son and moved over to the fire, nudging the coals with his boot and then warming his hands over the flame. It had been cold in the pub, and a couple of pints hadn't done a thing to warm him up. With a bad-tempered gesture he shivered, went into the kitchen, and banged the kettle on the light to boil. Years ago he had never felt the cold. In fact, he had been impervious to the bitter winds and enjoyed bragging about never needing to wear a vest. 'Only bloody nancies wear vests,' he used to say. Well, he wore one now, even combinations, long-legged woollen things, like all the old men he had laughed at when he was a boy. Bernard Mellor took down the teapot and out of the corner of his eye watched Alan reach for the biscuit tin . . . If Jane had still been alive he would never have worn a vest. Oh no, not if she'd been alive. A man had to keep up his appearance, didn't he?

She would have been getting on a bit now, he realised. Not quite the spring chicken she used to be, but still . . . His mind wandered up to the bedroom, remembering how it used to smell of floor wax, and how the window got banked up with snow around Christmas; remembering how he would lie with his arms around her until they got bloody freezing and he had to put them under the covers to warm them . . .

'That was our Zoe on the phone. She rang from New York.'

The kettle whistled and Bernard pulled it off the light with an impatient gesture. 'Oh aye. What'd she want then that couldn't wait until she got back?' he said, his tone irritable. 'That must have cost a packet, ringing from ruddy America.'

'She just rang to say hello . . . and she sent her love.'

Bernard Mellor grunted. He had never understood his daughter, but he knew that she was certainly doing well for herself. Just like Victor, the wily sod.

'She's going to a big auction tomorrow,' Alan said, his voice thick with excitement. He could never have gone, but he could imagine it, especially as Zoe would come home and tell him everything that had happened, giving him the catalogues and telling him about the dealers and the prices the paintings fetched . . .

His father interrupted his thoughts. 'Did she go with that old man?'

Alan turned to his father, his face crimson. He had been day-dreaming again, and it always embarrassed him to be found out. 'I suppose so . . . she always does.'

'He's too old for her. And he's married,' Bernard snapped, the cold making him even more irritable than usual. 'Bloody hell, Alan, why can't you get some coal in? Just because you're all right in that flaming garage with the electric fire burning out like an inferno every night, you could at least think of me once in a while — '

440

'I was working,' Alan said plaintively, wishing he had stayed in the garage out of his father's way. Now he was cornered because he hadn't expected him back so soon. He shuffled his feet uncomfortably, waiting for his father to finish; waiting to make his getaway.

'Working, my eye! You spend all your time in that garage. And what the hell for? Aye? Tell me that, what d'you do it for?'

Alan blushed, fearful that his secret would be dragged out of him. He glanced away from his father, his palms damp with sweat. 'I like working.'

'On what?'

He remembered the touch of marble on his lips. Cool, smooth. Without judgement or memory. 'You know, Dad . . . things.'

'Things?' his father repeated, spiteful with cold as he shook some coal on to the kitchen fire and rammed half a firelighter underneath. The match spluttered against it and then took, a weak flame battling against the damp coal and the downdraft of the winter chimney. 'What 'things'?'

'Statues and such like,' Alan said, moving towards the door.

' 'Statues and such like' he says. You great soft lummox, I know that! What I want to know is what are they *for*?' Bernard Mellor hissed, watching his son struggle for words. 'Cat got your tongue, Alan? Well, whatever it is you're doing, I suppose Victor's making money out of it.' He kicked the grate in frustration as the fire sputtered out. 'Aye, I bet our Victor's making a bob or two. Damn and blast that sodding fire!

441

I'm going to bed before I freeze to death.' He moved past Alan and then paused. 'Lock up, I'll not wait up for you.'

Shutting the kitchen door, Alan leaned against it and closed his eyes, relief washing over him. His father hadn't guessed about the statues. No one had. Without moving he listened until he heard the toilet cistern flush and his father's footsteps move into the front bedroom. After a bout of coughing the house fell silent, and minutes later, he could hear regular snores erupt from the sleeping Bernard Mellor. With a sigh of relief, Alan turned off the light in the snug and pulled the door closed, crossing the kitchen and only pausing to take half a packet of chocolate digestives from the biscuit barrel by the back door.

New York
Room 1498, The Waldorf

There was no sun that morning, just a hard sky and a spitting of snow. Zoe woke early and turned forgetting for a moment where she was. Then she remembered.

'I'd like scrambled eggs, bacon, and sausages,' she said, then changed her mind, her stomach rebelling. 'No, just make that a pot of tea, will you?'

This was her big day; the day she was going to get her own back on Victor — and after Victor, Mike O'Dowd. Oh yes, she thought, pulling the blankets around her, the time had come to settle some old scores. The snow floated past, finding its way amongst the dirty buildings· and the webbings of streets, falling on cabs and on the red sign of a liquor store. It might even be snowing in Rochdale, Zoe thought, bleaching the queue outside the dole office waiting to sign on, and landing noiselessly on the domed roof of the Essoldo . . .

A knock on the door shook her from her day-dreams.

'Come in,' she shouted, pulling on a dressing-gown as Harland walked in. He smiled, seeing her as he remembered her in the Manchester Art Gallery, younger, with less to lose. 'I thought it was breakfast,' she said. 'You're up early.'

'Couldn't sleep.'

She nodded towards the window. 'It's snowing,' she said, looking out. The buildings loomed above her, concrete and glass, the colours of the street crude against the tender snow while a solitary figure slid past on roller skates, hooded against the cold. 'Do you remember when I first came to New York?'

'You were very young. Very young and very sweet.'

She was suddenly vulnerable. 'Aren't I sweet any longer?' Zoe asked, turning to see Harland slip a tablet into his mouth. 'What's that?'

He tapped his chest. 'It's for my heart.' Zoe was suddenly anxious. 'It's nothing to worry about.'

He moved towards her and lifted her chin with his hand. The winter sun highlighted every wrinkle on his face and bored into his dark brown eyes to make them amber. 'I'm not going to have another heart attack. I promised the hotel, it was the only way I could get a reservation.'

'I'm very grateful to you,' Zoe said softly, her hands deep in the pockets of her dressing-gown, 'for everything you've done to help me over the years. I could never have come so far without you.'

Alarmed, Harland wondered if she was saying some kind of farewell, and said hurriedly, 'You've got the talent, Zoe, I just pointed you in the right direction. The credit is all yours.'

'But you put me in touch with the right people, and took me to the right places — '

' — and you made the most out of it. You're a natural and you've proved yourself. I trust your judgement about paintings — for fakes.' He touched his beard self-consciously. She wants to go, he thought. Oh God, she's going to leave me. 'Are you trying to tell me you want to move on?'

Zoe frowned. 'I was just saying thank you, you idiot,' she said, opening the door for Room Service. 'We're a team, aren't we?'

A team, he thought blindly. You're my world.

'I'm not going anywhere without you, Harland Goldberg,' she continued, her voice tender. 'Besides, you once promised me that you would be here as long as I needed you.'

The man hovered for his tip by the trolley.

'I meant what I said. I'll always be here for you.'

The man coughed.

'Promise?'

'I promise,' Harland said, smiling. 'Is there anything you want now?'

'Yes. A cup of tea,' she said. 'Oh, and tip the waiter will you?'

★　★　★

Hampton's auction house had thrown open its doors at two-thirty, in preparation for the sale at three-fifteen. The main hallway was thronged with people, wet coats dropped off at the cloakroom, the smell of damp wool permeating the crush. Following dutifully behind the men came the wives and mistresses, scrutinising each other for recent signs of plastic surgery, bejewelled hands raised in superficial greeting, the brief 'hellos' grating through extensive dental work. To be invited to this auction was the ultimate in social climbing and they knew it, pulling out small diaries and making reservations for lunch, gold pens skiing over the paper like mayflies.

In direct contrast the women who were there in a professional capacity were dressed in formal suits and wore their hair in long bobs or swept back from their faces. Aggressive gold earrings and heavy gold chains gave them the stamp of office, as did their black stiletto heels, designer legs, and the manicured hands which grasped the catalogue notes ferociously. New York women with New York habits, a drink or a snort hyping them up. Swing, ladies, the town's for the taking.

When she was seated, Zoe glanced round,

spotting Rupert Courtney-Blye, Tobar Manners and the inevitable Anthony Sargeant slipping a peppermint into his mouth, while several other dealers nodded to her in acknowledgement. So they are gathering, she thought, all waiting to hear what Victor has to say, all panting to see a fake exposed. The saleroom was comfortable, warm against the snowy streets outside, the auction staff taking their places, some standing by the bank of phones to take the bids which were phoned in during the auction, others at the back of the room, all watching the auctioneer who was still chatting listlessly, standing by the lectern on the platform. Knowing he was within everyone's sights he assumed an affected nonchalance, every expression enlarged slightly for the performance.

'Have you seen Jimmy van Goyen?' Harland asked as he slipped into his seat beside Zoe.

She shook her head. The Dutchman was on the skids, the rumour went, a series of poor exhibitions had hurt his business, and being caught out by several fakes had not helped. Zoe looked round, searching for a sight of his blond head and the recognisable pigtail.

'He's there . . . no, second row.'

She scanned the backs in front of her and then stopped when she saw van Goyen. He was alone, silent, his face rigid with anxiety, the set of his mouth hard. As she watched, Harland nudged her again and pointed across the room to where a full-breasted woman sat in complete silence as the waspish Tobar Manners flapped round her.

'It will do him no good. He's not her type.'

446

'He's not anyone's type,' Zoe replied, leaning forward to get a better look at the woman. 'Who's that? She looks familiar.'

'Suzie Laye,' Harland replied, flicking through his catalogue. 'Or as Leon calls her, 'Easy Lay'. He also calls her your rival.'

Raising her eyebrows, Zoe turned to him. 'My rival? Why?'

'She's well known in New York.' She knows you're coming up fast and apparently she resents it — watch out for her, Zoe, she is one bitch.'

Carefully Zoe studied the woman, trying to remember what she had heard about her and her gallery, the Conrad. She had inherited a fortune, her father having met with a fatal boating accident when she was only a child, her mother having converted to Catholicism and retired to live in Northern France. She'd also heard another story about her — that Suzie Laye had had a child years ago and farmed her out, the girl growing up in France with her grandmother, never referred to and never seen in New York.

'*Does* she have a child?'

Harland shrugged. 'So they say.'

'And she ignores her?' Zoe continued, searching Suzie Laye's face for any sign of cruelty. Mother, daughter. Love me, hate me.

'She doesn't want to know her. After all, it would be bad for her image to have a teenage child, especially as she lies about her age.'

With her eyes trained on Suzie Laye, Zoe hadn't noticed the man sitting behind her. Mike O'Dowd smiled and adjusted his glasses to read the catalogue. He had been aware of Zoe since

447

she walked in, and wondered what she was doing there. The thought engaged his attention almost as much as the back of the man's head two rows forward, the unmistakable ears advertising their owner the instant he sat down. Fully aware of the scrutiny, Leon Graves continued to write in his diary, his eyes fixed on the page while his ears took in every word exchanged within several feet of him. He had heard the rumour, the clever little snippet which had been going the rounds for nearly three days, and he had found it impossible to resist attending the sale in order to see the outcome for himself. Victor Mellor was going to uncover a forgery. Leon smiled to himself. If Victor Mellor was going straight he wanted to be there to see it.

The object of his thoughts was at that moment lighting a black Russian cigarette and straightening his tie in the mirror of the Gentlemen's cloakroom, humming to himself and imagining the triumph to come. Carefully Victor had done the ground work, sending out stories to prepare the dealers, all of whom were still desperate for revenge on the forger. Not that Zoe or Alan would come to any harm, he thought, inhaling deeply, no, the bust would just be exposed as a fake and then they would be forced to fade into the background while he was feted as a hero. Suzie Laye would be impressed by that, he decided, grinding out the cigarette, oh yes, even she would come to heel after this showdown . . . Victor smiled at his reflection and, satisfied, gave himself a mock bow and walked into the saleroom.

A whirr of excitement followed his arrival, and all eyes turned towards him. Victor paused, lit another Russian cigarette and, after carefully ignoring Suzie Laye, moved towards his seat . . . and saw Zoe. Brother and sister looked at each other for a long, slow instant, before Victor waved and moved over to her.

'Well, well, well.'

'Yes, thank you. How are you?'

He smiled wolfishly. 'I didn't expect to see you here.'

'No, I thought not,' she replied, her heart banging. 'You made quite an entrance, Victor, especially with that prop.' She pointed to the black cigarette scornfully. 'We used to get sherbet with those when we were kids.'

Victor bristled, he was really going to enjoy seeing her squirm. 'I'm afraid I have to get back to my seat.'

'Have a good sale,' Zoe called out after him.

Three-fifteen signalled the beginning of the auction as the auctioneer banged his gavel to get everyone's attention. Several hundred faces turned towards him at once, the rustling of the catalogues silenced as all ears waited for the bidding to begin — and for Victor Mellor's exposé.

'I have Lot 1 here, a very early Bernini sculpture of a Cardinal Mariozetti . . . what am I bid?'

Up went the first bid, the man's voice high with excitement as he strained forward in his seat. A woman's voice followed, then a phone bid, the figures galloping upwards like horses over Becher's Brook. Soon the atmosphere was buzzing, the air conditioning pouring in to warm the overheated audience. Minks were thrown off shoulders, catalogues were used as fans, and a sharp interchange of views nearly escalated into a free-for-all between an Italian and a bolshie Greek.

One by one the lots passed, the catalogue pages turning, jottings made in margins and reserves reached, or passed, money spiralling upwards and over the allocated figures. Even the auctioneer was affected by the excitement, his voice quick, his gavel slamming down at the end of a lot, as sighs of disappointment escaped a hundred mouths, or a roar of applause congratulated the successful bidder. Victor's pulse rate was rising by the minute as he waited for Lot 32. That was the number which would find him springing to his feet; that was the number of glory — 32. He whispered it to himself. It even tasted sweet on his lips.

It was tasting pretty sweet to Zoe too, as she waited, her eyes constantly moving between her brother and Mike O'Dowd who sat three chairs away from him. They were such good friends, she thought bitterly, it was a shame they couldn't sit together and let everyone know what chums they were. Dragging her eyes away, she saw Leon Graves's profile, and smiled to herself — still after the Irishman, she thought. You and me both.

Lot 30 came and went. The mahogany clock pulled the hour round to four-thirty-five. Time was running out.

'I have a bid for ninety-four thousand . . . ninety-four thousand dollars . . . Am I bid any more? Ninety-five . . . ninety-six thousand dollars . . . Going once . . . going twice . . . gone.'

Bang went the gavel; bang, the noise resounded in Zoe's head; Lot 31 came up, a nude raised on to the easel, the long full legs of the woman luminous under the saleroom light. No privacy, nothing left unexposed. Look at me, want me, buy me, she said . . . Bang, went the gavel again, the auctioneer pointing towards the back of the hall, a hundred heads turning simultaneously towards a whey-faced dealer from Geneva. Tobar Manners coughed. Zoe knew it was him, she could recognise the sound even above the agitated mumble of the auction crowd, and she could imagine his hands growing sweaty, the obese Anthony Sargeant beside him, rummaging for a peppermint in his pocket.

Bang went down the gavel again. 'What am I bid? Sir, yes, the gentleman at the back . . . one hundred and fourteen thousand dollars to you, sir . . . going once . . . '

Suddenly a telephone bid called in; the auctioneer's head turned, profile alerted towards the phone.

'We have another bid, sir. One hundred and twenty thousand . . . '

The bellow of the crowd. The circus is in town, and dressed in mink, Zoe thought ruefully, turning to look at Harland who was also caught up in the sale, his bright dark eyes sharp with excitement.

'One hundred and twenty-one thousand

. . . one hundred and twenty-two thousand . . . '

Up and up they went, the bids revolving and clinging and floating to the ceiling, as words . . . just words. Vocal money. Zoe shifted in her seat and looked for her brother, but there was no sign of him. She glanced around, Mike O'Dowd was there, his eyes unreadable as he watched the auctioneer, his stocky figure only feet away from Leon Graves.

'One hundred and thirty thousand . . . '

The man from Geneva blinked, his face waxy, expressionless, his eyes trained on the sensuous nude protrait.

'One hundred and thirty thousand, going once . . . going twice . . . '

The man from Geneva waited. She was almost his; his to hang on a wall and admire. Better canvas than flesh, so much less heartache.

'One hundred and thirty thousand dollars, gone . . . It's yours, sir.'

The rush of applause again, the rush of colour to the man's face; the unclasping of his hands as his possession is taken off the easel and leaves the saleroom. He smiles, accepts the congratulations, but his eyes remain some while on the doorway where she has passed, and without another word he leaves to follow his lady love.

Zoe's hands tightened on her lap as she waited for Lot 32 to be announced. There was a pause as the auctioneer read down the catalogue notes and then nodded towards the storeroom, off centre stage. As if on cue, Victor materialised, his face smugly confident, his tortoiseshell eyes turned towards the dais where the fake would be exposed. His breathing came rapidly, even though he tried to regulate it, even though he tried to stop his heart racing.

The auctioneer motioned to the porter again and the man emerged, carrying Lot 32 in his arms and thereby blocking any clear view of the sculpture. With practised care, he lifted it on to the dais in the same moment that Victor stepped forward. Overconfident, he had not even glanced at the sculpture. That was his first mistake.

'Ladies and gentlemen,' he began.

Leon Graves smiled; Mike O'Dowd's face remained impassive. Harland turned to Zoe.

'I have reason to believe that this lot is a fake . . . '

The room erupted, Ahmed Fazir jumping to his feet as Victor moved towards the dais. Zoe watched her brother. He was impressive, she had to admit that, even the auctioneer was silenced by his deadly assurance.

'Due to my own investigations, certain pieces of evidence have come to light which suggest that this work is nothing more than a cheap contemporary copy . . . '

Zoe flinched at the word. Alan might be a forger, but his work was never cheap. She smouldered as her eyes remained fixed on her brother.

'I also have reason to believe that the person responsible, although I do not know who that person is, has also been responsible for the rash of forgeries which has dogged the art world for months . . . '

Leon Graves was still smiling as Victor moved

453

towards the pedestal and caught hold of the cloth. He looked attractive, wealthy, worldly and savage, Zoe thought, as he tugged away the covering with one stylish gesture . . . There was no gasp of amazement. No applause. No congratulations. The saleroom was silent. No one spoke, they just watched him. And in that one second, Victor knew. His smiled jammed, and stiffly he turned towards the statue.

Two decades passed across his face in one look. Zoe saw him as a boy, then a young man, wilful, selfish, idle, greedy, feckless, dangerous, sensuous, cold. She saw every emotion pass across her brother's face, as, in the silence, he turned from the statue to the audience, and back again. The stillness yawned between him and the crowd. It yawned and stretched itself and then suddenly awoke . . .

'What the hell!' Harland snapped, jumping up and breaking the spell. 'That is an authenticated Frederic Leighton bust from my gallery. I have the provenance and the papers to prove it.' Victor's eyes moved from Harland's face to his sister's. 'How dare you insinuate that this lot is anything other than genuine — '

One row in front, Ahmed Fazir chimed in. 'You have no right to interrupt this auction with your stupid accusations, Mellor.'

Victor's face was stony, his mind racing. Breathing in deeply, he smiled at the multitude of outraged faces in front of him. 'There appears to have been a mistake — '

'And we all know who's made it,' Tobar Manners screeched from the fourth row.

454

'I came here in good faith to uncover a fake . . . ' Victor continued manfully, wondering *how* Alan's fake had been switched.

The uproar continued. 'You should leave such things to the experts,' someone bellowed from the back.

'What the shit does he know about it anyway?' van Goyen asked, his voice ugly.

'Is he a dealer?' another questioned loudly.

Harland was beside himself. 'I want an explanation!' he called out, afraid that his reputation would take a severe beating.

'Gentlemen . . . gentlemen . . . ' Victor said soothingly as the pandemonium increased.

With her hands clasped tightly on her lap Zoe was triumphant, her face luminous, but suddenly, within a second, the feeling faded leaving only a sense of pity. Covering her ears to block out the catcalls and the boom of angry voices, Zoe slumped in her seat as the auctioneer tried in vain to restore order.

With foolhardy stubbornness Victor remained by the dais, the damning Leighton sculpture beside him. At that moment, Suzie Laye began to laugh, a deep, languorous chuckle which galvanised Victor into action.

'All right, I've made a fool of myself today — '

'You can say that again,' Courtney-Blye interjected idly. 'You're no gentleman.'

The words were enough to push Victor over the edge. Humiliated and angry, he was more than eager to work off his temper with his fists. With a look of murder in his eyes, Victor pounded down the aisle, pushing several people back as he fought his way along the row towards the dealer. With a look of stark horror, Courtney-Blye beat a hasty retreat, stumbling over Anthony Sargeant's feet and cursing under his breath as a few people started laughing.

'Order . . . Order! . . . Gentlemen, please . . . ' the auctioneer pleaded, his gavel pounding down repeatedly as he watched an enraged Victor corner Courtney-Blye by the bank of hastily vacated phones.

Trapped, the dealer cringed. 'Don't hit me! Don't hit me!'

'Give me one reason why not,' Victor said bitterly.

'I'm . . . ' he stammered, then blurted out, 'I'm a haemophiliac.'

Victor's fist caught him just under the chin, and he crumpled like an empty bin liner.

With a deadly smile, Victor leaned over the man. 'Then that's all the more reason to mind your own bleeding business, isn't it?'

★ ★ ★

There had been a small rush of admiration for Victor from the perfumed brigade at the auction, but his ignominious departure from Hampton's was generally applauded, the novelty of someone being bounced from an auction assuring him a lasting reputation. And a ban.

'Stupid fool,' Harland said coldly, having assured the auctioneer repeatedly that the lot was genuine. The man had been understanding; besides, Victor Mellor was little more than a

456

thug, and who could possibly take a man like that seriously? 'He's an embarrassment to you, Zoe.'

He stopped talking and looked into her face. Quickly Zoe glanced away, but not before he had seen her eyes fill.

'He's no good — '

'I know that!' she said sharply. 'But he's my brother. Can't you understand that?' She had had her revenge, but it was sour and tasted of bile. Take me back, she thought, I never meant to hurt you. Any of you. I never meant . . . 'I'm sorry that he involved you in all of this.'

Harland sighed, eager to reassure her. 'You mustn't worry about me, Zoe, I have a good reputation and Hampton's knew that, so there's no harm done. No one really expected me to be dealing in fakes.'

Zoe smiled. I knew that too, she thought, and that's why I used you. I'm sorry, she wanted to say. I'm sorry.

'Victor can't hurt you either,' Harland continued. 'Everyone knows you have nothing to do with him, so don't think your reputation will be harmed. You just continue to keep your distance, and you'll be fine.' There was nothing she could say. 'Believe me, Zoe, Victor Mellor has learnt his lesson once and for all. His day is over.'

★ ★ ★

Leon Graves was waiting outside the back entrance of Hampton's as Victor came out,

457

sharply propelled by the toe of a size eleven shoe. Lighting a cigarette, he coughed and passed it to the sprawling Mr Mellor.

Victor looked up, rubbed the slushy snow off his suit and got to his feet. He then inhaled deeply and frowned. 'It's not my brand.'

Leon smiled and, folding his arms, leaned back against the brick wall. 'My, my, you did look a bit of a lemon in there, old man.'

'There was a fake — '

'There was a crooked man,' Leon said enigmatically: 'You blew your mouth off rather too fast and too soon,' he continued, glancing round. 'Ghastly places, alleyways. I do so hate snow too, it makes everything so very soggy.'

'What do you want?' Victor asked wearily, straightening his tie and inhaling again. 'Or did you just come to gloat?'

Leon Graves frowned. 'How could you be so suspicious, my dear fellow? I was merely lending a helping hand — and sizing up the opposition. After all, there you were, setting yourself up to uncover a forgery and I was merely hoping to pick up some tips.'

'Go screw yourself.'

'There's no reason to be unfriendly,' he replied evenly, without a touch of malice. 'I saw the appalling Mike O'Dowd at the auction too.'

Victor screwed up his eyes and shivered. 'So?'

'You should wear a coat, it's cold out.'

'I came with a coat!' Victor snapped. '*And* a bloody reputation.'

'The vagaries of the business,' Leon responded kindly. 'You mustn't let it affect you.'

Victor Mellor paused, his head down. In silence, he inhaled again and then stubbed the cigarette out in the snow. It hissed as it struck the grey slush. Oh no, he thought to himself, I may be down but I'm not out. So what if it didn't come off this time, there'll be other opportunities — if his sister didn't get in the way. He sighed deeply and thought of Zoe, savouring his anger. No, Mr Graves, I'm not helping you out . . . Besides, he thought ruefully, he had some explaining to do to O'Dowd, and that was going to be hard work.

'Thanks for the cigarette.'

If Leon Graves was disappointed, he didn't let it show.

'My pleasure.'

Victor moved off, tugging his suit jacket round him and walking down the alleyway towards the blare of New York traffic.

'Have a nice day.'

Victor's response was blunt and unrepeatable, and left Leon Graves laughing all the way to 42nd Street.

PART FOUR

Coup de Grâce

27

Rochdale
February, 1986

'I've missed you.'

Zoe sipped her coffee and glanced over the rim of the cup. The San Remo café was crowded with young people, too young for Steven Foreshaw, and in a way, too young for her. They were students mainly, some from the Holman Hunt College, some from the tech, some just hanging around, without jobs. The windows were steamed up with condensation, the tables Formica-topped, and smudged with dried-in Heinz ketchup stains. Outside, the snow had given way to rain.

'I'm only up for the weekend,' Zoe responded, trying to keep her voice light to avoid the inevitable argument. She had agreed to meet him because he had begged her over the phone — making her break her vow, dragging her back.

'We could go out tomorrow.'

She turned her head and wiped the window with her hand. A woman passed by, pushing a pram, her legs smudged with rain. 'I . . . have to work.'

He sighed extravagantly and she looked at him. In the eight years Zoe had known him Steven had altered, turned inwards, and faltered into middle age. Yet their affair had continued through those years — until now. Now she was a twenty-six-year-old woman, who could look back and wonder why she had stayed tied to him, and know the answer. Unsuitable as he was, she had been sure of him, and in an insecure world, that had been enough.

Naturally Steven pretended otherwise, priding himself on the fact that he had held on to her for so long. He knew, in his lucid moments, that she only pitied him, that the long burning of tenderness had faded to irritation. He knew it, and it didn't matter, because he still had her — it was to his bed that she came and in his arms that she sometimes slept. It was enough.

After the auction in New York Zoe had initially felt triumph, although it was quickly followed by a sense of self-loathing. Logic told her that she was justified in taking her revenge on Victor, but the deepest part of her grieved for the loss of him. Time passed, and Zoe progressed, becoming more in demand as a consultant, taking trips around England and abroad, alternately lonely or euphoric. Her achievements pleased her, but as her status grew she found herself more isolated, the acceptance she had longed for as elusive now as it had been for the shabby girl who had arrived at Harland's gallery many years ago. She knew that to outsiders her life seemed to be one thing, where as, in reality, it was quite another. People believed her to be Harland Goldberg's mistress, whilst all the time she had been the girlfriend of a poor art teacher up North. Grime, not glitter, Rochdale, not London.

I have no courage, she thought suddenly. I have accepted this relationship as enough for me, and it shouldn't have been. I should have had a suitable partner; someone respectable and respected; someone in my world. She glanced back into her teacup. Chipped china, a tarnished spoon — did I come all this way for this? she asked herself. Was this reality? Duplicity had secured her a place in the London art scene, just as the fakes had ensured her a secret means of cocking a snook and earning a fortune, deceit becoming her way of life — so why expect reality, when it had only ever brought grief?

'Where's your brother?'

'Which one?'

Steven frowned. His hair was beginning to grey, the white streak smudging into the rest without definition. Jack-the-lad Foreshaw, what happened to you? Zoe thought suddenly.

'I meant Victor. We were just talking about him the other day and someone said they hadn't seen him around for a while.' He sipped his coffee, his hands stained with paint, the same hands which had traced the outline of her breasts. 'He used to come up with you every other weekend — '

'He's abroad,' Zoe said abruptly. That was all she knew, that her brother had gone overseas to lick his wounds. And plot. With Victor, there was always a plot. But she hadn't expected him to be quiet for so long, for nearly four months. It was unlike him.

'I bet he's made some real money as a dealer.'

Zoe ignored the remark, and Steven continued. 'I bet you've made some real money too.'

465

The steam rose from her cup as she glanced down at her hands. She was wearing a simple raincoat and boots, her hair tucked behind her ears, her make-up light. Not wanting to draw attention to herself, Zoe had lessened herself, and when she glanced back towards the window, she saw her own reflection and stared . . . The image stared back, smaller than she expected, and totally divorced from the woman who travelled around the world giving opinions on valuable works of art. The hazy reflection taunted her — this is you in reality, it said, for all you pretend to be, this is you as you truly are. Zoe put down her cup with a shaking hand, the image watching her, as though someone peered in from the rainy street outside. She could be my sister, Zoe thought, but not me. Not me.

Unsteadily she rose to her feet, Steven's eyes following her. 'What is it?'

She glanced round the café, and wondered why she was there; why she had forced herself back, tied herself to a man who was unloving, and worse, ungiving. The reflection followed her as she snatched up her bag.

'Zoe, where are you going?'

'Back to London,' she said suddenly, turning towards the door. He remained in his seat, only a foot from her. 'Sorry . . . but I'm going. It's over, Steven.'

The image in the glass window mirrored her. As she moved, it moved; as she spoke, it spoke. Tiny, dull, weathered, as she had been as a child, staring out from a top window, banished, cut off from the rest of the family. Hearing noises below.

Let me in, I'll be good — crying late at night — *When I have children I'll be kind to them.* Waiting for the acceptance. Love me, hate me. *You can't feel that, Mother, can you?* No, you can't keep me here, Zoe thought, panicking. No one can keep me here any longer.

'Zoe — '

'Goodbye, Steven,' she said gently. 'Take care of yourself.'

The rain slapped her as she moved out of the door, and pulled it closed behind her. Quickly she turned up the collar of her raincoat and walked towards the town hall. For one instant she paused, and then glanced back into the café. She could see Steven Foreshaw hunched over his coffee; she could see the serving hatch, the students, the old radio on a stand by the door. But the watcher had gone from the window, there was no reflection any longer — because she was on the outside now.

★ ★ ★

Meanwhile the rumour mongers had begun their tortuous work throughout London again. A few innuendoes placed strategically, like firelighters, soon fanned the flames and before long a tidy little bonfire was burning. The theme was this — Victor Mellor had been gone for three and a half months and since his departure there had been no fakes on the market. Solution — Victor Mellor was either a forger or a man who dealt in forgeries. The premise was a reasonable one. The only trouble was that it left a very nasty smell

467

which was beginning to cling to Zoe. She was not slow to see the warning signs.

'The dealers are putting two and two together, Ron.'

Her brother turned round from the mirror. He was seeing Sally tonight and had brushed his hair four times already. 'You can't be sure.'

'Oh, but I can,' Zoe replied, unlocking the trunk and pulling out a small Corot. 'I can feel it in the air, and it won't do my dazzling career any good. I'd be guilty by association at least.'

'But you are guilty,' Ron replied lightly. 'Do I need a shave?'

'No, and thanks for the vote of confidence,' she replied. 'You see, Ron, much as I would like Victor to be forgotten, people are talking about the fakes, so I'm forced to protect him.'

Ron looked up at his sister. '*Protect Victor*? Are you kidding?'

'Before you fly off the handle, just think about it,' Zoe countered, turning away from him and looking at the Corot fake carefully. 'If I let a few forgeries back on to the market, all the attention will go off Victor — '

'And on to you.'

She shook her head. 'No, not if I'm careful.' She sighed, but the old feeling of euphoria was returning, the heady jolt of excitement. 'It would be a clever thing to do — and it would be fun.'

★ ★ ★

Harland had heard the rumours too, and he wasn't stupid enough to discount them entirely.

Besides, it seemed quite possible that Victor Mellor was dealing in fakes, and if Victor was, then Zoe might be also. They were brother and sister, after all. He felt uncomfortable suddenly and shifted his position, drumming his fingers on the arm of the chair as he waited for Myrtle. Not that he had been caught out by any fakes, and if Zoe had been dealing . . . He winced. Yes, of course, he should have known she would never have deceived him. She was too honourable for that. But was forgery honourable? He began to sweat lightly. He had heard too many stories to feel comfortable about the matter, and knew too many ruthless men. Wiping his forehead with his handkerchief, Harland forced himself to think back over the years, remembering especially the curious incident in Venice — Victor turning up out of the blue and being stabbed.

He forced himself to laugh at the idea, pouring out a stiff vodka and tonic and returning to his seat. It was too ridiculous, he thought suddenly. He was letting his imagination run away with him. Zoe couldn't be involved in forgery — she had too much to lose.

'You want we should have a crash before we get there?' Myrtle asked, walking into the lounge and spotting the drink in her husband's hand. She was ageing well. Having finally accepted that her husband's mistress was a permanent fixture, she was now actually capitalising on it, squeezing sympathy out of her friends and money out of Harland. For the moment the situation seemed reasonable, and a form of second-hand concern floated up to the turbulent surface of their marriage. 'The doctor said — '

' — that now and again I can have a drink.'

'Now and again isn't every night,' she continued, looking down at him. She was wearing a long bronze silk dress, her predatory arms poking out of the bell sleeves like orange sticks. It was obvious that she had been to the hairdresser, because her coiffure was ornate and piled high on the narrow head like a Roman helmet. 'My sister's having a party and you're already drunk.'

'I just — '

She interrupted him. 'I have a drunk husband downstairs and a heartbroken daughter upstairs.' She pulled on her evening gloves, stretching the material to the elbow. 'Erica's like me, unlucky.'

'What's the matter with her now?' Harland asked, sighing.

'If you took more interest in your child you would know!' Myrtle said savagely. 'It's that swine, Mellor. He's not phoned her for months.' She dropped her voice and leaned towards her husband. Her skin was smooth in parts, due to the avid attentions of her beautician, but here and there lines showed, like creases in a cushion. 'He's nearly killed her.'

'She'll get over it.'

Myrtle straightened up. 'We've never had any luck since that Mellor family entered our lives. First you, then Erica.' She sniffed, snatching up her sable coat. 'I've been too long-suffering, Harland. After all, what's sauce for the goose, is sauce for the gander. Maybe I should look up their father and have a little fling of my own.'

The image of his wife with Bernard Mellor flared up in front of Harland and he began to laugh, and he was still laughing as he drove his dark Jaguar out of the drive, Myrtle fuming beside him.

★　★　★

Alan had been used to working day and night in the garage, his overalls covered by a thick cardigan, his hands protected by mittens as he toiled into the early hours. But the previous November, after Zoe had told him to call a halt to the forgeries, he had been bereft, his world narrowing down and pressing in on him. Depression had followed, his shyness crippling him and preventing him from explaining his despair. Days had mingled with long aching nights. Nothing made any sense to him any longer, and his depression made him reclusive, a shadow man edging the moors, thinking.

Tom Mellor had grown old and found himself less interested in his nephew, so during the day they worked side by side and at five he scarcely looked up when Alan excused himself to go home. Not that he went home immediately, it was too early. Instead he walked round the town killing time, skirting the company which intimidated him. No one needed him any more. People avoided him. They didn't feel comfortable with the fat man from the stonemason's and on the few occasions Alan had ventured into the pub he had found himself shunned except for the sympathetic attentions of the barmaid. And those embarrassed him. Time dragged at his heels.

The garage was quiet. Even though Alan still went there, there was little to do, the tools laid on the bench unused, no rush orders to fill, no pats on the back from Zoe, no grudging words of admiration from Victor. Nothing. Only silence. Which was cruel. Even the statues lost their sorcery, their limbs stone now, not flesh, their solid eroticism mocking, no longer inviting. With a mixture of despair and disgust, Alan covered up each one of them with sheets, heads, bodies, faces hidden, like so many corpses in a morgue, throwing high shadows on the garage walls. Later, walking in the streets, steering clear of the groups of cheeky girls at bus stops, he returned home only to eat. Fish and chips from the High Street.

'One fish, two chips, a meat pie, no peas, ta,' he would say, a fat man in overalls. A butt of jokes.

In the cold garage he sat with a donkey jacket round his shoulders eating. It seemed like another time, the night they had all drunk champagne, and he had sung. He glanced up at the light and then flicked another bar on the electric fire, warming his massive hands, several nails blackened from chisel blows. The metal tools twinkled under the light on the tidy bench, the books lined up in rows on the makeshift shelves, the worn postcards from New York, Milan, Venice and Rome all peering down at him from the cork board.

That had been yesterday, when he had

belonged. The days had made sense when he had been busy and happy. He crumpled the fish and chips wrappers in his hands and bent his head. The silence crushed him and he hadn't even the energy to turn on his cassette player, the spools silent and unwanted, and each one wound back to the start.

* * *

Jimmy van Goyen was busy with his accountant, trying to reread the figures in a way which would make the losses seem less. He had been occupied with him all morning, the full impact of his situation descending like a wet sheet. The previous year had been a wicked one for the gallery, the accountant explained, and the last two exhibitions had not done well. Van Goyen glanced away and then straightened up, his back hurting him. Everything had gone hopelessly wrong, he thought, from being one of the luckiest and most successful dealers in London, he was now struggling to keep himself in business. He narrowed his eyes and thought of the fakes which had caught him out, somewhere some forger was gloating over him. The thought boiled in his head and made him dangerous.

By contrast, Anthony Sargeant was feeling delighted with the world and particularly with the Corot he was carrying under his arm. Allowing himself a slight smile, he entered the Courtney-Blye gallery. The place was empty as a muted bell rang out to signal his arrival and a large English bull terrier strode towards him.

'Hello, Harry,' he said nervously. 'Where's your master then?' he asked, catching a snatch of voices from the back room, and walking towards the sound.

'Another bloody fake!' Courtney-Blye said, his tone electric. 'I thought that maniac Mellor was responsible, but he can't be. Damn it!'

The Egyptian was more phlegmatic. 'We'll find out who's at the bottom of this — '

'But how much will it cost us!'

Anthony Sargeant moved towards the back of the gallery to listen.

'How many are fakes?'

Courtney-Blye calmed down a little. 'Only three have been found over the last two months, this one, a Gainsborough and a Corot.' Sargeant swallowed. 'Corots are always the easiest to fob off on to half-witted buyers,' Tobar Manners chimed in, his voice muffled as if he was the furthest away from the door.

The Corot under Sargeant's arm was suddenly leaden and boiling hot, its unwelcome frame digging into his armpit.

'I thought it was Victor Mellor myself,' Fazir conceded. 'In fact, I'll be honest and say that I thought his sister was in on it too.' There was an ominous silence. 'Thankfully such is not the case, or we would have looked complete bloody fools hiring her to find the forger.'

The humour of the situation struck Anthony Sargeant suddenly and made him snigger. Frightened that he might be caught out, he clapped his hand over his mouth — and dropped the painting.

Ahmed Fazir was the first out of the room, Tobar Manners following. The latter stood in front of the quaking Sargeant, his hands on his hips.

'Listening at doors again, Anthony?'

'I was only — ' He paused, and then, assuming a convincing expression of stupidity, said, 'I just dropped in.'

Tobar Manner's eyes raked down Sargeant's form and came to rest on the picture which had fallen against the wall. '*What* is that?'

'A Corot,' Sargeant whispered.

'What?' he asked spitefully. 'I didn't quite catch that.'

'A Corot,' Sargeant replied, burping. 'I've got indigestion now! Do let it drop, Tobar. I made a mistake that's all.' He glanced at the Egyptian, then at his partner, and then at the figure of Courtney-Blye lounging in the doorway, the dog beside him. 'I don't know what you're all looking so smug about, we all get caught out now and again.'

Tobar smiled grimly. 'Now and again, Anthony, that's true.' He tapped the painting with the toe of his polished shoe. 'Do correct me if I'm wrong, but wasn't that painting you bought last summer a Corot?' Sargeant's face coloured. 'So in short, Anthony, old chum, you have been taken for a ride. Twice. In fact, you have been taken for a ride so often you could qualify for a season ticket.' He jabbed the picture again. 'Now take that 'Corot' and — '

Anthony Sargeant's voice was faint, but steady. 'Tobar?'

'Yes?'

'You know you sent me off to that sale last week on your behalf?'

Tobar Manners was glassy-eyed.

'And you told me to buy something pretty, which would be easy to sell. Well, it was only twenty thousand, and it seemed genuine at the time. How was I to know? Tobar?'

★　★　★

Harland flicked on the lamp beside him and sighed. The rain had been pelting in with the occasional slash of hail since two o'clock, the sky a grumbling indigo. In the sullen light, the panelled walls crouched round him, the paintings in their gilded frames only half decipherable, the gloom making mysteries out of the English landscapes. Wearily he pushed the papers away with his hand and glanced back to the phone. It was cream plastic, ordinary, benign really. It was just the words which had contaminated it and made it repellent to him.

With what seemed to be a gigantic effort, Harland rose to his feet, the carpet muffling his footsteps, making him a ghost. He thought of death suddenly, wondering if that was how it might be in the end, an eternal walking amongst men, unheard. The thought terrified him and made him clumsy, his hand shaking as he poured himself some water from a glass pitcher. A sharp burst of hail rapped at the windows again, the lamp flickering instantaneously on the desk.

476

What had the man said? Harland asked himself. What was it he had said? The conversation came back in full colour, full sound, full implication.

'You don't know me . . . '

(I never wanted to.)

' . . . but I have some information which will . . . '

(Break my heart.)

' . . . be of interest to you. Zoe Mellor deals in forgeries.'

(Zoe, no. Not Zoe.)

'I know it for a fact. She even fakes some of them herself . . . '

(Fakes!)

'I saw one in her flat . . . '

(The words ripped at his gut.)

' . . . when I was, er . . . visiting her.'

(The implication was clear. Too clear. I've been a fool, Harland thought bitterly.)

' . . . I thought you should know. You should stop her . . . '

(Stop her?)

' . . . She's been using you. She doesn't love you . . . '

(I knew that, Harland thought. That's no surprise.)

' . . . she's a criminal . . . '

Silence on the line.

'Are you there?'

(Am I? Harland thought.)

'Please yourself, old man . . . I just thought you ought to know . . . '

The phone had gone down then, the connection severed.

Another rapping of hail on the windows shook Harland and made him turn. The sky was angry, an ill-tempered afternoon in early April, when the flowers should have been in bud. But instead it was out of sequence. Spoilt. He glanced at the photograph on his desk and frowned, turning Myrtle down on her face, her reproof too much to bear. After all, she had been right all along, Zoe Mellor *had* been using him. Bitterness thickened inside his mouth, his temper rising as a sharp pain in his chest made him pause and reach for his pills. He swallowed two and then took several deep breaths. I don't want to die, he thought quickly. I'm not ready to die yet. Under the unfriendly light he steadied himself, replaying the phone conversation over and over again. For a long time Harland Goldberg considered the information. He weighed it, assessed it, and then finally balanced it against the woman he knew. Zoe Mellor.

He had invited her into his world and enjoyed training her, taking a pride in her skill and her abilities, thinking that she had loved the work as he had. With a passion. He grimaced — he was respectable, honourable, a dealer whose word was his bond. The one dealer who was above suspicion. The one dealer who happened to be shielding a forger. The realisation skipped on his nerves painfully. I've been a bloody fool, he thought, for eight years I loved her and taught her and protected her . . . Harland smiled wryly . . . yet, if the truth be known, for the last two he had suspected her.

In fact, he had been waiting for such a call for

478

months. He had even begun to expect it. So why was he so upset? he asked himself, knowing the answer immediately. The caller had inferred a close relationship with Zoe, an intimacy which had obviously gone beyond Harland's . . . Yes, that had been the part which really hurt. She had had a lover, and kept it a secret. She had betrayed him. He frowned, acutely uncomfortable, and then with a shock realised that he didn't *care* if she was a forger — he only cared that she had loved someone else . . . The thought scalded him and his heart raced. I loved you, he said softly into the shadowed office, I loved you and you betrayed me.

But her lover had now betrayed her. He had tried to destroy her in a way which could mean disgrace and even jail. If Harland had been deceived, so had Zoe. His protective instinct welled up and obliterated everything else from his mind. The man had tried to hurt her, he thought again, remembering the bitter voice with its faint Northern accent — her lover had turned on her. His attitude shifted and, his sympathies aroused, Harland Goldberg reached for his address book and began scanning the numbers. He *had* to discover how involved she was in the fakes. It was a dangerous business, he thought angrily, running his finger down a list of names, he *had* to know what she was up to before he could decide what to do.

The phone was answered on the forth ring, the line from Amsterdam hazy. 'Hello?'

'Mr Hands?'

'Yes. Who's that?'

Harland dropped his voice automatically. 'My name is Harland Goldberg, I have a gallery in — '

'London, I know,' the voice replied easily, the Californian accent relaxed. 'You also have a fine reputation.'

At the moment, Harland thought grimly. 'I wanted to hire you to do a job for me, Mr Hands. Are you engaged at the moment?'

'Only with a long cold beer,' the American replied. 'When I've finished it, I'll be at a loose end.'

'Could you come over to London where we could talk?'

'Sure. I could be with you . . . ' There was a pause. He was probably looking up the plane timetables. ' . . . this evening, around nine. How's that?'

'Perfect,' Harland replied. 'If you could come to the gallery, it's number — '

'Oh, I know where you are, Mr Goldberg. I'll see you at nine.'

Harland replaced the phone and took several deep breaths. Mr Laurence Hands was coming to the rescue, he thought wryly. The cavalry was on its way.

The beer disappeared down Larry Hands's throat in one gulp as he hauled himself off the bed and walked over to the wardrobe, pulling down a suitcase and beginning to pack. Harland Goldberg, he thought to himself, that was a turn-up for the book. Why, the man was famous in the art world. Smiling, he whistled under his breath. He hadn't been to London since 1984, it was time he saw the old place again. Not that he hadn't done enough travelling since he had left the New York Police Department with a broken leg after falling off a fire escape. They hadn't thought he was temperamentally suited to the job, and he had reluctantly agreed. The trouble was that he was temperamentally unsuited to many things. His medical career had ended after the second year; then a bright future in business was cut short by boredom; followed by a try at the legal profession which was aborted almost as soon as it had begun. A miscarriage of justice, he thought drily. So he had gone into detective work. After all, he had watched enough episodes of the *Rockford Files* and seen the *Maltese Falcon* three times, so he reckoned he had the qualifications. With his easy, uncomplicated manner he had soon found clients and before long he was spending his time moving from country to country, tracing missing relatives, kids, and stolen property.

Not that his dedication hadn't earned him a reputation. 'Larry Hands can find anything' people said, and just like other people were born salemen, he was a born finder. Lose anything, and he would turn it up. It was a fantastic gift, and now, at the age of thirty-four he was at the peak of his profession, a *respected* private investigator — if such a thing existed. Not that he hadn't learnt to be careful about the jobs he took on, and by weeding out the tacky end, had succeeded in making a living while making himself high class. He grinned at the expresion — high class. How could he be high class while he still grubbed around? Or maybe the difference was that now he grubbed around in the higher echelons — like Harland Goldberg's. Whistling softly he turned on the shower and then slowly let the cool water run over him.

Harland was waiting inside the gallery as the taxi drew up at precisely nine o'clock. He watched as a man got out, pulling a case after him and turning to check the number on the bronze wall plaque. For some inexplicable reason Harland ducked back for a moment to scrutinise Larry Hands as he paid the cabbie, his tall frame bent towards the door. He was soberly dressed, with a head of dark blond hair which fitted perfectly, and a tanned face over which the flesh was drawn tightly. He looked fit enough to run ten miles with a lead backpack and he made Harland feel old.

'Please come in, Mr Hands,' he said, opening the gallery door and glancing up at the stranger. 'You're very punctual.'

Larry Hands smiled easily. 'I had a good flight,' he replied, nodding his head to the window. 'Isn't that an Augustus John portrait?'

Harland smiled, and then wondered ungraciously if he had had time to read the label before walking in. 'If you would like to come into the office,' he said.

The newcomer accepted a whisky and soda and leaned back in his seat, his coat falling open and revealing an inconspicuous suit and tie. Obviously he dressed to mingle and go unnoticed, Harland thought wryly. Not that a lean American stranger in London could go unnoticed — except by other lean American strangers.

'I have a problem . . . ' he began, trailing off.

The truth was that Harland had struggled with the situation all afternoon. He needed Hands to investigate Zoe's movements and tell him what she was up to. But he couldn't afford to take the man into his confidence and tell him about the fakes, because if Zoe was guilty, he would want to turn her over to the police. After all, he was an ex-policeman, wasn't he?

So he had decided on another tack, and breathing in deeply, began. 'I have a mistress . . . and I think she is seeing another man.' He gulped at his drink, certain that he was blushing under his beard.

Hands coughed discreetly. 'Well, I don't usually — '

'I know your reputation. I know that you don't generally like to get involved in . . . affairs of the heart . . . ' Harland staggered on, embarrassed, ' . . . but you are the best, and I do need someone discreet. The situation, you see, is embarrassing,' he concluded, his eyes moving towards Myrtle's photograph.

Hands was quick to pick up the hint. 'Why are you suspicious of her?'

'Myrtle?'

'She's called Myrtle?'

Harland blinked. 'Myrtle is my wife.'

'Your wife.'

'Yes . . . ' Harland replied, baffled, and then realising the misunderstanding, explained. 'My lady friend is called Zoe Mellor,' he said, passing

483

a photograph over to Larry Hands. 'I care for her very much.'

It was obvious why, the American thought as he looked at the picture, because although the young woman had been caught unawares glancing over her shoulder, the full impact of quirky charm was obvious in her unusual face. He studied it to imprint her features on his mind, the slanted eyes, the dark mass of hair . . . He wasn't surprised Harland Goldberg wanted to keep an eye on her, only that the dapper little man had such a mistress.

'Isn't she lovely?'

Hands nodded. Sure, she was lovely, but she was an old man's mistress, out for the money, a gold-digger, like the rest.

'Can you find out if she's seeing someone else?'

He should have told him to get lost and flown back to Amsterdam, but something in that photograph caught his imagination, and besides, he was tired of the Dutch capital, and the bicycles, and the drug problems.

'I charge — '

'I know your fee. I agree to it.'

And that was how it began.

The job was an easy one and Larry Hands soon found himself *au fait* with Zoe Mellor's timetable — from Palace Gardens Terrace to W1, then from the gallery home again in the company of her impressively proportioned brother. That was all. In fact, after two days surveillance, the only thing he had to report back to Harland was that his mistress was leading the life of a Chelsea pensioner.

'Well, things are quiet at the moment,' Harland explained, 'but at times we're busy. We travel around, you see, attending auctions.'

'Is there one coming up?'

'No, not for another two months. Then there is a very important sale on 17 September, but that's in London.'

'So you think she might be seeing someone while you're abroad?'

Everything was getting complicated, Harland thought suddenly. 'How could she if we travel together?' he snapped and then added quietly, 'I don't know. That's why I hired you.'

'Don't worry, Mr Goldberg, I understand.'

Harland was glad someone did.

The next week passed in this fashion, the lean American following Zoe from her flat, then tracking her easily across the warren of art galleries, and taking notes of all the dealers to whom she talked. It seemed unlikely to Larry that she was romantically involved with any of those men, and after seeing the likes of Tobar Manners and Courtney-Blye, he was certain she wasn't. But he wasn't so sure about Ahmed Fazir, who was obviously very attracted to her. He watched the Egyptian at the window of his gallery on Old Brompton Road, and saw that unmistakable look when Zoe Mellor walked in, her neat figure upright, composed, her eyes shielded by a pair of overlarge sunglasses. But her manner was abrupt and to the point, and even though he couldn't hear what she said, it was obvious that she had little time for the bulky Fazir.

By the time two more days had passed Larry was almost bored mindless. So when Zoe left the flat early on the Thursday and made her way to Victoria Station, he followed her avidly, in the hope of some kind of diversion. Having hired a beige Sierra, he tracked her taxi to the station entrance and was then forced to leave his car double-parked as he followed her into the train. Perhaps she was finally going to visit her lover, he thought hopefully, sitting down two seats behind Zoe and digging out his money to pay the guard. Totally unaware of the scrutiny, Zoe began to read her paper. She was, in fact, going down to visit the Baronet in Sussex, the same Baronet who owned the Peke and a selection of old English masterpieces which she had had cleaned, and swopped, and copied, and sent back — one third being replaced by glowing fakes. Not that the titled gentleman had noticed, any alteration in appearance he had merely put down to the cleaning, the intensity of the colours obviously brightening once the layers of grime had been removed.

The day was warming up as the train reached Brighton and Zoe hailed a taxi at the station, Larry in hot pursuit.

'Follow that cab,' he said, snatching open the taxi door.

A sleepy driver looked back at him with a slack smile. 'You are joking, aren't you?'

'There's an extra fiver if you don't lose her.'

Thus persuaded, the driver followed Zoe's taxi out into the countryside where the air was heavier, away from the sea. Totally relaxed, she leaned back, her head on the warm leather seat, and thought about Saltdean and the bungalow where Ron had spied on Victor, Lino Candadas and Noilly. She smiled thoughtfully, their little trick at the auction had certainly spiked Victor's guns, in fact, it had rendered him powerless. The sun nuzzled the top of her head. No one was going to take Victor Mellor seriously after that appalling gaffe, she was safe at last.

Blissfully ignorant of the taxi following her, Zoe's mind wandered while Larry kept his eyes fixed on the car in front, telling the driver to stop as it pulled into a long driveway.

'Wait here,' he said, leaning forwards in his seat. 'What's this place?'

'The home of Sir Leonard Compton-Lacey.'

'You're having me on.'

The driver mopped his head with his handkerchief. 'No, straight up. He's a Baronet, or something.'

Larry leaned back in his seat, the driver watching him through his mirror. 'What d'you want me to do now?'

'Just wait for me.'

Cautiously Larry moved towards the house, keeping himself obscured by the shrubbery, his eyes fixed on the open window on the ground floor which looked out over a moss-riddled terrace. If he could just get near enough to listen, he thought, then he would soon find out what Zoe Mellor was up to. He paused, his attention suddenly distracted as a wasp sidled next him and he flicked it away, his hand moving abruptly through the heavy air.

Hidden in the greenery several yards away, Ron watched him, chewing on an apple. Bloody big soft girl, he thought idly, as he scrutinised the American. Fancy being afraid of a wasp. He leaned against the tree from his own vantage point and wondered, not for the first time, what the hell was going on.

28

Zoe looked at her brother in disbelief. 'You're imagining things, Ron.'

'I've told you, there was a man following you.'

Absent-mindedly, she clipped on her right earring and glanced into the mirror. There was a private view that night at Jimmy van Goyen's gallery and she was going to attend, unfortunately without Harland who was holding a dinner party with Myrtle. 'Are you sure?'

'Sure I'm sure,' Ron replied evenly. 'He's the same bloke who followed you to work yesterday. I saw him by accident at first, but then I started to look out for him,' he continued, ladling some dog food into Peter's dish. 'He's a tall, lanky bloke.'

Zoe thought for a moment. Perhaps she had been too confident, too soon. If someone was watching her it could only be at Mike O'Dowd's instigation. She touched her throat, remembering the sound of the water under the bridge in Venice and the boats knocking together on the night tide.

'We're both overwrought,' she said, trying to convince herself as much as her brother. 'Things have been so frightening recently.'

'I didn't imagine it!' he said, aggrieved. 'And I'll prove it. You go out now and I'll wait until he follows you, then I'll tip you off.'

'How?'

'I dunno. I'll think of something.'

Twenty minutes later Zoe was leaving the flat, exchanging a brief word with a neighbour on the way out. The night was damp, and she stepped over puddles on her way to the waiting mini cab. The trees were already in flower, the cherry blossom coming into its own, although a sharp wind had dislodged some blooms and left them, easily sullied in the dark drains.

Feeling slightly foolish, Zoe glanced round, and then seeing no one, shrugged and stepped into the car. Ron watched carefully, Peter beside him, as the spare figure of the American moved out seconds later and followed the taxi. Sighing, Ron stroked Peter's ears thoughtfully, his eyes following the cab as it swept out of the damp street. There was no rush, he thought, because the man was obviously going to follow Zoe to the gallery so he had plenty of time to catch them up. Slapping his thigh for the greyhound to come to heel, Ron moved off.

He arrived forty minutes later and hovered outside Jimmy van Goyen's gallery looking for Zoe. All he could see was a selection of backs, and hear the occasional braying from one of the most inebriated patrons. Bored, Peter sat down and began to scratch his ear, a thin man in a dinner jacket coming out and giving Ron a bleak look. There was still no sign of Zoe or her pursuer.

'Can I help you?' a voice asked, the tone implying that it was the furthest thing from his mind.

'I'm waiting for someone,' Ron replied, embarrassed, his flat Northern vowels damning him further in the man's eyes.

'Whom?'

Ron was discomforted and unwilling to embarrass Zoe. On the other hand, he didn't want to be pestered, so stretching up to his full height and said, 'Do you want to make something out of this?'

In the face of two hundred pounds of solid muscle, the man retreated.

Satisfied, Ron leaned back against the wall, his face half turned towards the window. He saw a number of dealers he already knew by sight, the small figure of Mona Grimaldi, and the pigtailed Dutchman, looking anxious as he walked towards the back of the gallery, his hands deep in his pocket. He had just spotted Leon Graves when Zoe emerged, her face tight with suspicion. 'Well?'

'He followed you. Just like I said.'

She paled immediately, her face artificially white against the cream dress she was wearing, the familiar hunted look coming back into her eyes. 'Which one is he?'

Ron shrugged. 'I can't see him from here.'

'So come inside then.'

He baulked. 'Me, go in there? Aw, go on!'

Impatiently, Zoe tugged at his sleeve. 'Come on, Ron,' she said. 'If anyone asks what you're doing say you're my brother and then let me sort it out.'

Reluctantly, Ron left Peter waiting outside and moved into the teeming gallery. Smoke hung tented over the gathering, canapés of smoked salmon lying half eaten, catalogues smudged with ash and discarded phone numbers. The conversation was loud, and much concerned with prices, auctions, and scandal, Tobar Manners holding court by the fireplace, a bored Anthony Sargeant yawning beside him.

A young man, one of Manners's assistants in the gallery, materialised beside Ron. 'Champagne?'

He spun round, startled. 'I don't drink.'

'Maybe that's how you got to be such a big boy,' the man said admiringly.

Ron turned to his sister as she pulled him away. 'What did that mean?'

'Forget it,' she said, skirting Seymour Bell. 'Just point out the man who followed me.'

Obediently, Ron glanced about him. Having the advantage of height he could see over most people's heads and had already scrutinised half of the guests before his gaze came to rest on a figure admiring a Rossetti watercolour at the back of the gallery.

'That's him.'

Zoe looked over towards the tall man and studied him. Young, inconspicuously dressed, he looked at ease, just like any interested browser at a private view. Turning to Ron, she told him to go home, despite his protests for her safety, and then made her way through the crowd. 'What do you think of the painting?'

Larry Hands turned. Momentarily surprised he smiled and then feigned ignorance. 'It's great, isn't it?'

Zoe glanced at the Rossetti. 'He was a dope fiend.'

492

Larry blinked. 'Rossetti?'

'Yes, Rossetti,' Zoe replied, moving closer towards him. He could see the colour of her eyes clearly, and admired the outfit she wore which was obviously expensive and carried with some style. 'I know you've been following me . . . Who are you?'

He ignored the question. 'I *was* an admirer of Rossetti's,' he replied lightly. 'But now I'm not so sure.'

His manner infuriated her. 'For the second time, who are you?'

Deciding that honesty was the best policy, he answered her frankly. 'I was hired to investigate your movements. To find out about your boyfriend.' Zoe's face was blank as he continued. 'Your lover hired me.'

She thought of Steven Foreshaw and frowned. 'My lover?'

'Harland Goldberg.'

'Harland Goldberg,' she repeated, playing for time. What on earth was he up to? She had no lover, certainly not since she had broken up with Steven. 'He thinks I have a lover?'

'That's what he told me.'

The situation was ludicrous, and her tone implied as much. 'And what were you supposed to do about it?'

'Follow you and report back.'

The situation was suddenly apparent to Zoe. Harland must be suspicious about the fakes for some reason, and was using the story of her unfaithfulness as a cover to keep tabs on her. The ruse was clever, she thought admiringly, but she couldn't allow him to discover the forgery business. Not Harland.

'But I don't have a lover,' she said to Larry, adding for good measure, 'Apart from Harland, that is.'

He smiled. The champagne and the heat in the gallery were having their effect and he was pleasantly lightheaded. She was very appealing indeed, he thought, even if she was the old man's mistress. 'I know you don't. At least, I'm pretty sure. But then, I've only been following you for ten days.'

Ten days, Zoe thought, swallowing uncomfortably. Thank God she hadn't released any fakes lately. Thank God she hadn't gone home to see Alan in the garage . . . Harland would have had a field day. Not Harland, she thought again with a rush of anxiety, not him. I never wanted him to know anything, or suspect anything.

'I haven't been unfaithful to him,' she said quietly, the very words a double lie. 'But . . . ' she continued and then broke off, making her voice plaintive. If Harland wanted to play games, she would give him a run for his money. 'You see, he loves me very much and he gets very jealous.' She dropped her voice. 'He's old and very . . . well, you know . . . he loves me.'

The protective instinct in Larry Hands was immediately alerted. He moved towards her and touched her shoulder lightly. 'Don't cry.'

'I'm not . . . ' Zoe mumbled, burying her face in a handkerchief so he couldn't read the expression in her eyes. 'It's just that I'm upset that he thought such a thing of me . . . ' It was

494

all so easy, she thought, as she watched the man soften and fetch her another glass of champagne. Deceit was always easy, reality was the problem.

'Here, Miss Mellor — '

'Zoe.'

He smiled. 'OK, Zoe. Drink this, you'll feel better soon.'

She smiled gratefully, her radiance knocking him off balance. 'Oh, but I feel better already.'

Across the gallery Leon Graves watched them with avid curiosity, knowing who Larry Hands was and wondering who had hired him, and why. He also wondered why Zoe Mellor seemed upset. Thoughtfully he sipped his drink, nodding to Mona and noticing Jimmy van Goyen out of the corner of his eye. The Dutchman was standing by his office door, stooping slightly, his back obviously troubling him, his eyes fixed on his guests. Only feet away from him a man laughed loudly, knocking a glass off a table with his hand, one leather-clad foot grinding the shattered fragments into the polished floor. Leon glanced over to van Goyen and was suddenly alerted by the expression on his face. There was no trace of irritation or interest, the Dutchman's blank eyes merely glanced at the shattered glass and blinked, without seeing, as the champagne bled across the crowded floor.

Leon was still watching van Goyen when his attention was distracted by Ahmed Fazir, who greeted him warmly and proceeded to tell him a long story about his Cairo gallery. It was obvious from his dilated pupils and constant sniffing that he was back on cocaine, his voice thick with excitement, his tongue repeatedly licking his dry lips. As ever, Leon listened. He could find out much more when people were off their guard. Fazir's jowled face leaned towards his own, the expression befuddled and then startled, just as Leon's was when he turned suddenly and pushed his way into Jimmy van Goyen's office.

The Dutchman had shot himself through the mouth and collapsed over his desk, the white wall behind mottled with blood, a Gerrit Dou painting crudely splattered with wet crimson. Leon walked towards the body, Zoe following, her face stiff with horror, her eyes fixed on the gaping hole at the back of van Goyen's head, above the pigtail. She stared, transfixed as the hole darkened, became the black run to Buck's Lane in winter; the filth-smeared subway tunnels in New York; the dark alleyways either side of the bridge in Venice. The hole widened, gobbled her up, and grabbed at her — just as Leon Graves grabbed her the moment she fell.

★   ★   ★

In her Manhattan apartment, Suzie Laye was lying in bed with a sheet pulled up round her breasts. The sound of a shower from the other room was pleasantly soothing, mingling as it did with the taped music from the lounge. She yawned and stretched, satisfied, surprisingly so. Not many men satisfied her, at least, not for long.

'Hey, hurry up,' she called out.

The water continued to run and she pouted,

picking up a catalogue from the side of the bed. It had been her dream that her gallery, the Conrad, would be admired all over New York, because then she could be the queen bee, Art's First Lady. Oh yes, she wanted that; just as she wanted to be respected like that slanty-eyed bitch in London, Zoe Mellor. For a moment she burned with jealousy, and then relaxed. After all, success required dedication and long hours — and the only long hours Suzy was willing to put in were in bed.

But the feeling of guilt wouldn't go away. Having inherited a well established gallery, she had a real advantage over the opposition and should have used it. But hard work was hard work, after all. Suzie Laye was suddenly irritable — oh, what the hell! So what if the gallery got a little neglected? she thought, shifting her position and gazing at her bare legs, the situation could always be remedied. Yes, there was always a solution; another way to get what she wanted. The shape of her legs pleased her and made her smile. Well, maybe she *had* found a way. Sighing, she thought back to last night. Yes, he certainly was inventive, and very virile. She liked that. And he knew the art world inside out. Even if he was unscrupulous. Maybe she could realise her dream with him; maybe they could become Art's First Lady and Gentleman. Like the president and his wife. She giggled softly. They could even end up on the cover of *TIME* Magazine . . .

She turned over suddenly as he came back into the room and pulled her to him. With rising excitement, she felt his hands run over her breasts and murmured his name repeatedly. And as he kissed her, Victor Mellor glanced over and checked the time on the bedside clock.

★ ★ ★

Back in London, Leon Graves pushed everyone out of Jimmy van Goyen's office, locking the gallery doors behind them as he ushered them out into the street. Then he calmly called the police and took the phone off the hook. Zoe sat on a chaise longue, her hands tight on her lap, withdrawn and disbelieving, her mind constantly replaying the image of Jimmy van Goyen, the wound, and the blooded pigtail. To her, it seemed so horrific that she could not accept the Dutchman's death; to Leon Graves, the whole event assumed an aura of surrealism. That the dealer should choose to kill himself in the middle of a private view in such a violent way was incomprehensible, unless van Goyen wanted to make a final and lasting impression on everyone, the hole he blew in his head burning into their memories for ever.

Equally astonished by the turn of events, Larry Hands remained in the gallery, standing guard with Leon and shaking his head as he turned to the Englishman. 'Why did he do it?'

'He was badly in debt,' Leon answered, glancing over to the silent Zoe. She appeared not to hear, not to see, anything. 'He'd also been involved with fakes for years, robbing everyone blind. Unfortunately he got too greedy and lost a fortune.' Leon sighed and picked up a bottle of champagne, looking round for one clean glass amongst the dozens smeared with fingerprints or lipstick. 'It was bound to end up like this — or prison — it always does.'

It was bound to end like this — or prison — it always does, Zoe thought dully.

Larry Hands frowned. 'Hell of a way to do it though. I mean, blowing your head off in the middle of a showing.'

'He never had any class,' Leon said wryly, finally finding a glass and filling it. 'It was his way of getting back at all of us — 'look what you did to me'.'

Look what you did to me, Zoe thought, closing her eyes.

'I'll drive you home.'

Startled, she jumped and then looked up at Leon. It was just a game, she wanted to say, just a game. Nothing like this should have happened. But she remained silent even though his eyes seemed altered as he stared at her. Oh God, she thought despairingly, I want to get out.

'Zoe, did you hear me? I said I'll drive you home.'

'Someone has to stay for the police,' Larry Hands said. 'I'll take her home.'

No, Zoe thought, I want Leon to take me. I don't know this man.

But Leon agreed. 'Fine,' he said, helping her to her feet and walking her to the door. 'Mr Hands is going to drive you home,' he explained carefully, holding on to her tightly as the night air slapped at her and made her gasp. 'Will you be all right?'

She nodded, still dumb, and continued walking with the American up the street towards his car. When they arrived back at Palace Gardens Terrace he turned off the engine and looked at her. The street lamp shadowed her eyes and confused him, just as her silence did. Gone was the high-spirited woman at the private view, now she was shuttered away, the shock distancing her. Her vulnerability tore into him, the heady sensation of attraction displaced by a stronger feeling of responsibility. I can't leave this woman, he thought blindly as a bruised sprig of cherry blossom fell on to the windscreen and lodged by the wiper.

'Listen, we have to decide what to do.'

Zoe glanced over to him and frowned. What *was* he talking about?

'I could just report back to Mr Goldberg and say that you're not seeing anyone else.'

She tried to concentrate. What *had* they been talking about before Jimmy van Goyen killed himself? The red hole opened before her and she caught her breath.

'Hey, it's OK. I'll figure something out,' he said tenderly, stroking the line of her cheek. There was nothing sexual in the action, simply loving. Softly, Zoe began to cry and he held her repeating over and over again, 'It's OK, I'll think of something.' He leaned his face towards hers, her tears moving him, her anguish unavoidably his.

For the next few weeks Larry Hands reported to Harland Goldberg regularly, giving doctored accounts of Zoe's movements, telling him nothing about their talks, or their quiet dinners, never uttering a word about the fierce bond which had so rapidly tied them. Jimmy van Goyen's suicide shattered Zoe, and she blamed herself, thinking that her few fakes had ruined him, her guilt not allowing her to accept that the Dutchman had been losing money rapidly lately and had been dealing in O'Dowd's fakes for over a decade. In reality, she had no part in his suicide, but she convinced herself otherwise, wanting to punish herself and subconsciously prepare the way for an escape from the forgery business.

Larry Hands came into her life at the one time Zoe was completely vulnerable and she leaned on him gratefully. There was no possibility of her confiding in him, but his gentleness calmed her panic and enabled her to continue her life from day to day. To Harland she acted the perfect innocent, and he relaxed visibly, delighted that his suspicions about the fakes were unfounded. But the strain of deceiving both men, coupled with the gruelling guilt and anxiety about Jimmy van Goyen's death, left Zoe drained, her actions completed by rote, her nights invaded constantly by the sight of the dead man.

Yet her natural cleverness did not desert her altogether and in order that Harland should be completely duped she put a fake School of Tiepolo drawing into a small auction under the name of Miss Nancy Elliott. Because the fake was poor and they had been left a false address and phone number which could not be traced, the auction house soon discovered the forgery and word went around. By the end of the afternoon Harland came to hear of it, and because Larry Hands was supposedly following Zoe and had nothing suspicious to report, he concluded that she had nothing to do with it.

Meanwhile Larry was falling in love with a woman whose only crime was to be the mistress of an old man — and he soon forgave her that, as he forgave her frequent mood swings, putting them down to shock, the sight of Jimmy van Goyen's body unsettling her long after it should have done. He knew too that she had bad dreams, and that some mornings she was heavy-eyed, listless. Because he was eager to love her he accepted behaviour which, in another person would have seemed suspicious — he accepted it, but Leon Graves did not.

'She seems odd,' he said to Harland a while later.

'I know, she's been distant since van Goyen's death ... I don't understand why, she never liked the man.'

'She saw his body,' Leon answered, leaning against Harland's desk and choosing his words carefully. 'I was wondering — is there something else that she could be worrying about?'

Harland replied without a pause. 'Nothing,' he said. 'Don't worry, she'll get over it. It was a horrible thing to happen.'

Leon nodded, unconvinced.

A day later, Zoe arrived home early, changing into her dressing-gown and reading the note left by Ron.

'Gone out with Sally. See you later.'

Absent-mindly she paced the flat, the trunk in the corner looking at her, the lock shining under the overhead light. Open me up, it whispered, open me up and see what treasures I have. She turned away, trying not to think of the fakes but then turned back, finding the key and opening it. In a frenzy she pulled off the tissue paper — a Guercino drawing looking up at her defiantly from its wrapping. Her hands hesitated and then viciously she tore it up, the hours of work and skill ripped into pieces, the white paper falling on to the floor like bird droppings. With a sense of unexpected relief, Zoe dug down for the next drawing, her fever halted only when the doorbell rang.

Defiantly she ignored it, but it continued to ring and finally she realised that the caller was not going away. Frustrated, she slammed down the lid of the trunk and relocked it, going to the door and letting Larry in.

'Are you OK?' he asked, walking past her into the lounge.

'Fine. I was just . . . going to wash my hair,' she replied, smiling awkwardly.

'I'll do it for you.'

She backed off, suddenly alarmed. 'No, I can do it.'

'Let me. I want to,' Larry said quietly, stilling her, and leading her into the bathroom. He ran the water, nudging her on to her knees so that her head was over the bath, her hair falling forwards. Vulnerable and trusting, she felt his hands rinse her hair, and pour on the shampoo, massaging it into a lather and then running the clean water through it. Neither of them spoke, the act more moving to Zoe than anything any man had ever done for her, the gesture entirely loving. Finally he wound a towel around her head and knelt down beside her, wiping away the one strand of wet hair which had fallen across her forehead.

'I want to make love to you,' he said, noticing how she flinched at the words, 'but not now. When you're ready, tell me.'

'Larry — '

'No, you don't have to explain anything to me,' he said, leading her back into the lounge and beginning to rub her hair dry, her acceptance total. A child's gratitude. After a while she even relaxed and when he pulled off the towel she smiled at him.

'I could buy a place in London for both of us,' he said simply.

The panic nearly choked her. It was a physical reaction, a sudden realisation that she of all people, who lived and was excited by duplicity, was finally going to be caught. And by what? By love. The damning, despicable, power of love.

'But we don't know each other well enough.'

He had anticipated her answer, and was ready with his reply. 'Of course we do,' he said, leaning towards her and catching hold of her damp hair in both hands. 'I know everything I need to know about you.'

The irony rendered her speechless, and because he wanted to, he read her silence as acceptance. Carefully he drew her face towards his own, his mouth moving over hers. A heady excitement welled up in both of them, but as Zoe tried to draw back, he let go of her.

'I told you, I won't force you into anything. We'll make love when you're ready.'

And when is that? she thought. When was I ever ready?

For a long instant she looked at him and then sighed, nodding silently. With infinite tenderness Larry closed her eyes with the tips of his fingers and then kissed each lid. His breath seemed to burn her. Languorously, he undressed her and then himself, pulling her off the settee and on to the floor, turning and twisting with her as Zoe began to respond, her whole attention centred on the man with her. Eagerly she kissed him and touched him, and when she lay on top of him and looked into his eyes, her expression was so trusting that it startled and moved him. With one quick gesture, he stretched out his arm and pulled the lamp plug out of the wall, plunging the room into total darkness.

And that was what she wanted. The blessed darkness where she was safe. There were no eyes in the darkness, no ears, no terror, she thought. Then unexpectedly she cried out, her mind replaying the image of Jimmy van Goyen's head, only this time instead of his face she saw her own. Tightly she clung on to Larry, and from somewhere far back in her own childhood the memory of loneliness washed over her, spinning with the image of death, of her mother, of the limitless fear, and it spoke for her when she cried out, loudly and desperately, 'I want to go home.'

And he took her, the only way he knew how.

★ ★ ★

Mike O'Dowd was feeling decidedly mean-minded when he met up with Victor at a bar in the Lower East Side. The basement pounded with music, a TV switched on in one corner showing a boxing match, and a selection of women was lined up like battered skittles along the bar rail. O'Dowd blew his nose and settled in an alcove, his tinted glasses obliterating his eyes totally.

Victor arrived soon after, sliding into the seat next to him. 'How's things?'

'Don't piss about, Mellor,' O'Dowd said, his hands spread out on the table in front of him. 'I've waited long enough. After that bloody fiasco at the auction you're lucky I'm still doing business with you.'

Victor was unimpressed. His mind was on Suzie Laye and her gallery. He could see himself in a position of importance — he might even marry the stupid tart. Yes, he thought, if I owned the Conrad Gallery I would be someone to be reckoned with, and I could use it as a cover for the fakes. Victor Mellor, Director of the Conrad Gallery, New York. He liked the sound of it and smiled.

'What the hell are you grinning at?'

He turned to the Irishman. 'Why do you still want to work with me?' he asked. 'I can't get hold of any of Zoe's fakes any more, and besides, everyone in London's on to me.'

It was O'Dowd's turn to smile. 'Not quite. Your sister is very clever. After giving you a good

506

pasting at the auction, she was smart enough to let the odd fake come on to the market recently and take the heat off you.'

Victor raised his eyebrows. 'That was very sisterly.'

'No, that was very smart. She got you out of the way and then made sure that your name was cleared, which meant that hers was too.' He scrutinised his hands, the broad nails buffed to a shine.

'So what do we do now?'

'We wait until the time is right and then deliver the *coup de grâce*. I've been on to Candadas, and he's working his arse off in Wandsworth so we'll have a stock of fakes to put out on the market when everything has been sorted out. Why else?'

Victor thought for a moment. It had been profitable working with O'Dowd, but the time had come for him to go it alone. He could easily persuade Candadas and Noilly to work for him exclusively after he had cut the Irishman out of the picture. The question was, how was he going to get rid of O'Dowd without giving himself away?

'The Bracelet's still in town,' O'Dowd said suddenly.

Victor looked up. 'I know. I saw him after the auction.'

'He's up to something, Mellor, I can feel it,' he sighed, a dull sense of gloom washing over him. Maybe he was getting old, maybe he should just go for one last big kill and retire on the proceeds. After all, he'd made a bundle. His eyes flicked back to the TV screen, to the two boxers beating the guts out of each other, and he smiled nostalgically. He was not quite as quick on his feet these days. Not that he had lost his savagery, that never altered, but the appetite did. He sighed, thinking of Dublin, walking into Davy Byrne's and getting a pink gin, or watching the sun go down over the bay and savouring a pint of Guinness with fresh Dublin prawns, tasting of the sea. The images lulled him into silence and he thought of his children, his daughters in particular. All growing up like their mother, dark haired, cheeks full and red as apples . . .

'What's the matter with you?' Victor asked suddenly.

I can smell the air over Dublin, and feel the wet earth under my feet, O'Dowd, thought to himself. I want to see home again, you bastard, and I don't want to be looking into your yellow eyes.

'This time everything has to go right, Mellor. It has to be perfect. There's a big auction on 17 September, in London, and that's when we get our revenge on your sister. I want her out of the business, d'you hear me? I want her out, once and for all.'

Victor nodded. 'So who's arguing. The question is, how?'

O'Dowd sighed, he felt old suddenly, and missed the Irish rain. 'Think about it, Mellor. She's your sister after all. Just get her out of my way, or I'll get rid of you.'

Victor watched O'Dowd leave and then ordered a double brandy. He wasn't particularly bothered, even though he had an uncomfortable feeling that if he failed this time he would find his suit retailored with a nine-inch carving knife. Jimmy van Goyen's suicide had worried him, perhaps the Irishman had leaned too hard, for too long — but he couldn't intimidate him. Victor frowned, weighing up the pros and cons. After the auction Victor hadn't been able to sell any forgeries, a fact which had severely curtailed O'Dowd's income. A fact he had not appreciated. But the Irishman had stayed his hand and waited, knowing that the time would come when he was indebted to him. Now Mellor *had* to come up trumps. He had to retrieve the business and rid the Irishman of the troublesome Zoe.

Victor was in full agreement with the last sentiment. He felt again the hot flush of embarrassment he had experienced at the auction and winced. She had to go. Not that it would be anything overdramatic, or violent, simply a carefully orchestrated way to banish her — as she had banished him. Only in her case, it would be permanent.

Having made up his mind, his thoughts wandered to Suzie Laye and her gallery. He could picture the high navy-painted walls, and the balcony where they served drinks for rich collectors before a private view, the selection of cocktails almost as enticing as the women. He walked the gallery in his mind — down the wood-stained floor to the office at the end, turning the heavy brass handle and walking in to a wide room heavy with sunshine. But then there was always sunshine when there was money in the bank. There was also a safe tucked behind a painting of a Holy Martyr. He almost licked his lips as he thought of it and continued the tour in his mind. Up the iron staircase towards the upper gallery, the spotlights falling on glassed paintings, the chairs arranged at odd intervals beside expensive sculptures on plinths. Up he went to the second floor, to a lounge decorated with more dark navy walls — like moving around inside a bloody suit, he said to her — the furniture painted a shade of terracotta, huge bowls of flowers and busts in the same shade, the scent of orchids mixing with the faint smell of marijuana.

Quickly he swallowed the remainder of his drink. Marriage would never curtail his sexual activities, but it would mean financial security, a share in the business and the house down in Palm Springs. Oh yes, Victor thought, he could get used to the idea — providing that his wife-to-be never found out about his money in Switzerland, or his little sideline in the fakes. Yes, Suzie was lazy enough to let him have a free reign — she was like all women needing a man. Besides, if he kept her happy in bed, she wouldn't ask questions.

It seemed a small price to pay.

29

That summer the world was talking about Chernobyl, the threat of contamination looming from Russia, English sheep being spared the death sentence while tests went on throughout June. Yet the disaster seemed remote to Zoe, absorbed as she was with Larry, who soon afterwards reported his 'findings' to Harland for the last time, and experienced an acute sense of guilt at the man's generous response.

'You know, in a way I almost feel bad about taking this fee, Mr Goldberg.'

Surprised, Harland looked up. He would gladly have given Mr Laurence Hands twice his fee for the reassurance alone. Zoe was not involved in any forgeries or in anything criminal. The news was worth real money to him.

'Why?'

'It was an easy job and I didn't tax my energies,' Larry replied, flinching inwardly. He liked Harland Goldberg, but he had still betrayed the man. It was an uncomfortable thought.

'Well, whatever you think, I'm more than pleased with your services,' Harland said, writing out a cheque and passing it to the American. 'Thank you for everything you've done.'

He was blissfully unaware of the relationship between Zoe and Larry Hands. As lovers do, they soon developed that special language which was only for two, a secret fantasy world which often seemed foolish afterwards, when love had gone.

'What do you think about her?' Larry asked, as they sat on a bench in Kensington Gardens and watched the passing tourists.

Happily, Zoe screwed up her eyes and peered at the heavy woman passing in front of her. 'She could be Bette Davis in *Now Voyager*.' He frowned. 'You know, before she became all glamorous, when she was still the old maid.'

'What about him?'

The man walked under a huddle of trees and then crossed the cool grass, passing only feet from where they sat.

'Philip Marlowe.'

'Never!' Zoe replied, nudging him with her elbow. 'More like Steve Carella in Ed McBain's 87th Precinct.'

'Just a minute, that's cheating!' Larry said, turning to her. 'The game is to place people in movie roles, not characters in books.'

'I can't help it if I'm more literary-minded,' she replied, her tone pure Noël Coward. 'We English are intellectual, you know.'

'We English can be a pain in the ass,' he replied.

It was their secret game, casting strangers in famous film roles, a Calamity Jane here, a Captain Nemo there. Overheated tourists became Sherlock Holmes, a woman from Tampa, Florida, standing in for The Merry Widow. Fantasy and reality dipped and mingled in the sunshine and made them laugh, their laughter suspended when a look was exchanged, held, and fixed as one hand went out to clasp the other.

Throughout the summer they luxuriated in the affair, making love and enjoying each other's companionship in a way Zoe had never believed possible. Larry's kindness released her and made her view herself in another light. Gone was the rejected child, in her place was someone who not only knew how to love, but how to receive love. Contented for the first time in her life, she thought little of Steven Foreshaw, her father, or Alan, or Ron — in fact, even Victor faded into the background.

Happy as she was, her personality did not change altogether and as the memory of Jimmy van Goyen's suicide faded, Zoe found herself back at the easel, a drawing created over a weekend, and passed on to an auction the following week. Her lifelong habit of seeking excitement was too strong for her to deny entirely, the only difference was that the fakes were now few and far between. In fact, over the previous weeks Zoe had only released two small drawings supposedly by the eighteenth-century Italian painter, Tiepolo. As meticulous as ever, she had used hand-made paper stained by tea, and then scuffed the edges, even inflicting small tears to give the appearance of age. When the pictures were finished, one was placed in the steamy bathroom for days to allow the paper to buckle, while the other was held over a candle for the edges to brown slightly. The finishing touches were imperative and Zoe took particular pains with the Tiepolo signatures and the fakes certificates of authentication, knowing that although most of Victor's business was done through crooked dealers, she preferred to place her forgeries in auctions where there was less likelihood of her being discovered.

As before, nothing was left to chance, and after mounting the drawings, Ron secured them in suitably aged frames, Zoe filling out the forms for the auction house under her other false identity — Mrs Rachel Liebermann. Mrs Liebermann was doing very well, in fact, her account in Maida Vale was swelling impressively as the cheques kept dropping in from the auction houses — just as Zoe's other account, under the name of Belinda Noble, was growing too.

As were her reputation and her self-esteem. With love, the finishing touches were applied to Zoe Mellor and her beauty and confidence seemed to increase twofold. Harland was not slow to see the change, and put it down to success, security — anything other than love. About any love other than his own he refused to have any interest at all.

But he did have interest in her work and glowed with reflected glory as Zoe travelled abroad to see clients, giving opinions on their works of art, and advice on suspected fakes. Harland watched her, as did many of the dealers, and Zoe responded as to the manner born. She never felt at home with the dealers, but having clawed out a well earned niche for herself, she began to hope that her place was assured and the knowledge gave her some security. Only she knew that she was not what she seemed and that knowledge was her trump card, her secret: by day, respectable; by night, in the cold climes of the moon, deceptive.

The duplicity spiced her life and gave her the edge she needed. But *why* did she need it? she asked herself repeatedly, knowing that the answer was simple — there was always the possibility that Larry could leave her, that one day she would be cheated or deserted. She had been hurt before, and if it happened again, she wanted to be in a position to defend herself. Her greatest fault was that she had never escaped her childhood — and her greatest strength was that she knew it.

'Can you go over and see Marcella for me?' Harland asked her one day in early July.

Zoe turned to face him. 'Don't you want to come to Venice with me?'

He shrugged. If the truth be known the business was finally exhausting him. Little by little he had cut back his time at the gallery, passing over more responsibility to Zoe, giving detailed instructions to Leonard Phillips or Mona, talking to dealers over the phone, from home. That was the one real blessing. Now that his wife and daughter had decided to take a three-month cruise he had the house to himself, apart from the staff, and relished the quiet. It had been a brainwave on his part, and when the brochures had come through the mail he had understood his wife well enough to know what to say.

'What are those, Myrtle?'

'Rubbish!' She tossed the papers across the breakfast table. 'What would I want with such things? Cruises, hah!'

Her face was free of make-up, her hair flat on her head. She looks like a chicken, Harland thought ungraciously.

'I know what you mean, dear. No one would want to go on a round-the-world cruise. Stuck on a damn boat all the time with tourists — '

'They're not all tourists, Harland.'

He bit into some toast. 'You would hate it, you know you would. You never feel at ease with all those types — '

'What "types"?' Myrtle screeched uncomfortably.

'The stuffy lot that go on cruises. All the captain's table stuff. All that social climbing.'

'Social climbing, hah! Besides I'd love it.'

'No you wouldn't, you always resisted the idea when I suggested it. Anyway,' Harland said guilelessly, 'all the women go on those cruises to find a husband.'

The words had their effect. Surreptitiously, Myrtle slid the brochures back towards her as Harland kept his eyes on his food. He knew exactly what she was thinking — that their pining daughter might finally catch a respectable man, and might even have children. The thought made Myrtle's eyes shine.

'It would be expensive, Harland,' she said, her tone soft.

He shook his head. 'I don't mind the money, but you'd hate it, believe me.'

'Listen — '

516

'You'd loathe it — '

'I'm going whatever you say! You never want me to have any fun,' she responded, pushing back the dining room chair and going to call for her daughter.

The end result had been that two weeks later Harland found himself in Southampton, waving his wife and daughter off for a three-month world cruise, the summer opening out before him with the promise of quiet, and a rest he so deeply desired. Three months, he thought as the ship faded into the distance — I have until October.

Larry Hands could not believe his luck. For too long he had been rootless, shifting from country to country, and for what? Because there had never been enough of a reason to keep him anywhere. Now there was; now there was Zoe. Having been selfish all his life he found that her vulnerability allowed him to be kind, without embarrassment. Her need made him give; her aching loneliness made him tender. He understood because he chose to; he worried because he wanted to; he loved her because she never asked him to. And she loved him. With all her skill and talent she had picked *him*, just as her mother had picked Bernard Mellor. Not the man others would have chosen for her, but the one best suited to her needs.

Sometimes he wondered how she had managed to climb so far, so fast, but then he remembered the part Harland Goldberg had played in her ascent and dismissed the idea as being unworthy of her. To his astonishment, she wasn't like all the rest. Or was she? Cynically he could say yes; but when she was in his arms, or when she smiled, then he had to say no. Never. No way. This was love. So what the hell did it matter that she had been some guy's mistress? 'Had' was the operative word. Or was it? Was she *still* Harland's mistress, or had that relationship ended after theirs began? He loved her enough to try to be fair — Zoe had been with Harland for seven years, longer than many marriages last. She could hardly be expected just to walk away from him. But then again, the guy was seventy-four years old! Did he still sleep with her? Or was it more like a friendship?

The obvious solution would have been to ask her, but Larry didn't dare risk that. On the rare occasions when he had pressed her about her family, or her affair with Harland, she had lost her temper and flown at him, hurling suggestions that he didn't trust her, or thought she was hiding something. He hadn't, he had merely been curious. But not that curious. Not curious enough to risk losing her.

The facts were simple to him and he stated them. 'I love you.'

'I love you too.'

'Fine,' he said, turning over in bed. They had been in his flat and after spending several hours happily occupied, Larry had found himself too hopelessly in love with her to hide his feelings. 'So now what do we do?'

Zoe's face had registered nothing other than astonishment. 'What should we do?'

He sat up on the side of the bed. 'Listen, I want to be with you for ever. I don't want to let you go.'

'Who said I was going anywhere?'

She had looked lovely. Pale, but lovely. Fine arms, not too thin, and little legs. Zoe hated them, thinking they were too short, but he loved them. In briefs, from the back, she looked like a kid.

'We could get married.'

The words were out of his mouth before he realised he had said them. God damn it, was his first reaction, then a kind of deep satisfaction. He had finally asked someone to marry him. Without pressure.

'Married?' she had replied. 'Why?'

'I love — '

She had smiled and interrupted him. 'I understand that much.' Her hand went out to him, ran down his shoulder and along the small of his back. 'Oh, Larry, don't let's rush into anything.'

He had been crushed. Really disappointed. He had even wanted, for an instant, to shout at her and insist that they get married. OK, so he didn't have that much cash, and he didn't have a home, but he could buy one. There had never been the need before. He had enough to get them a nice place, and with all his contacts he could really make some good money. He loved her, so what the hell, wasn't it simple?

'I have to go to Venice next week,' Zoe said suddenly, watching as he turned back to her. I love you, she thought, I love everything about you, especially now, when you open your heart so easily.

'How long are you going for?'

'Only a couple of days,' she said, pulling on his dressing-gown and padding over to the bath-room. She could feel his disappointment and turned quickly. 'Do you want to come?'

★ ★ ★

Venice was another city. I don't remember you, Zoe thought, as the boat drew up and deposited them on the square, along with a couple of dozen tourists. The water smelt sour, the high summer smell of stagnancy, and the unexpected odour of cooking fat seeped out from the raddled cafés. A string of boats knocked randomly against each other, the sound echoing over the high water, the flocks of seagulls riding the tide and strutting across the squares, mottling San Marco with droppings. Heat made the paving stones steam, the water lapping indolently, like an old bath left to go cold.

She was to stay with the Marchesa, her elegant hospitality winging over the sweating crowds like a snowbird. Zoe had not wanted to go, preferring to stay with Larry, but it was impossible.

'I'll see you in the morning,' she said, stretching up to kiss his cheek.

'I'll miss you in a blasted hotel room,' he said impatiently.

'I know, but Marcella is a friend of Harland's —'

520

He silenced her with another kiss. 'Go on, I'll see you tomorrow.'

The Marchesa was dignified, welcoming, and beautifully attired in white silk, the dark villa as cool as a tomb, the high windows shrouded against the late sun as Zoe walked in. Behind the drawn drapes, the water lapped in the canals, the birds the only background accompaniment to the timeless sounds.

'You look so fresh and so pretty,' Marcella said, leading Zoe towards a sofa in the drawing room. 'I regret that Harland could not come, he must be so tired.'

'He's exhausted and his heart's been giving him some trouble,' Zoe said, sipping a glass of white Burgundy. Unaccountably, her head began to swim like the water outside, and a sleepiness settled on her.

'You look tired too,' Marcella said. 'I was only thinking of both of you the other day . . . ' Zoe's lids began to close 'and wondered if Harland might like to look at my painting of the . . . ' Ashamed of her lack of manners, Zoe tried to fight the tiredness, yet seemed unable to resist the lure of sleep. 'And I thought . . . ' Down I go, down I go, Zoe thought, as her limbs relaxed and her mind pulled her firmly to rest.

She woke hours later in a guest room, the high walls stuccoed with gold, gilded angels peeping down on her like artistic voyeurs, the windows opened to let in the coolness of the night. Embarrassed, Zoe struggled upright and shook her head, glancing at her watch. Eleven o'clock! she had been asleep for nearly four hours. She must have been exhausted by the travelling, she thought, as she moved out into the corridor, relying on her memory to guide her towards the staircase. But she chose the wrong direction and moved further into the villa where the corridor windows were closed, the drapes drawn and only a few candles left burning to give any illumination. Her feet sounded muffled on the carpeted floor, her eyes glancing round at the shadowed paintings and the faded frescos over her head. She wondered if she should call out to attract attention and then dismissed the idea — she would look a fool to be caught panicking, especially after her show of bad manners earlier in the evening.

Trying to get her bearings, Zoe stopped walking and looked around, and then remembered that the guest room she had used on her previous visit was on her right, a little down the corridor. Her spirits lifted as she remembered the layout. Only two doors from the guest room was Marcella's suite. Zoe walked along quickly and saw, with relief, that a faint light shone from under Marcella's door.

Zoe tapped on the door lightly. There was no response. She tapped again, more loudly. Again, there was no response. Finally she turned the handle and opened the door a few inches. The room was lit only by a fire burning in the grate, apparently the Marchesa felt the cold even on summer nights, and the dim light danced round a large mirror and skimmed across the picture frames. Cautiously, Zoe called out, and then moved further into the room. The bed was on her left, rising high and imperious towards the painted ceiling. Voluminous brocade drapes hung over it, shadows cast wide like a net on either side. The silence was total, but as her eyes became more accustomed to the dimmed light, Zoe could just make out the shapes of books in a cabinet and an array of white invitation cards over the mantelpiece. We request the pleasure of the Marchesa Marcella Rimimi on the occasion of . . .

At that precise moment, the Marchesa awoke and snapped on her bedside light. Zoe froze, caught out, guilty of nothing and everything. The woman in bed was momentarily angry and then turned away as Zoe took in every savage detail. The thin arms, the breast flat, flaccid, without support; and the face without its maquillage, an aged face without beauty; and her head small, narrow, the crown only partially covered without its usual hairpiece.

'I'm so sorry — '

The Marchesa responded in Italian at first and then as Zoe turned away, she called after her in English.

But she had already gone, feeling ashamed of herself for having taken away a woman's dignity. Almost running, Zoe rushed down the corridor, only stopping when she heard the feet behind her.

'Zoe!'

The word was a command and she turned.

The Marchesa was recovered, her coiffure restored, her face, although not made up, was, in the dim light, nearly perfect again. Imperiously she caught hold of Zoe's arm. 'Don't be afraid.'

'I'm so . . . sorry,' Zoe responded, trailing off.

The woman put her arm around her shoulder. 'People grow old. It was a shock to see you there, that's all.'

'But I feel so ashamed.'

The Marchesa laughed. The sound pooled in the dim light. 'Ashamed, why? Because you saw I was old? Everyone grows old. And I am very old now. As is Harland.' Her arm squeezed Zoe lightly. Affection restored. 'As you will be, one day. Which is why I say to you now, be careful and enjoy what you have.'

Zoe turned to look at her face. 'I try to.'

'Don't try! Do it,' she replied, walking Zoe towards the staircase and then towards the library. 'Do you remember how you came here that first time, before the auction?' Zoe nodded. The room was stern and smelt damp, the same massive globes planted on the floor, the walls frescoed, mottled brilliance. Leading them both to a seat, the Marchesa sat down with Zoe beside her. 'You were younger then, very young, I think,' she said, her voice low. 'It was a grand evening, a great success. But not for you,' she said, turning to the girl who sat with her. 'For you it was trouble, your brother, the stabbing . . . all that trouble. Trouble is like that, quick!' She snapped her fingers together. 'Quick and savage. It takes your breath away.'

'You were very kind that night,' Zoe said mechanically, wanting to change the subject and distance herself from the memory.

The Marchesa shook her head. 'I did very little.' She moved towards one globe and spun it gently. 'I remember that Harland told me he loved you — and that you were not his mistress.' She smiled over her shoulder. 'I was very proud of you then. I would have been so grateful for a daughter like you.'

Zoe glanced away, moved. 'I wished for a mother like you,' she said finally. 'For so long I wanted to hear my mother say she was proud of me. She never did. I never had the privilege of knowing she loved me . . . I would have been a different person if she had loved me.'

'You've done very well on your own,' Marcella replied, 'but everyone needs love, Zoe, and I don't mean Harland's kind of love. You need the love of a man who accepts you, and wants you, and will protect you.'

Zoe hesitated, finding it difficult to confide. 'I've met someone, but I don't know what to do. He asked me to marry him.'

'And do you want to?'

'I think so,' Zoe said, considering her future with Larry hands against her past with Harland Goldberg. 'I want to be with him. I know that much.'

'So be with him. What is stopping you?'

'Harland.'

The Marchesa pursed her lips. 'Harland Goldberg is a good man. He will want what is the best for you. Tell him.'

But something in Zoe resisted. A sixth sense which told her that he could never come to terms with the knowledge. 'I can't.'

She kissed Zoe lightly on the forehead. 'What makes you think he doesn't already know?'

★ ★ ★

Suzie Laye was in a temper. In such a temper that she had already smashed two glasses and was hurling another as she made her way down the staircase from the flat to the gallery below.

'How dare they write an article about her!' she screamed, the staff ducking as she reached the ground floor. 'Your bloody sister!' she said, turning on Victor. 'Why didn't they write an article on me! I've got one of the best galleries in New York! Why her?'

Victor pretended to be outraged, it was easier that way. Besides, he had spent months working Suzie into high dudgeon. When he finally edged Zoe out of the picture she would be so grateful that the gallery would be his for the taking.

'She's certainly getting well known,' he said smoothly, glancing across to the receptionist and noting the fact that she had good legs. 'There's no stopping her now.'

'But there must be!' Suzie howled. 'There must!'

'Calm down, it was only a piece in the paper. A fluke.'

'A whole page in The Times devoted to her brilliant career is no fluke. She's unstoppable.'

Jealousy always appealed to Victor. Besides, he could understand it. He was jealous of Zoe. too, but unlike Suzie, he had been jealous for years. Besides, he could live with it now that he had

526

devised a little plan with Mike O'Dowd for the auction on 17 September. Yes, soon Zoe would be out of the picture — he smiled at the pun.

'What the hell is so funny?'

'I have a little plan, darling,' Victor said, smoothly, linking arms with Suzie and beginning the long walk upstairs again. 'A neat little plan which will get my sister out of your hair.' She smiled at him gratefully. Little did she know that he was killing two birds with one stone — finish Zoe, stitch up Suzie. Women were all alike.

'I'll make you a drink, darling, and you just relax . . . ' he said soothingly, leading her into the bedroom and unzipping her dress, his hands stroking her thighs. 'Let's see if I can think of something to take your mind off things.'

★   ★   ★

Summer crept out, sullen and hot, ushering in a quiet September with the promise of luscious autumn. Zoe was truly happy for the first time in her life, in love with a man who loved her, and successful in her prestigious consultancy work, the fakes being cut back, forced into the background, like a lover whom she could not totally dismiss, but of whom she was ashamed. Unique and well known, Zoe Mellor was finally a name, her face appearing in magazines, her quotes everywhere, every opinion controversial and challenging. I am safe at last, she thought, the Mike O'Dowds are part of my past, as is Steven Foreshaw, as is the violence and guilt. She shook her head quickly to repulse the memory of

527

Jimmy van Goyen. No, she thought defiantly, that is past. Now I've made it, Zoe thought light-headedly, I've come out of the dark and found my place in life . . . And it was right and it was very good.

So when the phone call came through on 2 September she was unprepared, and listened, transfixed, her whole body shaking at the familiar voice.

'Your time's up, Zoe. It's not over yet.'

Victor was back.

30

Harland did not come into the gallery the following day. He was still working from home, leaving Zoe to run the business. At nine thirty-five precisely, Victor walked in, just as he had done all those years ago, when he had first come down to London. He even stopped at the mirror to check his reflection and smooth his hair, brushing imaginary fluff off the sleeve of his jacket. His sister watched with fury burning inside her, the sense of disappointment so strong that it winded her. She had not seen him for ten months. Any information she had received about Victor had come via the grapevine, and there had been precious little of that. People assumed, rightly, that they were estranged; that after the fiasco at Hampton's, Zoe wanted to have nothing to do with him. They had been correct.

She had played the game with consummate skill, allowing very few of her fakes on to the market. Since brother and sister had gone their separate ways, Zoe had concentrated on lesser-known artists, and after Jimmy van Goyen's death those had been very few and far between. She had been careful because she had a great deal to protect. Not only her name, not only her money, but her future.

Looking at her brother, Zoe thought about Larry and wondered guiltily why, after all their shared love and intimacy, she hadn't been able to confide in him. The answer was obvious — how could she admit that she had been lying all along? That she had never been Harland's mistress; that the ruse which had brought them together was a lie? How could she admit to deceiving him when he loved her so completely? When he thought she was so vulnerable, so innocent. How could she admit that she was involved in criminal activities?

The thoughts rankled on her and made her feel unclean, tainted. Which was exactly how Larry would feel if he knew the truth. He would resent her deceit; the little games they enjoyed, the love-making, the confessions of past hurts would all seem hollow, his suspicions constantly nagging at him. If she could lie once, she would lie again. It required little effort to imagine the expression on his face, the deep grief which comes after the realisation that a lover is flawed.

Zoe loved him and she was going to do her damnedest to keep him. Victor was not going to take her happiness from her, and as she looked at him she saw him for what he was — the one threat to her happiness and her security. Slowly she walked the length of the gallery, past Mona Grimaldi's empty desk, past the exhibition of Romneys and past the ormolu clock chiming nine forty-five. There were no visitors yet, it was too early, generally people didn't start arriving until after eleven. Only Leonard Phillips was at work, toiling in the basement below, out of sight and out of hearing.

'Well?' she said finally. 'What do you want?'

He turned round, looking smooth and clever,

with hardly a trace of animosity showing. He should have been furious — and that warned her. 'It's been a long time, Zoe, hasn't it?'

She was older, but she had aged well, matured. No hint of the give-away lines round the eyes yet, and no sagging flesh anywhere, in fact she was probably coming up to her best. The thought irritated him and he wondered if he looked as good in her eyes, and then wondered why it mattered. He was going to pulverise the little bitch into the ground. She had it coming after keeping him running around for ten months. For ten bloody months he had been treated like an idiot, and had to suffer the paranoia of Mike O'Dowd, and demands of the exhausting Suzie Laye.

'You owe me,' he said finally.

'Oh really? What do you want?'

'I want you to back off. Pack in the faking business for a while. You've had a good run, but it's my turn.'

Zoe's temper rose instantly. 'Listen, I've had a bellyful of you, Victor. All my life you have been a thorn in my flesh.'

He raised his eyebrows. 'Really? It's funny, but I was only thinking the same about you. You're an aggravation, Zoe. A little insect who wants squashing.'

She laughed and put her hands on her hips, defiant. 'And are you going to be the one who does it? I don't think so, Victor, you tried before and you failed hopelessly.'

'You were clever switching those lots at the auction,' he replied, taking his cigarettes out of

531

his pocket and glancing at the paintings on the walls. 'No, it was better than clever, it was inspired . . . That's a good painting, a Courbet, isn't it?'

She turned and looked in the direction he pointed. 'Yes, it's a Courbet still life.'

'What's it selling for?'

'What the hell has it got to do with you?'

'There's no need to be unfriendly,' he said.

The conversation was like a game. Words flying backwards and forwards. Ping, pong, ping, pong. Your serve, I think.

Victor smiled. 'You don't seem to realise the situation you're in.'

'I realise perfectly. I always have done, but you're in no position to come in here and dictate terms. No one is going to listen to you, Victor.'

His mouth set as he breathed in, trying to keep his temper. She wondered why he didn't let rip. 'OK, let's forget it. I've come here today to say let's live and let live. You give up the faking and everything'll be fine. You've got a good job here, for God's sake, and with that consultancy work, you don't need to earn any more. You must have made a packet already.' He changed the subject. 'Incidentally, I saw that piece in *The Times*. It was very good, although the photograph didn't do you justice.'

'Is that your aesthetic judgement, Victor?' she asked, sarcasm thick in her voice. 'You always had a good eye for a picture.'

Victor wanted fleetingly to choke her. 'Listen, Zoe, I'll say it one last time. Get out of the business. It's mine.'

'Why should I?'

'Because I tell you to.'

She laughed bitterly. 'Now let me tell you something, Victor. If you hadn't had *my* fakes — *my* drawings and *my* paintings — you would never have got anywhere. If you hadn't had Alan's sculptures to sell, you would never have had that car, that flat, those clothes and all your flaming tarts. You owe *us*!' she shouted, her voice high. All the years of resentment boiled up and bubbled over inside her. How dare he come here and say those things, how dare he! She was his sister, his flesh and blood, didn't that count for anything? Anger made her ugly, all gentleness suspended. You lessen me, she thought resentfully.

Victor lost his temper fast, walking over to her and shaking her. 'I'm giving you fair warning, if you don't get out of it now, you are going to come a cropper — '

'Don't threaten me, you bastard!' she cried, incensed, terror washing over her again. Get out of my life, Victor, she thought, leave me alone. 'You expose me and you'll ruin yourself. You can't go to the police, and you know it.'

'I want my patch back, and I've a little plan of action worked out — '

'With Suzie Laye?' Zoe asked coldly.

'What the hell has that got to do with you?'

'Oh, don't be so naive! I can read you like a book and I know you're sleeping with her — mind you, so is half of New York and most of the visiting dealers, it hardly puts you apart from the crowd — but if you've got big ideas about her, I'd forget it, Victor. She may look like an idiot, but I don't think she's that dumb or she wouldn't have that gallery — '

'She inherited it — '

'Yes, but she's hung on to it,' Zoe countered, narrowing her eyes. 'So that's it, is it, Victor? You want the Conrad.' A low laugh bubbled inside her. 'Such ambitions! Well, I wish you luck, but I don't think you'll pull it off. In fact, it might backfire on you. Look at Erica. You went for her when you thought it might get you in with Harland, but it didn't quite work. You left her crying her eyes out — '

'Oh, for God's sake!' he bellowed. 'You bloody women! I can't stand to listen to all your romantic crap. Why should I care about some two-bit Jewish tart?'

'She was in love with you — '

'So what! I didn't ask her to care about me. What the bloody hell does it matter to you anyway?' he said with disgust. 'Women! You all spend your time mewling and whingeing. You're good for one thing, and that's being used. You're all the bloody same, and you all make me puke.' He paused for a minute and then changed his tack. 'I came here to bury the hatchet,' he said, thinking about O'Dowd and pressing on. 'I don't want to see you hurt. You're family — '

'Hah!'

'All right! All right! But I'll say it one more time. You're family, so I'll give you the one iota of consideration I wouldn't give to any other bastard on this earth. I'm warning you — back off. This is a shitty business, so get out of it while you can.' He ground out his cigarette in the nearest ashtray. 'You're respectable, Zoe, so don't jeopardise your career. Don't jeopardise anything.'

She breathed in to steady herself. 'I don't trust you. Why are you trying to help me? Why? It's not like you. You wouldn't warn me of danger if my life depended on it. I'll go further, you wouldn't spit on me if I was on fire. There is *nothing* that you would do for me. Nothing that you have *ever* done for me!' Her voice rose. 'You have deceived and betrayed me and been treacherous, underhand, and bloody-minded every day I've known you. Every single time I have been involved with you, I've lived to regret it! You've cost me money and peace of mind. You've kept me awake at night,' she shouted at him, her voice almost hoarse. 'We had a goldmine, you stupid bastard, we had it here, in our hand. I was willing to work with you, had been ever since I was a girl. You had Alan too. Nobody anywhere can do work like his. You can go to Italy, to Rome, Naples, go and see all these forgers we hear about. Go to France, Victor, and what about Malta? Don't forget Malta, the forger who was so successful, the one who was found as stiff as one of his own ruddy statues — go anywhere, but you'll not find anyone who comes close to Alan.' Her voice was choked with anger. 'You had it all, Victor. A brother and sister who would no more have betrayed you than betrayed themselves — but it was too easy, wasn't it? Too damn easy. Like our mother loving you. Oh, she loved you, but that didn't matter, did it? Stuff her!'

'SHUT UP!' he shouted viciously. 'You're a bore, you're always harping on about that — '

'I harp on because it *matters* to me.'

'You want to grow up!' he said nastily. 'You're still talking like you were fourteen years old — '

'Christ! It doesn't get through to you, does it?' she said, flinging her arms up in exasperation. 'It makes no impact on that thick skull of yours. You don't give a damn about anything unless it has VICTOR MELLOR written on it in letters fifteen feet bloody high. Clean my boots, call my taxis, fill my bank account!' she shouted, driven beyond reason. 'Then it's OK, isn't it, Victor? But ask for anything back. Ask for *anything* from Mr Victor Mellor, Mr Slick Vic, and it's no, sir. Oh, dear me, no sir.'

Victor was moving towards her. He was really angry, his eyes yellow, almost like a tiger's eyes.

'Well I've had it with Mr Victor Mellor,' she said bitterly. 'I've had it once and for all. You can threaten me all you like, it won't make a damn bit of difference, because I shall live my life my way. And no one is going to stop me. Least of all you, because you're a creeping, conniving bastard — '

He struck her across the face.

She reeled and then immediately struck him back.

'That didn't even hurt,' he said, moving closer. 'I'll tell you something: you — are — on — the — ropes,' he said, emphasising each word for her. 'The game, my dear, is up. Finito. I tried to come here to warn you off. Wrongly, as it turned out. Well, it's not my bloody problem any longer. My conscience is clear — '

'Your conscience is clear!' she said, grinning with hatred. 'Don't make me laugh. The day you have a clear conscience you'll be in a coma.'

'Suit yourself. But very soon you will look back and remember this. You will *live* to regret it, and believe me, sister, you will have the *time* to regret it.'

'Get out!' she shouted.

'I'll go when I'm ready.'

'GET OUT!'

He smiled without humour. 'You're at the top of the midden now, Zoe, but your days are numbered.' He jabbed her in the chest with his forefinger. 'Enjoy the good life, kiddo, because it's not going to last.'

And with that he walked out of the gallery, the door swinging closed behind him as Mona Grimaldi walked in. As immaculately dressed as ever, she sidled over to her desk, delighted to see that Zoe Mellor was distressed. It was something to tell Anthony Sargeant later, embellishing the story a little so it would travel better down Albemarle and Bond Street. Her jealousy momentarily satisfied, she said to Zoe in a tone of mock sympathy. 'What's the matter?'

Zoe paused and looked in the woman's eyes. She and Victor weren't that dissimilar after all, she thought. 'You're putting on weight, Mona,' she said viciously, walking off.

★   ★   ★

537

Mike O'Dowd was sitting in a bar in the Meridien Hotel on Piccadilly. He eyed up a hard looking blonde, then decided that it wasn't worth the effort. He was too old and too tired. Even if she came back to his hotel room, he wasn't sure if he had the energy to do anything with her, and it would only cost money. Not that money was a problem with O'Dowd. He had made a packet and no one had caught up with him, not even that clever toad, Leon Graves. He smiled to himself. He liked Graves in a grudging kind of way. They had given each other a run for their money, and if it all ended tomorrow, he wouldn't be sorry. O'Dowd shook his head — what was he thinking? He was about to make a final killing and retire to Dublin. An image of the city loomed up at him, like a massive cue card. Remember me, it said. I'm an old man in a dry month, O'Dowd thought suddenly, remembering a quote he had heard somewhere, about three hundred years ago. An old man in a dry month, waiting for rain.

He could wax lyrical now and again, because he wasn't quite the ignorant Mick everyone took him to be. He liked poetry and could appreciate culture, that was how he could tell what was good and bad in the art world. Jesus, concentrate, O'Dowd! he said. You had to be on the ball these days. Younger, harder men were coming up, like Victor Mellor. Men who had to be watched, just like the plots and counterplots they hatched. It was all too complex — or maybe he was too old. He sighed and picked up his pink gin, the little round bar mat sticking to the bottom of the glass. God, he thought, now I look like a damn queer.

He moved in his seat and adjusted his tie. He looked smart tonight, in another Giorgio Armani suit. He had never thought, back in the old days when he was fighting in Dublin, that he'd ever be wearing cloth like this. No, he had come a long way. He smiled to himself — Michael O'Dowd, you are a star. He tried to buoy up his hopes, but the words had a hollow ring to them and within an instant his mind was already winging its way back to the salt spray and the bold wind, coming off the tide in Killiney Bay.

The following morning he woke refreshed and like his old self, putting down his previous night's gloom to bad food and tiredness. He showered, washed his hair, and dressed, and by the time he was back out on the street he felt good as new. Then on a whim he decided that he would treat himself to a good lunch. High with anticipation, he went to Fortnum and Mason's, a smart little Irishman surrounded by old women with Harrods packages, and the odd Arab with his overfed wife. Stretching his legs out under the table, he read the menu and ordered, glancing around the room.

He saw Zoe first, then flicked his gaze to the back of the angular man she was lunching with. His curiosity made him clumsy and he knocked his knife off the table, a white-aproned waitress hurrying over with a clean one.

'Here you are, sir.'

'Thank you, thank you very much,' he

replied, turning his attention back to the lobster he was eating, his mind running on. From what he had learnt over the years, Zoe Mellor was only involved with Harland Goldberg, although there had been some half-hearted affair with a shabby art teacher from Rochdale a while back. O'Dowd glanced at the couple again. They were animated, talking rapidly. So she had a guy, did she? And from the way they were being so lovey-dovey, it wasn't just a professional arrangement. Not content with having the family in on the act, she now had a bit of extra muscle. Damn it, he thought, he should have expected it. After all, with Victor out of the way, Zoe could bring in her own man. And he was her lover too. That was dangerous, he thought as he watched them, observing the man carefully, and wishing he would turn round. Young, obviously fit, and good-looking, O'Dowd thought grudgingly.

He listened avidly, hoping to pick up the odd word, hoping too that Zoe wouldn't turn round and see him. She didn't, she was too engrossed — and that was when he heard the man's voice and recognised it as Larry Hands. Christ! he thought bitterly, that was all he needed. Laying down his knife and fork, he wiped his mouth on the napkin and lit a cigarette. The more he thought about it, the more it confirmed his worst suspicions.

'Would you like a dessert, sir?' the waitress asked.

He glanced at her. Ginger hair, brown shadows under her eyes, hands with short nails the colour of seashells. 'Nothing, thanks, just some coffee.'

She moved away, and O'Dowd's mind ran on. He decided that a little warning was needed. It never hurt to let people know that you were on to them. He would simply scare Zoe Mellor a little, give her 'the gypsy's warning', as his mother used to call it. Satisfied, he inhaled again and then, to amuse himself, did the old conjuring trick, tucking the cigarette away behind his hand and then flipping it back. Now you see it, now you don't. He smiled, his nephew always liked that, it made him laugh. He used to be able to get an egg out from behind his ear, but he wasn't so good at that any more — mind you, he always had cigarettes on him, the same couldn't be said for eggs.

When the waitress returned with the coffee. O'Dowd smiled, and then wearily took off his glasses and rubbed his eyes. When he put them back on again, the couple were gone.

★   ★   ★

Rochdale was being pelted with a bad-tempered downpour, and Zoe had to wait twenty minutes for a taxi at the station. When one finally came she climbed in, her hair sticky on her head, her clothes smelling of damp wool. The driver was as depressed as the weather and said nothing, which suited Zoe as she was in no mood to talk. It had startled her to see Mike O'Dowd at Fortnum and Mason's the previous day. In fact she had done a double take, thinking she had been mistaken. But there was only one Mike O'Dowd, and seeing him back in London just after seeing Victor meant only one thing.

At least she knew who she was up against. The Irishman and Victor were working together. The thought hung on her as heavily, depressingly, as the rain pelting on the taxi windows. The previous night Zoe had determined on her course of action. In one last-ditch attempt to secure her future with Larry, she was going to make a killing at the auction on the seventeenth in London, putting in the two best fakes she had, the ones she had held back for so long. She knew they were of the finest quality, just as she knew they would fetch high prices.

The taxi stopped at some traffic lights and she sighed, trying to calm her nerves. She would leave with the money and with Larry, for California. It was the perfect solution, all she had to do now was to make sure her family was safe. The refuge she had chosen was Guernsey, and within twenty-four hours she had rented an old farmhouse in the countryside. It was a very quiet spot, and it was there that she was going to put all her family in safe keeping. Home safe.

She had obviously been thinking out loud, because Ron turned to her. 'What is it?'

'What? Oh, nothing, nothing.'

Peter was sitting on the seat between them as he stroked the dog's head. 'We're going to Guernsey, Ron. I've got us a place there and for the time being I want you and Dad and Alan to go. I'll follow later.' She didn't know *when* she was going to follow, but she wasn't going to tell him that. They had to be safe, that was her first consideration.

'I'm going nowhere without you,' he said flatly.

'Please, I want you to,' she begged.

'I'm not going,' he repeated flatly.

'All right, you can stay with me and we'll go together,' she said finally.

They pulled into Buck's Lane. It was muddy already and it wasn't even autumn yet. God, the place was seedy, she thought, glancing up at the house and seeing the rain smudges on the door and on the step. Little puddles gazed, open-eyed, up at the moody sky and when she got out of the taxi, a sparrow flew off, startled. As she had done since childhood she unlocked the front door and walked in, moving into the snug and seeing her father asleep. His mouth was closed under the white moustache, his eyes moving slightly under the lids, his hands clasped on his lap as though he was praying. I'll take care of you, Zoe thought, I'll keep you safe.

Gently, she leaned forwards and woke him. 'Dad, Dad.' His eyes opened, struggling to focus. He's old, she thought suddenly, old. 'It's Zoe.'

'What!' he snapped as he woke, his bad temper to the fore. 'What brings you up 'ere?'

Behind them, the front door opened again, a cold draft of air chilling the house. Alan had heard the taxi and run up Buck's Lane, his face beaming with pleasure. Zoe was back, and that could mean work for him. 'I didn't know you were coming up,' he said, hugging her and turning to his father. 'Look Dad, it's our Zoe.'

'You don't say,' his father responded drily.

543

Ignoring her father's sarcasm, Zoe hugged her brother. 'I'm sorry I've neglected you, but things — '

'OK, What's up?' her father asked bluntly. 'And where's Victor?'

'Victor isn't with me, Dad,' she replied, walking into the kitchen and turning towards her brothers. 'I want to talk to Dad for a minute. Can you leave us to it?'

They hesitated. 'But — '

'Please?'

Ron nodded to Alan and they left the room, the dog following behind. The old white enamel sink was filled with dirty dishes, the crockery chipped, the cold tap dripping on to a shaving mug lying on its side. A stained dishcloth hung from a plastic hook and a Brillo pad rusted underneath in a coronation soap dish Jane Mellor had bought decades ago. Zoe sighed; she had suggested that the Widow should visit a couple of times a week to keep things tidy, but Bernard Mellor wouldn't hear of it. His home was his territory, and he wanted it left alone.

'What's up?' her father asked, suspicion in his voice.

'Dad, listen, I've got a problem.'

His heart sank. Not that, anything but that. Please God, she's not pregnant, he thought suddenly. Where the hell was his wife when he needed her? He cut some bread unevenly and kept his eyes averted. 'What problem?'

'I've got us a place in Guernsey . . . '

It was worse than he thought, she was even

544

going to have the kid in another country.

' . . . and I want you to come.'

'Do me a favour!' he said, incensed.

'Dad, hear me out. Please don't argue, it's serious.'

'It bloody sounds it,' he said, horribly embarrassed. What was he supposed to say? 'Whatever it is, make it quick, I want to get to the pub.'

She sighed. 'I want us — you and Alan — to go immediately. I'll follow later with Ron.'

He opened his mouth to speak and then shut it. Zoe had never alarmed him before, in fact, she had done bloody well for herself apart from living with that old man. He coloured. Oh no, not the old man! Don't let it be his kid, at that age the child might turn out to be an idiot.

Zoe's voice was calm as she continued. 'Victor's involved.'

Her father's eyes bulged uncomfortably. Victor! Incest! Bloody hell — he'd kill him! He'd kill them both. The shame of it. Oh God.

Zoe rushed on quickly. 'It's big trouble . . . faking.'

Bernard Mellor breathed in deeply, light-headed with relief, and reached for the teapot. Zoe watched him, stunned. He was certainly taking it calmly, she thought, as he poured boiling water on to the tealeaves.

'I've been forging things, Dad. I've been doing the paintings and Alan's been making the sculptures.' She trailed off as he pushed a cup of tea across the table towards her.

Accepting it, she sat down. 'I have to get you out of here. Tomorrow. To Guernsey — '

'Not bloody likely!' he said suddenly. Not that he was really bothered. In fact, compared with the horror he had been expecting, it sounded like a good wheeze. Fat Alan a forger! He *was* a dark horse. Not that he hadn't been suspicious that something was going on. But forging . . .

'Dad, you have to, please, for me.'

'Are the police involved?'

'Not yet, and they never will be if everything goes according to plan,' Zoe replied evenly.

'But you could go to jail if you were caught?'

The word rocked her. *It had been only a game*, she thought she heard herself say.

'Yes, I could go to jail if everything goes wrong. But I don't intend to let it.' She sounded confident and surprised herself. 'Victor is going to try and hurt me, Dad, and he might do it through you. So I have to get you safe, because if I know you're all safe, then I stand a better chance. Do you understand?'

'Just a minute, I'm not so sure about all this!' her father said defiantly. 'What are people going to say? Jesus wept, it could even get in the *Rochdale Observer*!'

'Dad, you don't seem to understand — '

'I understand!' he said, raising his voice. 'What do you think I am? Some daft old bugger with half a brain? Good God, I'd have to be an flaming idiot not to have got wise to something. For years you've all been creeping around, in and out of that garage, and for what? Not bloody tea dances, I'll be bound!' He pushed back his

546

seat and got up. 'And I know Victor well enough to know that if there was anything he could do to make money, he'd do it. That boy couldn't play it straight if his life depended on it. But you . . . ' He paused to look at her. 'I thought you were cuter than that.'

'It's forgery, Dad, not theft. I'm not robbing anyone who can't afford it. It's the art world, the dealers, and they've been cheating everyone for years.' The image of Jimmy van Goyen loomed up before her. 'They deserve it. After all, I was just redistributing their wealth a little.'

He wanted to smile, but restrained himself. Well, well, well, his little girl leading them all by the nose.

'Listen, I know how it sounds to you, but it all started as a bit of a game. Victor suggested — '

'Victor.'

'Yes, it all began with Victor,' she explained. 'And Dad, if I don't watch out for all of us, it will end with him too.'

'Why?'

'I don't know.'

Her father looked at her for a long time and then said, 'Don't you, luv? Well, I do. That brother of yours is what is known as a right bloody toerag. I never could stand him when he was born, a mewling little bugger at the best of times, and I loathed him when he grew up.' He leaned back in the kitchen chair and folded his arms. 'He's got a chip on his shoulder the size of the ELK mill. And you've really pissed him off.'

Zoe looked at her father in total surprise. 'Why?'

547

'Because you're successful and you're a girl!' he laughed wheezily. 'And you're smarter.' He continued to laugh. 'You've got guts, and you can mix with all the nobs, all the snotty upper-class buggers who wouldn't give our Victor the time of day.'

He trailed off, running his hand across his mouth, his eyes shiny with good humour. 'And d'you know the thing which really creases me?' She shook her head. 'He knows he's always going to be a common working-class spiv, and all the money in the world won't change it. He knows it, and worse, he knows that every other bugger does too.'

'Dad,' Zoe said softly, 'you have to go to Guernsey with Alan tomorrow — '

'Bloody hell — !'

'No, don't argue,' she said firmly. 'I'll go with you and get you settled. It won't be for ever.'

'I like it here.'

'Damn you!' she shouted suddenly. 'You *have* to go! I never asked you for a thing in my life. Never. I never complained, or asked why you didn't stand up for me. You always took Mum's side,' she said angrily, 'and never wondered how I felt. This bloody house was hell for me when I was a child.' He blinked, silent in the face of his daughter's anger. 'I was excluded by Mum and by you. Well, now you *owe* me, Dad. I want you to go to Guernsey. I'm begging you.'

Father and daughter looked at each other across the table. Bernard Mellor was thinking that the trip might be a lark, a break. Things had been so flaming quiet since he retired, he'd like a change of scene. It might be good for him, pep up his life a bit.

'Does it rain there?'

'Not as much as it does here,' she said evenly.

For a long moment he said nothing then he nodded and picked up his coat from the back of the chair. 'Right then, I'm off for a pint.' He paused at the door. 'I'll go, but if you think I'm doing the bloody packing, you've had that.'

The door closed after him and Zoe sighed with relief glancing round and then taking off her coat. Carefully she washed the dishes, cleaning down the cooker and then vacuuming the carpet after emptying the full cleaner bag. Completing the work she had done since childhood, she wound up the cheap clock on the fireplace and filled the washer, sorting out the shabby underwear from the bed-sheets and searching under the sink for washing powder. The actions soothed her, taking her back, and by the time an hour had passed the kitchen smelt fresh again, as it had done when Jane Mellor was alive.

The screech of car brakes was so sudden that Zoe jumped, the noise exploding in the small kitchen, the hurried shouts outside alerting her as she ran down the muddy track of Buck's Lane. Out on the main road she looked round, a set of tyre tracks streaking the wet road, Alan's huge figure already crouched down beside an abandoned car. She ran across, her mouth drying with fright, her brother's face turning towards her.

'Alan, are you all right?'

He said nothing because all that either of them could hear at that moment was a low whimpering, coming from under the car. It was a noise unlike anything Zoe had ever heard, full of pain, the whines becoming screams and riding the wet air.

'Oh God,' she said, crouching on her knees, 'oh God, Peter.'

The dog lay on its side, half hidden, one leg bent at right angles. Quickly Zoe reached out, tears starting in her eyes as she tried to touch him. But he was too far under the car to pull out and in despair she turned to Alan. 'Do something, for Christ's sake, do something!'

In shock, he gazed at his sister, then hurriedly clambering to his feet, leaned down, his hands gripping the metal underneath. With one almighty heave, Alan Mellor tried to lift the nearside of the car off the dying dog. It shifted only an inch.

'Try, Alan, do it!' Zoe cried out as the dog's whimpers of pain filled the air. 'Again, Alan, again!'

He shifted his grip and leaned down once more, his face contorted. Slowly, agonisingly, the nearside of the car began to rise, Alan's arms shaking with the effort. As soon as she had room, Zoe gathered the animal in her arms and lifted him out from under the car. Red-faced with exertion, Alan lowered the vehicle and leaned against the bonnet, looking down at his sister who was cradling Peter in her arms, his face bloodied, his eyes already rolled back in the silent face.

6 September
Guernsey

The journey to Guernsey was a nightmare, Peter's death providing the final proof of the danger they were all in, Ron's reaction shattering all of them. The previous night he had returned from his walk calling out for the greyhound and running down Buck's Lane looking for him. Zoe had heard him and remained in the kitchen, Peter's body in his old dog bed, silent by her feet.

Moments later Ron had entered, his face puzzled. 'Have you seen Peter? He's run off somewhere.'

She had rehearsed what to say, but now that she was confronted with her brother the words failed her.

'Zoe?' he said simply, and then, on instinct, glanced down at the dog bed. His face changed slowly as he realised what had happened, his grief making him incoherent as he sank to his knees and threw back his head, a long scream of agony pouring from him as he cradled the dead animal in his arms.

'Ron . . . ' Zoe said simply, kneeling beside him and clasping hold of her brother.

Sobbing uncontrollably, Ron closed his eyes against the image of his dead pet, his body shaking, his hands pressing into the dark fur.

'Who did it?' he asked finally, turning to his sister. His eyes were red, swollen, his mouth bitter with grief. Zoe could say nothing and merely watched as her brother laid Peter down in his bed and tenderly stroked his face. 'I want to know who did it.'

Still Zoe remained silent. Impatiently, Ron turned to her. 'Tell me! Was it Victor?'

She shook her head.

'Mike O'Dowd?'

Again, she said nothing.

'Bastards!' Ron said vehemently, his voice breaking as he continued to stroke the dog's head. 'I loved him,' he added, bending down and resting his face against Peter's, his tears washing the blood from the greyhound's face. 'I loved him . . . Why did they do it? Why?'

In the morning Peter's body had gone and when Ron returned later, no one asked where he had taken him, although Zoe suspected that the greyhound had been laid to rest up on the high moors so for evermore he would look out over the streets and hills he had walked so many times.

The event shattered all of them, but altered Ron. He became distant, revengeful, talking repeatedly about Victor as they made their journey across to Guernsey and the small farmhouse surrounded on four sides by fields, a dirt road running down to the village a hundred yards away, where there was a pub. They discovered that fact the first evening they arrived, Bernard finding the journey exhausting and moaning bitterly about wanting a pint.

Ron had already gone off for a walk alone, leaving Alan to soothe his father. 'What about a can of lager, Dad?'

'I said bloody beer, not witch's piss,' he said

irritably, moving to the door. 'I saw a pub down the road, so I'll see you later.' He went off down the path, his cap pushed back on his head, his sleeves rolled up as the evening was warm.

'Will he settle?' she asked Alan.

He shrugged. 'I dunno. But I like it here.'

He had every reason to. Behind the house there was a barn which could easily be converted into a studio, the space offering unlimited potential for work. Bedazzled, Alan had walked in and gaped, the late sun pouring in through the top windows and smudging the myriad dust mites which hovered in the still air. A smell of dry grass and earth curled round him as he touched every surface and ran his hand along an old table, once a proud possession, now relegated to the barn. He breathed in to steady himself, his mind filling with images, the old sensations stirring in him.

'Will it do?' Zoe asked.

He turned away, instantly embarrassed. 'When can I start work again?'

She looked away. 'I don't know, Alan.'

His disappointment was palpable. Maybe nothing had changed after all, he thought, maybe it was just like Rochdale, only warmer.

'In time we'll start again,' she said softly, 'but for now we have to be careful.' There was no response as she walked over to her brother and touched him on his shoulder. 'Alan?'

''In time' means never.'

The sun speckled her hair and mottled the brown eyes. He looked at her and hung his head. 'It was . . . you know, like everything to me

553

... knowing that people bought the stuff ... '
He trailed off, incoherent. 'I felt good, that they
liked them ... proud like.'

Zoe sighed, dreading the effect her words
would have on her brother, the long sigh into
depression. 'Alan, we can't risk doing any more
fakes yet.'

He moved away, opening the tea chests and
pulling out his tools, laying them down on the
table in useless rows, his fingers smudging the
film of dust. Zoe's throat tightened as she
watched him lift out books that he would no
longer read, or use; book after book which
previously had been poured over, their contents
consumed and translated into stone. Beyond
comfort, Alan seemed oblivious to her presence,
working automatically on some wood carvings,
filling his time, and as she walked out the sun
startled her and made her momentarily blind.

10 September
London

Seven days to go, Zoe said to herself. Just seven
days to go and she and Larry would be off to a
new life. He moved beside her and she touched
his back, looking at his face. Unshaven, younger
than she expected, fast asleep. No trouble with
his conscience. Only ten days. She shifted round
in bed, finding sleep difficult, even though she
knew that her father and brothers were safe, even
though she knew that she was soon going to start
a new life. A safe life. Larry moaned in his sleep

and turned over. She touched him again to soothe him. Sleep darling, stay asleep, I'll watch for both of us.

The early morning light lifted outside the curtains. Pulling the sheet around her, Zoe wondered for the hundredth time if she was wise to enter the auction, and then, as ever, she reassured herself. The two lots she had entered for sale were good enough to fool anyone, a painting of a small Watteauesque scene and a Boucher of nymphs and water gods. They were the most ambitious forgeries she had ever entered at auction, but they needed to be superb because they were going to be studied and their faked provenances examined minutely. Both lots had been entered under a false name, a name derived from a headstone in Venice of a woman long since dead. But the address was a real one, and it was that of Marcella's summer home near Naples.

Only days before, Zoe had phoned the Marchesa and asked her for permission. 'It is a huge favour and one for which I feel guilty asking.' It was true, she had never liked using people, but she had to cover her tracks thoroughly. Besides, it was the last time.

'Anything you want. Just ask.'

'I just need to have a cheque sent to your Naples address.' She had already opened an account in the false name, so the cheque would be passed without trouble wherever she cashed it.

'What an unusual request.'

'It's very important and won't harm you in

555

any way,' Zoe had replied. After all, if she was caught she would simply say that she had used the Marchesa's address on a whim.

'I never thought it would,' Marcella had answered. 'Has this got anything to do with your young man?'

'It has everything to do with him.'

'Then your request is granted, my dear. Good luck.'

16 September
5.00 p.m.

One day left, Zoe thought, smiling at Larry, her cases already packed. 'I can hardly wait to go.'

He bent down to kiss her. Neither could he; in fact, he wondered why they couldn't leave now and send someone else to attend to the auction.

'Why couldn't Mona Grimaldi go?'

Zoe kept her voice steady. 'It's my work, and it matters to me. People expect to see me there,' she said. 'Besides, after the seventeenth we'll have all the time in the world together.'

'What about Harland?'

She glanced away. 'I've told him that I want a long break from the gallery, two or three months. By then I'll have been gone so long that he'll be more used to the idea of my being away.'

Both of them knew that was a lie. 'He'll miss you.'

'I know,' she said guiltily, 'but I'll still see him and do business with him. I owe him that much.'

Larry nodded, satisfied. He was prepared to

wait another day for her; in fact, he could hardly comprehend his good fortune. Soon he would have Zoe all to himself, he could take her to all the places he loved and show her his country. Flaunt her. He looked at the clothes she was packing and if he did notice any nervousness in her manner he put it down to their going away together. Romantic, last-minute nerves, he thought. But they wouldn't last after tomorrow, he thought, relishing the idea of Zoe in California — it was almost too good to be true.

The phone rang suddenly and he leaned over to answer it. 'Yes, she's here. Just a minute.'

He passed it to her immediately, knowing then that he should have dealt with it himself; knowing instinctively just what it was going to do to her.

'I'm Zoe Mellor — can I help?'

The words drilled down the line and made her sit down suddenly. 'I'll be there as soon as I can.'

She moved to the door quickly, snatching up her bag as Larry followed, running down the steps after her. 'Zoe, let me come with you, Zoe!'

The words were lost on the air as she hailed a taxi on Kensington Gore and leaned back into the seat, alone. It was all happening at once, she thought, one by one the chickens were coming home to roost.

The driver pulled back the dividing screen. 'Where to, lady?'

'The Harley Street Clinic,' she said, 'and make it quick, please.'

The specialist explained that Harland had had a second heart attack and that he was seriously ill, but holding his own. He also told her that he was under sedation in a private room off the Intensive Care Unit. Zoe nodded dumbly and went in to sit with Harland. He was tiny, she realised with horror. Aged. He had never looked so small before; so utterly segregated from the world. Sitting down, she wondered if she should tell the nurse to contact Myrtle on her cruise and then leaned close to his ear and whispered, 'Harland, wake up. It's Zoe.'

Nothing. No response, only a sense of *déjà vu* — I've done this before, she thought, in New York. Years ago.

'Harland, I'm in trouble,' she said. 'I'm being selfish, you see, putting myself first again. I want you to live because I need you. Especially now, when so much is at stake. Anyway,' she added childishly, 'you promised me that you'd live as long as I needed you. And I need you.'

There was no response. Harland, Harland — *whisper their name and call them back*, someone said — Zoe blinked with tiredness. Where had she heard that? Could you call them back? Harland, Harland, come back, come back.

Her eyes closed and she dozed for an instant, waking and thinking for a blessed moment that the auction was over and she was in California. But she was in London, and beside her Harland Goldberg slept on. The corridor was quiet outside, the nurse having looked in minutes earlier, when Zoe lifted the sheet and, slipping off her shoes, lay down beside the sleeping man, one arm laid protectively across his breast, her head inches from his, their breathing in unison.

17 September
12.30 p.m. London

The previous day had been mentally exhausting
for Zoe, not only because of Harland's illness,
but because her two fake lots had been on view
to the public. The policy at Lister's was that the
whole sale was exhibited before the auction, in
this case, the many important 'French Masterworks', so that interested would-be buyers could
come in and browse.

So did the likes of Leon Graves, Mike
O'Dowd and Victor Mellor. Zoe was there
herself looking at the catalogue and searching
for her lots. They were listed under the name
of Signora Claudina Ghiberti — their lot
numbers 12 and 43. Damn, Zoe thought
suddenly, why couldn't they be together? Then
she could get it all over with quickly and
leave. Now she had to wait around until nearly
the end of the sale, and waiting was
dangerous. No, not dangerous, she thought.
Victor would never expect her to have the
nerve to try and sell any fakes now — and
that was what she was banking on. She had
always had more nerve than her brother, even
when they were kids. Victor would never
expect her to gamble with so much at stake.
And why? she asked herself. Because he would
never risk so much himself.

Besides, the forgeries were too good to be
spotted. All Zoe had to do was to turn up at the
sale in her own right as a consultant and
assistant partner at Harland's gallery. People

would expect her to attend an important auction and possibly bid for some of the lots. No one would know that as soon as the sale was over, Zoe Mellor was catching the big silver bird across the Atlantic with Mr Laurence Hands. They might even get married, she thought suddenly, and then she could continue to work as a consultant in America. After all, they would have enough money to live well, so there would be no need for the fakes any longer.

The minutes ticked past. She *could* have resisted the sale — she had more than enough money already. But she couldn't resist the gamble — and she prayed that Victor would think otherwise.

2.30 p.m.
Lister's Auction House
London

'You look well, very well,' Courtney-Blye said as Zoe passed him and slid into her seat on the front row. 'I was only saying the other day to Ahmed that you were positively blooming.'

'Which is more than can be said for Harland,' Zoe said bitterly.

'Oh yes, I forgot — how is he?'

'Holding his own.'

Stung by her tone of voice, Courtney-Blye moved away to his own seat beside Anthony Sargeant and Tobar Manners who was engaged in a fierce conversation with a bellicose Italian collector. Zoe unfastened her Dior jacket and leaned back in her seat, nodding in acknowledgement as people called out greetings to her or asked after Harland. To all intents and purposes she seemed composed, perfectly at ease, but inside her nerves were taut, her skin crawling with tension.

A hand materialised from nowhere and clasped her wrist. She turned to look up into the face of Leon Graves. 'So sorry to hear about Harland, my dear. I've just popped over to the clinic to see him and he seems better. Sent his love.'

She nodded. 'He was brighter when I saw him earlier. Thanks for going, Leon.'

'Oh, it was nothing, Harland and I go back a very long way.' He still had hold of her arm. 'Are you going to be bidding for anything today?'

Zoe glanced down at the catalogue, a look of careful disinterest on her face. 'I don't think so, there's nothing that would be right for any of our clients.'

He frowned. 'What an exquisitely patronising remark, Zoe. Don't you realise that Lister's think they have laid on a mouthwatering array of goodies that no one can resist? Hoping that everyone will get carried away in an orgy of consumption and that the whole sale will develop into a gigantic pig-out.' He glanced away and then looked back at her. 'Well, whatever you think, Zoe, some people seem interested, not many sales bring Miss Laye over from her lair in New York.'

Zoe's mouth dried as she followed his gaze. Suzie Laye was in deep conversation with Victor

561

in the fourth row. Transfixed, she watched them, and then her brother looked up and spotted her. Smiling, he raised his hand, then turned back to his companion.

'Suzie Laye . . . ' Zoe said softly.

'Yes, the lady herself,' Leon continued. 'Although I use the term lightly. What a common dress,' he said, his voice scathing. 'Suzie Laye and your brother — a match made in heaven, no less.'

Leon Graves moved away soon afterwards to his own seat, as Zoe kept her eyes averted from Victor. Having seen the American woman she was worried; she knew how much Suzie Laye resented her; and she suddenly realised how much capital Victor would have made out of that envy. Her palms felt sticky, and she swallowed. Come on, Zoe, don't let them get to you.

A moment later the auctioneer climbed on to the dais and banged his gavel to quieten the audience before he began. A huge monitor reproduced him in glorious Technicolor, as it would each individual lot as it came up for sale, and there was the inevitable bank of phones clustered underneath, each manned by an autocratic member of the Lister's staff. Zoe glanced up and saw the huge digital board which announced the currency rates for the foreign bidders, and the mass of wiring which kept every piece of machinery running. Mechanised art, she thought drily.

'Ladies and gentlemen, Lister's are pleased to announce that their sale 'French Masterworks' is about to commence . . . ' Up came the first lot, a

562

Manet. 'Do I hear ninety thousand pounds
. . . ninety-five thousand . . . ' Up went the bids,
the same spiralling Zoe had seen and enjoyed so
many times. The excitement pooled in her, the
buzz of the audience and the heady and
intoxicating mixture of art and power.

' . . . you, sir, at the back, three hundred
thousand pounds . . . '

Away we go, thought Zoe, further than the eye
can see. Further than I ever dreamed in
Rochdale. Years ago.

' . . . four hundred thousand pounds . . . is
that a bid, madam?'

An animated hum from the crowd.

' . . . thank you, madam . . . we have four
hundred and fifty thousand pounds . . . '

This is the last time, Zoe thought. From now
on, no fakes, no fear of exposure, or jail.
Nothing, just contentment and love. She glanced
up at the auctioneer. I have risked myself too
long, she realised, too long.

' . . . going once, going twice, gone . . . it's
yours, madam . . . '

It's yours, madam. Mine, Zoe thought, it's
nearly all mine now. My man, my career, my
money, my new life. She sighed inwardly. Just
keep your nerve. It means nothing that Suzie
Laye is here, it's just Victor showing off. That's
all.

'Lot 12.'

She refused to look over to Victor, the image
of Jimmy van Goyen flicking up in front of her
eyes. Oh God, Zoe thought, let me get away with
it once more. Just once more.

'Here we have a fine Watteau pastoral scene . . . thank you, sir, fifty thousand pounds . . . a bid at the back, sir? Thank you . . . seventy thousand pounds . . .'

Hurry up, Zoe thought, hurry up.

'Thank you, madam . . . was that a bid? No . . . very well . . . one hundred and twenty thousand pounds . . .'

Up we go, climbing up. Just as I did, Zoe thought, crawling, scratching, but climbing. She remembered Harland in the Clinic, and remembered too the time they had first met in Manchester, when he was carrying the china cockerel. She smiled to herself gently — Harland, get well, I miss you.

'Thank you, madam, two hundred thousand pounds . . .'

Zoe sighed, the atmosphere washing over her as she detached herself, locking herself away, her nerves momentarily stilled. She thought back and remembered Todmorden, the days she went 'knocking' with Victor. No, *dealing*, she thought, smiling to herself.

'Two hundred and fifty thousand pounds . . .'

Buck's Lane floated before her eyes, the garage, Alan's callused hands working skilfully on the stone Victor brought from Italy or France. If she concentrated she could smell the marble dust and feel the hot sun on her arms the day she went up to Tom Mellor's . . .

'Two hundred and seventy thousand pounds . . .'

That's enough! Zoe thought suddenly, remembering other times. Her mother's face, the fall of the Christmas tree, the high ceiling above her while she waited for her punishment as a child. Her attention came back to the present with a jolt and she glanced over to Victor, looking away immediately. Don't expose yourself, you idiot! she thought angrily. He doesn't know it's a fake, he can't know. Relax.

'Three hundred thousand pounds . . . '

A roar of approval went up from the audience and the auctioneer smiled. The Watteau was reproduced on the giant monitor, glowing, fabulous, like a magical bird winging above their heads. Three hundred thousand pounds, Zoe thought, her head swimming. We're home and dry, Larry, home and dry.

'Going once, going twice . . . gone . . . '

One down, Zoe thought, one to go.

But out of the corner of her eye she saw Victor lean towards Suzie Laye and flinched as he looked across to her.

3.30 p.m.
The Interval, Listers

Three hundred thousand pounds, Zoe thought triumphantly as she glanced over to the woman who had just bought her fake Watteau. She scrutinised her, the fine legs, the full almost heavy hips and breasts. Suzie Laye, you have just given me my ticket to freedom, Zoe thought ironically, getting to her feet and walking into the foyer where the interval was in full flow. It had been an innovation of Lister's Auction House, although at first the dealers said that breaking off sales in the middle would mean that people returned cold, and unwilling to bid. They were wrong. By providing a generous bar, the buyers returned merry and not a little reckless, and Lister's profits had risen considerably.

The tension was taking its toll though, and afflicted by a sudden bout of dizziness Zoe made her way into the ladies cloakroom, dabbing some tepid water on her neck and closing her eyes. Maybe I should pull out now, she thought suddenly, withdraw Lot 43 and leave. The thought was dismissed immediately. It would look suspicious and might even give her away. The Bracelet would be on to that kind of trick immediately, as would Victor. No, she was surrounded by enemies now — she *had* to see it through. Fear prickled her skin, mixed with a real excitement as she thought of her brother. I'd match my nerve to yours any day, Victor, she thought grimly. So you and Suzie Laye want me out of the business, do you? Well you've got a fight on your hands.

Reapplying her lipstick, Zoe left the cloakroom and walked back towards the hall, catching sight of Ahmed Fazir talking to Seymour Bell and Anthony Sargeant drinking what looked like an Alka Seltzer. She smiled at them, triumphant, and then froze as Victor walked towards her. Her heart thumped, he can't know, he can't, she thought, otherwise he would have warned Suzie Laye about the painting. Panicking, Zoe watched his approach. She should never have tried it, it was stupid . . . Oh God, why was he coming over to her?

People only congratulated the buyer or the seller.

'Zoe.'

She looked up. Yellow eyes. Unfathomable. Oh, no.

'You look pale.'

'Harland's ill,' she said, by way of explanation. 'He's had another heart attack.'

'He's an old man, what do you expect?'

The conversation was stilted. Unfocused. Underwater words.

'Do you want some air?'

'No.'

'What do you think of the sale so far?'

'It's . . . '

The auctioneer's voice loomed out of the saleroom and hustled down the corridor towards them. 'Ladies and gentlemen, the auction is about to recommence. Please return to your seats.'

Victor caught hold of her arm and then pointed to the stocky figure of Mike O'Dowd standing by the saleroom doors. 'Time's up, kiddo,' he said.

He's only bluffing, he's only being Victor, Zoe thought, trying to calm herself as her brother walked off and Ahmed Fazir slipped his arm around her waist and ushered her back into the saleroom. Surprised, she tried to pull away, but the Egyptian was holding her too tightly and saw her to her seat, waiting until she was settled before bowing sarcastically and moving off. By this time truly frightened, Zoe looked round her. Leon Graves looked back, as did Tobar Manners,

Courtney-Blye, Anthony Sargeant, Ahmed Fazir, Seymour Bell, Suzie Laye, and Victor — they know, she thought blindly, that's why they're all here, waiting to move in for the kill. I left it too long, too late. I lost.

The lots poured past, Lot 34 . . . 38 . . . 39 . . . Applause, congratulations. Pecks on cheeks, red pens scoring out entries in the catalogues. Zoe remained in her seat. Everywhere she looked it seemed that someone was watching her. All the people who had bought her fakes over the years, all the people she had duped were now arrayed behind her. My jury, she thought bitterly, close to panic. Lots 40 and 41 came and went, then 42, and then it was Lot 43 — her fake Boucher, tiny, precise, an oil in an oval frame, a pastoral scene. It flashed on the monitor, yards high and wide, luminous, clever . . . but not clever enough. She swallowed, the saliva balling in her throat. Come on then, let's get it over with.

'Here, ladies and gentlemen, we have Lot 43, a pastoral scene by François Boucher . . .'

Zoe's eyes never left the auctioneer's face. What was happening? Was he going through with it after all?

Then suddenly the auctioneer paused as a man on one of the telephones lifted his hand to get his attention. He walked slowly, agonisingly slowly, towards him. Words were exchanged, as was a disbelieving shake of the head, and a gesture with the hands. Oh God, time's up, Zoe. This is it.

He returned to the platform. 'Ladies and

gentlemen, a most unusual thing has occurred today . . . '

I know, Zoe thought, I know.

'We have a gentleman on the line who says that this lot is a fake . . . '

There was a blaze of photographers' flash-bulbs as the press leapt to their feet to take pictures of the astounded audience. Dealers glanced frantically at each other, and at Zoe, each one more alarmed than the next — except for Victor, who was calm as a millpond. The *coup de grâce*, Zoe thought bitterly as the auctioneer continued.

'Normally Lister's would not allow such a sensational charge to be made by phone, neither would they interrupt a sale unless the word of the person involved was sufficiently respected to be accepted . . . '

The press kept scribbling in their books as the atmosphere tightened. Respect, Zoe thought wryly, who has respect for Victor Mellor? They are all hypocrites, to a man.

'The gentleman on the phone has some vital information . . . '

The murmur of outraged voices continued.

' . . . and the caller is going to tell us the name of the person responsible for this fake and for others which have been distributed over the last few years. However, the name will only be divulged on the condition it is announced to all of you here and now . . . '

All the dealers leaned forward in their seats, and waited. The silence was absolute, even the press paused, the photographers poised. I'll pose for your pictures, boys, Zoe thought, I'll be your pin-up girl.

'The name of the person responsible for the fakes is . . . Harland Goldberg.'

The room exploded into a roar of noise, people shaking their heads, turning to one another. As if moving through a dream, Zoe glanced over to Victor and saw him, pale, shaken, his hand clasped by an enraged Suzie Laye.

I would have bet my nerve on yours any day, Zoe thought dully, and I would have won.

31

Harland was awake, and turned his head slightly as Zoe walked in, his eyes fixed on hers. The room was shaded, the curtains drawn so that the drowsy London daylight came through subdued, the heat of the sun muffled. By the side of his bed flowers loomed up like sentinels in uniform hospital vases, their perfume still speaking of gardens, while next to them a small gathering of letters fanned out, some read, some waiting for attention. Death was not too far from this room, and both of them knew it.

'Why did you save me?' Zoe asked quietly, taking his hand. 'It was too grand a gesture. You should have left me to fight my own battles — '

'And go to prison?' he asked, his voice almost firm. 'I couldn't let you do that.'

'Why not, if I deserved it?'

His fingers grasped hers. 'It must have been a marvellous experience, Zoe. All that excitement, all those dealers duped . . . ' He laughed softly, his eyes alert. 'I had my suspicions, that's why I hired Laurence Hands to follow you, but when he came back with nothing to report, I thought I was on the wrong track.'

Zoe had the grace to look discomforted. She didn't know how much Harland knew of her relationship with Larry, or if he understood that she had duped them both. She didn't want to know either — suddenly she didn't feel clever any longer, only foolish.

'It was Leon who tipped me off,' Harland continued. 'He'd been watching Mike O'Dowd for years and found out that he and Victor were involved and that they were going to expose you at the auction. He was a good friend to you,' Harland said, asking carefully, 'How long have you been faking?'

She answered evenly. 'Eight years.'

'Eight years!' Harland repeated, amused. 'I was suspicious for the last few years, but I never thought it had gone on so long. So you began before you met me?'

'I did a little,' Zoe said impatiently. 'But what does it matter any more? You lost your reputation saving me. Your *reputation*, Harland! For which you worked so hard all those years.' She was moved beyond words. His sacrifice had been too huge to accept, even though she had taken it willingly, grateful that she had escaped at the eleventh hour. 'Your work was your life, Harland.'

'No,' he said firmly. '*You* were my life. You were my whole life from the first moment we met, and when you came down to London my existence was altered beyond measure. Every day I woke happily knowing I would see you. Every time you smiled or talked to me, my heart moved in a way it never had before. You were, and *are* my world.' He smiled. 'What is a reputation by comparison with that? I would have lost a hundred reputations willingly to save you and fulfil the promise I made — that I would live as long as you needed me.'

'I still need you, Harland.'

'No. I've played my part. Now there's a man who loves you as you should be loved, and you must go with him.' He touched her face with his fingers. His hand was cool, dry. 'Go with him, Zoe, it's time you were really happy.'

She shook her head. 'I'm not going anywhere. I'm staying here to look after you. The press are on to it, Harland. They were there at the auction and they'll be here and pester you now. They'll want statements and photographs . . . I can't let you do this for me.'

'I want to do it.'

'No,' Zoe said, straightening up. 'You've always given me everything I needed, without a second's thought. I abused your kindness and your trust, Harland — '

'No, you meant no harm. Besides, you protected me, you never sold me any fakes, or used me. You could have done, but you didn't, and I admire you for that.' His hands shook slightly as he relaxed back into the pillows. 'I don't give a damn for my reputation. Why should I? When I die, who will care for the gallery or the paintings which meant so much to me? Who will care, Zoe, apart from you?' He was angry. 'Will Myrtle care? Or Erica? No, they don't care now and they never did.' He sighed and then glanced back to Zoe. In the subdued light she was frail, hardly a woman at all. 'Do you really think I made such a sacrifice? What better way was there for me to show my love, than to throw away the one thing I held dear — until I compared it with you.'

Zoe shook her head. 'The press and the dealers will pester you, Harland. They'll run you into the ground — '

He closed his eyes. 'No. No, they won't.'

Gently, she leaned over and kissed him on the mouth for the first time. 'I love you.'

Smiling, he nodded and then said softly, 'Some day, Zoe, tell your young man that we were never lovers.'

She shook her head gently. 'No, Harland, we were the *best* of lovers.'

He sighed softly. 'I dreamt last night that you came to me and lay in my arms, here in bed. I dreamt we made love,' he said . . . and died a moment later in her arms.

★   ★   ★

Larry Hands hadn't wanted to hear their conversation. He had arrived just after Zoe, following her into the hospital room and had been about to speak but she was already deep in conversation with Harland and oblivious to him, to the man who moved behind the screen, and listened. I didn't want to hear your conversation, Larry thought again. I didn't want to know that you had lied to me and made a fool of me. That you and Harland had made me the joker in the pack. He shook his head and walked down to the waiting room, a tall angular man in his prime. An American detective, the type women fall for. Once upon a time. But not Zoe. She had started out lying to him so maybe she was lying now. A cheat, saved by the bell, a woman who had deceived and used him. Duped him — *come into my bed and I'll spin your head round, confuse*

574

you, make you blind with love — but not deaf. Not any more. Because he had just heard that conversation. And it had changed his life.

★ ★ ★

For thirty minutes Zoe held on to Harland. Long after she knew he was dead, long after she should have rung the bell and alerted someone. Instead she held on to him and talked to him, about the gallery and the paintings she had seen, about Leonard Phillips and his retirement. She told him about her home in Rochdale, describing Alan and the garage and telling him about the farmhouse in Guernsey.

'You can go and look at it, Harland. You can go anywhere, now. Go and tell me what you think.'

She even told him about Mildred Cross, the Widow of Salford, and the mynah bird, Albert, and the stonemason's, and Tom Mellor's pink eyes, and his rabbits, that didn't have pink eyes. For thirty minutes she welcomed him into her past and her home, telling him all her secrets and loving him.

★ ★ ★

'Larry?'

He stood up and looked at her, without offering comfort. Surprised, Zoe moved away and walked down the corridor. Within the space of a silent hour they were back in her flat. As strangers.

'What is it?'

He flinched, the words cut him. 'I heard your conversation with Harland before he died.'

I lost after all, Zoe thought, a real feeling of despair flooding over her. 'I see.'

'Do you?' he shouted, his temper immediately roused. 'Well, I don't see at all! I wanted to marry you, Zoe, I wanted you to go away with me. I wanted the woman I thought you were, not some liar.'

'Yes, I'm a liar,' she replied, turning away. 'I can't deny it. Does it mean that you don't want me any more?'

He shrugged. 'I love you. I thought you loved me.'

'I do,' she said dully. 'Harland's dead, Larry. I can't think clearly.'

'Harland Goldberg saved you at that auction, didn't he?'

She said nothing.

'*Didn't he?*'

'Don't shout at me!' Zoe snapped, walking towards the packed suitcases in the middle of the room. 'I did it for us,' she said, trying to explain and knowing then, from the look on his face, that it would be impossible. 'I did it for *us*. My brother was going to expose me and ruin me — '

'You should be exposed,' he said bitterly. 'You're a crook.'

She sucked in her breath. 'I did it for us.'

'Why?'

'So I could make a killing, get some real money together and we could start a new life — '

'Why did we need this money?'

She turned on him. 'Because I've been bloody poor, that's why! Because I've been at the bottom and I didn't like it, because I wanted something grand and wonderful and because I wanted the security of being rich.' She dropped her voice. 'Larry, the money would have meant a real life for us. A good life.'

'And where did the money come from? The fakes? That's theft, Zoe!'

She raised her eyes. 'Theft? Is that what you call it? Well, I don't. Those art dealers are the real thieves every time they say to some old woman, 'Well, it's not that good an example of his work, but I think I can give you a few hundred' and then sell the painting on for thousands. Every time they puff up reputations, fake provenances, and create false markets. *They're* the thieves. Do you know what 'burning' means, Larry? It means that when a picture has embarrassed them by falling short of its reserve at sales, they put it away until everyone has forgotten it.' She looked into his face. 'Believe me, for every honest dealer there are twenty dishonest. *That's* why I wanted to get back at them. For every man and woman who's been cheated I wanted to cheat the dealers in return, and why? Because I've been an ignorant layman and I've been an expert, and believe me, the latter is better. I identify with the people they cheat.'

'How very humanitarian of you,' Larry said snidely, tapping one suitcase with his foot. 'It's just a shame that you didn't donate the money to charity.'

Zoe turned away from him. 'You better go.'

'Why?'

'You despise me and I can't stand that.'

He hesitated. 'I can't despise you,' he said dully. 'But I have to know something — were you lying when you said you loved me?'

Zoe did not answer immediately, she was too frightened of losing him, of being thrown back into nothingness. Now Harland was dead, who would care for her? Or was it her destiny to be committed to her family, the long yearning of love following her down the empty years?

'I wasn't lying. I do love you. At the beginning I wanted to make you fall in love with me so that you wouldn't report back to Harland, and wouldn't be watching me. I had to protect myself . . . surely you can see that?'

He couldn't, and a look of incredulity passed across his face. Zoe was suddenly transported back to Rochdale, the cycle of rejection almost complete.

'I did it for us,' she said pleadingly.

For a long moment he looked at her and then took her in his arms. 'I don't know why but I still love you. I still want you.'

But as he kissed her, his mind was running on. If she had cheated him before, she might do it again. She could begin faking again, or lying . . . anything. He pulled away and looked into her face, into the slanted eyes.

'Zoe, I want you to tell me everything. Everything.' She nodded. 'On tape.'

Her surprise was intense as she tried to read his thoughts. 'What for?'

'For me. If you love me, you'll do this.'

'And put myself at risk? A tape could be discovered, I could be caught.'

'No, it's just for me. I need it as a guarantee.'

Angered, she shook her head. 'What kind of guarantee is that?'

'If I have this tape, you can't leave me. You will come to America with me and make a new life. I will have a hold over you.' He kissed her suddenly, wanting her. 'I have to have you, Zoe, I have to.'

She stiffened and then relaxed against him. He wanted a tape spelling out the story of the fakes, of the parts played by Candadas, Noilly; the places mapped out, Wandsworth, Venice, New York, London; and he wanted to hear about all the personalities, the dealers she had duped, the men she had fallen foul of — Leon Graves, Mike O'Dowd, and Victor. His love demanded a tape which would describe the death of Jimmy van Goyen, one which would ruin her if it ever fell into the wrong hands. He wanted the tape so he could use it to damn her and keep her. Zoe leaned her head against his chest and thought for a long moment. The tape could ruin her — or secure her lover.

She made the tape — her way.

The following day
Heathrow Airport

The flight was due to leave at five o'clock, and Zoe was already supposed to be in the departure lounge. Larry glanced up at the clock and

579

frowned. She was late at the gallery, sorting everything out before the grieving widow returned that evening. Harland Goldberg rest in peace, he thought grimly, at least you missed Myrtle. Meanwhile Mona was grieving publicly, making phone calls and begging for sympathy, the gallery filled with the sounds of her Technicolor bereavement, her father failing suddenly now that Harland Goldberg, one of the last of their generation, was gone.

Larry waited at the airport. He was impatient but not worried. Zoe had made the tape the previous night, explaining everything, and left nothing out — at least, nothing he knew of, although there was no mention of Ron, Alan or Rochdale, not one word to connect her family with the forgeries. As ever, they had to be protected and kept safe. All of them, except Victor.

When the tape was finished Larry had locked the precious and damning evidence away in his hand luggage, convincing himself that it was merely a precaution, not admitting that his pride was so damaged that he demanded revenge. He didn't know how long he was going to keep hold of the tape; in fact, he had already mused over the possibility of destroying it and simply pretending to Zoe that he still had it in his possession. But something stopped him. In the end he decided that time would tell. Time and love. He did love her, but he didn't trust her and she knew it. There was a lot of repair work to be done on their affair and this way he had the upper hand. While he had the tape she would never leave. She might fall out of love with him, but she would never leave. Besides, an ex-policeman could get his own back nicely with such ammunition. Not that he would — he loved her.

Larry glanced at his watch again and frowned, looking up as the Tannoy burst into life. 'Will Mr Laurence Hands please come to the information desk? Mr Laurence Hands.'

Uneasy, he rose to his feet and walked to the desk where a young woman handed him an envelope. The writing was Zoe's. He ripped it open and read.

Darling Larry,
It's not on, is it? You would always be suspicious of me, and I would resent it. I do love you, my darling, but I can't change. I thought I could. I thought I would want to settle down and make a new life, but it's not true. You deserve a better woman.

My love, to my love,
Zoe

Larry knew immediately what he had done and remembered the tape, realising with horror that it was in his hand luggage — the luggage he had left in the departure lounge. Panicking, he rushed back and snatched the case up with relief, snapping open the locks and rummaging through the papers. It was still there. Sighing, he sat down, his mind finally registering his loss. He couldn't believe that it was over and remained in the lounge for several minutes until he summoned the energy to walk to his car. The sun hummed on the bonnet as he leaned against it, he had loved her and already missed her, his anger and disappointment mingling with a real sense of grief. Heavily he slid into the driver's seat and pulled out the damning tape, turning it over in his hand. That had been his master stroke, and the thing which had lost him Zoe. He should have trusted her, he thought bitterly, slipping it in the cassette player and leaning back in his seat.

He wanted to hear her voice. To listen to her and imagine her in his arms. Slowly the tape wound back to the beginning and then, with a dull heart, Larry Hands leaned forward and pressed the start button. The music startled him, and he glanced down at the cassette box in surprise. His writing was on it as he expected, but although the box was the right one, the tape wasn't. The music ran through a chord and then, as Flight 409 to Guernsey passed over him, Frank Sinatra sang, 'Come fly with me . . . '

Flight 409, First Class
Destination Guernsey

High up in the wide blue yonder, Zoe smiled and finally relaxed. She had made her decision and surprisingly didn't regret it. I loved you, Larry, but not enough, she thought, and certainly not enough to risk myself. The cassette tape was light in her hand as she looked at it, and when the air hostess offered her a drink she ordered a bottle of champagne to toast herself. A new life and a new start was suddenly possible thanks to Harland. Thanks to his sacrifice she was free to live again. In fact, she was really looking forward to seeing the farmhouse and her father and brothers . . . Her attention shifted suddenly as a feeling of unease settled on her. What good was her triumph? What good was *anything* if love was gone? Harland was dead, her first and last ally was dead and she was left, successful and powerful — but alone.

The inescapable sense of loss swamped her and she reached out for the champagne bottle, filling her glass again, blotting out the thoughts which would fill her life from now on. Money, success, prestige, what are they without love? What do they matter when there is no one to share them?

She was so distracted that when the hand appeared from nowhere and grasped her wrist she lifted her head with a jerk — and saw Leon Graves.

'My dear, Zoe, how lovely to see you again.'

'Leon,' she said simply. 'What are you doing here?'

He slid into the reserved seat next to hers and smiled hugely, the good-tempered face and over-large ears as familiar as ever. 'A little diversion,' he explained. 'I wanted to see you after the auction, but things got so fraught.'

So near, and yet so far, Zoe thought. The game was obviously up, and yet strangely, she felt relieved.

'You know, Leon, if anyone had to catch me, I'm glad it was you.'

He raised his eyebrows. 'Harland came to the rescue in time, didn't he?' he said, helping himself to some of her champagne. 'Such good timing. You were lucky there.'

She felt no resentment. It was surprising in the end how little everything mattered.

'He was always a gentleman.'

Leon nodded. 'Always. Harland was a man to take people on trust, not like some insensitive souls, always wanting security, guarantees.'

Zoe turned to look at him. Did he know about the tape which Larry had insisted upon? she asked herself, remembering what Harland had said all those years ago. *Leon Graves is a clever and dangerous man, the most dangerous man I know.*

'Are you listening to anything interesting?' Leon asked, pointing to the cassette in Zoe's hand.

'Not really,' she said, smiling. She had been right after all, in the end it was only a game. 'It's rather dull actually.'

He raised his eyebrows. 'Really?'

'Yes, really,' she replied, slipping it into the pocket of her jacket.

Carefully, Leon filled up Zoe's glass with champagne and ordered another bottle and a glass for himself.

'What happens now, Leon?' Zoe asked, without rancour. 'You must have all the evidence against me, or you wouldn't be here.'

The smile he bestowed on her was beauteous.

Apparently, Leon Graves was enjoying himself tremendously.

'Evidence is always so very useful,' he continued, sipping his drink and stretching out his long legs into the aisle. 'Especially when used correctly,' he continued, pulling a pair of glasses out of his pocket. 'Recognise these?'

They winked up at Zoe. A pair of tinted glasses blinking in Leon Graves's hand.

'They're Mike O'Dowd's,' she said, turning to him with astonishment in her voice. 'How did you get them?'

'When he was in Rochdale, running over your brother's dog,' Leon answered evenly, 'I went to see him — we're old sparring partners — and suggested that he could either retire prematurely or face charges relating to his forging business. The result of which would certainly be jail.' He raised his eyebrows. 'It does seem incredible, but he chose retirement. Killiney Bay, I think he said. I thought I would keep these ghastly opticals as a memento.' He turned to Zoe. 'Put out your hand.'

She did so, and he dropped the glasses into it.

'Leon . . . aren't you going to give me away?'

He leaned back in his seat and scratched the lobe of one large ear. 'No.'

'Why not?'

'I've enjoyed the game too much,' he said simply. 'You're good for me, Zoe. In fact, I'm almost sorry that you're giving up and going straight. You've had a hell of a run.'

'I've broken up with Larry,' she said suddenly.

'Well, he wasn't up to much,' Leon replied

smoothly. 'Good hair, mind you.'

'I'm going to stay with my family in Guernsey for a while.'

'Splendid.'

She felt a dull sense of anticlimax. 'I don't know what I'll do after that.'

'Get married and have children, I presume,' Leon said, closing his eyes. 'Or buy a little house somewhere and create a marvellous garden. I do so love a garden — '

Zoe interrupted him. 'I could go back to work.'

He opened his eyes suddenly.

'Legally, Leon, I promise. Strictly above board.'

32

New York City
August 1990

The television interviewer was dazzled by Zoe
Mellor, and found it difficult to remember his
questions. Naturally he had heard of her, and of
her career, all the world knew of the famous
English connoisseur and collector. But he had
never dreamt of interviewing her.

Zoe was composed, the charming hostess in
her massive brownstone house in the middle of
the very best part of town. New York City had
taken her to its heart, she was invited to parties,
to premières, her fame and intelligence flinging
the doors back on their hinges. It also amused
society to find that she had no snobbery, and
that she was not afraid to say what she thought.
They were intrigued by the close ties she had
with her family, who lived with her; her elderly
father, now partially paralysed with a stroke,
firmly ensconced on the third floor, and her two
brothers, Alan and Ron, with their own suites.

Zoe took pains to cultivate her image, relaxing
only in the farmhouse in Guernsey which had
now been restored to its former glory, the barn
made into a studio, the garden packed with
blooms in summer when the family fled there,
away from New York City. Zoe's other house, in
England, was often used too. The dark, stone

house on the hillside outside Rochdale. 'Gloom Home', she called it airily, loving it as a permanent reminder of her youth.

In fact she visited it every few months, Ron travelling with her, his grief over Peter's death extending down the years so that every time they returned home he went to the grave of his beloved pet, buried high on the blank moor, under the granite sky. Otherwise Zoe's anxiety was centred on Alan. Her much loved brother, the one most needing, most likely to take the same route Jane Mellor had taken, the one to slip away from her into the never-never-land of dark depression. Take away his work and you take away his life, she had thought, but a few years ago it had been the only solution; the fakes had had to be stopped. It was the only way to keep them all safe. Zoe had understood that, but Alan hadn't.

Her mind moved back to the present as she blinked into the camera lens, the high, white light flashing on to the map of her face. Serene, the wide, slanting eyes, fascinating, even mesmerising on television as she made the medium work for her. And it did. Across magazines and screens flashed the icon which was Zoe Mellor; her words filling columns, her thoughts dissected over breakfast tables and in bars. For years she climbed steadily, and altered. Safety was now certain, she knew, but she realised with biting clarity that it was not enough for her.

It had been a viciously hot day in New York when she decided. The time was two o'clock, and the place her lawyer's office. Calmly she signed the contract to take over the Conrad Gallery and screwed back the top on her pen. It had taken a while, but she had finally revenged herself on Suzie Laye for trying to usurp her, the lady having unfortunately lost a fortune after buying a series of expensive fakes . . . You and Victor wanted to ruin me once, Zoe thought, well now I have ruined you.

When the deed was done, Zoe walked languidly out on to the boiling street and turned. The gallery looked back at her. Glass windows, high, wide and handsome. I own you, she thought, seeing herself reflected, a small figure on a New York street, a long way from home. Zoe shaded her eyes and glanced up to the windows of the flat where she would make her office and from which she would run her business. For herself and her family. As ever, as always . . . and that was when she knew. The deciding moment when she knew for certain and, turning, made her way back to the house and called excitedly for Alan.

'So, Miss Mellor,' the interviewer said, dragging her thoughts back to the interview, 'you're now a very hot property on the art scene and your opinion carries a lot of weight. How does that feel?'

She smiled and the man was beguiled — just as she had meant him to be. I'm safe now, she thought, and I am finally myself. 'It feels extremely pleasant.'

'I'm not surprised,' he went on. 'You certainly have a wonderful reputation. In fact, some would say that you're probably the most powerful woman in the art world.'

'I think that might be an exaggeration,' Zoe said graciously, crossing her legs and remembering the night of the auction when Mona Grimaldi had tricked her, and the humiliation at Courtney-Blye's.

'Is your family with you at the moment?'

'Yes. My father, as you know, isn't very well, but he's making some progress. My brother, Ron, is usually with me, but Alan likes to stay in Guernsey for the summer. He finds it so hot here.'

Especially when he's working, she thought to herself, especially when he's busy, his clever hands working, chipping away at the marble. Making a little putti, which looked suspiciously like an early Rennaissance piece.

'But don't you have another brother, Victor Mellor?'

Zoe's face set hard on screen. Hard as marble. Victor had stayed with Suzie Laye for a while, until she lost most of her finances, and then the gallery. When he heard that his sister had bought it, he moved out of New York and set sail for Europe, trying his luck in the green pastures recently vacated by Mike O'Dowd. Leon Graves was delighted to have a new adversary, and watched, and waited, and knew that Victor Mellor would slip up — one day.

But he didn't. Instead he became more clever, and certainly more careful. Zoe knew he was still trading in fakes and suspected that he was working with Lino Candadas, until the forger was imprisoned in Naples for the attempted murder of his lover, Noilly, who had been found with his genitals mutilated with a chisel. After that, Zoe lost track of her brother, although she heard rumours often enough as his reputation grew. Immoral and ferocious, he achieved the status of anti-hero, and the stories which circulated about Victor Mellor became staple fodder for gallery openings and private views.

A legend was born, and as with all legends, myths abounded. The story went that Victor had limited his business to a few dishonest dealers, who knew a great many unscrupulous collectors round the world. The latter could be relied upon not to ask too many questions and had one thing in common — greed. Victor soon perfected a method which never failed. He would take the collector to a gallery and show him a painting, whetting his appetite and promising that he could 'obtain' it for the man's collection. Independently, Victor would go to the gallery as an expert and ask for the painting to be taken down so that he could look at it. When it was in his hands, he would attach a blank canvas to the back of the picture and then invite the collector once more to the gallery. In a show of good faith, Victor would then ask him to put a chalk cross on the back of the picture. Naturally, when the canvas was removed and the copy made and taken to the collector, the avaricious connoisseur would see his mark and think he had the original.

It was dangerous work, and required nerve

and skill. But Victor was used to that and became greedier and craftier as the years passed. But clever as he was, he was also overconfident and when his sister's power grew and she bought the Conrad Gallery in New York he thought he would look in on her and beg forgiveness. Smirking, Victor imagined the scene, and the lucrative outcome as he crept back into favour. He had always known how to handle women, and Zoe was a woman, after all, so how difficult could it be?

But when Victor arrived at the house in Guernsey he was met by Ron, not Zoe, and as he got out of his Daimler and stretched his lean body in the cool evening air, his brother watched him carefully.

'Hello, Ron. Where's Zoe?'

Ron's face was unwelcoming, hard. 'She's away,' he said. 'Anyway, she didn't know you were coming.'

Victor frowned. 'She must have known. I sent a letter.'

With a slow movement, Ron pulled a crumpled sheet of paper from his pocket. 'Oh yeah, so you did,' he said blandly. 'I must have forgotten to give it to her.'

'Now, look here!' Victor exclaimed, moving towards his brother, his anger apparent.

The blow struck him full on the nose. Stars. Music. Lights. A whole chorus of singing angels reverberated around Victor Mellor's head as Ron's fist landed on target. He dropped like a stone, his suit smudged with dust, his face covered in blood.

Ron looked down at his brother. 'That's for Peter,' he said simply, walking off and slamming the front door behind him.

Ten minutes later Victor Mellor drove off cursing, with a handkerchief clenched to his nose.

Back in New York, Zoe considered the interviewer's question, and then replied carefully. 'Unfortunately, Victor and I are not close, so I'm afraid I can't tell you what my brother is doing at present,' she said. 'There was some talk of his having gone abroad. Australia, I think.'

Aware of the chill in Zoe's voice, the interviewer changed the subject tactfully. 'But your husband's involved with the art world, isn't he?'

'Very much so. In fact, he's always looked after my best interests,' Zoe replied, flicking back some hair from her face and glancing into the camera lens.

At that moment the door of the lounge opened and a small child rushed in. Ignoring the cameras and the interviewer, he clambered on to the settee beside his mother and put his arms around her. Pride, as always, rushed up in Zoe. This was her son, her child.

The interviewer smiled. 'Have you any plans for your son's future?'

Zoe smiled brilliantly and the man's heart lurched.

'Well, he's only very young, of course, but he's good with his hands and we all hope he'll follow in the family business.'

'Art dealing?'

'Naturally,' Zoe responded calmly. 'Whatever else?'

They both looked at the child. He was tall for his age and very good-looking. In fact, he was quite a remarkable boy, almost perfect. Except for his rather prominent ears — which made him his father's child.

We do hope that you have enjoyed reading this large print book.

Did you know that all of our titles are available for purchase?

We publish a wide range of high quality large print books including:
Romances, Mysteries, Classics
General Fiction
Non Fiction and Westerns

Special interest titles available in large print are:
The Little Oxford Dictionary
Music Book
Song Book
Hymn Book
Service Book

Also available from us courtesy of Oxford University Press:
Young Readers' Dictionary
(large print edition)
Young Readers' Thesaurus
(large print edition)

For further information or a free brochure, please contact us at:
Ulverscroft Large Print Books Ltd.,
The Green, Bradgate Road, Anstey,
Leicester, LE7 7FU, England.
Tel: (00 44) 0116 236 4325
Fax: (00 44) 0116 234 0205

Other titles published by Ulverscroft:

THE WITCH MARK

Alexandra Connor

Alison had been blessed by nature all her life — only I knew the other, darker side of her character. And only I knew the pain — the torment — of a jealousy that could never be assuaged. Throughout our childhood, she stood in golden light, centre stage, while I, blinking through heavy spectacles, looked on ... As we grew to adulthood, it seemed that the path fate had charted for her was smooth and straight and clear. Gradually I resigned myself to staying in her shadow, playing out the role of second sister. I would have been content that way — if only she had not fallen in love with Mark Ward ...

THE SOLDIER'S WOMAN

Alexandra Connor

In Oldham in Lancashire, Faith and her brother James are raised by an aunt following the untimely death of their parents. While James works in their grandparents' photographic studio, Faith befriends the characters in the rag trade. But a sordid encounter causes Faith to mistrust men. However, she finds love with the charismatic wanderer Samuel Granger. Then during the Great War, despite being posted 'missing, presumed dead', he returns to her and baby Milly seriously injured. Struggling financially, Faith takes in a lodger, a Frenchwoman — a war widow with a baby. The two women become close friends. Then tragedy strikes, and Faith realises her trust has been betrayed. She wants revenge and determinedly sets out to reclaim the greatest love of her life.

THE WATCHMAN'S DAUGHTER

Alexandra Connor

It is 1930. Life is harsh growing up in Preston's poorest area, but Kat Shaw's family is a loving one. Then tragedy hits them, triggering the return of her father Jim's alcoholism. With Jim unfit to do his night watchman rounds, Kat secretly covers for him, but it's when she takes on work for her uncle that her reputation is ruined. However, Andrew Pitt, the landlord's son, doesn't judge her — Kat is soon in love, and there are plans to marry. But catastrophe follows, and the nickname the Watchman's Daughter becomes infamous in the North-West. Kat embarks on a desperate course to protect those who depend on her. It seems hopeless, but Kat is determined to get back the man she loves.